From "Sitting Shiva" by Judith Tarr

I put Sarge to bed, pull off her boots, and think about the rest, but I'm not so sure of my hands yet. I'd rip something. She hasn't stopped talking. It's quieter now, a mutter that gets faster, then slows down, then speeds up again.

If something was wrong, the techs would be there, making fixes. There isn't even a yellow alert on her file in the net. This is normal, then—within the parameters.

Some parameters.

I start to head back to my own quarters, but one way and another I end up sitting by Sarge's bed. I don't need sleep; I've got a module that takes care of that. Fifty hours to go before I have to access the dream files, process and purge them. So I sit, and I watch Sarge.

Sarge and I go back a long way. Sarge bailed me and half a platoon of peacekeepers out of a major breach of the peace on No-Name. I got Sarge out of trouble on Seljuk, when that pretty boy announced he was having their baby and she was going to marry him or be flayed by a committee of mullahs. No-Name's slag now. The boy on Seljuk decanted the baby and robbed the mosque and headed for the Rim, where he's seducing Rimmers and running a handy little blackmail business on the side.

And Sarge and I are on Sheol Four, getting an upgrade. They'll ship us out, who knows where, wherever there's peace to keep. Time was when I'd be wild to get back out there, walk on thin edges, negotiate or fight. That's long time since. I'm an old hand, been everywhere, seen everything, died often enough to know there's no guts or glory in it.

It feels like hell.

Women at War

EDITED BY

Lois McMaster Bujold

AND

Roland J. Green

A TOM DOHERTY ASSOCIATES BOOK
NEW YORK

WOMEN AT WAR

Cover Art by Nicholas Jainschigg

A Tor Book
Published by Tom Doherty Associates, Inc.
175 Fifth Avenue
New York, NY 10010

Tor Books on the World Wide Web:
http://www.tor.com

Tor® is a registered trademark of Tom Doherty Associates, Inc.

ISBN: 0-812-54458-7

Library of Congress Card Catalog Number: 95-35362

First edition: December 1995
First mass market edition: June 1997

Printed in the United States of America

0 9 8 7 6 5 4 3 2 1

MUSTER

Introduction

Lois McMaster Bujold

An earnest young (male) fan once blundered up to me at a convention to offer his own impression of my military science fiction tales: "Ms. Bujold," he said, "you write like a man." To which I should have replied (but didn't, because I don't think fast on my feet—that's why I'm a writer, the pencil waits) "Oh, really? Which one?"

I'm still trying to work out whether or not it came to a compliment. In all, since I write most of my adventure books from deep inside the point of view of a male character, Miles Vorkosigan, I've decided it's all right; if I'm mimicking a male worldview well enough that even the opposition can't tell for sure, I'm accomplishing my heart's goal of writing true character. The comment worried me for a long time, though. A trip through the essays of Ursula Le Guin also shook my self-confidence. Was I doing something wrong? But then I wrote *Barrayar,* returning at last to the full range of a female character's point of view, and I haven't been troubled by such comments since.

When Roland Green and Marty Greenberg first pitched to me the project of co-editing *Women at War,* which would be a collection of original military science fiction stories by women writers, my initial thought was that this was a concept that would have been startlingly original—twenty-five years ago. Then the idea began to grow on me. As one of the world's more pigheaded writers (as my own editors can testify), it seemed to me absolutely necessary to give our own invited authors the maximum possible scope and range over which to work while still embodying the given theme. That way, I reasoned, we would get not work-to-order but the best possible stories, from the heart's passion and the mind's most fundamental convictions. Thus the reader will find here a mixture of both science fiction and fantasy, light (and dark) adventure, and deeply pondered themes, short and long, from as many different worldviews as Roland and I could round up and cram in.

So, I'll turn my earnest young fan's comment on its head—What does it mean to "write like a woman"? Not one damned identifiable thing, as far as I can tell. As any competent statistician can testify, from a general statement about any group of people (such as a gender) nothing reliable can be predicted about the next individual to walk through the door. The pleasures of editing this anthology have proved it to me: writers, if they are any good, write like themselves, and like no one else. And I thank them for it.

Introduction

Roland J. Green

Dealing with Lois McMaster Bujold on this anthology was an unalloyed pleasure until there came the moment to write my introduction. As is usually the case when Lois expresses herself on a subject, she has left very little for anyone to add that would not be gilding the lily.

What I can add is a historical note. I have been writing and reviewing military sf and fantasy (among other fields) for a good part of the twenty-five years Lois mentions in her introduction. I will respectfully suggest that twenty five years ago, this anthology would certainly have been much more original and much less feasible. The Vietnam War, cultural attitudes, a dearth of women writing sf and fantasy at all, and a shortage of good popular military history were all acting against it.

Now the Vietnam War is at least not on the six o'clock news. Good research material abounds (I review military history too), fewer cultural barriers exist to women sitting down and scarfing up the latest ten volumes on the War of the Lower Slobovian Succession, and hardly any barriers at all remain to their writing sf and fantasy.

As a result, this anthology has not only become feasible; it could have been half again its present size without exhausting the supply of qualified writers. (Whether Tor Books' patience would have survived equally well is another matter.) Nor was I any more surprised than Lois when we got a wide, even exhilarating range of concepts and treatments. Delighted, definitely, but not surprised.

We hope readers will feel the same. We also hope they will join us in thanking our collaborator, Marty Greenberg, our agent, Eleanor Wood, our editor, Patrick Nielsen Hayden, and all the rest of the Toroids.

We may even do it again.

One of the more pleasant tasks of an anthology editor is deciding in what order to present one's bag of tales, even while realizing that for the large fraction of readers who dip into anthologies at random or in order of favorite authors or some other scheme it will be work tossed on the wind. I knew from the first moment I read it that I wanted Jennifer Stevenson's story to be the first word, even as I knew that I wanted Elizabeth Moon's to be the last.

The writer lives in Evanston, Illinois, with a husband and a cat, and likes gardening and crows.

About "The Purge" Jennifer writes: "This story came out of a dream just like the narrator's. Which is more real, more authentic, the dream or the story the waking mind makes of it? If the dream is not about me, is it still my story?

"I've always been fascinated by soldiers. Not war, or the act of killing, or the politics or any of that, but the soldiers themselves, the survivors. I am indebted to Barry Longyear for showing me how to write about them without, er, overstepping my authority."

—LMB

The Purge

Jennifer Stevenson

It was the most horrible dream I have ever had.

I couldn't wait to get it into form, get something physical under my hand where I could control it. Until then I would feel defiled, invaded, somehow guilty for the creature's filthy touch on my clothes. There was risk in form, but that was a faint fear beside the need to purge myself of its utter vileness.

If it were going to be reproduced I would have cast it. That was a temptation. A clay model would feel cleaner, be finished with sooner, and then there would be only the making of the intaglio mold, pouring the resin, breaking the mold and releasing the creature. I'd still have to paint it no matter how it was built. But a mold would take less time than the right way, and I might be tempted to refrain from breaking the mold. A cast piece can always be recast. I didn't want reproductions. In the dream it reproduced itself quite handily. I shuddered, nauseated.

The right way was the slow way. I wanted to think about it, deeply and completely, once. Just while making it. Then I could cleanse myself, knowing the job was done.

I started with a wire armature, black and heavy but soft, life-size at ten inches high, soldered to a forty-pound lead base. Something heavy was needed. This critter wasn't going anywhere once it was built. The armature did most of the show work, too: all scrawny limbs and joints like a mantis or a grasshopper. It sat on its haunches, foreclaws to its mouth, gnawing, a pest, a parasite. I soldered on the sharp hooked spurs at forearm and shin, remembering how terrifying it had been to feel a tug on a leg of my uniform's pants, look down and see its feral face, half-rat, half-insect, see it climbing me with those spurs.

In the dream I had not noticed if it was scaly or bald or chitinous; as I painted on layers of resin I compromised, etching on scales with a dental tool on one layer, then painting it with a wash like dirty dishwater, then over that another translucent layer of sewage-colored resin etched with a few coarse hairs in large pores, then a wash like oil on a wet tarred street, building up the thickness of the strong thighs and upper arms, the bulb of the head. Color went on in washes. The effect was to be pearly and obscene, and the viewer would remember it black, as I did, though it was many colors.

In my head as I worked I saw it scamper through cratered villages to pick up a bit of charred skin, a child's finger. I saw its bullet head, all eye and mouth, swimming strongly in the latrine, and my sphincter squeaked as I drew back unemptied. I saw a bulge in the belly of my friend, dead two days and unburied under the shrieking yellow sky, the bulge and a busy, squirrel-like tugging and pecking under the skin as it maneuvered in the little room it was making inside him, working its way toward his genitals. I feared it in the bellies of the living. Who will die next? What will he do first? I never saw one dead or stretched to its full length.

I positioned the foreclaws close to the head, mouth parts askew in the act of chewing. Chewing what must remain ambiguous. For that I used a piece of green pepper partly coated with resins, knowing that the pepper, rotting, would leave the resin convincingly shredded-looking, with a lingering odor. The creature took shape, rubbery and durable, squatting, with a flattened cigarette wrapper under its hind claws, completely at home.

I had no business submitting it to the veterans' show on Halsted Street. I knew that. I photocopied decoration certificates from a library book, forged a signature on the entry form. I could more easily have put the beast in one of my regular galleries, where I would rub it in the public nose, if it had any validity at all.

But what if not? I Couldn't bear the idea. What if it was my dream alone? I believed in my monster completely, but I wasn't quite sure of the war. I didn't have that nightmare and do this work to make a bogeybeast for white chicks from the suburbs.

They didn't question me. I walked among the authentic photographs and the helmets painted by genuine veterans, my hands in my pockets and dread in my heart, watching for a reaction to my work. There must have been a dozen men in the gallery. Some still wore the rags of their uniforms. My guilt lent me second sight. Blinding fire shimmered off them, granting them vitality that made my eyes water and my throat tighten.

The first man stopped in front of my creature. He swayed.

That was the most satisfying gallery experience of my life. He looked for a long time. Then he looked toward the card. I said, "Mine," without thinking, and he looked up at me.

"You saw it too?" I said.

"All over the goddam place," he said, shuddering, his gaze shocked and inward.

I should have kept quiet. I should have left. "What was it called?"

He faced it again. In his eyes I saw the echo of my own reaction to the thing: shame, defilement, invasion. He swayed again. "Nothing. I never saw one—so close." His eyes narrowed on it. I wondered if for him the memories returned, sputtering over reality with a horrid paintbrush. He shook himself. "It isn't real, you know."

This is the exquisite moment. No hunter takes greater satisfaction in the capture. I exulted, for now I knew, as I had suspected, that our nightmares were the same. Joy rushed out of me toward this man, and toward the thing I had made, the unknown parasite, eater on the dungheaps of war. We shared that. That justified everything, the horror itself, my impertinent illustration. That justified him. I wanted him to know that. I wanted to say, I did this for you.

Then he saw me. How young, how female and unscarred. "Hey, you weren't there!" His face reddened. He swelled with anger.

I hung my head. I felt disastrously exposed and ashamed of myself.

"Who do you think you are? This isn't your war!" He shouted and shouted at me. "You don't know what's real! You can't just come in here—" The other men came to listen. I felt their scrutiny, damning me deafeningly. They saw my work, they heard him accuse me. I said nothing. He pushed me. I stumbled against the pedestal. I put up my hands, mortified. I still saw their faces, stripped and angry. The pedestal rocked, but the piece stood solid. I had screwed it down.

They stood around me now, the fire radiating out of them, an anger that knew how to express itself.

"Who told you about it? Who? Come on!"

Cringing, I whined, "I dreamed it." *Stand up or he'll smash you,* I thought. In a stronger voice, "I dreamed it."

"Easy now, easy now." The gallery owner pushed forward. He looked at me and at the card pinned to the pedestal. "Who's this Andy Franco? Your father? Your brother?"

"My brother?" I echoed, dazed. "The papers—" I stammered, but they only looked at each other and I stopped, sour fear in my mouth.

"He checked out," the gallery owner said.

Relieved, my harasser demanded, "So your brother made this?"

Oh no you don't, I thought, *I know what you're doing.* I was still desperately ashamed of myself. I shouted, "What does that matter? Can't anybody believe in the war?" My belly cried, *Never mind all that, get out or get hurt.*

The gallery owner stepped between us. "You can get out now," he said to me. His jaw unclenched. Grudgingly he added, "Thanks for delivering it anyway. Andy did good." He turned back to the listening men. "Settle down. She's leaving."

One by one, each man gave me a hot look and turned his back. I had to dodge around my creature, screwed forever to its pedestal, to get to the door. There was a small tearing sound as I opened the door. When I looked back, the card with the false name on it lay on the floor in four pieces. Beyond, a barrier of implacable dirty green coats.

The beast sat its pedestal at the end of a dark tunnel. It looked, suddenly, impossible. Fresh air blew in past me. My skin felt less sticky, my mouth less sour. My shadow scuttled across the floor, fleeing the sun at my back, and disappeared into the bodies of its rightful owners. For the first time since my dream I felt clean.

Rebecca Meluch is the author of seven science fiction novels, including one of my personal favorites, *The Queen's Squadron;* I'm still trying to figure out how she made me fall in love with a torturer who had the unlikely name of Penetanguishene. Her bachelor's degree is in communications, and her master's is in ancient history from the University of Pennsylvania. She holds a second-degree black belt in tae kwon do. She lives in Westlake, Ohio, with a husband, a tankful of fish, and two ferrets.

About "Traitor" Rebecca writes: "Interstellar distances would certainly complicate matters of military intelligence in any sort of space warfare. I have a habit of picturing ships in space as I see them on book covers—as if I could see them at all in the blackness between stars. Computer-enhanced images of sensor readings might afford you a visual image, but what is that sensor detecting and how fast does that signal travel? If the ship is eight light-minutes away from you, when do you become aware of it? And how fast can you get a message to it? Even after you have found ways around these obstacles, what do you do with the information that you do manage to receive? Words often arrive safely while leaving their meaning in baggage claim. Barring telepathy, what one being says and what another hears will never be exactly the same. Understanding what a message means is less a matter of knowing the words than it is of paying attention to what the speaker intended them to mean, especially if she is an alien."

—LMB

Traitor

R. M. Meluch

Elizabeth Stone had been called captain most of her life, from captain of the swim team in school, captain of the Texan Olympic team when she brought home the gold round her neck, a field rank on Trinity Alba when anyone senior was dead, to ship's captain, and now, as rear admiral of the Second Fleet, she was still captain of her own ship, the huge quarter-gun *Castor*. She had grown accustomed to the title, and it was what she answered to. A ship's captain, especially out here on the frontier, was its god.

The captain had been counted beautiful when she was young: tall, with a command presence measured in stellar magnitudes. Still striking, she was not called beautiful anymore. Time had weathered her face and given her a rugged rangy look. She was supremely comfortable in her authority and wore it like her battered jacket—familiar, well used, and utterly hers. Her soft Texan drawl was the voice of absolute command.

"I need a traitor," said Captain Stone.

"And you thought of me," said Vallary. Her eyebrows lifted, disappearing into her shaggy bangs. The coarse bushy mane of her dark hair disguised the size of her skull. "No one loves a double agent."

"No one loves you anyway. That's never bothered you."

The alien Vallary was entrenched in the big chair in the captain's cabin, her booted feet dangling over one padded arm. Her eyes were fixed on the highball glass balanced between her eleven fingertips, as though meditating or listening to her head buzz.

Vallary's was an unsettling gaze. She seldom deigned a direct glance, but she could see, hawklike, everything to her side, banded fovea within opaque black irises taking in a half circle with the clarity and resolution that a human would focus on a single printed word.

A small *woof* that was little more than a snort begged attention. Vallary shifted her drink to her six-fingered hand, reached down with the other, and scratched the dog's thick ruff. She got on much better with dogs than with anything she could talk to.

Dogs were common fixtures on shipboard. Characteristic smells had been added to leakable gases, which dogs could detect in parts per billion with an efficiency that put any device to shame, and they were infinitely better for morale. They were no one's personal property, but Beth Stone had appropriated this one, an Alsatian-husky-malamute mutt. Balto was *her* dog.

And Vallary, so it was said, was her bitch. No one else could control her. She was physically stronger than most Earth women, but she still hadn't quite the bulk of a human male. Agile, athletic, haughty, she could be said to be attractive, but she had angered too many people for anyone to say it. There were few humans Vallary did not make a concerted effort to *alienate*.

She remained an enigma, a source of grave concern, a pain in the ass ever since she'd come flying out of a stargate four years ago.

Even she could not say how far she had come. All anyone knew was that her map was not on United Earth's map—which extended light-millennia beyond where their ships could travel—and that the stargate through which she'd come had since shut with cataclysmic finality, so there was no going back for more data.

She should have been more alien, that was all there was to it. It was not the differences but the similarities that jarred, considering that she was not of this galaxy, maybe not even from this dimension or this universe.

She had more chromosomes, but the odd thing was that she had chromosomes at all. She had been equally dismayed to find Earthlings so much less than utterly alien. As she had explained once, "If each of us had only one hundred characteristics mapped in our genes, and if those genes allowed only two choices for each of those hundred, then there would still be more than a nonillion possible genetic combinations for our get. But point of fact, we don't have a hundred characteristics. The possible characteristics for human beings alone run into staggering numbers, and for life on your planet the possibilities are as close to infinite as you get in real time. And that's just for carbon-based life."

"I know of no other," Captain Stone had answered.

"That explains much," Vallary had said.

Earth treated her like a diplomat, the ambassador of her kind, though she never pretended to be one. She was a soldier, not an envoy, not a scientist, not a missionary. Her little ship was armed. She was here to survive and to learn, not to make friends. A scout, a watcher. There was no one to report back to anymore; and still one sensed her watching.

The creature without a country had parked herself for the moment on the Sagittarian frontier aboard the flagship *Castor,* which was seldom far from a war zone.

"So who am I to sell out to? Is there anyone left in your galaxy who wouldn't shoot me first? I have a great aptitude for taking people off."

"An extraordinary aptitude, I'd say," said Stone.

"Extraordinary. All right."

"Monumental even."

"I have admitted to extraordinary. Don't push it. So who have I missed?"

"Conrad Arthur."

Vallary spread her left hand in a six-fingered shrug. "What planet?"

"Earthborn," said Stone. "Nowhere now. He's an anarchist."

"I may have heard the name."

"More and more you have. I want him silent."

"You're sending me on a shoot?" said Vallary. "You have ten boyfriends to do that. What's wrong with SanSebastian? He's your shooter."

"Not just dead," said Stone. "Silent."

"You lost me."

"When he was just a guerrilla he was unfightable," said the captain. "You can't inflict a killing blow on guerrillas, but they can't organize, either. Well, he's grown big and organized, and like any higher organism he's developed a nerve center. Now there's a target. I need you to shoot him in the head."

"His com/com center," said Vallary. Command/communications. "I take it we don't know where it is."

"We don't. And we're pretty sure it's mobile. It's gotta be a space station. His transmissions are all bouncing bubble so we can't trace them. It's a moving needle in the big haystack." She circled with her finger to indicate outer space. The biggest obstacle of modern warfare was finding one's target. "Intell says they found his campfire once." Campfire was what Intell called the heat residue and dumped garbage left behind when a station or a ship parked for any length of time. "There was no trail in or out, so the station is probably jump-capable, which makes it damn near impossible to corner even if we do find it."

"You need to find it just after a jump," Vallary finished for her. Something the mass of a space station could not manage two jumps in quick succession. Until the station's graviton engines recharged, FTL would be its only means of escape. And while Fleet could not track a vessel through a jump, anything traveling FTL normal *Castor* could easily track and overtake.

"I need him shut down and turned off," said Stone. "He's become more than himself, it seems." Then perplexedly, inward, she said, "A lot more."

Vallary caught something in her tone and she sat up. "Is this personal, Beth?"

"No. It should be. But it's not." She confessed herself at a loss: "They tell me I knew him. I don't remember him. He remembers me."

She raked her fingers through her hair. It was still pixie short, as she'd worn it in the jungle, a darker silvering blond now, and her bright blue eyes were held almost always in a squint these days. She pressed her palm heels to her head, as if she could push vanished thoughts back in. "I don't remember him. Hell, I don't remember him. A quarter of a lifetime ago. But still. Hell, how do you forget a messiah?"

"It's not like you to forget your own," said Vallary.

"He wasn't mine." Stone shook out her hair. "His name is on the courier record as the one who used to bring me top-clearance communiqués on Trinity Alba. Once upon a time Conrad Arthur was a loyal citizen with a snow white record."

"Is it the same guy?"

"Intell says yes. I can't even picture him. I've seen the Intell recordings and nothing triggers." Finally she had to admit, "Shit, Val, I never looked at him."

"How do you know he remembers you?"

"Intell tells me he reported me 'bout fifteen years back."

Vallary broke a bright predatory smile. "You did something interesting? Straight-shooting Elizabeth Stone?"

"I've done things I'd rather Jenny and my grandboys never hear about. If I had to do them over, I'd do just the same. Sometimes you just flat-out run out of choices. I count my casualties by name, but if the lifeboat is full, I can make the hard decisions. They used to call me Less, for my middle name."

Black eyes narrowed in thought. *Elizabeth R. Stone.* "Your middle name is not Lessa."

"My middle name is Ruth. Nothing came of Arthur's report. Intell brushed him off like the class tattletale. But he knows me and how I work. That makes my next trick damn difficult."

"To shut him down?" said Vallary, bemused nearly to smiles. "Should be simple! Wait for entropy to work! How do you organize an anarchy?"

Stone smiled despite herself. "I know. Amazing, isn't it? Of course it's not an anarchy; it's a personality cult. Conrad Arthur has been hailed as the Second Coming. People *love* this man. His core is mostly a lunatic bunch of intellectuals whose biggest crimes are desertion and stealing the spaceships they escaped with. If that was all there was to him, I'd leave him to Stellarpol. But his sympathizers are past counting, and they're pissing me off. Arthur's message to the masses—to those 'not ready for pure anarchy'—is to live by their conscience. This translates to tax resistance and draft dodging. Basically, if you don't like the law, you don't have to obey it." Beth's voice grew softer and softer as she grew warm on the subject. "I've got my butt out here on the frontier trying to fight off Antarean sharks, Crown kamikazes, and Sag ghosts, and here's this *mailman* chewing off my supply line at the roots. Yeah, I want him dead."

"Dicey work, Beth, killing a Second Coming."

"That's why I need to take his communications core out with him—before some well-meaning idiot Fleet sniper can martyr him. Take him out so people won't even know he's dead till he's been silent for a while, everyone's cooled off, and it's all old news. I want you to join him. There's no one else I trust who he would believe could turn on me."

"You trust me?" said Vallary. "To what?"

"Not to turn. He's seductive."

Vallary gave a long cat-stretch. "Bestiality is not numbered among my vices."

"Not seductive as men are to women. Seductive to the soul."

Vallary looked annoyed. "How long have you known me, Beth?"

"You have been drinking my hooch and passing out on my cabin deck regularly for three and a half years. I have never known you."

"I am immune to ideologies, that much you know. Especially to stupid ones."

"Counting on it."

"But I think United Earth's ideology is stupid too."

"And you've let everyone know it. You're a natural for this."

"But I'd be suspicious, were I this man. Especially if he knows you at all. People call you and me friends."

"If someone knows he's being baited, then you feed him what he can't afford to ignore," said Stone. "Already on the table you're showing a sophisticated technology, and even I don't know what you're holding in your hole cards. If you put hydra into the stakes, Conrad Arthur will deal himself in."

Vallary's hydra. There wasn't a planet-nation in the known galaxy that didn't want a good look at Vallary's little ship. "If this is to be remotely believable, I should have a motive other than caprice. I have free run of this Fleet. Why would I cash in big bad United Earth for a small-time anarchist?"

"With the stargate's shutting, and you cut off from your homeworld, you've been bucked down from sole representative of a sophisticated spacefaring race, down to 'vanishing species' status. You've got no cavalry, Val. You've lost your intrinsic worth to Earth. The rare technology of your ship is all that's left. Your days of prancing through Fleet like brat royalty are done."

Vallary blinked, stunned. "Have I really been?"

"No. Your stock is tied to mine. But Arthur could buy it if you sell it."

Vallary did not like the answer. Brittle-voiced, her back rigid straight, she said, "Why should I?"

"I don't pretend to know why you do anything, Val, so I can't answer that. I made the suggestion. The choice and reasons for it are entirely up to you."

Vallary never told what she was thinking. And guessing was like trying to guess what a dog thinks. Even when she spoke, you were still left in doubt. She tossed out things with double meanings and messages underneath the words. She would say one thing while telling you another and dare you to catch it.

Stone ended with a backhand gesture of dismissal, "Or you may stay here and drink."

Vallary had been doing a lot of that, much more since the stargate shut nearly six standard months ago.

"I'm taking the hydra," said Vallary.

"No," said Captain Stone.

True startlement escaped Vallary's perfect alien containment, followed by a slow menacing arch of her brows.

Unruffled, Stone explained, "I've impounded your hydra in the name of United Earth, and you want it back. Come get it." Then, as if in afterthought, she added, "Oh, and bring help."

Vallary nodded in comprehension. Her voice was hard. "It is very believable that I would turn on you, were you to take my hydra . . . seeings how that's all I'm worth. Whose plan is this? United Earth? Fleet? Or Beth Stone?"

"Guess."

"Oh, it's pure B.S."

"You knew."

Fleet tolerated Vallary with gritted teeth, but they would never send out a loose cannon on an independent mission.

"But," said Stone. "The order to hit Arthur comes from the top."

"Who else knows about this plan?"

"Only my old squad." The hardest of corps. "And Auriga." Her first officer.

"I need to get something off my hydra," said Vallary, standing. She had accepted the mission.

"I can arrange that," said the captain.

"And I want a dog," said Vallary. "This dog." She thumped the husky mutt, Balto.

"No," Stone said too quickly.

Vallary's eyebrows shot up in a very human look of severe skepticism, sensing danger in the refusal. In a near-whisper she said, "Is there a part of this plan that I don't know?"

"Take the dog," said Stone briskly. "Bring him back."

"Aye, Captain."

Vallary had to wonder if it was a sign of good faith. Or had the dog just jumped into Ruth's lifeboat?

The hydra crouched in one of *Castor*'s cavernous hangars that had been built to house corvettes. Vallary's boots sounded a muffled tread on the metal grid of its deck. Balto padded after her.

All in sleek silver-grays and black, the little ship, like its owner, spoke nothing of its origin. When Vallary first arrived its artificial gravity had been set to 1 g, its cabin pressure to 14.7 psi, and its temperature to 22 degrees C: all Fleet standard, betraying nothing of what would be counted normal to her.

United Earth and its Fleet had a great interest in hydra—not that it was the fastest ship; it wasn't. Not because it had superior firepower; it didn't. But it was stealthy; its alloys were beyond Earth capability and apparently durable, because hydra never needed maintenance beyond what its pilot could give it; and its sensors were extraordinary. Where Terran ships left heated particle trails in their wakes and mapped out wide infrared targets on enemy scanners, the hydra left a scant trace and was all but invisible.

The ship's construction was indecipherable. Unlike Fleet ships whose parts snapped out and back in for quick maintenance, removing anything from hydra was like removing a lung.

The alloys of which it was made were so dazzlingly intricate they were unique in this galaxy, complex as brain cells. Terran labs hadn't managed to catalog them all yet, much less duplicate any of the substances. Their attempts were a constant chuckle to Vallary.

But what Earth most wanted to decipher were hydra's sensors. Aboard hydra Vallary had been known to do the impossible—follow a ship through a jump. Vallary had let slip that she needed to know the mass of her quarry in order to do it. Overnight, the masses of things Fleet-wide had become classified information.

Vallary refused to show anyone how to use hydra's instruments. She had been the only one able to detect the presence of the stargate by which she'd come until it had become spectacularly unstable for all to see and then collapsed, trapping Vallary on this side, the sole specimen of her kind.

She had never let anyone so much as peek through the stargate for the nearly three years that it had lain open. And she still didn't, now that it was shut and Earth could pose no possible threat to her home.

Balto's heavy tail quickened its lashing thump on the deck. An easy stride, sounding somewhere between a stroll and a strut, rang on the grid. Vallary spoke without turning. "Hi, Beth."

"Taking the keys?" said the captain.

"Maybe."

When Vallary turned, Beth Stone was leaning in the hatchway, hands in her pockets, one foot crossed over the other. In passing, Vallary withdrew a component from her pocket to show what she was taking from hydra, as if expecting a veto. It was a solid piece of metal from the end of a control column.

Stone glanced at it and addressed herself to something else, "You destroyed all your biopsies in the med lab."

Vallary pocketed the control stick and kept walking.

Stone turned and walked down the ramp with her. "You shouldn't have. If you ever need blood—and the way you live, that's likely—we can't have any on hand."

"I have a horror of cloning," said Vallary with a secretive curve to her lips.

Commander Auriga, looking as usual like a forbidding slab of half-carved stone, greeted them at the base of the ramp. He frowned as he always did around Vallary. "Clone you? That's got to be someone's idea of a doomsday device."

Vallary ran a fingertip down his broad chest, simply because she knew he hated her to do it. "I shall clone a doomsday device for you."

"You don't know how to clone," said Auriga, then to Stone, less certainly, "She doesn't know how to clone."

Captain Stone said to Vallary, "Half of everything you say—the big half—is crap."

"Only half?" said Vallary.

"The other half," said Beth, "is encrypted."

Vallary had taught Stone the true meaning of one-half. With eleven fingers, Vallary's natural count was in base eleven. "Gotta make for a pissy monetary system," Stone had observed. The square of eleven was not divisible by two. If it followed an Earth pattern, it gave a base monetary unit that did not divide in half.

"Of course it does," Vallary countered. "To you, half means down the middle. To us, it means you break something in two, and half is one of those pieces. There is nothing in our word *half* that denotes or implies equality. That word is *pshin*. It's a math expression like your zero-point-five. We don't use it in everyday speech, any more than you ask for point-five of a candy bar."

"Point-five of a candy bar, Val?" Beth had offered.

Vallary put out a palm.

Stone broke the chocolate bar. "Oops. Here. Take half."

Auriga complained to the captain, "I checked the armament on the stinger you're giving her. She's packing twenty-two rpg."

Stone turned to Vallary. "You were allotted twenty per."

Vallary gave an ingenuous smile with a spread of her excessively fingered hands. "And twenty is what I have."

In base eleven.

Stone let the guns pass.

"Where do I find Arthur?" said Vallary.

"At the moment he's gone underground," said Stone.

"You lost him," said Vallary.

"We lost him. As soon as he makes another public appearance we'll let you know."

Auriga said, "And just how are you going to introduce yourself to him, once you catch up with him? Me, I'd shoot you."

Stone began, "SanSebastian came up with several scenarios—"

"I know he did," Vallary cut her off. "Just find him. This ceases to be your operation. You gave it to me. It's mine now."

A heavily armed stinger in United Earth Fleet colors came up in the FTL blind spot behind the anarchist carrier, so no one knew it was there until it nosed up to a hangar bay door and opened communications with a voice message: "Open up or I'll huff and I'll puff."

At once the carrier yanked in all its sensors in a convulsive motion in preparation for a jump, which did not occur. Several moments later, the hangar doors opened. The diminutive stinger moved in to dock inside the anarchist carrier *Rosalynd.*

When the hangar bay pressurized, Vallary and her dog disembarked to a ring of ready anarchist guns.

One of the anarchists darted in gingerly to snatch the beam gun from her holster, and the one from her boot, and the one behind her belt under her short jacket. The dog growled, but she bade him stay.

Though she had come in a Fleet ship, she was not in Fleet dress. Her gray boxy jacket and black trousers did look like some sort of uniform. She wore black gloves, neatly fit to her tapered fingers, all of them. She showed no fear, not even nerves. She and the dog both looked as if they traced their roots back one very short step to wolves. She faced the ring of armed anarchists and said quite coolly, "Take me to your leader."

Vallary's first words to Conrad Arthur were, "You don't look like a messiah."

He seemed off-balanced at the comment. Some Second Coming. He looked no more imposing in person than he did in his broadcasts: Caucasian, tall, probably forty-five years old, with a decent face of disarming boyishness. There was a sparkle in his eyes that otherwise were of a nondescript color. His hair was ash brown and a little thin and wispy. An instantly appealing man, but not an especially powerful one. He looked around, then shrugged whimsically. "How many have you met?"

"A few."

Vallary's black eyes took in her surroundings without appearing to scan. The clothes of those holding the guns spoke with a medieval accent—tunics and cloaks, hoods and wimples: probably comfortable, since the ship was cold.

To Arthur she said, "Why didn't you take a shot?"

"I don't like killing people," said Arthur. "I really don't. Especially when they haven't done anything to me and I haven't even seen their face. I thought you wanted to join me. Do you?"

"Shooting first is safer," said Vallary, ignoring the question.

"Shooting first is safer. It's not very fair."

"And what's fair got to do with anything in realtime?"

Conrad Arthur looked her up and down in surprise, and then once over again. He said, "You're Vallary!"

"You know me." It could have been a question or a statement.

Arthur's manner was all gushing enthusiasm. His eyes lit up. "Anyone who has been paying attention does! This is wonderful! I've been wanting to meet you."

"Then you haven't been paying attention," said Vallary. "*No* one is happy to see me."

"Stone sent you?" said Arthur.

"Is there a doubt in your mind?" She nodded past him to the armed ring of his followers. "I want my weapons back."

Conrad Arthur signaled to his adherents that it was okay.

Those holding the guns stirred in consternation.

"If she wanted me dead, we'd all be dead," he coaxed. "Come on." Then to Vallary he said, "You want something else."

"I do."

Her weapons were not forthcoming, so Arthur collected them himself and returned them to her. As she reholstered her arsenal, Arthur offered his hand for Balto to sniff. "I have to admit, if I've got Admiral Stone's attention I am a very very very nervous man. Life expectancy on Elizabeth Stone's hit list is not long. What does she need first before you bring her my head?"

Vallary straightened her jacket over her holster. "What she wants is utterly beside any point. Coming here was a convenient order to obey."

"How is that?"

"I need a bug-free tractor. I'm willing to trade." She nodded backward at the ship she had arrived on.

Surprise and skepticism ringed her. A stinger for a tractor was too good an offer to trust.

Receiving no answer, Vallary said, "I want to turn in a sword for a ploughshare. What say ye?"

"It's tagged!" one anarchist blurted a guess. "That's it, Arthur! Trojan Horse! It's tagged! As soon as she's away, in come the homing torps!" His fist smacked an open palm. *"Boom!"*

"Then scan it," said Vallary, in nettled impatience. "If it's dirty, clean it. I don't know why it should be tagged. As far as Captain Stone knows, I'm working for her."

"Who are you working for?" said Arthur.

"The only cause I ever believed in."

A scanner sounded a low whirring as a technician inspected the stinger. He snapped the instrument off and reported, "It's dusted."

"No, it's not," said Vallary.

The technician showed the handheld scanner display to Arthur. Vallary moved to look too.

A faint spattering on the stinger's belly glowed red on the screen.

"Can you clean it?" said Arthur, but other anarchists had already taken the task upon themselves and were rounding up the equipment to expunge the resonant tag.

A homing torpedo would stalk a tag until it caught it. And since the tags were resonant, distance bought you only time. The torpedo still knew where you were, and moved relentlessly toward the tag.

Vallary had fallen into brooding silence. She moved away from her ship. Conrad Arthur prodded her for comments, but she had none. The flashing of a wall beacon panel washed intermittent green on her fair skin. Arthur noticed the beacon for the first time. "How long has that been flashing?"

"Since around the time she showed up," said an anarchist.

"Anyone call in?" Arthur asked.

Arthur's followers beckoned him apart from Vallary. They whispered, uncomfortable with her presence. "We've got a real problem, Arthur. They're moving Helena to a real prison. In forty-eight hours this goes from a simple grab to a mission way the hell over our heads. It's forty hours to Cygnus."

"Then let's be on it," said Arthur.

"What about *her?*"

The anarchists kept glancing to see if Vallary was trying to listen, but the alien seemed more concerned with supervising the decontamination of her stinger. She had crouched down, arm around her dog. It seemed the wrong animal was wearing the collar.

The technicians cleaning the stinger shut off their equipment, took off their gloves and visors, and pronounced, "Clean." One ran a scanner over it again to make certain. "You can go now," he said to Vallary, eager to be rid of her. "No charge."

"I want a tractor," said Vallary.

Arthur broke in, "I don't want her to go yet." To Vallary he said, "I want to talk to you. I don't have a tractor on board this ship. I can get one, but you've caught me in the middle of a commitment—"

Balto began to bark sharply, his ears held back.

"And you have a problem," said Vallary as the wall beacon changed color to red. Alarms sounded throughout the carrier.

Arthur hit the intercom to the bridge. "What is it?"

"Red sign!"

"Parallax!" he demanded.

"Parallax from sensors five and sixteen . . ." It took a moment for the monitor to translate the infinitesimal angle of arc into a distance, and another to believe it. "Fifteen light-minutes."

Gasps sounded. "Jesus God!" said someone.

They had never detected a ship that far away. It must be huge.

Arthur looked to Vallary. "Friends of yours?"

"I don't know who it is, but as I told you: I found you on Captain Stone's intelligence."

"Dimension!" Arthur demanded through the intercom.

"Angle we've got toward us is three hundred meters."

"Jesus God."

"That's *Castor,"* said Vallary.

"Ready jump!" Arthur ordered. The wall panels began to flash alternate red and white.

Rosalynd reeled its sensors back in again like the tendrils of a startled anemone.

"Has she seen us yet?"

"She's got a fifteen-minute–old image of us. Still thinks she's in our blind spot. In twenty-five seconds she'll know we've turned and that we've spotted her."

"Jump status!" Arthur demanded.

"Not yet," a strained voice answered.

"What about *her!"* Someone pointed at Vallary.

Arthur pointed at the stinger. "Is that clean?"

"Yes," said a technician.

"Then she's with us."

Someone else said, "Stone wouldn't shoot with her on board. Would she?"

"We're going to find out in ten seconds," said Vallary. "A little flat on your jump readiness, aren't you?"

"Status!" Arthur called to the bridge again.

"We've got a sensor stuck!"

Someone was counting softly, "Five, four, three, two—"

"Shut up!" another screeched.

The voice from the bridge called, "We've been sighted! Torpedo fired!"

"You mean torpedo fired fifteen minutes ago!" the technician cried as the other anarchists dropped to their knees in prayer. "It's FTL! Where is it *now?"*

Arthur opened his mouth, mute, round-eyed, and answerless.

Vallary said flatly, "It's seconds away. It's seeking. Erasing the tag bought you a few moments to say good night."

Arthur found his voice. "Jump status!"

The voice from the bridge was shrill. "Ready! Ready! We're ready!"

Vallary crouched down on the deck and hugged her dog, who had hunkered down too, as if he knew what was coming, whether destruction or jump. Arthur was shouting into the com as he gripped a railing for balance, "Destination computer random. Go jump! Go jump!"

They were already going. Vallary closed her eyes with the disorienting sense of being rent from her place in reality as she and the anarchist ship *Rosalynd* around her vanished.

* * *

On the bridge of the quarter-gun *Castor,* Rear Admiral Elizabeth Stone received the news of the anarchist carrier's disappearance with singular lack of surprise. Her crew was chagrined to report that they had lost the ship they were stalking and that their homing torpedo was wandering around lost. "I'm sorry, Captain. They jumped. And it looks like they erased the tag."

Captain Stone gave an order to detonate the lost torpedo and to step up security around the hydra, which was berthed in *Castor*'s Hangar 19. Then she left the bridge.

All was proceeding according to plan. Even so, she could not shake the residual fear she hadn't felt since she was a rookie—the gnawing sense that a fatal salvo is off course and bound for only God knows where.

The anarchist carrier *Rosalynd* unfurled the long tendrils of her sensors as the navigator set about determining where it was that the computer pilot had jumped them to. Technicians suited up to go out and inspect the cantankerous sensor retractors.

The rogue alien Vallary was still to be found on the hangar deck, searching her stinger. The technician who had taken it upon himself to watch her was expecting her to relay their new location back to *Castor* on the resonator, but it eventually became apparent to him that she was searching for bugs and homing transmitters and hidden reson dust.

"We cleaned it," the technician said testily, taking personal insult at her redoing his job, as if she questioned his competence.

Vallary continued her inspection without deigning to answer or even acknowledge his presence.

When Arthur returned to the hangar deck the technician appealed to him. "Arthur, the ship is clean. I'd stake my life on it."

Vallary was, by then, taking Balto's collar apart and running a scanner over the dog.

"She shot at you," said Arthur.

"You think she didn't know the tag was erased when she launched that torp?" said Vallary. "Stone lets you find one. That's so you stop looking. The real one will be under it, not easy to find, and not so easy to remove. *If* she's really tracking me."

Arthur waited a moment. "Find anything?"

Vallary closed up her scanner and stood. "No. Are your people always that hysterical in a crisis?"

Arthur smiled. "Pretty much. Yeah. We got away, didn't we?"

"Oh, she let you go," said Vallary. "It was a cheap stunt. She mustn't think much of you."

"Or of you?" Arthur hazarded.

"I told you. She thinks I'm working for her."

"I came down here to tell you we're coming into *Camelot.*"

Vallary drew in her chin. "We're coming into *where*?"

"Probably what Stone sent you to look for," said Arthur, and beckoned her to come with him.

She followed him to the conning platform, where still nothing showed on the monitors but stars and blackness.

Arthur spoke into an encoder. "Hello, *Camelot.* This is Arthur, coming into red orange."

The scrambled return signal fed through the decoder a challenge: "Where is the Grail?"

Arthur answered, "Look within yourself."

The return message was warm this time. "Welcome home, Arthur."

Arthur beamed. A dim dot in the starfield began to take on dimension and form: the space station *Camelot.* The anarchists on the bridge brimmed with excitement.

Vallary crossed her arms. Second Coming indeed. She muttered, "It's not the Second Coming of Christ. It's the return of King bloody Arthur!"

The space station was a hulking piece of reworked salvage, an old D479-style torus a full klick in diameter. Once upon a time it used to rotate. It had since been refitted, artificial gravity installed, its interior gutted so that now its denizens walked on the old walls. Add-on structures stuck out every which way, like a crust of coral on a sunken wreck. Hangared in it and docked to it were ships of many different makes. They were painted in the heraldry of the anarchists.

As the station had artificial gravity, and no one was swearing Vallary to secrecy, these could only mean one thing. "Yes, she's jump-capable." An anarchist had anticipated her question.

FTL ships used artificial gravity to neutralize the force of acceleration inside the ship. Sharp turns that would otherwise flatten crew and contents on the bulkheads like so many road wafers—or cause the ship to break up entirely—were reduced to give a mild sensation of movement.

The same graviton technology, taken a step further, allowed a ship to jump—to cease to exist where it was, and instantaneously come into being elsewhere. No vessel could jump twice within thirty minutes, and nothing the size of this space station could do so within about forty-eight hours.

Camelot had evidently not jumped in the past few days. It stood ready and able to vanish should a hostile ship come to call.

Out of the corner of her eye, Vallary saw Arthur watching her, pleased and proud to show off his secret. It was impressive enough, if ugly and held together by anarchy.

Vallary spoke. "Your round table?"

Arthur nodded. "The master computer's name is Merlin."

"Oh. Jolly good," Vallary said dryly.

"I get the feeling you're laughing at me."

"I am," said Vallary. "Anarchy as a viable form of government. You don't see the humor in that?"

Camelot filled the screens of all the monitors. Arthur said, "This is funny?"

The view had become so enormous that Vallary had to turn her head to take it all in. Torn between skepticism and amazement she said, "This is hysterical."

The carrier, too big to fit inside a hangar, moved in to dock at a flexible lock-tube.

Arthur said, "Rule here is not by law but by personal responsibility for your own actions. We live by morality—or by ethics, if you have no God." He spoke with quiet passion, seemingly genuine, with great pride and a sense of humility both.

Vallary had watched his transmissions in the briefing room aboard *Castor* and had assumed then that the man was a sapsucker, or a charlatan. In person she was picking up the strange impression that he was for real.

When docking was complete, Arthur returned to a joyous welcome in *Camelot.* It was fortunate that the station no longer rotated, for the flocks of people clustered at the dock would have thrown the great torus off-balance. Arthur met each with the anarchist's greeting. They'd seize each other by the head, touch brow to brow, and beam at each other. The women kissed him and cried.

One sober and quiet young man in this rankless society came across as a second-in-command. Arthur called him Brandon.

Brandon didn't smile. He muttered, "Arthur, we're cutting this very close."

"I know, I know," said Arthur. "I'm still on."

"Who's this?" Brandon looked beyond Arthur to Vallary. From his manner, she knew at once that she did not fit Brandon's profile of a likely convert.

"This is Vallary."

"Oh God."

Arthur turned to her. "Vallary, I'm sorry I have to neglect you for a few days. I have a mission. It can't wait even for you. Promise you won't sabotage my station while I'm gone."

"Oh yeah," Vallary said curtly. "Certainly. You have my word."

"Good enough," said Arthur and turned to go on his way.

"Idiot," Vallary shot at his back.

Arthur gave her one of his loopy grins over his shoulder and left her at her word.

Vallary took a walk once around *Camelot.* The station was cold, and people spoke in frosty puffs. Birds fluttered around loose. Balto gave a small *woof,* but Vallary would not give him leave to chase.

Life in the anarchy was hard and supplies short, but a cheerful cooperation reigned. Volunteering appeared to be a competitive sport. Under a printed slogan on a wall, The Proud and the Free, someone had added, in longhand, *The Cold and the Skinny.* They did in fact see that this was funny. And they were laughing.

She heard music, played live, with clapping of hands and thudding of dancing feet, and singing. She was struck by the sense of community: defiant, buoyant, cohesive. The anarchists smiled at the stranger but allowed her her distance, for Vallary had always carried herself with drop-dead aloofness.

An old woman offered her a hooded cloak, thinking she must be cold in just her short jacket. Vallary wasn't, and she declined. She heard herself thanking the woman—a strange word for her. Vallary was not polite by nature or by training.

Eventually she broke into a run and clapped her hands. "Balto! Find Arthur!"

The dog ran ahead until he came to a closed door where he scratched at the deck and tried to push the door in.

Vallary admitted herself, blustering into a conference room where a mission briefing was convened amid maps and pictures and frowning strategists, and addressed herself to Arthur as if no one else were there and nothing else mattered. "I look like you, but never presume I think like you. I need to know. This human concept of the value of one's *word.* It's agitated air! What worth can there be in a spoken word?"

Supremely patient while having his meeting crashed, Arthur explained, "If words are breath and breath is life—rather a lot."

Vallary then looked around at the maps and pictures. She pulled a chair out from the wall and sat herself down in the midst of the strategy session. "What are we doing?"

The others stirred edgily, mistrustful, but Arthur's kindly manner never wavered. "We're trying to rescue someone, Vallary. There's a woman who hid her son from the colonial draft on Cygnus Erie. She's been imprisoned for obstruction. Her son wants to turn himself in so they'll let her go. That's not what Helena wants."

"So why are you in this?"

"These people are being forced under penalty of loss of freedom not only to fund a war that they oppose on moral grounds, but to send their sons and daughters to defend that immoral system. Helena resisted. She followed my tenets of civil disobedience. I got her into this."

"Where goes your tenet of taking personal responsibility for one's actions?" said Vallary.

"Helena's paying for hers," said Arthur. "Now I'm taking responsibility for mine."

"You," said Vallary with a sudden light dawning. "When you say you're going to rescue her, you mean *you* are going."

"That's right."

She stared at him, astonished. He waited with a smile for her either to say something more, or leave them to their planning.

"You are possibly the most naive *Homo sapien* I have ever met. I'll just take a tractor—I noticed *Camelot* has a few—and be on my way."

"But you can't! There's so much I want to tell you. You've been among Fleet since you arrived through the stargate. You should hear the side of this conflict that's not United Earth."

"And what makes you think I give a gorzan's ass what happens in your bullshit universe? I'm not entirely convinced, you see, that you even exist. I don't think I ever made it through the stargate. I'm lying in sick bay in a coma. In my delirium I've created a counteruniverse in my own image except that they count in tens, and now I've made up King Arthur. Twice! I've lost all grip and so have you. You see some imagined higher nature in me that everyone else in your universe missed."

"I'm good at that."

"I want a tractor."

With one of his most endearing grins, Arthur said, "I'm going to give you what you want. But you have to endure some agitated air first."

Vallary translated: "I have to sit through the sermon if I hope to get a tractor."

"That's it in a nutshell."

"Just where it belongs."

"I have to do this first." He pointed at his maps and waiting strategists.

Vallary sat back down. "Then let's get this done."

Eyebrows arched round the table like synchronized inchworms.

"I'm *not* staying here," said Vallary. "Anyway, I'm the only professional in the lot of you."

There was a general hesitation, then one blurted what the others felt: "I don't want her at my back, Arthur."

"Not necessary," Arthur reassured them. "She'll be at mine."

Vallary, Arthur, the pilot, and the dog Balto boarded a swift little quickjumper that was armed with benign stun bombs. Vallary and Arthur wore uniforms of colonial prison guards.

"Secure your dog and strap yourself in, Vallary," said Arthur, preparing for launch. "We're about to cut grav."

Vallary reacted with a quick jerk of her head. "This is a mechanical separation?"

Arthur nodded. "Nobody powers in and out of *Camelot*'s hangars. It's a push-out/reel-in system. We won't power up till we're clear of the hangar."

"How archaic," said Vallary, coaxing Balto into a net. "How interesting."

"Straightforward, old, reliable. Nothing to go wrong."

Vallary strapped herself in. The artificial gravity released and her hair floated up. Balto looked like a wooly bear. Once the air leaked out of the hangar, the outer doors opened to the stars. At the end of a countdown, the catapult under the hangar deck gave a gentle shove. The g forces sank Vallary into her seat as the little ship pushed free of the hulking space station *Camelot*.

Nothing simpler. A push. The ship goes this way, the station goes that way. Simple physics.

Clear of the station, the quickjumper re-established artificial gravity under its own power.

Finally under way at FTL normal, Arthur asked Vallary, "Was Stone demoted? You called her captain."

"On her ship, that's what they call her. A ranking captain on board Rear Admiral Stone's ship is another word for ballast."

"Did she tell you why she's out to get me?"

"Why should she not?" said Vallary. "You're gunning for her."

"I'm not," said Arthur. "I'm just trying to survive her."

"Why'd you report her to Intell?"

Arthur paused. "That was a long time ago. I was stupid."

"Past tense?"

"I was also warned at the time not to go looking for bones in Captain Stone's closets. I said, 'You're afraid I might come to harm?' They said, 'No. Who gives a shit about you? This department is nuts crazy about Captain Stone.' That's when I realized it's all a game. The first trick is to find out which rules are the real ones. I really was the most naive *Homo sapien* in the galaxy back then, and I regret doing that. Elizabeth Stone is not evil. It's the system. It's a dog-eat-dog system, and Elizabeth Stone knows how to eat dog.

"United Earth is a collection of nations whose concept of justice is a game of lawyers. A jury does not decide who is right and who has been wronged, but whose lawyer better played the game. Truth never enters into it. And the lawyers, the guardians of justice, contrived a language unto themselves for the game, which necessitates the hiring of one of them to serve as translator. Any hope of justice requires money, lots of it, to engage a lawyer. One slip of a word and you've lost your turn. Those not proficient in the language lose the game. The rich fly. The poor rot. Guilt or innocence doesn't enter into it."

"You just woke up to this?" said Vallary. "I didn't need you to tell me that. You want honor? You want knights? They're not just dead. They can't die because they never lived. Knighthood is a fairy tale."

"The idea of knights lived," said Arthur passionately. "And the idea of knights never died. The idea of knights gives me hope. First you conceive what you want to be. Then realize it. King Arthur brought law to the land. I've come to take it away." Then with a loopy grin he presented himself. "I am the Anti-Arthur."

Vallary stared at him straight for several moments, as if expecting him to change. When he didn't she said, "Stone is the devil I know. You, Arthur, are an alien." She turned to look out at the stars, one of them taking on size—the system of Cygnus Erie, where they were bound. She groaned. "This is going to be a dangerous grab."

"Captain!" *Castor*'s first officer urgently requested Stone's attention in a secure room. "Vallary killed a colonial guard!"

Stone reached for the report. Blue eyes flicked back and forth as Auriga told her its contents: "Conrad Arthur staged a raid on a provincial prison on colony Cygnus Erie to spring a minor criminal. There's pictures. It's Arthur in person, and *that's* Vallary with the tracking gun. The victim's name is Sergeant Mustafa Gann of the Cygnian Colonial Guard."

Stone murmured, "Looks like Val is making her bones with the anarchists."

"She killed one of our own while under your orders," said Auriga. "You don't have to tell me that this is war and people die, but friendly fire usually means an accident. She aimed and shot the guy!"

"Get me the names of the family," said Stone, her tone one of dismissal.

"Captain," Auriga demurred. "Permission to speak."

"Take it."

"Vallary is not bound by United Earth law or Fleet regulations, and you knew that when you sent her. That gets her out of any legal culpability, and United Earth isn't liable, but I have to say: you knew, Captain. You knew."

Captain Stone turned her head slowly, a glint of menace in narrowed blue eyes. She said softly, "Don't you ever tell me I'm not in pain just because I won't scream for you. Are we clear on that?"

"Aye, Captain."

"Anything else?"

"Aye, Captain," said Auriga. "Are you sure she's still working for us?"

A straightforward raid had gone vastly awry. The anarchists had approached the freeing of Helena the same way the colonial police would have freed a prison guard taken hostage—stun the whole facility, walk in, and carry out the one you want. When the unaccounted-for backup systems sprang into action, it had fallen to Vallary, always armed to excess, to shoot, blast, and burn their way out.

When the first barriers had slammed down, Vallary had glanced over at Arthur and found him bone white, sweat beading on his lip, eyes glassy. But he'd never frozen, never even hesitated, and he would not drop Helena for the life of him.

Now that Helena lay sleeping off the stun in a hammock aboard the quickjumper, Arthur sat gripped by severe shaking, in shock at the danger just passed, his face wet and pasty-colored.

Vallary waited, glaring at the king of the anarchists, trying to be contemptuous but more puzzled. "Didn't you have any reports on this place before you decided to hit it?"

"We did." Arthur wiped his face with trembling hands. He managed a smile. "Bad ones." He glanced at Vallary. "You could have turned me right over to the M.P.s."

"Provincial police," Vallary corrected. "They were shooting at me, if you didn't notice. And I can't get back to *Camelot* without you."

He smiled outright. "You protest too much."

She shook her head. "Still looking for a higher motive where there is none? No. The rest of the galaxy isn't as loath to shoot first as you are. And you want to take away all law? What are you thinking?"

Arthur's tremors subsided and he returned to his normal color as he found himself in his element—defending his creed. "Eventually. Not overnight. I'm sure civilization would have fallen apart into mob rule if the world had suddenly turned democratic overnight in 500 B.C.E. It wouldn't have worked. That doesn't mean democracy wasn't the right way to go. You have to start on a small scale and spread the idea. *Camelot* is Athens 500 B.C.E. , the first working society of its kind. It's where we'll all be three thousand years from now. Right now I'm holding this spark cupped in my hands. There's a heavy wind and rain, but it'll catch. I know it'll catch." His eyes were alight. "Law is only a means to an end. Like training wheels. Children will always need law, to teach them to be responsible adults. But there comes a time to take the training wheels off. Ours have stayed on too long. The law has become a crutch, and it's stunting us. The conscience atrophies without free exercise. As it is now, people do what the law allows, right or wrong. If it's legal, it's okay. If it's legal, do it, even though something tells you it's not really right. But if, instead, you're bound only by conscience and honor, then there's nowhere to hide. You have no choice but to choose what is fair. When the training wheels come off, then at last we'll live by our sense of right and have true equality."

"Equality!" Vallary cried, and the dog Balto gave a startled bark. "Where's the hat you pulled that one out of? You have this weird concept of equality and axiomatically think that's the way it's supposed to be! Let me tell you what will really happen when the wheels come off: the wheels will come off! There's no equality! One-half does not mean right down the middle! If you had a proper complement of fingers you would know that! *This* is half and *this* is half!" She held up her five- and six-fingered hands. "But you were born with two small halves. Not only were you shorted, but you have this unnatural sense that all is supposed to be equal! In any two, someone gets the short end, and that's a law of nature. Nothing ever breaks down the middle!"

"I never said equality grew wild in nature," said Arthur. "It must grow in civilization."

"Must?" said Vallary. "There's no historical precedent on your world."

"That's like saying we can't behave in a restaurant because of our past performance as a one-year-old sticking peas up our nose. We have grown. It's time to stand up as an adult civilization."

"This is truly cute, Arthur. Your vision of the world says more about your lenses than it does about the world."

He grinned at her. "You're arguing with me. I thought you didn't care about our bullshit universe."

"I don't. Have I heard enough sermon yet? Can I have a tractor now?"

"Yes."

Vallary felt as if she'd been tugging on a rope with all her might and it had abruptly given way, leaving her staggering for her footing. She marveled at him. He colored people with his own value system. All humans did, but his colors were different. The swindler does not believe in the existence of honesty. The promiscuous cannot credit that anyone could be celibate by choice. The liar knows he's being lied to. And here was Arthur. His failure to credit the base nature of humanity could only mean that Arthur was as noble-hearted as his loony message. She'd had a hard time crediting it: *He believes it! He's an idiot!*

"The difference between us, Arthur," she said softly. "The main difference is: you know what you're living for."

And I like him.

Arthur and Brandon came to the dock to see Vallary off from *Camelot.* Balto was racing around their legs, in the mood for games. "Balto. Mush!" Vallary clapped her hands to command him to board the tractor.

"I give up," said Brandon. "What are you going to do with a tractor?"

"Captain Stone has my hydra. I'm going to get it away from her."

"With a tractor?" said Arthur, stumped. "Isn't it too slow?"

With a pained shutting of her eyes, as though to an imbecile, Vallary said, "A hydra can summon another hydra idented to the same pilot."

"But there's only one hydra," said Arthur.

She patted the tractor's hull. "So I'll get another one."

"I don't understand. How, if the gate to your universe is shut?"

She let the silence shout. She boarded the tractor and the hatches sealed after her. Lights changed color to signal she was launch-ready.

Brandon exited the deck at Arthur's side, murmuring low so as not to be overheard. "Did she just say that the stargate is open?"

"I . . ." Arthur opened his arms with a shrug. "I guess we'll wait and see. And count hydras."

A deep clunking resounded within the hull of the quarter-gun *Castor,* as if a lot of boulders were rolling around loose within the titanic ship, rousing Captain Stone to the bridge. "What the hell is *that?*"

The duty officer gave an uncertain stammer. How to say it? He blurted, "The hydra is trying to get out."

Commander Auriga arrived out of breath. "Damn hydra's powered up in the hangar. It set off the fire alarms. The hangar sealed off automatically. The outside doors opened to put out what the ship thinks is a fire, so now we can't get into the hangar. The deck locks are holding the hydra down, but it's rocking them loose."

The clangor re-echoed within *Castor*'s hull.

"Who's on board?" Stone demanded.

"No one," Auriga said grimly.

"What?" Stone said. "Is it a tractor beam?"

"No. It's under power. A program or remote control."

The proximity alarm sounded. "What've we got?" Stone demanded.

"Unknown," said the lookout. "Distance—" He began, broke off in disbelief, then reported, "Distance . . . ten meters."

Auriga pushed the lookout from his station to check his readings. "Eight meters," Auriga verified, then looked up on the display as he fed in the view where the sensors said the intruder was. "We should be able to see him."

A dark shape. Barely visible. Even the starlight slid around it. It showed no heat trail, no running lights. *Castor*'s sensors had detected that pattern before, but the computer did not credit the identification because the location of the only one of its kind was locked in *Castor*'s hangar 19.

A lookout breathed, "It's a hydra."

"Override that fire emergency program," Stone ordered. "Get the hangar doors shut. Hand-crank them if you have to! That hydra doesn't leave this ship." As Auriga got on the intercom to relay the orders, Captain Stone opened an outside com. "Vallary!" She looked to the signalman. "Is she receiving this—Vallary!"

The deep banging emanating from the hangar was shaking the ship. "Shit."

"She's going to pull out the hangar deck," said Auriga. "We may have to let it go."

"We will not," said Captain Stone. "And secure *that* one!" She pointed at the dark image as it slipped off the screen. "Get a tractor beam on that ship."

"Yes, sir!" the weapons officer said with relish, but in a moment reported in distress, "Can't get a lock, Captain. Sensors are having a tough time deciding that there's anything there."

"Then tag her and lock on that."

"Yes, sir!"

Her. They knew who this was.

The weapons officer reported in mounting frustration, "She's avoiding the jets." They had lost any vestige of a visual image moments ago. "She's too close to angle one on her."

There came a low *thunk* of hulls touching.

Stone muttered a growl. "Hell, I could spit on her from here. Open a window." She hit the squawkbox to the ready room: "Scramble outriders. A and B flights. Tag hydra. Don't shoot her unless she shoots first. Scramble now."

But the chutes to launch the outriders were no sooner uncapped than the second hydra vanished.

Stone spun away from the display. *Shit!*

The shaking instantly ceased with the last thump of the captive hydra dropping inertly back into place on the hangar deck.

The captain's eyes narrowed to bare slits that seemed to contain blue fire. Stone was vibrating, riding out the enormous implications of what she'd just seen.

Two. There were two.

Auriga cut to the core and spoke her mind for her, his arms folded across his broad chest. "You wanted a traitor, Captain. Looks like you got one."

"A second hydra?" Conrad Arthur received the report with disbelief.

"One inside *Castor,*" Brandon affirmed. "And we have a low-placed sympathizer aboard *Castor* who verified that it's still in there. And one somewhere out here."

"Hoax?" said Arthur, afraid of being too eager to believe this.

"I assumed so," said Brandon. "Even we can project an image."

"But something has changed your mind," Arthur observed.

"The only thing stealthy as a hydra is a hydra. Our proximity alarms haven't gone off, and I don't know how long that's been sitting there." He pointed past Arthur and out the clearview bulkhead.

Arthur turned to see what Brandon was looking at. He saw only what *Camelot*'s sensors saw: nothing but starfield.

Then, looming like an uneasy shadow, black as eternal night, not even winking the stars, a shape suggested itself. "I see it. . . . I think." He wasn't sure until a voice transmission from the void set off all the alarms. "Open up, or I'll huff and I'll puff."

Rear Admiral Elizabeth Stone gathered four of her trusted ten around her, those who would come to *Castor* on no notice, for a hastily summoned conference. They came without question. When Beth Stone called for help it meant her hand was on the button.

Commander Auriga related all the events to date, then Stone summed up: "Given that (a) the gate to Vallary's homeworld shut nearly six months ago; (b) only one hydra was stranded on this side of the gate with her; and (c) there are two hydras now; then . . . then what?" She gave up the floor.

"Then either a, b, or c is false," said Auriga. "They're mutually exclusive."

"Well." Senator L'Abbe rubbed his dark, bristly cheek. Stone had called him back from his vacation. He was trying to grow a beard and it itched. "Since (c) just attacked you, (c) looks like a given."

SanSebastian spoke aside to the captain, "That part from the hydra that you let her take with her. Know what that was, Beth?"

Stone shook her head. "I *thought* it was a *stick*." She sat up straight. "There's one more given here: Vallary is a games player. She tells me things in riddles just to see if I get it. She probably told me to my face what she's doing now; I just fucking missed it."

L'Abbe scratched his chin. "You've got to wonder about a race of people who'd send out a vanguard like Vallary. They can't be peaceful. Ever consider her name could be an Earth word?"

"It is," said Stone. "That one did not get past me. The first Roman soldier upon the enemy rampart to take the emplacement was awarded a crown of gold, the vallary. It would be just like her to introduce herself as the first invader," she said. "And maybe that was the original intent—but she got up on the wall and the ladder got kicked away. She's alone here now."

"Is she?" said SanSebastian. "What makes us so sure the stargate is shut?"

"Fleet sensors recorded the gate shutting," Carver Baldwin noted.

"No, sir," Auriga said. "Fleet sensors recorded things for which they had no referents; Vallary told us what they meant, and we accepted that."

Stone cut off this discussion. "I am sure the gate shut with *one* hydra on this side." As she said it, a challenge rose from deep within where all the darkest monsters dwelled: *Why?*

She remembered the day. The self-sufficient, callous, fearless, imperious creature came to her seeking oblivion. Vallary came to the captain's cabin and drank till she passed out on the deck, curled up with the captain's dog. Tears glistened on Balto's fur. Balto had whined and licked the alien's face.

No one could convince Beth Stone that Vallary had not really been stranded. She would doubt everything else first.

"I'm not done with this line yet, gentlemen. Run with me a while longer. I'm looking for alternatives. No matter how improbable, assume a, b, and c are all true."

There was a long silence. Auriga was scowling.

"Two thoughts," said L'Abbe.

"What've you got, Dana?"

He tossed out a possibility. "The stargate reopened?"

"There's a thought," said Stone. Even Auriga had to admit he'd missed that one. "I sure don't like it. What else you got?"

Dana L'Abbe folded his dark hands over his wide stomach. "Just this. How do you know she's not playing out the scenario?"

Stone ignored Auriga's snort. "I would dearly love to believe that. That's why I'm afraid to believe it. Armies have been run straight into the ground by that kind of leadership and empires into the dust. A second hydra changes everything. It means . . . What does it mean?"

"It means she lied to you, sir," said Auriga.

Stone pursed her lips behind her knuckle. Odd to be so uncertain, so out of control. *Two hydras. Two hydras.*

You launched her. Either trust her or don't. Make a decision.

"Shoot the flare, Beth," said Baldwin. "The big one."

All eyes turned inadvertently to the panic button that would send a direct resonant signal to Earth: Alert. Invasion imminent.

"No. I got us into this." *Stand by your original trust. Ride it into the ground if need be.* "This is my quadrant. My fleet. My command. My war if this be war."

"You could take Earth down with you," said SanSebastian because it needed to be said by someone other than Auriga.

"My decision."

"Sir!" Auriga nearly burst. "Sirs, Mr. Senator, Governor Xixan. I am aware that I am at the bottom of this brass birdcage, but I want to be on record. Captain, I admire you and I know you got to the top by being a high roller, but you're staking things you have no right to risk. There is evidence of a powerful hostile alien armada that knows Fleet workings, and we know nothing of them. Except that their ships can be on us before we see them. A report upstairs is required!"

"Thank you, Auriga," Stone said quietly. "Anyone else?" Something did not fit here. Something was wrong with all of it. She looked to Governor Xixan. "Chuck?"

Charlie Xixan shook his square slab of a head minutely. There was too much unknown. "You know the lady and we don't. What's your call?"

"Hold course. Maintain secrecy." And before Auriga could wedge in an objection she had stood to accept their salutes. "Conference closed."

Auriga held back to ask Captain Stone alone, "You're sure?"

Evenly, without blinking, she said, "I'm sure."

Auriga stalked to the bridge. Alone, Beth hugged herself and questioned her certainty.

All reason was telling her that it had blown up, the galaxy might be facing invasion, and she was leading them deeper into disaster with every silent moment. *You know the lady and we don't,* Charlie Xixan had said. *I* don't *know her,* Beth admitted. And still instinct told her to stay the course, certain that the stargate was shut. *Why? Why so certain?*

Because she wanted to believe Vallary? Because the alternative was unthinkable?

Because you saw her cry?

As soon as the bay pressurized, as many curious anarchists as could wedge onto the hangar deck squeezed in to greet the hydra. The mob of them parted as best they could to let Arthur through to the fore.

"You came back," Arthur said.

Vallary had nowhere to stand but in the hatchway of her craft. "What was meant to be a simple grab went wrong. I—" she broke into a graveyard grin. "Didn't account for the backup systems."

"But you got your hydra," said Arthur.

"This isn't my hydra. This is a new one. Stone still has mine. I still need help getting it back, and you can't afford to leave it in her hands, so you're going to help me. Sooner or later she's going to realize just what she has." Her tone was ominous.

Arthur was still trying to credit what he was looking at. Even in the bright glare of the docking bay hydra seemed to vanish into shadow. He climbed up the ramp. Brandon came with him. "Where did this come from, if you can't go home?"

The pause stretched. He answered himself. "That's what you told them. We all assumed that card had been removed from the deck."

"I made you assume what I wanted you to assume," said Vallary harshly. "That's what I'm good at."

Arthur nodded. How better to protect the security of her home from the imperial curiosity of United Earth than to make Fleet believe the door was gone?

Arthur ventured aboard the hydra. Its newness shrieked. No smudges marred the control surfaces. There were no dog hairs, no grimy film, no scratches, no grit, and no supplies. It was so new it wasn't even properly rigged out. What it had, Arthur recognized, had been carried over from the tractor.

"What else do you need from us?" he said.

Vallary looked agitated. "I need to get away from here and you need to move. A hydra can find a hydra keyed to the same pilot, which both of these are. I know where Stone is as long as that hydra is aboard *Castor*. Sooner or later she's going to figure out that she can find *me*."

"That's all right," said Brandon. He seemed to be *Camelot*'s self-appointed chief of security. "We don't have to move yet. We can see *Castor* coming fifteen light-minutes off. And maybe hydra can sneak up on us; but hydra's not known for its firepower."

"She's not going to send *Castor* OR hydra," said Vallary. "What will show up will be a bomb load. Here." She made an X on hydra's deck with her foot.

Arthur protested. "United Earth Fleet doesn't have pinpoint jump bombs. No one does."

"Stone does! Whether she knows it yet or not." Vallary felt herself for substance and, finding herself in one piece, concluded, "Evidently not yet."

Arthur's face and those of the anarchists in hearing range at the hydra's hatch slackened in dread comprehension. "On board the hydra," Arthur said.

"A hydra can find a hydra," said Vallary. "And there's a whole rack of jump bombs on the one she has."

"Bomb her first!" someone cried.

"*I* don't have any!" said Vallary. "I don't have anything. I'm flying a skeleton here. I have no weapons at all save beams. HQ was not keen on the idea of sending good bombs after bad. Now. I've put a bull's-eye on your station. I have to stay in motion. I can't fly in a straight line for as long as she lives. And you, you have to jump this cow over the moon."

"This is intolerable!" said Brandon. "How are you going to get the other hydra out of Stone's hands?"

"I tried! I am open to suggestions!" said Vallary. "Even yours!"

Brandon thought out loud, "If we can't jump bombs to *Castor,* maybe we can get *Castor* to jump into bombs. A mine field."

"You have mines?" said Vallary.

"We have mines," said Brandon.

"There're a lot of people on board *Castor,"* said Arthur.

"There're a lot more on *Camelot,"* said Brandon. *"Castor* is a ship of war."

Arthur nodded. "Can you get Stone to jump into a mine field?"

Brandon offered to Vallary, "In case it helps, we're in a position to leak some false intelligence. A warning flag went up on a coded transmission twice today. Fleet has just broken our Code thirty-seven."

"That sounds perfect," said Vallary.

"It does?" said Arthur.

Brandon explained, "You're never in a stronger position than when the enemy thinks he knows your secret language. We can feed them all kinds of crap and they'll swallow without chewing."

Arthur said, "I'm not going to underestimate Elizabeth Stone. I think she'll chew whatever we feed her."

"In that case you feed her what she can't afford to ignore," said Vallary. "Someone taught me that."

"What sort of information are you going to leak?" said Arthur.

"How about the supposed rendezvous point of *Camelot,* me, and a whole squadron of hydras? We'll give her short notice, so she has no choice but to spend a jump. And *I'll* really be there—zigzagging around the mines—so it will look real in case she figures out how to track me."

"What if she jumps wide of the mine zone?" said Brandon.

Vallary took a big breath. "Well. What can you give me to hit something the size and armor of the *Castor?"*

"We have some shipkillers," said Brandon, reluctant to part with them. "You'll lose your stealth if we hang them on you."

"There's no stealth between hydras. I need hitting power. Hang 'em."

Arthur exchanged looks with Brandon, who shrugged. "This could work."

Vallary said, "Hurry and load me, give me your broken code, and get the hell out of here."

When the new hydra was loaded with mines and hung with shipkiller missiles, Vallary eyed it skeptically. "I'm not sure I can jump with this load. Weigh me."

The anarchists cleared the hangar deck and measured the mass of the loaded hydra plus the pilot and her dog. The technician passed her a data note with misgivings. It read: *9071.903 kilograms.*

"I can work with that," said Vallary.

Arthur and Brandon moved back onto the hangar deck. "I've heard that a hydra can track a ship through a jump," said Brandon.

"True," said Vallary. "If I know your mass."

Arthur laughed and even Brandon actually smiled. "The mass of the *Camelot?"* said Arthur. "We haven't a clue."

"I wasn't asking," said Vallary. "Let me out of here."

Vallary boarded her hydra. The hangar was sealed off and depressurized, then the outer doors opened. Vallary addressed her ship in her own tongue. "Computer. Mark: the space station. Mark: hydra. Mark: stationary object in my crosshairs." She had sighted a piece of debris beyond *Camelot*'s wide torus. The computer located the object indicated. Vallary instructed, "Note relative positions. Record: space station's velocity and hydra's velocity relative to stationary object. Keep recording through separation. Finest possible resolution."

Artificial gravity quit. Vallary signaled to *Camelot* that she was ready.

A push sent the hydra out of the hangar and beyond *Camelot*'s wide wheel. "Stop record," said Vallary. Clear of the station she engaged the ship's engines.

"Computer. Give me some numbers."

The response glowed on the computer readouts: *Velocity hydra, 9.001001 meters per second. Velocity space station,* 4.858801×10^{-4} *meters per second.*

Vallary fed in the data the anarchists had given her. "Compute," Vallary ordered. "Velocity hydra times mass hydra; divide product by speed space station."

As the computer answered her, Vallary stared at the empty space from which the *Camelot* had vanished. There were some laws even anarchists had to obey.

Auriga woke up Captain Stone at midnight absolute time to hand her a message. "Surveillance intercepted this. Resonant signal, so this is realtime. It's in anarchist code, newly cracked."

Stone squinted at the printout and frowned.

Hello Camelot. *This is hydra 2. Have located Liz Stone. You are safe to jump to rendezvous with hydra squadron at 0020 hours absolute at Quadrant II: 48° 39′ 59″ by 142° 27′ 13″ by 8,793.*

"Hydra squadron," Auriga said severely. But the captain was looking at something else glaringly wrong. "Liz Stone?" she said, her voice graveled with sleep. "Liz? *Liz?*" She looked up at Auriga. "We were meant to decode this."

Auriga looked at the message again in new regard. "Ambush?"

"No doubt," said Stone. "But whose?"

The first one you're meant to find. The real one is underneath it and much harder to see.

When *Camelot* received hydra's message, Brandon inhaled sharply. There was a kind of shock in relief.

"Where does she say we are?" said Arthur.

"Kiloparsecs away from here." Brandon handed him the readout. "We're really at Quadrant II: 52° 43′ 4″ by 167° 29′ 14″ by 11,577."

Arthur covered his face. "My God, I almost want to warn them."

Brandon paced the conning tower like a caged baranta for the next minutes. Then he cried, "Arthur, I'd give anything to see what is happening. Can we send a robot to Vallary's coordinates to see if *Castor* hits the mines she's laid?"

Elizabeth Stone glared at empty air, her blue eyes fierce as she wrestled with the message. What did it really say? She had escaped Vallary's barbs while everyone else was fair game simply because Stone listened to her. What was she saying now?

"Half of everything Vallary says is bullshit," she said aloud. She looked at her two hands. *Which half? I don't have enough fingers.* "What time is the rendezvous?"

"0020 hours. It's 0006 now. Shall I set jump?"

"0020 hours," Stone muttered to herself. "Twenty. *Twenty.*"

"Sir?"

"Give me that." She took the printout and began scribbling numbers on it. "Mr. Auriga. Set jump to these coordinates. Engage at 0022 hours. Have the gunners ready all weapons."

"Captain? These are not the coordinates in the message."

"Yes they are," said Stone. She grasped his sleeve and looked him straight in the eyes. "Vallary left here with twenty rpg and we don't have enough fingers."

At 0022 hours, proximity alarms sounded aboard *Camelot.* "Sighting!" the monitor cried. "Big one!"

"Parallax!" Arthur demanded.

"Don't need it. We can *see* it. It's a quarter-gun! Coming in under the deck!"

"*Castor?* Can't be!" He opened the intercom stationwide. "Siege stations!"

"Second sighting!" the monitor reported, voice going shrill. "From the top!"

"Identity?"

Lifelessly, the monitor said, "Can't make it out. But it's loaded with shipkillers." It was loaded with enough shipkillers to take out something large and well defended.

On the bridge of *Castor,* Commander Auriga's face read open shock at the scene that greeted his eyes as he came out of jump: a huge torus of a space station, and a ship coming up on the far side of it that was only visible on account of the load it carried—a near invisible ship bristling with shipkiller missiles. Vallary.

The captain's soft drawl yanked him out of his startled daze. "Mr. Auriga."

"Weapons!" he barked. "Locate all targets." And he looked to the captain questioningly: how many targets were there here? He still didn't know.

The captain said, "Stand by to return fire." She didn't know either.

Auriga ordered the lookouts, "Keep an eye out for other ships. And don't discount other hydras."

And they waited. Seconds crept by.

Beth muttered into her hand, "Okay, Val. Run up your colors."

The lookout reported, "Shipkiller launched from the hydra."

"Track shipkiller," said Auriga.

"Tracking."

In moments the lookout turned to his commander. "Shipkiller headed toward the station."

A spate of defensive fire erupted from *Camelot* as the shipkiller missile drove toward it.

"There it is," said Stone with a signal to her exec.

"All weapons!" Auriga barked. "Lock on the station!"

"Station targeted and locked!" weapons acknowledged.

"Fire," said Captain Stone.

"Fire!"

Balto's lashing tail announced Captain Stone's approach to the hangar deck. Vallary's greeting was less enthusiastic. "Why'd you dust my stinger, bitch?"

"I always tag my own," said Stone. "My daddy taught me when I was a very little girl that any weapon you carry can be turned against you."

Vallary tossed the component she had taken from the first hydra. "Vanishing species status, my ass."

Stone caught the stick, not quite comprehending. The piece was, as she had originally thought, only a solid stick of alien metal. She looked at the second hydra. New. It bore the scars of only one battle. Stone's blue eyes shifted, uncertainly.

Vallary spoke, "You were expecting wildly different life-forms from the far side of the stargate. You wouldn't recognize one if it flew up your hangar! You were so busy fucking me over you forgot the horse I rode in on! Did any of you *ever* stop and wonder why I named the damned thing *hydra!*"

Stone turned the strange alloy in her hand over and over. "You cloned it."

"I told you I had a horror of cloning. Did I say of me? You supplied the object."

"Then each cell must know the map of the whole . . . like DNA."

And that's only carbon-based life.

I know of no other.

That explains much.

"It's alive," said Stone.

"Define life, then we'll talk."

"How did you do this?"

"No," said Vallary. "You tell me who my stock is tied to."

"You made your point," Stone said evenly. "In nines."

Vallary had reasserted her worth and her untouchable status. "Brat royalty?"

Stone tossed off a salaam with a wave of her hand. "Your Highness."

Satisfied, Vallary started out from the hangar deck. At her back Stone said, "For a while I really thought you'd turned."

Vallary stopped, then stalked off the deck without a word or a look back.

The mopping-up took some time. Captain Stone spent a long day in chasing down the survivors of *Camelot* in their small ships and escape pods or even just floating loose in spacesuits. A prison ship was summoned from the quadrant base to collect them. It would arrive in a week.

Conrad Arthur numbered among the dead.

Stone left the rest of the cleanup to Auriga.

The smell of alcohol and the thump of her dog's tail greeted her upon her return to her cabin.

"How are we, Val?"

There was a glazed shine in alien eyes. "Mimsy as a borogove."

"Liz Stone?" said the captain. *"Liz?"*

"Knew you'd get it," said Vallary.

A refugee crow from *Camelot* rode the captain's shoulder. Beth had always been good with animals. Vallary glanced up at the bird. "POW?"

Stone shook her head. "I brought Auriga lunch." She moved the crow to perch on the back of a chair. "I thought you needed a ship's mass to follow it through a jump."

"I do," said Vallary. "I got it."

"How?"

"Conservation of momentum. If I knew mine, I could figure theirs. Shit, I even got them to weigh me." Her head lolled to one side. "They heard the same coordinates you did, and I gave them twenty minutes to evacuate in case they were really listening to me. They weren't. They just sat there." Her hands dropped, limply.

Beth hadn't seen this much emotion out of Vallary since the stargate's shutting. Vallary's anger wandered about the cabin like a homing torpedo without a tagged target.

Vallary's brow pinched. "The knights are dead."

She had no lord, no liege, no country, no commander. She did not even know if her God made it over to this side of the gate. Her loyalties now, such as they were, were personal. Stone had known that. And as she herself had said, the movement wasn't an anarchy, it was a personality cult.

Stone watched her warring with her confusion. "Know anything about brainwashing, Val?"

"No. We don't take prisoners."

Stone said, "The first step in recruiting for any cult is to remove the subject from all that is familiar. You cut them off from everything they know. That was already done, and thoroughly, when I sent you out. I am sorry."

Vallary shrugged. Arthur's aura, the captivation, was already fading in the light of shipday like the hysteria of a crying jag. She could not recapture what first triggered it. It faded in the presence of the familiar—what had become familiar—*Castor,* Earth Fleet, Captain Stone. Balto.

Vallary ruffled the dog's mane. "I told him I didn't know what I was living for. Does that sound like someone who can go home again? He wanted that stargate to be open so bad. He didn't listen. I told him that I made him assume what I wanted him to assume. He still saw what he wanted, heard what he wanted, believed what he wanted. He had the same information you did. Except he knew where the mine field was."

"What mine field?" said Stone.

"The one at the coordinates I sent. In base ten."

Captain Stone leaned forward, hands clasped, elbows on her knees. "You would have jumped me into a mine field?"

"Knew you'd get it." Vallary took a drink. "Liz."

"What if I hadn't?"

"Then," said Vallary. "Then we wouldn't be here, would we?"

When we pitched the idea of the *Women at War* anthology to Holly Lisle, she offered us the choice of two ideas: a serious or a funny one. With one voice—a glad cry—Roland and I leaped on the funny one. Irony we had collected in abundance by that time, but humor itself was thin on the ground. If there's one generalization I can make, it's that women don't find war very amusing. It's true that all the wars in history so far, tragic or at best dramatic, have been won by men. Maybe if women ever win one, it will be a comedy. Sounds like an improvement to me.

Holly traveled widely in her youth as the child of occasional missionaries, held the usual eclectic mix of odd jobs, then spent ten years as a registered nurse (medicine is the inverse of war, I sometimes think). Unlike Medwind she has collected only one husband, but two children and many cats. She was a final nominee for the 1993 Campbell Award for best new writer.

About "A Few Good Men" Holly writes, "I didn't plan Medwind Song. She showed up on a bridge in the pouring rain in my first novel *Fire in the Mist* and proceeded to try to steal the book. Not satisfied with that, she demanded her own book, and I gave her *Bones of the Past,* and probably should have given her more of it than I did. She is, after all, a headhunter, and not someone to be argued with. I can't get rid of her. She's bossy and argumentative, and she adores men, and she doesn't get along very well with her gods; in other words, she's a lot more like me than any other character I've ever written. Now she's back, after pestering me to tell the story of how she acquired so many husbands and went to war over a goat."

—LMB

A Few Good Men

Holly Lisle

Medwind Song lay very still with the bedskins pulled over her head and refused to open her eyes. She was surrounded by the sounds of the Huong Hoos camp—old men swapping lies; children running and shouting; two of her six husbands whispering hopeful endearments in her ears.

It was that last which kept her feigning sleep.

Stefet, nuzzling against her right ear, whispered, "Myet'je, sweet little goatling, wake up and let me pleasure you."

Kostis, burrowed under the kidskin cover, murmured against her belly, "Dearest Medwind, softest Medwind, your hair is like silk and your breasts are sweet as honey."

Rub, nuzzle, fondle, lick.

At least there are only two of them this time, she thought grimly. *No telling where the other four are—maybe sleeping off last night so they can be sufficiently enthusiastic for this one.*

It was her own fault, she thought. She should have killed the last three; anyone else would have. But she hated to waste perfectly good men. They were always so handsome, so muscular, so . . .

She rolled over on her stomach when Stefet began nibbling, and swatted both husbands away.

Two husbands had been wonderful. Three had been even more wonderful. Five had been a bit more than she'd bargained for, and she'd determined she would take no more husbands. But then she'd had to decide on Stefet—and his eyes were the blue of an autumn sky, and his hair was the russet of a prize stag.

Thus she came to discover that six husbands were entirely too many.

She knew six young men were going to be randy—in fact, initially she'd considered randiness a point in their favor. But she had not anticipated their competitiveness.

Even in her dreams she could not escape their brags. "Let's see how wild we can make her," they said. And "I'm ready every night." And worse yet, "*I'm* ready twice a night." And *especially* "I can go all night long."

Maybe it isn't too late to turn them into drumskins now, she thought darkly. *If I had six drums instead of six husbands, I could get some sleep.*

Stroke, rub, nibble, tickle.

Etyt and Thiena, she prayed, *rescue me.*

Her gods, who had ignored this same prayer or variations of it for what seemed like forever, finally heard her. At that instant the thunderous roll of the Enemy Drum sounded throughout the camp.

"A war!" she shouted happily, and bolted from her sleeping mat. She pulled on staarne and breeches and boots, and raced out of her b'dabba and away from her husbands like a woman chased by demons.

Hoos warriors dashed from all parts of the camp to the Great B'dabba—from the sacred huts and the gaming pits and the corrals. Shalle Song met each at the b'dabba flap with the terse message: "A Song women matter."

Many of the warriors turned away, but Medwind was both woman and Song; she passed inside, where incense curled out of the mouths of the vha'attaye, the smoke already thick and pungent. The dead were not yet wakened, but her Song sisters knelt cross-legged on the thick felt mats and drummed and sang. Medwind chose a *sho* from the hanging forest of sacred drums and joined them.

The women's voices melded, interwove dark melody with counterpoint and harmony as the ancient words filled the b'dabba. They sang to the skulls that lined the low shelves, gleaming yellowed bone painted with bright patterns. Incense smoke curled out between the vha'attaye teeth; the skulls waited, silent.

Mekaals-koth dla-aavuaba'kea . . . the women sang. *For what shall I have let you die* . . .

The song wound on and in and out of itself—the words a reminder to the dead of all they had left behind and of how much they were needed by the living. The melody was wistful, yearning, haunting. The tempo of the drumming picked up. The women swayed and rocked; their voices grew husky as they sang.

And slowly, the green glow of false life covered the bony visages of the chosen vha'attaye with ghosts of their remembered flesh. The warriors fell silent, and the brief hush of the b'dabba filled with creaking bonevoices as the waking dead left the place between the worlds and joined their children.

The glowing eyes of long-dead Song women blinked open.

"Alive," the vha'attaye whispered one by one in their rasping deadthing voices. And they looked into the faces of their heirs. "For what do you call us back from the cold and the darkness, daughters?"

The Hoos warriors fell silent, and Shalle Song, her hands clenched together in anger, said, "Beloveds, ancestors, advise us. In the night, strangers crept among us, beat the goatmaiden senseless, and stole the Song women's sacred goat."

The hiss of indrawn breath from nearly thirty living women greeted the news.

Medwind felt the shock of that pronouncement as deeply as a physical cut. The expressions on the faces of the women around her and the horror in the eyes of the Song vha'attaye reflected her own dismay. The sacred goat . . .

Not the sacred goat. That was disaster!

Who could have stolen it? she wondered. *And, more important, why?*

The vha'attaye conversed softly among themselves, their hoarse creaks and dryleaf whispers too faint for mortal ears to comprehend. Their voices were the rattle of the breeze through the branches of leafless trees on a winter night; the soft hiss of leather boot soles over ice; the faint and shivery whisper of swords drawn from scabbards—cold hollow voices, stripped of all humanness. The vha'attaye were ancestors, but they scared Medwind and everyone she knew spitless. She tried to read their intentions from the expressions on their faces, but she could see nothing but growing fury in their eyes.

The warrior women sat motionless and silent, respectful of the dead, waiting. The ghostwhispers wore on, rising and falling cadences and rare snarled epithets audible to the listeners, but nothing else. Medwind's back began to ache, but she did not move. Any movement while seeking audience of the vha'attaye was disrespectful.

At last, the greatest Hoos warrior woman who had ever lived, the long-dead Taithe Song, grandmother's grandmother to them all, said, "It is decided, daughters. Hear my decree."

The warriors leaned forward slightly.

"No man may know the value placed on the Song women's goat. No man can be permitted to suspect its purpose. Therefore, though a large war would admirably serve the needs of justice, the needs of secrecy are, in this instance, by far the greater."

Taithe's already quiet voice grew softer yet.

"The Song women may not gather for war to rescue the sacred goat. Instead, one woman alone will wage this war for all of you."

The warriors did not move, but Medwind felt the powerful urge to look at her comrades, to see if she could possibly have heard Taithe aright. One woman, alone, against unknown numbers of the enemy—with the retrieval of the most prized of all the Song women's prized possessions resting on her shoulders.

"Grandmother's grandmother," Shalle said, "it is too late for this to be secret. I have beaten the Enemy Drum. All the camp knows something has happened."

Taithe Song frowned. "Then you must lie. Disguise another goat as the sacred goat, and tell the goatmaiden she must say only that she was beaten. If anyone should ask you, you must say that, after discussion with your vha'attaye, you have decided the matter of the beating was between the goatmaiden and the one she wronged. The warrior who goes off to rescue the sacred goat will win no war-necklace, and will get no public honor. She will never be able to brag in the war-brags about great feats she may accomplish in this secret war, and no matter how many warriors she kills, she will get not even one more war-bead to sew on her staarne-saaid. She will be gone as long as she is gone, alone, her life forfeit, her absence from the tribe unexplained, her public honor forever after questioned."

When Taithe fell silent, none of the living spoke. Medwind sat, breathing in the incense, considering the vha'attaye decree.

Shalle Song buried her face in her hands and groaned. "Oh, by Etyt and Thiena—we must have our goat back. But how can I command an honored warrior to rescue our goat, when I cannot offer her those things that are a brave warrior's due?"

"You cannot command," Taithe said. "But one among your number will volunteer."

Taithe looked briefly straight at Medwind Song, and then away.

Medwind was, for an instant, appalled by the idea of volunteering alone for such a terrible war. Trekking, alone, over the Hoos domains in search of a single stolen goat. Fighting, alone, for the honor of all the Song women. But then she saw in her mind's eye the Hoos domains—the deep, rich red-and-gold fields and fruit forests of the Chak Hoos lands to the north; the rolling, grassy plains of the Huong Hoos domain; the bleak, forbidding beauty of the rocky barrens and steep fjords of the realm of the Stone Teeth Hoos to the south. She could see the Kéle Sea pounding against the cliffs of the Stone Teeth, or rolling onto the warm, wide, white sand beaches northward.

Riding, tracking, camping—alone. A day or two—maybe even three—tracking the thieves, a bit of danger when she killed them, and another few days riding home. The beautiful sound of wind rushing over the tall grasses and the scent of sun-warmed earth and crushed greenery rising up from beneath her horses' hooves. Nights spent under an open sky, staring up at the stars. A campfire with a fresh-killed burrie roasting on a spit. Mountain water fresh from a spring.

The serenity of lonely wilds. Silence. No one to talk to but her horses.

"I'll go," she said, and her voice rang loudly in the silent b'dabba.

The other warriors started, and a few were so shocked they actually turned away from the vha'attaye to stare at her.

One of the women said, "Well, yes, I suppose you would. You have more to lose than the rest of us."

No—more to gain, Medwind thought. But she said nothing.

Shalle Song said, "You will have the secret gratitude of all the Song women, young or old, warrior or priest or mother. You will have our eternal thanks, in place of the glory you deserve."

And Medwind simply smiled.

I'll give up glory, she thought, *for a good night's sleep.*

Medwind packed her camp gear and weapons and gathered supplies for herself and her horses. She bid her husbands good-bye without explanation and rode out of the village uncheered, leaving like an outcast instead of a hero—her face unpainted and her feather crest packed, when it should have been waving brightly from the top of her head.

The silence followed her, and though she knew her sister warriors held her in their prayers—as all the Song women would hold her in their prayers—that silence hurt. She faced the greatest challenge of her life, and even if she succeeded, she could never tell.

It was a fact best not thought on, she decided.

The trail Medwind followed led south. It veered once, at the point where it crossed a streambed. Until that crossing, it had been so faint and so carefully hidden that she had not been certain she was following the right one. But when the thieves crossed the stream, she could see where the horses and the goat—only one goat—had stopped to drink; could see where thieves had walked upstream to get their own water. On the muddy bank, she finally saw that the horses wore shoes—and the Stone Teeth Hoos shod their horses because their terrain was rocky and hard on their horses' hooves, while the rest of the Hoos tribes left their horses unshod.

The boot prints were all large and indented deeply in the earth—tracks made by men, not women. She paced off three squares where the prints were clearest as the thieves headed away from the bank and while they were remounting, then counted and compared footprints within each of the squares. For every three sets of tracks she got in her three squares, she counted one man. She was following at least five people; she reminded herself that some of the thieves might not have dismounted, so there could be even more. With them, the men had easily twenty horses—the prints crossed and overlapped, making an accurate count nearly impossible. And of course she found the tracks of the single goat.

She swung back into her saddle and trotted out after them. She was worried.

The thieves' trail kept steadily south, over a low ridge and down into the basin of the Kaabali Plain.

Medwind stopped at the top of the ridge, wary. Twilight would not be long in coming, and the Kaabali, the Demon Plain, was rife with predators adapted to the tall grass. It was home to a number of deadly things that lived nowhere else. She nocked an arrow and looked down the slope, alert for movement.

For a moment, she neither saw nor heard a thing. But then, when she felt sure her enemies had been swallowed up by the Demon Plain, she heard a noise so impossible, for an instant she felt certain her ears deceived her.

From the depths of the tall grass, the sound continued. Whistling.

And the terrible stories came back to her—the stories of the whistling demons who haunted the Kaabali.

The darkals, harbingers of nightfall, flitted through the skies in search of insects. Down below her, in the tall grass, a shaarni coughed. Medwind heard horses whinny in the farther distance, and knew the men she stalked were gaining on her—getting away across the basin. Bloodsuckers hummed and buzzed around her, coming out in clouds as the earth cooled and the sun rolled down to the horizon. Medwind had no wish to challenge the demons for passage, though. She began backing her horses so that she could go the long way around the haunted ground.

And suddenly, the whistling changed to loud singing, and Medwind stared down into the basin, overwhelmed by sheer disbelief. The singer was a woman—and from the sound of the words, an outlander.

Medwind kicked her horse to hurry him away from the basin. An outlander in the haunted places was worse even than just demons—the warrior could feel the crackle of magic beginning to build around her; she could taste the metallic tang of demon-smoke gathering in the air like storm clouds. Doom hung heavy in the twilight sky while the outlander sang cheerily in the tall, tall grass below.

"Around the Kaabali," Medwind said to herself. "Around, then pick up the trail on the other side—and hope the demons don't eat the goat before I get him."

But she hadn't time to get away. Out of the clear sky, demon lightning flashed directly beside her, and thunder cracked, and her string of horses plunged down the slope into the demon-plagued hollow. Medwind gripped her mount's round sides with her thighs and sawed on the reins and swore, but the lightning nipped at the horses' heels again and again as the demons herded Medwind and her string into their domain. The horses pounded over the plain, heedless of the ground beneath their hooves; Medwind prayed to Huuwer, god of horses, that her beasts would not fall into any holes and break their legs—or her neck.

Dust devils swirled up from the ground, pale, twisting, sickly white in the darkness; dust clogged her nose and gritted in her eyes and mouth. Then all around her the demons began to answer the woman who'd summoned them—whistling. The earth glowed golden beneath her horses' hooves and cracked open in front of her and behind, and out of the cracks in the earth sprang the demons. Medwind tried not to look at them. It was common knowledge that demons stole the souls of those who saw them; but the demons were too beautiful, and they were everywhere. They glittered like sunlight on water, or like the sparks cast up by a crackling fire; they twisted through the air in curls of glowing smoke.

Medwind wished she knew what her soul felt like, so she could tell when the demons stole it. She hoped it was something she wouldn't miss very much.

The demons twisted around her and licked along her flesh, still whistling—and their icy touch brought her skin to chillbumps and left her shuddering. Her riding horse trembled with fear and fell over dead; she leapt free, narrowly avoiding being crushed, and pulled her sword from her sheath as the demons chased after her, slipping along on the night air. Whistling.

Then her string of packhorses toppled one by one as the demons touched them—all dead, either of demonic magic, or from sheer fright. Medwind's pulse pounded in her ears and her blood raced and she wondered if her own heart was about to burst.

She heard shouts in an unknown tongue—or perhaps the shouts were gibberish. Or a spell. She recognized the voice of the singing madwoman—the one who'd whistled up these nightmare-spawned fiends—the woman was no doubt commanding the demons to destroy Medwind. To steal her soul.

Medwind's mouth went dry and her palms sweated. She gripped her sword two-handed and crouched, her stance wide. She longed for her feather crest, for her war-garb that gleamed with its silver studs and clanked with war-beads, one for every warrior she'd defeated. She yearned for the weight of her war-belt around her waist, clattering with the bones of her slain foes—for if she died at the hands of demons, she wanted to die as a warrior, with her face painted and blood on her blade.

"By Etyt and Thiena!" she shouted, "I'll slay you all!"

It was sheerest bombast, but the words made her feel better.

She fixed the images of her gods in her mind, and charged forward, slashing at the glowing phantoms.

They slipped around her blade unscathed—they could have been smoke for all the harm she did them. The demons whistled, and the blowing dust grew thicker, and the wind fiercer, so that she had to fight for breath and could not keep her eyes open.

She lost all sense of direction. Blind, she staggered over the uneven ground while the tall grass, wind-whipped, lashed her and cut her skin and clothes. She sensed a change in the tone of the demons' whistling, then—as if before they had been unsure what to make of her, but now they knew. Now they mocked her, and she lost her temper, and flailed blindly for them with her sword.

She gasped for air, and tears streamed down her cheeks. She pulled the hem of her staarne up over her face so she could breathe through the filter of the cloth. It wouldn't be long until sand and grit clogged the fabric. If the demons hadn't killed her by then, suffocation surely would.

Deeper, distant thunder rumbled in the distance, and Medwind felt dampness in the wind that blew around her: a storm approached. She stumbled forward, step by staggered, clumsy step, swinging the sword toward the loudest whistling; she grew angrier and more frustrated as her blade met nothing but air.

Then suddenly and without warning, something grabbed at her ankle and pulled, and she toppled to the ground. Her sword flew out of her hands and she only just escaped smashing her face into the ground; the palms of both her hands felt as if they'd been flayed, and her wrists throbbed.

"Die, fiends!" she bellowed, and scrabbled blindly after the demon that had tripped her.

A wooden staff smacked across Medwind's knuckles. She yelped, and a raspy voice shouted in her ear: "Hush—to be quiet and sitting still!" The accent was atrocious, and foreign, and completely unfamiliar to the Hoos warrior. "Am to making gone the sky-devils."

Medwind crawled away from the place where she guessed the woman and her staff to be; she sat sucking her knuckles and trying to get the sand out of her eyes. She discovered the dust-devils no longer blew around her—and she realized, as well, that something had muted the demons' whistling.

Her eyes burned—the sand had stung them raw. But she began to see things again; at first, only the difference between light and darkness, and then, gradually, details of the place in which she found herself.

She saw that the grass of the Kaabali Plain continued to whip back and forth while the demons danced over it, their muted whistles furious. Medwind discovered she sat within a pale circle of light into which the demons did not cross. She wondered what power could keep the demons away.

Medwind turned to study her rescuer. The woman crouched, wild-eyed, over a small fire that burned in a brazier—her thick red braids waved over the flames, unheeded, and occasionally the tip of one or the other would dip through the fire and out again, unburned. The woman muttered ceaselessly and made passes directly through the flames with her hands.

She stared at the outlander, astonished. Medwind had seen magic before; the Huong Hoos had priests, of course, who drummed and chanted and rode the terrible River of Time back to the days of the ancestors. And Hoos warriors sang the vha'attaye to life. Medwind herself had an unexplained talent for making the weapons of her enemies leap out of their hands at inopportune moments—a talent that did much to balance the inequity she found when battling bigger, stronger male warriors.

But to hold off demons with a bit of flame and some words . . . that was a wonder the likes of which Medwind had never even imagined. She leaned forward to stare more closely at the fire, which did not consume the things it touched, and reached out a tentative finger.

A bolt of lightning slammed into the ground entirely too close to her—real lightning—not the tricksy stuff made by the misbegotten demons. Its ripping sound was followed by a roar of thunder that shook the earth under her feet. She jumped, startled, and her hand knocked over the brazier. The fire went out.

The circle of light that kept out the demons died, and they slipped in to lick against the women, their shrill whistles once again loud enough to drive even a warrior to madness. The dust blew thick and damp—it stuck more horribly than before.

And then the true storm broke, and torrents of rain poured down like rivers freed from the sky. Medwind gasped for air; across from her, the stranger's mouth gaped open like a fish's, and she wiped frantically but uselessly at her eyes.

The golden wraiths ceased their whistling; they began to wail, and to Medwind's amazement, they guttered like flames put to water, and smeared and ran through the air, down to the earth. The ground around Medwind and the stranger glowed faintly for several moments as the demons washed back into it—and then they were gone, and the two women were left in the cold, wet darkness.

Both women just stood there for a moment, unable to decide what to do next. Then the stranger shouted over the roar of the storm, "This maybe not such good-for-camping place after all, how you think?"

The only response Medwind could manage was a weak laugh.

The demons should have been her only problem, Medwind thought. If the gods weren't such uncaring fiends, they would have thought the demons enough.

Problems . . .

The woman, who introduced herself as Rakell Onosdotte, had kindly offered to share her tent with Medwind for the night, seeing that the Hoos warrior was without one. The offer was meant in kindness—

—But Rakell's tent leaked. In fact, as far as Medwind could tell, the only purpose the tent had served had been to collect the rain and hold it in place so both women could stay wet after the storm passed by. By morning both women were soaked to the bone.

The outlander stomped around in a foul humor. "How people live in tent like that, I not even to imagining."

Medwind's remark that no one in their right mind would live in such a tent elicited a snarled comment that the Hoos warriors who sold it to her swore it was a genuine Hoos b'dabba. Medwind laughed—the outlander glowered and muttered something in her own tongue that Medwind didn't think would translate kindly.

They packed Rakell's mules, and then the outlander spread her arms and smiled. Evidently, Medwind thought, all was forgiven.

"Where we to going now, Medwindsong?" she asked.

Medwind stopped, flabbergasted. "We?" she asked. "*We?* No, no. You will go where you must go, and I will continue on my journey."

Rakell's face fell. "You to traveling alone, and no horses, and no food—very bad. Very bad. I to going with you, to sharing all foods, and you to taking me to Hoos village."

"I'm going into war to save our goat, and you aren't coming with me," Medwind said.

The outlander's eyes widened—and then she frowned, her expression one of bewilderment. "I to thinking I not understanding good the words—I hearing word 'war,' I to thinking 'fight many people.' I hearing word 'goat,' I to thinking little animal to going 'baaa-baaa' what to walking four-legged and having"—she waggled her hands on her head, mimicking goat horns—"things on head."

Medwind nodded. "That's right."

Rakell leaned against her lead mule and sucked in her lower lip. "Oh. Goat war." She closed her eyes. "Mmmmm. Ha." She opened her eyes. "Why?"

Medwind sighed. She needed to get to her dead horses, to see what she could salvage from the previous night's disaster. She needed to figure out some way to relocate the goat thieves, since the rain would have washed away all her sign. She needed to get moving—and the little outlander with her endless questions would slow her down.

"It's a secret," the Hoos warrior said. "The sort of secret you keep from your husbands."

Rakell frowned again. "Oh. I not having husbands."

Medwind waved a hand dismissively. "Lovers, then."

"I not to having lovers."

Medwind arched an eyebrow. Perhaps the woman didn't understand the words. "Men. Your *men.*"

"I not to having men."

Ludicrous, Medwind thought. She'd never heard of anyone over the age of the change who hadn't had men. Even the ones who preferred women had always tried a man or two. The outlander was just misunderstanding the word, she decided.

"You are a woman," she said slowly. "I am a woman." She pointed to the two of them. "Women. Men are . . ." She frowned, and pantomimed the distinguishing characteristic of the male. "Men are . . ."

"I to knowing what men are. I not having men. Not to having women, neither."

"Well . . . but you've had men before," Medwind insisted.

"No."

"Not ever?" the Hoos warrior asked.

"Not never."

Now it was Medwind's turn to express disbelief. "Why not?"

"I to making deal with you," the little outlander said. "You to telling me what for you needing goat-war, I to telling you what for I not to having men."

Medwind decided it wouldn't really matter if the woman followed her part of the way to the Stone Teeth domain. She could insist that Rakell let her share the mules—certainly having pack beasts would speed her trip to the Stone Teeth Hoos domain.

"Come on, then," Medwind said. "I have to see what the demons left of my things."

They hadn't left much. The demons—or perhaps the mundane denizens of the basin—had devoured everything of the horses but polished bones. With Medwind's packs they'd been only slightly less voracious. The b'dabba remained, as did her war-dress, and her cooking utensils. All of her provisions were gone, though—cleaned out as if they'd never been.

Rakell looked at the remains of Medwind's things, and then out at the waving, flat sea of grass in the Kaabali. Medwind saw her shudder.

"Bad, very bad things in this place," she said slowly.

Medwind, busy transferring her few remaining belongings to the backs of the mules, snorted. "You just realized that, did you? This place would have been dangerous even if you hadn't whistled up the demons."

"Whistled—up—the demons . . ." Rakell frowned. "But the Hoos men, they to telling me this place very good for to camping place. They to telling me whistle for to keeping away—" She growled and curved her fingers into claws.

Medwind shook her head. "Hoos men *told* you to whistle on the Kaabali Plain?"

"Yes."

"Were these the same Hoos men who sold you that tent?"

Rakell nodded vigorously. "Same men."

Medwind shook her head, awed. She stopped packing and looked at the little woman. "What did you do to them? Did you try to steal their goats—or tell them their mothers were sheep and their fathers were shepherds?"

Rakell shrugged. "I to not knowing. I to looking for Hoos village. I asking them, 'Where to finding Hoos village?' They saying, 'You to looking for husband?' and I telling them not. They to smiling at me with pointy teeth and saying, 'You to sleeping in tent with us, we to telling you where is village.' I saying, 'No, thank you,' and they—" Rakell shrugged, imitating the men. "They to saying all is good, all is happy—they to selling me tent, they to telling me I finding village here. They to saying, 'Remember—must to whistling.' " She shrugged again.

Medwind chuckled and went back to her packing. "Next time men want to bed you and you tell them no, don't buy their tents or ask them for camping advice afterward."

Rakell chuckled ruefully. "I to keeping that in my thinking."

* * *

They got out of the Kaabali as fast as they could, which meant backtracking toward Medwind's village, and then going around the basin rim. The rim was a vile place—most of it rough ground, with the steep decline into the basin itself on one side, and jagged, upthrust rocks all around. Medwind hated staying so close to the Kaabali, but she figured the Stone Teeth thieves had gained at least a couple of days on her as matters stood. If she worked her way out to more hospitable land, she could lose them altogether.

Medwind and Rakell led the mules, and Medwind tried hard not to miss her horses—her fine, fast, lovely horses that had been so afraid of the demons they'd fallen down dead. She tried not to worry that while she and the little outlander walked, the thieves on their horses were pulling farther ahead—every step took them farther ahead.

And she discovered that trying not to worry was exactly the same as worrying, but with more guilt. So then she tried not to feel guilty; that made things even worse. The next time Rakell made an effort to start up a conversation, Medwind greeted it with genuine relief.

"So you to warring for goat. Now you to telling me why?"

Medwind felt the goat was too close to her problems. "First, tell me why you have no men," she said.

Rakell shrugged. "I am not to knowing all the words. The making of thing to happening by—" She waved her fingers in front of her, and Medwind recognized the movements as being similar to those that had so fascinated her the previous night.

"Magic?" she offered.

The outlander shrugged. "Maybe. I am to teaching"—she stumbled over the word —"*magic* at the . . . big house for women—" She snarled something and threw up her hands in a gesture of frustration. *"University of Daane,"* she muttered.

The sounds she made were alien to Medwind, and the Hoos warrior shook her head to signify that she did not understand.

"Is a place to learning." Rakell sighed. "I to hating your language."

Medwind nodded and laughed. "I don't think it likes you, either."

The outlander frowned for a moment, and then caught Medwind's meaning, and laughed with her. "Maybe—or not. But for to doing magic, and to making magic stronger, must not to having men. No—" Words failed her again, and once again she resorted to gestures.

Medwind caught her meaning, and forced herself not to laugh at the bawdy pantomime. Instead, she sifted through the hundreds of Hoos words relating to the subject. She picked the least specific of them. "Sex," she said helpfully.

"Word to sounding like two cats fighting on roof," Rakell muttered.

"Cat sex is 'myaakfissu,' " the Hoos warrior said.

"I not to wanting know that word. I to explaining—for *mage*—word for me is *mage*—the sex is to being bad thing. So no sex."

Medwind frowned. "That's terrible. Did you do something terrible?—Or don't your gods like you?"

"Sex and magic not to mixing. I want to doing strong magic, so no sex."

Medwind made a rude noise. "Then I'm glad I'm not a"—she recalled the word the outlander used to describe herself—"a *mage*. I have six husbands—and lots of sex."

"But you not to doing magic, so it not matter."

Medwind felt suddenly challenged by the other woman's dismissive attitude. She stopped and glared down at the little outlander. "I can do magic," she said. "Watch."

She focused on one of her spare axes, which she'd packed on the outside of the mule's baggage. The trick she knew was easier to do in battle—perhaps because she needed it more—but she could manage well enough without the added pressure. She waved a finger, and the ax worked its way out of the pack and floated to her hand. She grasped the cool, smooth bone handle, and turned to the outlander. That was the only trick she knew, but it was real magic—and it had saved her life more than once, which, as far as she was concerned, made it the best kind of magic.

She was astonished by the expression on the other woman's face.

"That to being impossible," the woman asserted. "That to being big magic—not little magic. To doing again." Rakell crossed her arms over her chest and frowned at Medwind.

"I don't have another ax out where I can get it," the Hoos warrior protested.

"Then to putting that one back."

Medwind shrugged, and recreated the bright line in her mind along which she floated the weapon. It was harder sending the weapon back—perhaps because she was tired, or perhaps because, having done the trick once, she didn't see the point in doing it again—but she did manage. When the ax settled itself back into its carrier, she turned to the outlander.

"So it's not impossible, you see?"

Rakell nodded. The expression on her face was unreadable. "I to seeing. Is why I to coming this place. I to finding other magics, and other ways."

They walked along in silence for a while, along the rim of the Basin. In the tall grass far below, Medwind noted dark shapes moving. She thought of the predators that hunted there, and she shuddered. To the Hoos warrior, even walking along the rim seemed like begging disaster to strike. She mentally damned her quarry to an unwarlike death, so that they would never be permitted the eternally green plains of Yarwalla, for taking the route they'd chosen.

Rakell sighed. "Now you to telling me why is so important this goat."

Medwind plodded along the rocky terrain, her head down. She said softly, "Husbands are important to Hoos women—good, virile husbands, who produce children and pleasure their wives. We brag about them in the women's b'dabbas, and tell the tales of their sexual feats to win status over our sisters. To my gods, war and husbands and children—" Her voice broke at that last. Medwind had no children. Her lack—her failure—grew in importance to herself, to her sister warriors, and to her gods with every month that her belly remained flat.

"The goat," Rakell prodded. "You are to telling about the goat."

Medwind studied the outlander's impatient expression and clicked her tongue. "This is about the goat. The Song women are famed for the virility of our husbands. Of all Hoos women, we are held in highest regard because our husbands are the most virile, and the"—Medwind sought for the perfect word—"the horniest. If a Song woman courts a man, all the women in the village will lust after him because then his manliness is assured." *Except for me*, she thought. *I can't even lure a lover from my own tribe because I have no babies—and no other women desire my men.*

"The goat," Rakell growled.

"I'm getting to that." Medwind shook her head in bemusement—among her own people she was thought appallingly direct and tactless. The Hoos woman thought the outlander would go mad listening to Hothmir the Taleteller spinning one of his stories—no one *ever* accused him of being direct.

"We Song women have a magic that makes our men randier," she said. "We choose the finest young billy goat from all our flocks, and by magic, we bind his lust to the lust of our husbands so that they acquire his amazing prowess."

Rakell's already pale skin seemed to Medwind to grow paler while the outlander's mouth flapped open and closed in a fashion the warrior found droll. "Insane," Rakell muttered. "To making hornier the men, who are bad-bad horny already."

Medwind chuckled. "No such thing as bad horny." Then she thought of her six husbands waiting for her at home and amended her statement. *"Most* of the time."

Rakell rolled her eyes. She obviously found the idea of wanting sex from men inconceivable. "So, what to happening now your goat is took?"

The Hoos warrior felt the bleakness of impending doom settle again on her heart. "It depends on what the Stone Teeth Hoos do with the goat. Just by taking him away, they will weaken our men's lust. The farther they take the goat, the less our husbands will desire us. The distance that controls the power of the spell is no bad thing when we are far from home and warring on enemies, for then our husbands who are warriors must sleep in the men's place apart from us. They must think only of war, as we who are also warriors must also think of war." She sighed and picked her way past fallen rocks that littered the path. "To have the goat far away and the men at home—that is a bad thing."

"That to sounding a little bad," Rakell said, looking like she didn't mean it. "There is something worse?"

"Mmmmmmm." Medwind didn't really want to think about the worst possibilities. But she nodded. "If they do magic on the goat, or kill him, it would make our men—" The Hoos warrior nibbled on her lower lip and looked over at the outlander. "You know the word *geshfuda?*"

"No."

"Is a man whose balls are cut off."

"Oh." Rakell looked suitably impressed.

"All the husbands of the Song women will become *geshfuda.* Their balls will dry up and fall off, and the Song women will have no more husbands, and no more children."

"Not good."

"No," Medwind agreed. "Not good at all. So I have to get the goat back."

"So why you alone? How come you not got all the Song women with you? And I to thinking the men *help* you get that goat back," Rakell remarked. Medwind noted the outlander's single raised eyebrow, and the way she only smiled with half her mouth.

"Our husbands don't know about the goat," Medwind told her. "And I don't want to think of what they'd do if they found out."

Medwind looked from the rocky, uneven terrain around her to a bird that flew overhead, and swore softly.

"Is to saying bird to molesting goats?" Rakell asked. She looked puzzled.

"It's profanity," Medwind told her. "I just wish we could fly like that *dleffing* bird. Then we could catch the thieves."

The little outlander looked up at her, and the pale, freckled face grew thoughtful. "Fly," Rakell said softly. She, too, stared up at the bird, but her eyes held something in them besides envy. Medwind didn't recognize the look.

Rakell stopped and sat on a rock. She rested her chin in both her hands, and when Medwind cleared her throat preparatory to asking what the outlander thought she was doing, said in peremptory tones, "Shutting mouth. I to thinking."

Medwind didn't care for Rakell's tone, nor for the content of her demand. She wondered if telling the outlander about the shelf of skulls lining her b'dabba back home would improve her manners.

"I to thinking maybe we can flying," Rakell said abruptly.

Medwind wondered how common insanity was among the non-Hoos.

"There is"—the outlander held her hands out, imitating the flight of birds—"things what flying with people in them in land of my home. I not knowing how that magic works. Is *saje* kind of magic. But I to thinking maybe make mules to flying. That is *my* kind magic."

Medwind studied the mules; she thought they looked incredibly unbirdlike. They looked back at her with stubborn, unhappy expressions. They were balky, finding the rock-strewn, grassless terrain not at all to their liking. They stamped and snorted; shook off flies; kicked peevishly at one another.

"I to having this idea once long, long time ago, but not so sure how good idea is to being. But now we must to hurrying so your husbands' balls not falling off. You to holding first mule."

Medwind evidently didn't move fast enough to suit the little outlander. She stood, stomped angrily to the mules, and staked all but one to the ground. She glared at Medwind while pulling the packs off the lead mule and dumping them angrily on the ground. Then she grabbed the lead mule by his halter and yanked him over to the warrior. "To holding him now. Not to letting go, understand? Not for nothing!"

Medwind held the mule and kept silent—but she began to imagine the outlander's pale, freckled skin stretched over a little two-headed drum. Pale skin like that was probably very thin and fine—and would surely make a nice, musical, high-pitched sound, she thought. As she mentally transformed the outlander into drumheads, she started liking her better.

Rakell sat herself with an air of righteous indignation back on the rock and pushed her nose against the mule's. She stared into his eyes. She started to mutter under her breath, in her heathen outlander tongue.

Medwind watched, fascinated.

For a long time, nothing seemed to happen at all. Then two bumps appeared, one on either of the mule's sides. Medwind worried—she hoped the outlander wasn't doing something that would kill the beast; the hideous bulges on its sides were growing larger and more fatal-looking by the moment. They developed sharp edges and knobs, and she began to believe the mule had swallowed a demon the night before, and the demon had chosen this moment to try to get out.

Then membranes of skin flexed in between the growing knobs of bone, and Medwind realized she was seeing wings. Not the feathered wings of birds, nor the scaled wings of darkals—but fur-edged wings, with leathery skin stretched between the bones so fine and thin she could see the mule's sides underneath it as the wings grew.

Magic. She watched the outlander and recalled her own little trick with the ax, suddenly ashamed she had believed it to be such a wondrous thing. Yearning grew in her soul—a hunger to learn the magic this outlander knew. And the outlander said she taught magic.

Medwind stared at the mule; its legs tapered and grew thinner, as did its barrel sides and blocky head—and the Hoos warrior felt the beast was shrinking to feed its spreading wings. The wings grew wide, wider than the wingspan of any creature Medwind had ever seen.

The mule began to twitch the huge wings. It shivered, and Medwind could see the whites around its eyes. Its nostrils flared, and it snorted and stamped its hooves nervously.

She understood. She tried to imagine herself sprouting wings and empathized with the poor beast. She would have been frightened, too.

Rakell opened her eyes, and pulled her face away from the mule's. She whispered something in her heathen language and smiled up at Medwind. "To being beautiful, is not?"

Medwind nodded slowly. The mule with wings *was* lovely. She wasn't sure, though, how well the creature would fly—or how happy she was about the idea of riding while it did. What the outlander planned was evident.

"Next mule," Rakell snapped.

Medwind unpacked and led over the second mule, and watched as the *mage* altered the second beast.

Without being asked, she led away the second and got ready to bring the third, but the outlander stopped her. "I to being too tired," she said. "Two enough for us. I to sleeping now." And without further comment, she staggered over to the packs, pulled out her bedroll, and spread it on the ground without even bothering to first clear the rocks underneath.

As fast as that, she was on the ground and asleep, curled into a ball and snoring heavily.

Medwind sighed and stared at the mules, two slender-boned and winged, and one stolid and heavy and tied to the ground. She thought of the thieves, getting away, the Song goat their captive—and the Song women's husbands and lovers as much their captives as the goat, though all unknowing.

I could take one of the mules, she thought. *Fly after the thieves, with my bow and arrows and axes, and strike them down from the air. The outlander would still have two mules—and here on the rim, nothing would bother her.*

But the warrior didn't move to take one of the winged mules. She could not bring herself to steal from the woman who'd worked to help her. She was more than a little terrified of the prospect of getting on the back of a mule with wings and launching into the air like a bird. And, as much as anything, she was drawn by the wonder of the magic—greater and more wonderful magic than she dreamed possible.

She wanted that magic for herself.

If the winged mules flew, then Medwind would catch the thieves quickly. If they didn't, she was losing little more time than she'd already lost.

While she waited, Medwind unloaded the packs from the third mule and fed all three animals out of the outlander's meager supplies. Then she pulled her warrior's garb from her pack and put it on. She braided her hair through the upstanding bone spikes of the feathered war-crest, and striped her face with esca in the cat patterning of the Song warriors. She donned her war necklaces, and her red, black, and silver staarne, and the warrior's belt from which her enemies' bones dangled, clattering softly. She did not don coin bracelets or bell earrings—the bells and jangles made a wonderful sound when a hundred Hoos warriors rode over the crest of a hill but eliminated any hope of using the element of surprise. A hundred Hoos warriors didn't really need surprise—but Medwind figured she might.

The sun moved only a short way through its rolling arc before Rakell woke. She sat up abruptly, rubbed the sleep out of her eyes—and then she looked at Medwind. She yelped. Medwind watched the outlander glance from the bone sslis in the warrior's nose to the red plumes that curled out from the top of her head; she watched her take in the weapons—short straight sword, vha'atta ax, bow and arrows. The Hoos woman felt a smile pulling at the corners of her mouth as the outlander's gaze fixed on the bones at her waist.

Rakell took a long, deep breath. "Fine," she said at last. "So. You to having weapons, I see. Now we must to going. Must to hurrying, Medwindsong." The outlander pulled a few items Medwind didn't recognize out of her packs and placed them in a pouch at her waist.

Medwind nodded. The outlander flipped her braids back over her shoulder and scrambled onto the back of the smaller winged mule, leaving the larger for Medwind. "We now to saving your husbands. Then you to taking me to Hoos village." Her eyes were wary, though—as though she thought she went to sleep with a little cat and woke only to discover a lion by her side.

Medwind nodded again and walked cautiously to the mule, which glared at her. She stepped to the beast's side. It flailed out with its wings, struck Medwind hard across the chest, and knocked the warrior over backward. Medwind landed on her rump on the rocky ground, and swore.

The mule snorted at her and stamped its hooves.

Medwind stood and growled at the animal, low in the back of her throat.

"Not to being afraid," Rakell demanded. "Just to getting on. Now, please."

The scrapes on both Medwind's palms were bigger and deeper than they had been the night before, and they hurt. She told the mule, "If you do that again, beast, I'll cut your ears off to wear at my belt."

The mule's ears lay flat against its head, and it bared its teeth at the warrior. But Medwind knew beasts. She grasped the lead rope tightly, took a firm grip of the mane at the withers, and vaulted onto the animal's back, settling herself high on the withers in front of the wings.

The mule had sharp, bony withers. It was a damned uncomfortable position.

"Now what?" she asked Rakell.

The little *mage* exuded confidence. "Now to riding very fast, to leaping in air, to flying to goat stealers."

Medwind nodded. That made sense. "You go first," she told the other woman. "I'll follow right behind you."

Now that the moment was upon her, she found herself hoping the mule would not be able to fly. She tried to imagine the ground falling away beneath her feet, and shivered.

But the outlander seemed fearless—and Medwind, a Hoos warrior, could appear to be nothing less. So when Rakell kicked her mule in the sides and shouted it forward, Medwind did the same.

The mules took off in a leisurely amble.

"Haaaayaaaiiiii!" Rakell shouted, and smacked her mule on the rump. Medwind imitated her actions.

The mules moved into a grudging, bone-jarring trot; then, when Medwind was sure she'd never again have a reason to care whether her husbands' testicles fell off or not, dropped back to a walk again.

She sucked in air through her teeth and wished she'd thought to pad the ax-blade-humped mule with the clothes she'd been wearing.

Rakell looked annoyed. "We must to"—she looked over the edge of the Basin, then at the rock-strewn ground around her—"to poking with sharp things," she said. "To making the mules go faster." The outlander pulled a little dagger out of a sheath hidden in the front of her shirt, and pricked her mule's hindquarters with the tip.

The mule's head went down between his forelegs, his hindquarters launched into the air, and the outlander flew over the mule's neck and landed on the ground with a thud.

Courage was a thing to be emulated, the Hoos woman decided, but not lunacy. "No, I don't think I'll try that," Medwind said thoughtfully.

The outlander got up, muttering. "Unmothered beasts," she snarled, and glared at the mule. "Mules to being too smart—horses much better."

Medwind preferred horses, too. But if the outlander had poked *her* in the rump with a dagger, the Hoos woman thought, she would have taken the woman's thighbones for drumsticks. She thought the mule showed admirable restraint in only throwing Rakell.

The outlander climbed back on the mule, still muttering.

It was obvious, Medwind thought, that mules with wings weren't going to get her to the thieves—which meant the goat was farther away than ever, and her chances of getting him back safely were less than they'd ever been.

"We might as well repack the mules and start walking again," she said, but the outlander wasn't listening. She was sitting very still on the mule's back with an expression on her face so stubborn it made the animal look like the more reasonable of the two. Suddenly, Rakell shrieked in her mule's ear, yanked the lead rope around to one side, and kicked the mule in the flanks, all at the same time. The mule jumped, twisted—and fell off the Basin rim.

"Oh, gods," Medwind whispered. The mule with the woman on its back toppled toward the Basin floor, and the warrior watched them, dismayed. The crazy outlander was going to die because she'd tried to help Medwind—and then the mule spread its wings. And flew.

"No," Medwind muttered. "That's crazy."

Below, the mule flapped its wings and gained altitude. Medwind heard the outlander's triumphant shout.

"Oh, no," she said, staring down at the mule in the Basin, and then at her mount. "She doesn't think *I'm* going to do that, does she?"

"To hurrying, Medwindsong!" the outlander shouted. The mule had gained more altitude and was now circling in the Basin about eye-level with Medwind. "Goat is waiting!"

Evidently she did.

Medwind commended herself to the gods, and told them, "This is the *same* as battle! If I die on this damned mule, you still come get me and take me to Yarwalla." She tensed.

"Yeeeeeeeaaaaaahhhh!" she screamed, and jerked the mule's head cliffward, and dug her ribs into his sides.

The mule bolted, jumped—

Medwind tangled her fingers in the mule's mane, locked her legs around its sides, closed her eyes tightly. The wind, whistling up around her, was the only sound she could hear. Her stomach felt as if it were going to crawl out of her throat and take her morning meal with it, her heart seemed to have stopped—she was going to die.

Medwind had never been surer of anything in her life.

The wind kept roaring past her, terrible and loud and hungry.

And kept roaring past her, though the direction seemed to have shifted.

It was certainly taking her a long time to smash into the ground, she thought. She squinted through one eye. The ground below was a very, very long way away. She closed the eye again, regretting having peeked.

"Medwindsong, why you to flying that way?" shouted the execrable outlander. "We to going the other way!"

She was going to have to open her eyes. Warriors didn't fear the things that noisy little outlanders faced with courage. She opened both eyes, and made herself keep them open.

Gods, but it was a long way down. She pulled on the lead rope to turn the mule's head, and was surprised to find that even in the air, the rest of the mule followed.

Medwind picked out a landmark she knew and aimed the mule toward it. She concentrated on the horizon, which looked the same as it always did, and refused to look at the ground beneath her feet; *that* had become as horrible and different as a once-familiar thing could ever be.

The thieves were moving into Stone Teeth Hoos territory when Medwind Song and Rakell Onosdotte overtook them. The two women kept their mules high in the air, hoping with sufficient altitude they would look enough like birds not to draw attention.

There were twelve men in the party. She was disconcerted to discover she'd so badly missed her estimation of their numbers; few of them had dismounted to drink. She wondered if they had avoided doing so only to mislead trackers about the strength of their numbers. If that were the case, the ploy had been damnably effective.

Medwind studied the lay of the land ahead of them. The gently rolling plains of the Huong Hoos domains had given way to the rough, crumpled terrain the Stone Teeth claimed. She was fascinated by the shapes the ground formed when viewed from high up. She could see passes and cliffs, paths and . . .

She caught Rakell's attention and pointed down. In the direction the Stone Teeth thieving party was moving, through a pass and tucked into a valley, she saw signs of a permanent camp. She and the outlander left the thieves behind them and soared to it.

"This to being where they coming, you think?" Rakell shouted.

Medwind nodded. She circled the camp once at a lower altitude, noting the twelve painted dwelling b'dabbas set up around a central meeting hut.

Twelve. She frowned. Very odd. There should have been more—villages never sent all their men out on a raid; not even the Stone Teeth, which Medwind considered the stupid branch of the Hoos. But there had been twelve thieves, and there were twelve b'dabbas, and from the air, Medwind could see no sign of life in the camp below.

She located an even-looking stretch of ground nearby.

"Back to the ground," she shouted, and pointed at her chosen landing site.

Rakell nodded her understanding, and the two women angled their mules toward the ground. It approached with alarming speed, and Medwind, her mind replaying the terrifying takeoff, wondered if perhaps she should close her eyes.

The mule backwinged, and the approach of the ground slowed.

Ah, good, she thought, relaxing.

So Medwind wasn't braced when she and the mule hit the ground. The mule bucked and tried to keep its feet under itself, but when it locked its legs, forward momentum threw the beast rump over nose and tossed the warrior to the ground in front of it.

Medwind lay staring at the glittering stars spinning an arm's length above her. No part of her body didn't hurt, but some parts hurt much worse than others. Her left leg, for example, pained her terribly instead of just a lot. She looked down and discovered that the spike of her head-hunting ax, which was intended as a convenient place for carrying the severed heads of enemies, had driven itself completely through the back of her thigh.

It's really *going to hurt when I pull that out,* she thought. She carefully moved her feet and her hands; everything seemed to be in working order. She forced herself to sit up, and braced one hand against her thigh, and the other against the ax. She gave one sharp jerk, and the spike came free. Blood poured from the wound.

"Yehhhgh." The outlander sat on the ground halfway across the clearing, watching—she had crashed, too, but looked none the worse for it. "Leg to looking bad."

"Doesn't feel very good, either," Medwind grumbled. She started digging through the supply kit strapped to her hip. She had a bit of dried goat dung to pack the wound with, and some hide to hold the packing in place.

The outlander shrieked when Medwind pulled the dried dung out of the kit.

"Not to using! Not to using! I to having fix for hole in your leg!" She scrambled toward outlander and waved her hands frantically.

Medwind worked her boot off and untied the ankle strings that kept the baggy breeches tucked in. She rolled the thin goat leather up, and studied the wound. As holes went, she'd seen bigger. It was a bloody mess, but she didn't think she'd done irreparable damage. "A little dried dung to cover the hole, and—"

"You *crazy!*" The outlander shook her head, and from her pouch pulled out a little bag of white powder and a bright blue stick. "To holding still!" Rakell demanded.

Medwind didn't think she liked the idea of an outlander working on the wound—but she considered Rakell's magic. She wondered if, in the outlands, people had magics for fixing holes in the leg.

She discovered they did. Rakell drew big circles around the holes on both sides with her blue stick, then sprinkled powder over the stick itself and, without any warning, jabbed the smooth, waxy rod in through one side of the wound and all the way out through the other. Medwind yelped as fire hot agony burned from the inside of her leg outward. She stared at the twin holes. First, they stopped bleeding. Then the edges of the wound turned black, and puckered. And then, to Medwind's amazement, the wounds sealed off.

"Hah!" the outlander said. "Better than goat shit."

Medwind had to agree. She moved the leg cautiously, and found the wounds stayed closed. The leg still hurt—but pain was nothing of real importance. She was relieved the leg wouldn't turn green and fill with pus like Kother Song's leg did when he got stabbed. Medwind had always wondered if the dagger Kother's enemy used had been poisoned, but the idea that it might *not* have been had always frightened her even more.

"Thank you," she told Rakell. "That's very good."

"Simple. If I to showing you how, probably even you to doing it—you with your six husbands. Pah! Easy magic."

They stood.

Medwind looked at the mules, grazing at the far side of the clearing, away from the camp. "Will they come when you call them?"

Rakell stared at Medwind, then laughed. "A joke!" she said. "They to being mules. They not to doing anything when you to calling them."

The Hoos warrior sighed. "We'd better catch them, then."

Rakell said, "I to having a little *candy* in my pocket. They to liking *candy."*

She handed a piece of something red and slightly sticky to the warrior. Medwind sniffed it thoughtfully. "What is this?"

"It is to eating. To trying it."

Medwind licked it once, then closed her eyes. She'd never tasted anything like it in her life. "Oh," she whispered. "This must be what the food at Etyt and Thiena's table tastes like. How did you get it?"

"Candy to being common in Ariss. Everybody to eating it."

Medwind popped the piece of *candy* into her mouth, and let it melt on her tongue. To go to a place where she could eat the food of the gods and learn magic . . . *That is something I must do someday,* she told herself. She sighed and smiled at the outlander. "What a wonderful place your Ariss must be."

Rakell shrugged. The expression on her face suggested she was not overly impressed. "It is a place."

Medwind laughed. "As is my village, which you want to see so much. And in my village, we have no *candy,* and only a little magic." She sighed. "You will be disappointed, I'm afraid. But now I have eaten the *candy,* and the mules are still over there."

Rakell said, "You to going left, I to going right, and we to pretending we have *candy* in our hands. The mules, they to knowing what it is."

The Hoos warrior tried to picture a place where even mules ate the delectable sweet stuff. Yarwalla could not be finer, she decided. "Someday, you must take me to your city. I'd like to see this wonderful land for myself."

"You to scaring the pants off the Arissonese." Rakell laughed and walked toward the winged mules, one hand out, clicking her tongue. She swung right while Medwind, emulating her gestures and sounds, swung left.

The mules' heads came up and they eyed the approaching women warily.

"Here, mule," Medwind murmured, and proffered the imaginary sweet. "Come get the *candy.*"

Both animals backed up, then, as Medwind and Rakell got closer, turned and galloped away. In midstride, the mules lifted into the air. Medwind and Rakell stared after their vanishing mounts with dismay.

"Interesting," Medwind said as the mules disappeared beyond the line of hills. It occurred to her that their braying as they flew away sounded very much like laughter. "Perhaps you have some magic to fix this problem?"

Rakell shook her head sadly.

"Well, then," Medwind said, and sighed. "I suppose this means we'd better win."

The thieves arrived on the tail of darkness, trotting into the tiny, empty camp with shouts of triumph and laughter. They staked the Song women's billy goat next to the central b'dabba, then went about the routines of opening up their camp. They lit a fire, passed around drink and meat, and settled down on logs to talk.

They were all young, all blond and green-eyed in the manner of the Stone Teeth Hoos. When they smiled, their point-filed teeth gleamed in the firelight.

Medwind found them sexy. She thought it a pity she was going to have to kill them.

They ate and talked, frequently looking back the way they had come.

One of them finally sighed and asked, "How long until the women come after us?"

Medwind almost didn't catch the question. The Stone Teeth dialect was different from that of the Huong Hoos. She'd used it for a while when she was breaking in her fourth and fifth husbands, but dropped it as soon as they were both fluent in Huong.

"My sister thought they would follow us right away—I can't understand why they didn't."

One young man chewed on a strip of dried fish, and poked at the fire with a stick. "Maybe they came a different way. Or maybe the men are coming with them."

The man with the sister shook his head vehemently. "Shoshu told me the women would never let the men know what they've done with their goat."

Shoshu! Medwind thought of the captured Stone Teeth woman who had become a Song man's wife, and a friend of the Song women. Shoshu was never permitted in the Song women's secret ceremonies—but one of the sisters must have told her about the goat. Perhaps, Medwind thought, one of the Song women had even spelled Shoshu's husband for her so that he would be certain to keep her satisfied.

Beside Medwind, the outlander shifted impatiently. "Why we not to killing them now?" she whispered.

"Shh. I'm listening to something."

The warrior returned her attention to the thieves.

"—can't kill the goat, but we could cut off his balls."

"Shoshu said no. She wants her husband intact."

Which meant they didn't steal the goat to exact revenge for Shoshu. Medwind frowned.

One of the thieves stood abruptly and threw the rest of his meat into the center of the fire. "I want a woman!" he snarled. "You said if we did this, we could get women without having the whole Huong village after us!" He glared down at the man with the sister. "They were supposed to follow us! They didn't!" He stormed off toward one of the smaller b'dabbas.

Another of the thieves stood. "He's right. We did this so we could get laid—and we aren't getting laid. I say we kill the goat, and too bad what your sister wants. *She's* getting laid."

Medwind realized then what the thieves were. They were the young-bucks—the men of the Stone Teeth tribe who were too old to be children but too young to challenge the Stone Teeth elders for their harems. The elders kicked them out of the main tribe when they started looking like a threat to the nubile women, leaving them to roam wild and cause trouble for everyone else.

Of course, it also meant that Stone Teeth young-bucks made wonderful husbands if they could be safely caught.

Medwind looked at them, and slowly licked her lips. They really were very fine. Broad chested, lean hipped. Probably, she thought wistfully, well hung.

Killing them would be *such* a waste.

"They was all together where we could to killing them," Rakell huffed. "Now they to getting away."

Medwind came to a decision. "We're not going to kill them," she muttered.

"Not?"

Medwind shook her head slowly. "Not if I can help it."

Rakell tried to press for details, but the Hoos warrior put her finger to her lips and glared the outlander to silence.

They crouched in their hiding place in the darkness, only steps away from the main camp, and waited while Medwind's feet fell asleep and her legs and thighs burned from the enforced stillness.

The men debated killing the goat, or neutering him—and finally agreed to wait another day, to see who might show up in their camp. The man who won the debate argued eloquently for his sister's continued happiness; Medwind thought he would make an especially good husband.

For someone else, she told herself firmly. *Not for me. For someone else.*

The men banked their fire, and all but the single guard finally went to their lonely bachelor huts for another womanless night.

Medwind grinned in the darkness. At least, that was what *they* thought.

"Now, Outlander," she said, "I'm going to do some Hoos magic. It's going to be dangerous. Will you help me?"

The outlander rolled her eyes. "I not to having many choices, am I?"

The warrior gave the outlander a sunny smile. "Not a lot."

They crept in a circle around the camp, following the path of the sun. The outlander had offered some advice on this portion of their magicking, and so as they walked, they sprinkled a powder behind them that Rakell insisted would make their spell binding.

They were especially careful passing the guard, who sat morosely by the campfire, eyeing the Song women's goat. Medwind found the guard mightily attractive, and did not wish to have to shoot him or cut his throat. The women were silent as zephyrs over stony ground—

Even so, the guard froze, and stared toward them, into the darkness surrounding his campfire. He nocked an arrow in his bow and frowned.

Both women froze.

Medwind held her breath, and thought—*sit down, sit down, damnable man.*

The guard drew the bow and stalked forward.

Medwind sighed. She focused on her one war trick, and slowly, slowly, lifted the arrows out of his quiver, and gently, gently, floated them away on the night wind. Then she threw her head-ax into the brush away from herself. It made a soft thud as it hit the dirt, and the Stone Teeth guard swiveled, shot the arrow perfectly into the place where he heard the sound, and reached over his shoulder to his quiver for another arrow.

His next reaction was a natural one. He patted at the air where his arrows should have been. Then he turned around to see what had become of them.

In three running steps, Medwind was upon him with her knife to his throat. She twisted his arm behind his back with her free hand, and pulled it up between his shoulderblades so high his upper arm bid fair to pop out of the shoulder joint.

"The Song women have arrived, you *kako*-sucking goat thief," she hissed in his ear, "and we're really mad. If so much as a whisper escapes your mouth, we'll cut out your tongue first, and take your balls after. Understand?"

His eyes bulged, and he nodded vigorously.

"Down," she snarled.

He knelt, and Rakell sauntered out of hiding, shoved a scrap of cloth in his mouth, and bound it in place. He watched her, his green eyes round with fear.

"So you wanted women, did you?" Medwind growled.

He nodded his head affirmatively, but the Hoos warrior could see from the look in his eyes that he was already doubting the wisdom of his wishes.

"Well, you've got women now. Cut his shirt off," Medwind said to the outlander. Rakell nodded, and with a very large knife, sliced the young man's shirt away. His eyes rolled wildly, but he kept quiet. Without being told, Rakell cut the soft leather of his shirt into strips and bound his ankles, and then his wrists. Then, with a grin, the outlander made an extra twist in the leather and tied wrists and ankles together behind his back.

Medwind tipped him facedown into the dirt, and she and the outlander exchanged grins. "Finish the circle for me," Medwind said.

She crouched by the thief, not trusting him to stay silent if she was out of reach. She knelt over him, maintaining her fierce attitude—but she couldn't help thinking he was gorgeous. His skin was smooth and brown, his nose as straight and sharp as a blade, and his eyes were as green as the plains in springtime.

She sighed—

And felt the press of a knife against her own throat.

"So," a gravelly voice whispered in her ear, "the Huong women worry about their goat after all."

Damn all, she thought.

She tried to think of a way to disarm him.

Nothing came to mind.

Then she heard a shuffle and a thud, and the weight of the man's body dropped on top of her, knocking her onto her captive.

Feels just like home, Medwind thought as she struggled to roll out from between the two men. The second man, the one with the knife, was unconscious. Medwind checked to make sure he wasn't dead. He breathed and his heart beat—but the Hoos warrior noted the egg-size lump on his skull and thought he wouldn't be happy when he woke.

Rakell stood above the three of them, holding the thieves' cooking rock in her hands.

"I not to hitting him too hard," she said.

"That was just right," Medwind told her. "Thanks."

"He to coming out of that tent right beside you, and you not even to seeing him." The outlander gave the Hoos woman a knowing look. "You to needing pay closer attention."

Medwind snorted. "What I need to do is fix the damned goat."

She rubbed the billy's head—she was fond of him. He did a good job for her—though of late perhaps he did too good a job. But that, she told herself, wasn't *his* fault.

The outlander finished the circle, then waved at Medwind from safely outside of it. The warrior nodded. She took her dagger and nicked her finger with it, then let one drop of blood fall onto the dirt, and one fall on the billy's nose. She whispered,

"Like unto like
Etyt and Thiena—
Who lead me in war and in bed,
All within this circle
I claim and bind.
I call lust to greater lust,
Men to women—
That they be merry to rut,
Merry to bed."

The two red drops of blood glowed briefly with a pale white light. Then the light faded, and outwardly, all within the circle remained unchanged. But Medwind patted the goat on the nose, knowing better.

She walked to the fire and picked up the stick one of the thieves had been playing with earlier. Stick in hand, she went back and stood beside the goat.

"Draw your weapons, warriors," she shouted. "Let's teach these thieves a lesson."

She listened, and instantly heard movement within the tent.

An arrow landed mere inches from the first head that peered out of a b'dabba.

Medwind was impressed. Rakell hadn't even known how to hold the bow when Medwind handed it to her. Either the outlander learned fast—or the gods held the young thief's life in their favor.

"Come out and fight, you cowards!" Medwind yelled. "*Kakos* eaters, goat molesters!" She gave them her most telling insult: "Plowers of the earth!"

That did it. They flew out of their b'dabbas, wielding swords and axes and bows, and looked around. The first of them saw her, realized that she was only holding a stick, and charged.

Medwind smacked the goat vigorously across the testicles, then jumped quickly out of the way.

The goat went wild.

The thieves grabbed at their crotches and rolled on the packed earth, writhing and groaning.

"The Song women will teach you!" Medwind yelled. "First lesson—guard this goat with your life."

The twelve men, the goat, and the two women made a pretty parade riding into the village. Medwind earned herself a necklace for the capture of the twelve Stone Teeth young-bucks, even though she didn't get anything for the goat.

But in the secret meeting of the Song women afterward, Medwind discovered her mothers and sisters were not as pleased with her catch as she'd hoped they'd be.

"What are we going to do with twelve more men?" Shalle Song rested her head in her hands and sighed. The rest of the Song women knelt in the b'dabba, watching Medwind.

The men, their wrists still bound, knelt outside the b'dabba, awaiting the verdict of the Song women.

"I mean," Shalle said, "you won back the sacred goat—and for that, you have our undying gratitude. But, Medwind—what in the name of the gods were you thinking? Have you decided to start collecting them?"

Medwind winced. "I didn't bring them all back for me," she said. "I thought everyone else might want one or two."

"Why didn't you just *kill* them?"

The Hoos warrior sighed. "They were"—she cringed—"cute."

"By Etyt and Thiena!" Shalle sputtered, her exasperation clear. "All men are cute when they're young. It passes."

Medwind nodded gloomily. "I just didn't want to waste them."

One of the Song women sighed. "They really are lovely, though. I suppose I could take one. You did say you've bound them all to the goat."

Medwind nodded again.

Another of the Song women said, "I could use an extra husband for myself—and one for my daughter."

Several other women agreed to take on an extra man.

But when the women were done, there were still three Stone Teeth young-bucks left.

"We can't give them to any of the other women," Shalle said. "They're already bound to our goat. They're Song men now. They'll be so far superior to the other men . . ."

"Kill them," one of the warriors said. "I need some new drumskins. And these men aren't all scarred up. They'll tan nicely."

Another patted Medwind on the shoulder. "Don't feel so bad. You did save most of them," she said.

Medwind hadn't wanted to save most of them. She'd wanted to save *all* of them.

She groaned. "Don't kill them. I'll take the last three."

The rest of the women stared at her, and a few snickered.

"Did someone accidentally bind you to that goat, too, Medwind?" one asked.

Only Medwind didn't join in the laughter that followed.

Medwind put up with her nine husbands for two weeks. They were the longest, most exhausting two weeks of her life.

When Rakell Onosdotte came to her b'dabba, and said, "I to finishing study of the women's magic here. I just to wanting say good-bye," the Hoos warrior was on her feet and at the outlander's side in an instant.

"Take me with you," she begged. "Teach me outlander magic. Let me come to your Ariss. Please."

The outlander frowned. "Medwind, at the *university,* there to being no men. No sex. You could not to bringing your husbands with you."

And all Medwind could do was smile.

Judith Tarr began her writing career in fantasy and historical fantasy, producing a dozen novels and a couple dozen short stories. She has collaborated on novels set in Jerry Pournelle's War World, for Baen Books. Recent historical novels published by Forge include *Lord of the Two Lands,* about Alexander the Great, *Throne of Isis,* about Cleopatra, *Pillar of Fire,* about Akhenaten, and *The Eagle's Daughter,* set in tenth-century Byzantium. The following short story, however, is science fiction with a vengeance.

Judith lives in Arizona with two cats, two dogs, a goat, and three Lipizzan horses. She received her master's degree from Cambridge University in England, holds a Ph.D. in medieval studies from Yale, and is the least-handicapped deaf person I've ever met. She finds the computer net a boon, at last giving practical use to her telephone.

About "Sitting Shiva" she writes: "This was supposed to be a different story. The war, the soldier, the boy she left behind her—the usual. In the way stories have, it mutated. The old story is still embedded in the new one, but there turned out to be a whole lot more that needed to be said about Sarge and her war."

—LMB

Sitting Shiva

Judith Tarr

Early late darknight on Sheol Four: Kosinski and Mwalunga and Sarge and I close down the bar. There's just us and the sweepermech and the bartender rolled up in his coffin, with a sound like a snore to tell us he's on standby till closing time. Kosinski does something to the console that pings us another hour, Mwalunga stands us round number we-all-forget, and Sarge props her chin on her fist and says, "Old stories. Old, *old* stories. Same old stories."

Mwalunga's a Radical Semioticist, so maybe that would get him spinning off on a litany to Saint Derrida, but he's busy deconstructing the formula for the perfect tequila fusion reaction. Kosinski is figuring out how to fit the bar through a transdimensional warp without including the bartender. That leaves me, and I don't argue. The last augment got rid of my vocal apparatus. Temporarily, the techs said. Just till the shunts finish rooting. Then they'll install a new and improved set. After that I'll be the finest peacekeeping machine in six systems. Except for Sarge, of course. And Kosinski and Mwalunga. And a classified number of other advanced-model peacekeepers under construction in Peaceforce's labs on Sheol Four.

Doesn't mean I can't think. Doesn't mean I can't listen, either. I'm the best listener in the system. Enhanced hearing and all. Increased processing capacity. Eidetic memory.

"There are no new stories," says Sarge. She's not drunk, high, or blissed. Her augments take care of that. What she is, is augmented into a roaring blue funk.

"No new stories," she says. "No new ones at all."

Sarge is adapting to new dotware. Ethical module, the net says when I ask. We're peacekeepers. Not soldiers. We don't make war. We wage peace. We have ethics built in.

Ethics, if you ask me, are a pain in the ass. But nobody's asking, and I couldn't answer if they did. Sarge is rocking on the stool, back and forth, back and forth, glaring at something the augment's showing her.

"Remember," she says suddenly. It bursts out of her—the augment talking, putting roots in new portions of the wetware. "The day we took Babylon: old whore of cities opens her legs and we ram right in. Nobody screams. Nobody dies. Right, so we rape a few. Pay your coin, tell 'em it's for the goddess, take 'em right in the street and what can they say? We've got the big spears."

I shiver, somewhere in back of my thermal-control module. She's got the big one, the bad one, the one we're all whispering about. She's got the module that's so secret it's not even classified. Nobody can tell you exactly what it's supposed to do, except make better peacekeepers. Lots better. Real kick-ass peace-of-the-action boysngirls. Go right in there, smile the place to slag, beat swords into agribusiness, and on to the next little breach of the peace.

"Blood," says Sarge, "is the most beautiful, beautiful color. We poured it out in rivers, there in the Wilderness. Remember how the creek ran red? I drank from it. It tasted cold, like iron. Then that Yankee fell in it and it tasted like shit."

She's remembering, is what she's doing. Programmed memory. Might as well be past-life regression, which they tried, but either it didn't work at all or it worked too well, depending on who's telling it. Subject crawls up his own asshole and goes to sleep with his thumb in his mouth.

Might *be* regression, I think, watching Sarge. But if it's that, they found a way to focus it, and she's been through history's greatest hits.

"Shadows on the wall," she says. "Ash. Inferno. You don't feel the rads, they swear you don't, but even in the suit, my skin feels weird. Like it's crawling. Everything's burned. Everything. Blasted—blown to hell and away."

Kosinski's dimensional warp is a little swirl of not-quite-there in the middle of the table. Mwalunga is finishing off something poisonously green. I shoot them a look and reach for Sarge. Got to be careful not to break her the way I broke the first glass tonight, picking it up in fingers that don't look any different but by Waldo are.

She's just a little thing, always was. She doesn't fight, and good thing, too.

She could throw me through the wall if she wanted to. I ease her up and point her toward the door.

She's still talking, still swaying, on her feet now, never quite falling down. "Great king," she says. "King of kings. King of Hatti. Come—I have need—your son—" Then shifts. "So kill the little bastard. So kill him dead. Put a bullet right through his brain." And shifts. "And we took Acre, we held it, we drove out the Saracen—for God and Holy Sepulcher."

I put Sarge to bed, pull off her boots, and think about the rest, but I'm not so sure of my hands yet. I'd rip something. She hasn't stopped talking. It's quieter now, a mutter that gets faster, then slows down, then speeds up again.

If something was wrong, the techs would be there, making fixes. There isn't even a yellow alert on her file in the net. This is normal, then—within the parameters.

Some parameters.

I start to head back to my own quarters, but one way and another I end up sitting by Sarge's bed. I don't need sleep; I've got a module that takes care of that. Fifty hours to go before I have to access the dream files, process and purge them. So I sit, and I watch Sarge.

Sarge and I go back a long way. Sarge bailed me and half a platoon of peacekeepers out of a major breach of the peace on No-Name. I got Sarge out of trouble on Seljuk, when that pretty boy announced he was having their baby and she was going to marry him or be flayed by a committee of mullahs. No-Name's slag now. The boy on Seljuk decanted the baby and robbed the mosque and headed for the Rim, where he's seducing Rimmers and running a handy little blackmail business on the side.

And Sarge and I are on Sheol Four, getting an upgrade. They'll ship us out, who knows where, wherever there's peace to keep. Time was when I'd be wild to get back out there, walk on thin edges, negotiate or fight. That's long time since. I'm an old hand, been everywhere, seen everything, died often enough to know there's no guts or glory in it.

Sarge is in deep dreamstate. Her muttering's gone subvocal. I don't bother to listen to it. I've got an eye on her, an eye on the net where she's a tight small node, security-tagged till there's no Sarge left to find. That doesn't upset me. She'd find the same thing if she tried to access me. I've got codes that could get me straight in. I don't try them.

I do an end run instead. I wiggle past a couple of nodes, slide under a nexus, and come in the back way.

It's a battle. Don't ask me where. When is easier. They're at the AK-and-napalm stage, and they're killing one another with brisk efficiency. Everybody's in desert camouflage. No telling who's who. It's blistering hot. It's bloody. Something next to my foot turns out to be a fragment of skull and a wide, surprised brown eye.

This is your standard taped-memory sequence, subspecies Horrors of War.

Except there's an emphasis that I haven't seen before. It's the small things that come into focus. The skull fragment, the eye. The flies on a corpse. The corpse's hand, stretching toward a low stone cylinder that might be a well.

I can smell the blood-and-shit-and-sweet stench of death. Dust, sweat, something sharp that goes with ancient projectile weapons. I can't tell you how I know that. Taped in, then.

Still, that's fairly standard. We're supposed to know why we keep the peace. War has no glory. Death by violence has no honor. The best death is death in old age, in bed: a peaceful letting go.

What's different is how it feels.

It feels like hell.

Hell's a superstition. Hell's also a place—anyplace that's been a killing ground. Hell's the killing, and the quiet after the killing.

Sarge is in hell. Hell that doesn't stop. Doesn't let up. Killing ground after killing ground. Men in furs killing one another with clubs. Men in iron killing one another with spears. Men in camo killing one another with guns. Men in ecosuits killing one another with beamers.

I rip myself out by the roots. It's that bad—that deep. I almost trigger the alarms, but some reflex keeps me going along the right pathways, back and out and into the safety of my own aching head.

I have to sit and breathe for a long time. Just to feel the air blasting in and out of my lung implants, the creak of reinforced ribs, the twitch of servoed hands into fists.

Sarge hasn't moved. She's deep in her private hell. Her augment that nobody knows about. Her experimental ethical module.

I get up. She twitches, but not at anything I'm doing. I get out of there.

I find Kosinski in bed with Mwalunga. Mwalunga's on top. I wait for a pause in the proceedings. Mwalunga says something uncomplimentary in Derridan. Kosinski says calmly, "Next time you come in, watch out for the timeloop by the door."

I hadn't even noticed it. Not that I'd have noticed if I had, if you know what I mean. Timeloops are infinite, unless someone shuts them off.

I check the chrono in my head. No, no loop delay. Luck's a bitch, but sometimes she's a lazy bitch. She hasn't given me the back of her hand. This time. Took Peaceforce to do that, abducting my vocal apparatus and not putting it back when I need it.

I do what I can with what I've got. I pull them both to their feet. They're class 10 augments to my class 40: featherweights.

Kosinski blinks. Mwalunga's still pissed, but he asks me, "What's wrong? You've got the subtext from hell."

I nod so hard my head near pops off.

Kosinski says, "Don't do that. You'll blow a module."

And Mwalunga says, "You've been hacking again. They've upped the ante for that. Third offense, termination."

I passed offense number three a long time ago.

The net's there. The whole planet's a network, with nodes wherever there's wetware. I can't use it, even using hacker's tricks. What I'm thinking about can't go anywhere there's a chance I'll get caught.

Mwalunga and Kosinski exchange glances. Kosinski's hand moves in front of his prick. He could be scratching his balls, or he could be telling me in quicksign, *Sarge. We know.*

My hands are still present and accounted for, even if my larynx isn't. *What's going on?*

Mwalunga goes to the cleaner to wash his hands. They're answering me while he scrubs the sex-sweat off. *Experiment. New peace initiative. Teaching module. War's hell, right? Nobody believes it, everybody wants it. This shows them what they're really wanting.*

Mwalunga doesn't hack the net. He doesn't spy, either. Mwalunga reads subtext. He reads subtext like nobody else but another adept-class Radical Semioticist. Peaceforce knows that, it's what they use him for, but I don't think it quite processes the datum that Mwalunga doesn't stop reading subtext when he's told to. He keeps right on doing it till he gets to the bottom of it. If there is a bottom. Which is a religious argument on Derrida, and not something I need to worry about right now.

My head's aching worse than ever. I scrape my hands through the stubble on my scalp. *Why Sarge?*

Teacher, Kosinski signs, flopping back on the bed. You'd never know he's got plasteel bones, or much of any bones at all, the way he moves.

But she's trapped. I'm so agitated I forget to be sneaky, come right out in quicksign. *She's in a loop. She can't get out. It's* hell *in there!*

War is hell, Mwalunga signs, with the qualifier that says *cliché,* squatting on the floor to comb his mane of hair and put it up in a braid.

I snarl and squat to face him. I'm bigger. Was to begin with, even before the augments. I know I look mean. Mwalunga doesn't pay any attention. My subtext has all the menace of a kitten's, Mwalunga told me once. That's why, he also told me, I can be as big and ugly as I am, and still make it as a negotiator. Intimidation goes just so far; some people don't care if you kill them, as long as they stick to their brain-dead principles. But a big, ugly, killer-augmented, sweet-talking peacekeeper can work them around.

I can't even talk at the moment, except in sign. *They'll break her,* I tell Mwalunga.

They don't think so, his fingers say, working his hair into its plait.

They don't think so, I sign, so ferociously I almost knock myself down.

Mwalunga shrugs.

I swivel till I'm head-on with Kosinski. He's playing with himself, kind of absent, kind of meditative. Saying in quicksign around his big ruddy cock, *If we interfere, we're in shit, pure grade.*

I'm too disgusted to say anything. I lever myself up and head for the door—veering around the timeloop and barely evading the nexus that Kosinski didn't bother to warn me about.

It's almost firstlight. A couple of moons are up. Sun One's on its way. Sun Two will take a while yet. I can see the sky from Sarge's quarters. She has an outer berth, with windows that she keeps turned on all the time. She likes to see out, she says. She's a claustrophobe. Blanked walls make her nervous.

Sarge hasn't changed much since I ran out on her. Maybe she's a little grayer in the face. There's no alert on her net-signature, no more than there was before.

It's not disconnected. I check that first thing. She's logged on. No error codes. No loose connections. As far as the net knows, Sarge is in perfectly normal and acceptable condition.

I suppose she is, for a peacebreaker sentenced to a term in hell. She's not in any physical pain. Her indicators are all in the safe range.

None of them measures psychological or psychic damage. The net doesn't monitor for that. Freedom of will, you know. Thought control is a crime under Peaceforce regulations.

And what, I'd like to know, do they call this?

She's talking again. Same words as before. "Old stories. Old, old stories. Never a new one. Always old. Old."

I take her hand. She doesn't rip my arm off; doesn't respond at all.

"Burning," she says. "The burning ground. Shiva dances in ash and embers. Dances sitting. Sitting shiva. A god mourns the dead, and mourning, laughs."

Teaching module, Mwalunga said. I laugh, a hiss in my empty throat. Ethical module, the net told me. Teaching ethics. Teaching hell. They'll put whole worldsful of savages through this, make them into keepers of the peace. Or punish the peacebreakers, educate them with a perfectly nonviolent and profoundly convincing distillation of human history.

Who was it who said that the essence of humanity is hate?

Never mind.

"Hell," says Sarge. Her voice is clear. She sounds like herself. I start, and grab at hands I'm already holding so tight the bones would break if they weren't plasteel. She's still in the dreamstate, still trapped in her loop. Her voice got loose, that's all. "Hell is perfect boredom," she says. "Hell is red horror repeated until it grays into ennui. I'm bored, Hamid. I'm bored out of my skull."

Hamid is the name of the boy on Seljuk, the boy with the beautiful face and the blackmailer's heart. So she remembers him. I didn't know.

He'd be a perfect candidate for this new module.

She's running a fever. Her indicators show it, mark it, but don't tag it for treatment. She's quiet for a while, her breathing short and sharp.

She was all right last night. Twitchy, I remember. Pale, a bit. Short-spoken, but Sarge isn't your sweet-talker, not like me when I've got the equipment to do it with. We're all rough around the edges when we're post-op, anyway. She got strange near closing time in the bar, when she started talking about stories. Stories are Mwalunga's game. Sarge doesn't tell them, or talk about them. She lives them.

That's what she's doing now, if you want to think of it that way. Living somebody else's stories. Old ones. Old wars, old battles. Old hells.

I don't read subtext, like Mwalunga, or twist the fabric of the universe, like Kosinski. I fight when I have to, negotiate when I can. And I watch, and I see what the net won't register. Sarge isn't going to make it out of this loop.

I fire the datum through the net. The net doesn't send anything back.

I don't expect it to. The message is a formality. Going by the rules. Following procedure. Grasping at straws.

I can't do a thing. I can't do a damned fucking thing. Blow up Peaceforce Central? Crash the net? Sabotage the C-in-C's vat?

Sure, and see what good it does Sarge. That's another thing they did to me. Installed a failsafe commonsense module. A good peacekeeper not only knows when to fight and when to negotiate, she knows when there's nothing she can do—nothing that will make the least difference in the worlds.

I can't scream. I can pound my head against the wall, but that gets tiring after a while. I file protests with every office I can get an access code for. I charge Peaceforce with injustice, ineptitude, incompetence, the sheer incomprehensible randomness of an experiment gone to hell and dragging a good soldier with it.

All it gets me is another headache.

"Enkidu," Sarge says. "Enkidu, my brother, my heart."

She's gone deep, deeper than it would ever be safe to follow. I tell myself she's not talking to me. She doesn't even know there's a world outside of her module.

"We'll live forever," she says. "We two. Do you remember, Hephaistion? The tomb, the sacrifice: Achilles and Patroklos in the same grave. They never died, not in memory. No more shall we."

Her voice is getting thready. The net registers something, finally: dip in power in the pulmonary system.

Every alarm in the net should be going off. System failure—I know what it looks like. We all do. But not here on Sheol, in the quiet, with no enemy but the net, and no weapon but the module.

I'm doing things. I don't remember them any longer than it takes to do them. Desperate things. Futile things. Things that never work, not for complete systemic shutdown.

* * *

Peaceforce is shocked. Peaceforce is apologetic. It had no idea its experimental module would run a shunt around the safeguards in the hardware and the wetware—cancel the alarms in the net, lock the subject into a permanent downward spiral.

I'm cynical, I suppose. I don't believe much of what they tell me. Except that Sarge is dead, and won't be brought back. Can't, they say. The module took too much out of her template. They suspect a sequence of code somewhere in a subroutine. Instead of protecting the personality matrix, it ate holes in it, wrote itself over them, and then imploded.

The experiment failed, Peaceforce tells me. They regret, it's a shame, how unfortunate, they recommend a catharsis module. I still don't have my larynx back, but I show them where they can stuff their fucking module, and net-hack myself a berth on a ship going out, I don't care where.

Kosinski and Mwalunga and I close down the bar the night before my ship heads out. Peaceforce gave me my larynx back, with modifications. I'm supposed to go easy on it. I haven't, in fact, said a word. I've got used to not talking.

Kosinski and Mwalunga have got used to me not talking. They sit across from me at the table we always sit at, over by the bartender's coffin. Kosinski has figured out a potable version of null-space, a kind of anti-anti-matter. Mwalunga is reciting the *Angalta Kigalshe* in Sumerian. He told me the refrain in Standard before he started chanting:

From heaven above to hell below,
To the Netherworld she descended.

I drink Kosinski's creation, which tastes like nothing and everything, with a touch of primordial soup, and listen to words as old as human memory. Inanna went down to hell to rescue her lover, and gave up everything she had, and died horribly. But she bribed her way free, and her lover too, and they came back to the land of the living. Like us—most of us—when we're killed in the line of duty. They ship our templates back to Sheol Four, and they reconstruct us, augments and all, and we go out again, and die again, keeping the peace.

When Inanna was a goddess in Sumer, when Nineveh was new, when Tyre was a raw young town on a rock in a sea that boiled off in a firefight a thousand years ago, that's not what they called it. They called it waging war.

I drain my cup of nothing and everything, and prop my chin on my fist. Mwalunga's eyes are shut; he's chanting like a monk, for the pure sound of the words. Kosinski has got into the bartender's innards, over the bartender's feeble protests, and started tinkering. There's no space where Sarge should be. Just memories. And stories. Old stories. Stories so old they're new again.

I get up. Mwalunga doesn't notice. He's chanting the refrain; I've got so I can recognize the words as they repeat. Kosinski shoots me a glance, but he's too busy to talk. I quicksign him the Peacekeeper's good-bye. Him, and Mwalunga. Sarge, too. Sarge more than either of them.

Die well, my fingers say. *Live forever.*

This anthology seems to have more than its share of multitalented writers, not to mention people with medical backgrounds. Mickey Reichert is a pediatrician, a veterinary technician, a horse trainer, a computer programmer, an Iowa farm girl, a wife and mother, and incidentally has parents who actually are rocket scientists. Her writing credits include the five-book *Bifrost Guardians* series, the *Renshai* trilogy, *The Legend of Nightfall,* and *The Unknown Soldier,* in addition to numerous short stories. She sold her first novel and graduated from medical school in the same year, at the age of twenty-two.

About "Homecoming" Mickey writes: "While a medical student, I spent two years working with Vietnam veterans in an inpatient psychiatric hospital. Amid the schizophrenics and the manic-depressives, I met a number of regular guys who had lived through a hell most of us could not have invented in our wildest nightmares. At that time, very few people had written about the war, and those mentioned little or nothing of the personal atrocities of ordinarily good and moral people driven to acts of evil by war, and the guilt such acts inspired. Shame kept some silent, and, for some, the necessary secrets became too much to bear.

"My first novel, and this story, were born of a need to communicate the pain, remorse, loneliness, and rage of so many forced into a war that seemed causeless and senseless, invading a country of strangers when their own had nothing at stake. Post-traumatic stress disorder did not begin or end in Vietnam veterans, but it definitely claimed more than its share of victims from that war. My curiosity about what made this war and its warriors different from their predecessors led to an inspection of glory and honor that spawned this story."

—LMB

Homecoming

Mickey Zucker Reichert

The Vietnamese jungle enwrapped Paul Yamashita like a damp blanket. He took a long drag at his joint, its sweet, acrid taste a warm comfort despite the heat. Four hours earlier, he had opened the manila envelope that should have contained his orders to return stateside. "Two weeks left in my chit, and the screwed-up record shows six months." Smoke wafted from his mouth as he spoke, its fragrance clinging to sweat-plastered, black hair. "I won't get home by May fifth. Happy fucking birthday." Tears welled in his eyes. He took another drag at his joint, but this time the flavor failed to soothe. "Damn army."

Yamashita doubted he could stand another six months of watching buddies get blown away. He wanted to forget them for a while. He needed to get stoned or to find a whore, though the latter meant scratching crabs for a month. The drawn faces and hungry eyes of the local girls held little attraction for him. Nothing in this place felt like home except, oddly enough, the jungle.

From Yamashita's first day in Vietnam, the sounds and odors of the rain forest seemed as familiar as the mountains back in Pennsylvania. *Sure, walking by myself in the jungle is dangerous. Guys alone get fragged by locals all the time. But even dying is a way out of this hell, and I couldn't hardly go AWOL with five other guys.* He took another hit.

A loud rustling behind Yamashita startled him. *There's something in the brush, big and coming fast. Friendly or not, I can't afford to be discovered.* He searched frantically for cover, found a rotting deadfall, and dove beneath it. Stabbing out the joint, he flattened to the ground, still as a stone. A Charlie in black pajamas broke from the undergrowth and staggered awkwardly onto the trail. With an animallike moan, the VC fell to his knees, then rose, clutching a gray arrow protruding from his shoulder. The VC ran unsteadily down the path. A bloodstain remained where he had fallen.

Impossible. Yamashita trembled on the edge of hysteria. *Who would hunt VC with arrows?* His heart raced. His muscles knotted, and he clamped his hands to tight fists. Alone, AWOL, and carrying only a side arm, Yamashita pressed closer to the log and hoped the shadows of the jungle would shield him from the archer.

Without warning, three tall men emerged from the foliage. They resembled actors from an old Errol Flynn movie. Even their color, or lack of it, fit the image. They moved with an alien silence; their swirling, pepper-colored cloaks contrasted starkly against their pallid skin. Yamashita dared not believe what he saw. *Hallucination.* He squeezed his eyes shut. *Gotta be a fucking hallucination.* He opened his eyes. The strange men were searching the path where the VC had fallen.

Sweat tickled down Yamashita's forehead. One of his buddies had died from poisoned grass. Yamashita shook with rage. *If I get back, I'll kill the bastard who sold me this.* He dropped the joint and watched, transfixed, as one of the strange-looking men knelt and studied the bloodstain on the path. A slender finger flicked forward, touched the blood, and delicately raised it to ivory lips. A shiver racked Yamashita.

The man who knelt sniffed the air several times and moved his mouth soundlessly. Suddenly, as one, the three strangers turned toward Yamashita. He saw their full faces for the first time, the grotesquely high cheekbones set over pointed chins. Their tiny, black eyes seemed to stare through the log directly at him. Revulsion welled within Yamashita. Something deep and instinctive compelled him to destroy these loathsome beings, but fear stayed his hand.

The three pale men crept toward Yamashita. His gut knotted in horror. *They smell the damn doobie on me!* Cursing, he leaped to his feet and raced recklessly into the forest. An arrow whizzed silently by his ear. Panic gave him speed but not direction. He sprinted onward, mindlessly ducking branches and leaping brambles. Another arrow lifted the hair on one side of his head. He ran deeper into an unfamiliar part of the jungle. The ground cover thinned. Without the heavy undergrowth to foil his pursuers' aim, he would make an easy target.

Yamashita weaved through the jungle, seeking cover. He dove behind a gnarled bush. With a trembling hand, he worked the slide on his .45 and wondered how he would fare against three bows. Exposing his head only enough to aim, he poked his pistol through the foliage. As his pursuers entered the dense thicket, Yamashita braced the heel of his hand against a root and waited. The leader emerged, though neither he nor the brush made the slightest noise. Light filtered through the thick canopy of leaves, tinging his cloak green.

Yamashita steadied his sights on the man's chest and squeezed the trigger three times. The bullets passed through the stranger as if he had no more substance than a reflection and thudded into a tree behind him. *Huh? How?* Yamashita continued to shoot until the .45 dry-fired. None of his bullets struck flesh. He dropped the gun and ran.

My first three shots should have hit! Yamashita's wits exploded in terror. *They did hit, but they passed right through him. How can I fight what bullets can't hit?* Fear gripped tighter. He fled blind, like a hunted animal, back twitching in anticipation of pain. At any moment, a shaft could end his life with the abrupt finality of a sniper's bullet. His side ached, and his head pounded. He forced himself onward.

Smaller trees gradually replaced the broad-leafed giants of the jungle. The forest became as alien and soundless as the men who hounded him. In his haste, he tripped over a white-barked root and sprawled on his face. The dirt and stones of the trail bit into his palms. As he rose, he darted a panicked glance behind him. The strange men still followed. In the open sunlight, their cloaks shimmered forest green and their hoods looked gold. *How?* The color changes had to be hallucination, a drug-inspired movie spliced from black and white to Technicolor. With a howl of frantic terror, he raced along the path.

The sun beat down on Yamashita. Though his hair and cammies dripped with sweat, his skin and mouth felt parched. The throbbing pain in his head warned of impending heatstroke, yet he had no choice but to continue running. Birch trees with cadmium yellow leaves flickered past him on either side. He struggled frantically against his failing body to maintain his reckless pace. He tried to glance backward and stumbled. He rose, staggered forward, and fell. The cycle repeated itself, rise, stagger, and fall, until, one time, Yamashita kept falling.

Yamashita's gummy eyes pulled open, and he looked up through the long shaft of an abandoned well. The sun's rays shone nearly vertical, and they illuminated the upper third of the hole. Dust swirled through the beams and around thin vines that had eased his fall. His left ankle throbbed, but he doubted it was broken. *Where am I?* Memory returned in a painful rush, spurring another question. *How long have I been out?* No answer came this time. He rubbed gluey grit from parched, aching eyes with a sleeve, blinking to fully restore his vision.

The stone wall that encircled Yamashita remained in surprisingly good repair, except for a crack in the north side. Pressed tightly to the stone, he squeezed through the fissure and entered a chamber beyond it. He probed for the back wall through the impenetrable darkness. The smooth stone sides continued northward, and Yamashita followed them with his hands. As long as the cavern hid him from searchers at the well mouth, he did not care what lay at its far end.

Yamashita stopped, unscrewed the lid of his canteen, and gulped its contents with a greedy thirst. The water felt warm against his tongue, but it soothed the intolerable dryness of his throat. He emptied the canteen. *Trapped in some nightmare episode of "The Outer Limits."* He sat, back against the cool wall. *Who or what chased me?* He could not answer his own question. *Those creatures seemed to gain color as the woods changed. And why were they so damned quiet?* He stuck his head through the crack and glanced up the long shaft that isolated him from the outside world. *Let them try and follow me through that.* He leaned back with scornful defiance.

A rope dropped through the torn foliage.

Shit! They're coming down. He leaped to his feet so suddenly he bashed his head against the ceiling. Dazed, he staggered into the tunnel. With every movement, wet clothing peeled away from his skin and stuck in a different position. He could not guess what lay ahead, but he would find only death if he remained. *I'd rather crawl through a nest of VC than face those bastards.*

Yamashita escaped farther into the passage. The ceiling pressed lower as he went until he could no longer stand. First stooped, then on hands and knees, he scrambled through the tunnel. He heard no sounds of pursuit, but the silence did not comfort him. Even when the pale men had chased him through the dense underbrush of the jungle, they made no noise.

Yamashita crawled deeper into the darkness until his cammies wore through and his knees bled. His shoulder struck and toppled some unseen object. The rattle as it hit the floor echoed hollowly through a large, high-ceilinged chamber. He clawed instinctively for his .45 and found the holster empty. *Smart move, Paul, you idiot. Threw away your only weapon.*

Yamashita huddled against the wall and waited to be attacked. Only the distant drip of water answered his fears. He reached into the thigh pocket of his cammies, withdrew his cigarette lighter, and flicked the wheel with his thumb. Through the tenuous light of its white sparks, he looked into the twisted steel face of a horned man. A scream strangled in his throat. The wick did not catch. Yamashita scuttled backward and sought anonymity in the darkness.

Shaking uncontrollably, Yamashita crouched in silence. The wait for the death stroke he could not see became maddening. He struck the flint again.

The wick sputtered and caught. Its flickering light played over the woven red and black of Japanese armor. *Empty.* His fear abated, and he gathered enough courage to look away from the steel gray face and examine the object he had overturned in the darkness. A stand lay on its side, the three swords it had held scattered across the floor. The scabbards were crafted from ivory with a single flower etched delicately on each. On the handles, golden silk braided over a small, silver dragon.

Memories rushed down on Yamashita, Grandfather's stories of his ancient ancestors who carried weapons like these swords into battle. He did not puzzle over how he knew that the name for the dragon beneath the braid was *Menuki,* nor why he recognized *katana, shoto,* and *gu* as the Japanese words for the long and short swords and the armor. Now he had a weapon.

Yamashita's hand closed around the hilt of the *katana.* Reverently, he drew it from its sheath. The braid rested comfortably in his hand, and an inner calm suffused him. He laid the scabbard carefully on the stone floor, gripped the *katana* in both hands, and awaited the inevitable battle. The peace and confidence within him seemed alien, yet right.

The yellow light of a lantern bobbed in the tunnel. Yamashita turned to face it. Abruptly, one of the three strange men emerged from the shadows, clutching a sword. Yamashita's assurance ruptured into sudden panic. *What the hell am I doing? I don't know how to use a sword.* An urge seized him to hurl the *katana* at his attackers and run, but his body would not obey. Sweat stung his eyes as he tried to force his body to retreat. He could not gain control. His body responded to some force outside his will, and his mind followed helplessly. As if of their own volition, his arms swung the *katana.* The blade struck his opponent beneath the shoulder, the force of the blow aching through Yamashita's hands. Flesh gave with a sickening tear, and the whetted steel severed bone as well.

The other two men swept forward, swinging at Yamashita. He dove beneath their blades and rolled to his feet. One lunged. Yamashita redirected the thrust aside and down, drawing the man off-balance. Yamashita's foot smashed into his attacker's ribs. The *katana*'s blade slid along his throat, cutting a straight trail of scarlet. Blood splashed Yamashita's eyes, stinging. The stranger fell, dead.

Still enmeshed with the thing controlling his body, Yamashita faced his last assailant. He drew the *katana* close to his waist, blade parallel to the floor. Both men circled. Lines creased his opponent's face. The tiny black eyes shone cold with fear, but he did not run. The tip of Yamashita's *katana* leaped, in a feint, for the alien face. The man raised his sword to block. He recovered too late. Yamashita's cut arched toward his enemy's unprotected thigh. Terror reflected from the man's eyes. Steel wrenched through bone. The man fell.

Blood ran over the smooth floor. Two of Yamashita's opponents still writhed, clutching their wounds. Their mouths gaped, but their screams made no sound. Stomach roiling, Yamashita tried to avert his eyes, but he could not. Isolated from his own body, he could not even swear in frustration. Mechanically, he cleaned blood from his *katana* and checked the blade for nicks.

The force possessing Yamashita donned the armor, wedged the three swords into the left side of his belt, and made him crawl back through the tunnel. He fought to find a shred of reality to anchor his drifting consciousness. The portion of the *gu* covering his hip chafed as he crawled. He focused on the discomfort with the desperation of a drowning man. Only the pain lay between Paul Yamashita and insanity.

The weight and bulk of the armor rendered movement difficult, but Yamashita managed to climb up the rope and out of the hole. He shuddered violently. His arms and hands tingled as he felt control of his body return. His mind filled with vivid pictures of the creatures' grotesquely angular faces twisted in soundless shrieks. Memory of the brutally efficient being that had possessed him made his skin tingle and crawl. He screamed. Stomach cramps doubled him over. He collapsed to his knees and vomited. Unable to comprehend the strange abilities his body had manifested without his mind, he dropped to his side and wept himself to sleep.

Paul Yamashita slept restlessly, plagued by a dream with peculiar overtones of reality. Alone in a manicured garden, he sat with his feet tucked beneath him in the *seiza* fashion. Birds flitted between branches bent from the weight of abundant blossoms. In spite of the distractions, he turned his mind inward.

Although Yamashita's eyes remained closed, he felt the presence of another man in his illusory garden. Yamashita rose and walked past the carefully trimmed shrubbery toward the intruder, an old man dressed in traditional *gu* who waited by a pond beneath a cherry tree. Both men watched blossoms drift down to the surface of the pool. As the blossoms struck the water, circular ripples widened until they encompassed his entire dreamworld.

The old man's voice held an unnerving calmness. "Paul Yamashita, the time has come for you to begin the way of the warrior."

Vacantly, Yamashita stared into the pond and watched a hummingbird's reflection as it darted among the flowers. Most of his grandfather's stories revolved around the *musha shugyo,* a warrior's search for personal enlightenment through martial arts and combat. As a boy, Yamashita idolized the samurai, Miyamoto Musashi and Kusunoki Masashige most of all. But they lived in a very different time. They faced the men they fought, not specks on a landscape a thousand feet below or a green shadow moving through a starlighter infrared scope. And they never killed women and children.

Yamashita rolled to his side, caught in the ether reality of his dream. As if the old man read Yamashita's mind, he continued. "Your world is different. The skills you use in battle take months to learn, not lifetimes. The path to accomplishment lies in honorably facing a man superior to yourself and rising to his level of ability. Your culture reduces men to equals in combat. You have taken the glory from war." He paused. "But you are no longer in your world." The old man added one thing more. "When the time comes to return there, you must block sound and color from this world. Do not lose vision fully, though. Beyond your world, nothing exists."

Lost in illusion, Yamashita contemplated his situation in the waking world. If he accepted the existence of the nightmare place into which he had fled, he admitted insanity. If he refused it, he committed himself to the reality of Vietnam. Any option, other than death, was more inviting than another six months in Southeast Asia. His choice seemed too easy; he wondered what insanity entailed. He imagined he would discover the answer soon enough. One thought still bothered him. "Who are you?" he asked.

The old man rubbed his thighs. "I am the one who will start you on the path to enlightenment. I am your grandfather's tenth grandfather." His voice gained a strange power. "You must avenge an act of dishonor against our family."

Yamashita wondered whether insanity still represented the better choice. "What must I do?"

The old man turned from the pool and stared into Yamashita's eyes. "First you must listen to a story. Then you must kill a spirit."

Surrounded by the atrocities of war, the assignment seemed too routine to Yamashita. He sat *seiza* style and prepared himself for a tale from a less familiar grandfather.

The old man closed his eyes. Wrinkles from a long life in the sun creased his face. "Many years ago, Miura Benkei studied the physical aspects of strategy and set out on his own *musha shugyo.* Though young, he fought many duels and faced death bravely on every occasion. Soon, he neared the final stage of enlightenment when he would see all creations and their opposites as one. His sword would become 'no sword.' He would face himself in the cold, harsh light of truth and find ultimate harmony."

After a long pause to collect his thoughts, the old man continued. "Benkei's wanderings led him far south of Japan, near where we now sit. He, too, inadvertently entered this realm where spirits have color and sound. There, he discovered an *ikiryo tengu* formed from the evil notions of Ikuru-Tayotami, a lord once killed by an ancestor. Foolishly, Benkei challenged the creature to a duel. The *tengu* demon-lord accepted. He arranged to hold the combat in his imperial gardens at sunrise the following day."

The dream-Yamashita listened in silence. Only the old man's mouth moved. "When Benkei approached the site of the contest, nearly a score of demon guards ambushed him. He cut down several. But, faced with more enemies than he could possibly defeat, he fled." The ancient eyes opened wider. "The *tengu* lord named Benkei a coward. He offered a reward for the young man's head. Though Benkei tried to avenge himself, the spirit defenses stood impenetrable. Rather than lose face and be hunted down like an animal, he committed *seppuku* and died honorably."

Yamashita's ancestor shifted slightly and braced his hands on his thigh. "Benkei's swords had served his family for generations; and he would have dishonored the swords, their craftsman, and his ancestors if he allowed them to fall into Ikuru-Tayotami's ignoble hands. To protect his weapons, he built them a shrine in a long-abandoned well. While escaping spirits, you discovered Benkei's shrine. Now, to fulfill your destiny, your sword must become 'no sword.' You must complete Benkei's *musha shugyo* by killing the *tengu* lord. Meet him in his garden, unannounced, and finish the duel."

Finish the duel; finish the duel. The old man's words trailed through Yamashita's mind and haunted him into the waking world. He awoke shivering. A pale sliver of moon lit the forest like day. Forcing aside recollections of his dream, he adjusted his armor to a comfortable position. His fire base lay to the east, and he would start back at first light. He propped his back against a tree and waited. But he did not remove the *gu*.

The bulkiness of the armor enwrapped Yamashita like a cocoon. The feel of the swords at his side inspired a sense of confidence and returned his thoughts to the dream. After a year in Vietnam, he had grown inured to death; but the thought of killing another man with a sword revolted him. Grimacing, he recalled the sickening drag as his *katana* opened the *tengu*'s throat in Benkei's shrine.

No matter how many times he had witnessed or caused another man's death, Yamashita's own had always seemed distant and unreal. Now, his own demise felt all too imminent. He imagined the agony of his skin tearing as a sword blade slid along his throat. His mind rebelled against the image. *I don't want to die.*

Despite twelve months of combat, Yamashita had never accepted his death as inevitable. Everything in Vietnam happened too fast. A soldier never saw the lethal bullet or the dynamite taped to a child's back. In comparison, Yamashita's sword battle had seemed painfully slow. Every enemy stroke needed to be countered with immediate skill. He recalled the wild gleam of horror in the eyes of his last opponent when the demon realized he could not parry the fatal blow.

The heroes of Grandfather's stories chose personal combat as a way of life. Suddenly, Yamashita's childhood idols seemed little more than men trying to destroy themselves. *Hell of an attitude for a kid to admire.*

Still, Yamashita knew it must have taken raw courage for a man to accept inevitable mortality. He unsheathed the *katana* and rested it across his knees. The sword gleamed in the first tenuous rays of dawn. A tempering line ran parallel to the gently curving edge. *What type of bravery would it take to wield a sword against an enemy?* Without the force that had possessed him in the shrine, he could not have faced the demons he had killed.

Yamashita's hand closed around the *katana*'s hilt. It felt unnaturally comfortable in his grip. He stood and swung the blade. His arms and body worked in conjunction, as if the force still controlled him. Near panic at the memory, he resheathed the sword. Leaning against a tree, he tried to understand why the force had disappeared but its skill remained. Curious, he drew the sword, cut upward, reversed the blade, and returned the *katana* to his sheath in one fluid motion.

Yamashita explored his newfound proficiency. He practiced feints with the *katana;* the blade flickered about him like an old friend. He drew a *shoto* with his left hand and added its skill to the dance. Like an echo of reality, he remembered a swordmaster's lesson: "There is no dishonor in dying if each of your weapons has been unsheathed." *That's not my memory!* Dread trickled through Yamashita, and he froze. The recollection must have come from the same source as his weapon mastery.

Yamashita suspected the old man from his dream was the source of both remembrance and skill. He tried to picture his ancient ancestor as he had appeared in the dream, sitting *seiza* in a garden before a pool reflecting a cherry tree. Yamashita recalled his grandfather saying, "The sword is the soul of the samurai." But the old man of his all too-real illusion carried no sword. Yamashita looked at the *katana* and *shoto* he held as if for the first time. Without the doubt of normal speculation, he knew they belonged to the old man in his dream.

"Now I'm believing nightmares," Yamashita mumbled, shaking his head at his failing sanity. "If this doesn't earn me a section eight, nothing will." He walked toward the rising sun, watching for demons with the caution of a point man on sniper patrol.

When the sun hovered directly overhead, a dark line of mountains stretched before Yamashita from one horizon to the other. He had not crossed mountains as he ran from the *tengu* the previous day, and no range lay east of the fire base. He was lost. Recalling stories of men in the wilderness wandering in circles, he chose a peak in the mountain range and headed directly for it. The view from its summit would command the entire area. If he was near the fire base, he could see it from the mountaintop.

The lack of underbrush in the alien forest made progress easy. The terrain and the armor had an unnatural calming effect on Yamashita's nerves. He daydreamed while he walked. In his mind he became the warrior Miura Benkei, seeking enlightenment with courage, skill, and three sharpened swords. The blades skipped around him in silver arcs, guided by his callused fists. Enemies slashed and defended, the chime of steel becoming music, the combat a reckless dance. Every movement, of his own or his foes, funneled his identity one step closer to truth and understanding. Suddenly, honorably facing death at sword point seemed a fine and noble fate.

The miles passed swiftly while Yamashita amused himself with his imagination and memories of tales of courage. Twilight bathed the sky dull gray when Yamashita arrived at the foot of the mountain. A vague familiarity troubled him, despite his strange surroundings. Forcing uneasiness aside, he searched for shelter. He descended a slope and discovered a stream bubbling through a rift. A gnarled pine rose from the rocky soil at its bank. Its branches sagged to the ground.

The place seemed ideal to prepare camp. The tree would provide shelter and the creek sustenance. He cut away several of the pine's lower branches with his shoto, hacked the boughs to even lengths, and carried them to the stream. He pushed the sticks into the streambed until they formed a solid V-shape. His fish trap complete, he returned to the tree and waited.

Yamashita crawled beneath the net of hanging branches and settled at the pine's trunk. His thoughts returned to his ancestors who sought death in order to understand life. During his shift in Vietnam, he had watched people die almost every day. Some of the casualties were friends, but most were nameless villagers. For all the witnessed destruction, he felt no wiser. *What did my fathers find in war that I cannot understand?*

Again, a memory of the swordmaster's teachings rose in Yamashita's mind. "Benkei, the only mystery to life is death. You must find it here." The wizened man tapped his own chest. "Once you do, you will not fear. You will act in harmony with the universe and know all things as one."

The significance of the master's words was lost on Yamashita, but the name he spoke was not. Benkei was the man he had faced in his dream, the ancient ancestor whose swords now swung at Yamashita's side. Realization struck like madness. *Benkei died a young man, yet his visage in the garden looked old. How? And why do I have his memories as my own?*

Unable to comprehend the mysteries of Miura Benkei, Yamashita crept from beneath the tree to check his fish trap. A trout wriggled, caged between the stakes. He pinched the trout beneath the gills and tossed it to the bank. The fish flopped helplessly while Yamashita removed enough sticks to make the trap inoperable. Turning, he gutted the trout with his fingers and returned to camp.

The sun dropped below the horizon. Darkness surrounded Yamashita as he savored the delicate, pink flesh of the trout. Then, finished with his meal and tired from his long journey, Yamashita fell asleep.

A low growl awakened Yamashita. Instinctively, he drew both *shoto* and crouched. Pale pink dawn light spilled through the tangled web of boughs. Near the stream, an otter growled a final warning and dragged fish entrails beneath the water. Yamashita laughed at his paranoia, sobered suddenly by the realization he had drawn the swords without thought, with the natural ease of a samurai.

Terrified by the bizarre merging of his sensations with those of Benkei, Yamashita fought to empty his mind of thought. But memories of flying steel and glory rushed down upon him like nightmares. The grim philosophies of ancient swordmasters beat aside recollections of murders, rapes, and tortures in Vietnam until the former seemed reality and the latter only dreams.

Benkei's remembrances dispersed swiftly. Yamashita sheathed the swords, rose, and pushed through the sagging curtain of pine. Afraid for his tenuous identity, he concentrated on the mundane aspects of breaking camp. He drank, filled his canteen at the stream, and hid all evidence of his recent presence. He took a deep gulp of air and held it like smoke from a joint. Releasing his breath with a high-pitched hiss, he quelled his uncertainty and started up the tree-lined mountain trail.

Sun glared from boulders in the sparse growth of forest. The climb soothed Yamashita's raw nerves like a Sunday drive in the States. Death seemed distant and hazy, though it remained crouched like a predator at the back edge of his thoughts. Benkei's presence became more familiar, almost soothing for its memory of the terrain. Yamashita was not surprised when he reached the summit at midday.

A hundred feet beneath him on a mountain spur, a small palace with a tended garden commanded a strategic view of the valley. A regal-looking man with high cheekbones, a narrow chin, and piercing black eyes paced the gravel paths of the garden. A knot formed in Yamashita's stomach as he recognized the *tengu* lord.

An eerie composure overtook Yamashita. His mind and body felt in harmony as they never had before, and wielding swords seemed as natural as dying. Placing each foot carefully, he descended the rocky slope and neared the garden. No great spark of insight revealed the truth, but peace suffused Yamashita, an all-encompassing joy that swept from core to skin. He no longer felt torn, afraid, or possessed. He accepted his own death, and his sword became "no sword."

Yamashita crawled through a gap in the shrubbery that surrounded the garden and entered the world of his dream. Stunned, he stared at the smooth bark of a cherry tree and its reflection in the pool near its roots. He sat *seiza* beneath the tree and watched for Ikuru-Tayotami.

Soon, the *ikiryo tengu* rounded a bend in the path. His blue velvet cloak rippled in the breeze, and a thin sword bounced at his side. Yamashita rose and stepped to the path in front of the spirit he intended to kill.

Though obviously startled, the *tengu* drew his sword quickly. His brows arched in question over cruel, dark eyes. "We haven't seen your kind here in centuries. Let's retire to my chambers and discuss what brings you to the spirit world." Friendly words and invitations could not soften the ruthless set of his eyes.

Recalling the *ikiryo*'s treachery against Benkei, Yamashita knew he must refuse. He spoke with unfamiliar courage. "I've come to avenge the honor of my ancestor Miura Benkei. I offer you a fair duel, more than you deserve."

Lord Ikuru-Tayotami's mouth stretched to an angry gash. He unfastened the silver clasp at his throat and let his cloak fall to the ground. "Are you in such a hurry to die?" His sword cut precise arcs through the air before him. "I've had centuries to perfect my technique. Your kind no longer uses swords. There shall be precious little excitement in this duel." He laughed derisively.

Yamashita said nothing, eyes locked on his enemy's hands.

Ikuru-Tayotami continued as he closed on Yamashita, as if the combat seemed too trivial to require his full attention. "No answer? You're as much a coward as Benkei, then." He lunged.

Yamashita unsheathed his *katana* with a reverse grip, and struck the thrust aside. He made a countercut at the *tengu*'s wrist.

Ikuru-Tayotami leapt back, out of range, and never stopped talking. "I shall slay you now." He bowed. "I am warning you so that you may appreciate the intricacies of swordwork while you die." He lunged again.

The *tengu*'s speed shocked Yamashita. He barely blocked the thrust. To gain more distance, Yamashita gripped the *katana* normally. He drew one of the *shoto* and prepared for the next attack. He dodged a feint to his head, caught the main thrust on the flat of his *shoto,* and spun. The *katana* whipped toward the *tengu*'s head.

Ikuru-Tayotami ducked and again lunged for Yamashita. Yamashita's *shoto* forced the stroke high. Delicately, he swung the tip of his *katana* beneath Ikuru-Tayotami's guard. The blade sheared through the *tengu*'s sword belt and disemboweled the lord.

Ikuru-Tayotami pitched to his knees and dropped his sword. Clutching bleeding viscera, he stared into Yamashita's face. His eyes rolled white and his tongue protruded as he collapsed, face first, in his own blood.

Oblivious to the violence, cherry blossoms floated placidly on the surface of the pool. Triumph, not nausea, overwhelmed Yamashita. Smiling with satisfaction, he crawled back through the hole in the bushes and climbed toward the mountain summit.

For more than a fortnight after the duel, Yamashita tried to return to his world. *But how?* Old Benkei's words and memories of the demons' quiet colorlessness in Vietnam gave him only partial answers. Apparently, different dimensions distorted certain senses. If he could eliminate hearing and color vision, he felt certain he would return home. Yet, although he had altered taste, smell, and touch and peered briefly into their corresponding worlds, hearing and vision seemed beyond him. For the sixtieth time, he sat *seiza* and concentrated on sight and sound.

Yamashita counted each breath and imagined a circle slowly spinning against a black background. The meditation techniques muted the world around him. He focused his attention and eliminated sounds, one by one, until a fabricated silence enclosed him.

Yamashita dared not open his eyes. Ice particles in a bitter cold wind bit into his exposed skin. Fighting excitement, he concentrated on removing all color from the world. Gradually, the stinging hail abated and a familiar warmth surrounded him. He opened his eyes and stared into a soundless Vietnam.

Gray flames licked the sky. Panicked villagers ran toward the jungle. Men in black held assault rifles and gunned down the townspeople as they ran. An old man threw his arms toward the sky in a gesture disclaiming life. Children fell bleeding to the muddy streets. Smoke billowed toward the clouds.

Yamashita watched, dazed. Gunfire rang around him. A VC carrying a rifle smashed his gun's butt into a pregnant abdomen and ran toward Yamashita. Smiling with twisted joy, the VC pushed the tip of the barrel into Yamashita's face. The muzzle flashed as Paul Yamashita took sight from the world.

Yamashita's consciousness floated, disembodied, through a vast blackness. Unsure whether he had died, he surrendered himself to the void that encompassed him. Without change, time lost its significance. Minutes became millennia, and he drifted through eternity. His only reality consisted of his own memories and those of Miura Benkei.

At first, Yamashita recalled scenes from both lives equally, but a childhood in a Pennsylvania coal town quickly palled before the pageantry and excitement of a samurai in feudal Japan. Every moment of Benkei's life replayed a thousand times, until Paul Yamashita accepted his ancestor's heritage of violence and honor.

On a whim, Paul Yamashita imagined Miura Benkei on a familiar road, in the Iga province of Japan, without sound and color. A gale whipped Benkei's hair and drove leaden clouds across the sky. A warrior on horseback rode toward him, a dark silhouette against the rising sun. Yamashita recognized the man as Benkei's older brother, although the scene itself seemed unfamiliar. Suddenly, Yamashita could no longer feel the void around him. He stood on the mountain road in the person of Miura Benkei.

Benkei's brother raised his spear in a gesture of recognition. Wind ached through Yamashita's ears, and hair danced and tickled across his forehead. Satisfaction and a sense of completion accompanied the change. Although twenty generations had passed, he had fulfilled his *musha shugyo* and returned to Japan alive. In four hundred years, he would sit opposite a young American soldier in a mystical garden and tell Paul Yamashita a story that would change his life. Benkei laughed and returned his brother's salute.

Paul Yamashita was declared missing in action in the jungle near Bong San on May 5, 1968.

Jane Yolen is another of our astonishingly multitalented contributors. She has written well over a hundred books, for adults, young adults, and children. She is also a formidable editor, according to her writers, editing among other things her own Young Adult line for Harcourt Brace. She is a past president of the Science Fiction Writers of America. She is a heart-stopping oral storyteller, and a considerable authority on folktales. School librarians fall at my feet when they find out I've had lunch with Jane Yolen. She also, according to rumor, came very close to being the third member of the folk trio Peter, Paul, and Mary back in Greenwich Village in the early fifties. Peter, Paul, and Jane? When her daughter was in her teens Jane confides she dreamed of protecting her in a glass case with piped-in rock music till a handsome prince with the right degree came along. But her daughter grew up to become a private detective, proving once again that in parenting, example is more important than precept.

About "The One-Armed Queen" Jane writes: *"Sister Light, Sister Dark* and *White Jenna,* both novels of the Dales, were finalists for the Nebula Award and the World Fantasy Award. This short story begins after the great hero of the Gender Wars, White Jenna, and her husband, King Carum, have disappeared, and their three children—Jem, Corrie, and the eponymous one-armed queen Scillia—are fighting over the throne. Scillia is the oldest but is an adopted daughter, which goes against her in some quarters, and the Gender Wars seem ready to begin all over again. After writing this short story, I became so intrigued with Scillia that I am now turning her tale into a novel called—also—*The One-Armed Queen.*"

—LMB

The One-Armed Queen

Jane Yolen

The Myth

Then Great Alta took the warrior, the girl with one arm, and set her in the palm of Her hand.

"There is none like you, daughter," quoth Great Alta. "Not on the earth or in its shadow. So I will make you a mate that you might be happy."

"Why must I have a mate to be happy?" asked the one-armed girl. "Do you, Great Mother, have a mate? And are you not happy? I would be your blanket companion."

"To reach too high is to fall too far," Great Alta replied. "I have neither blanket nor companion."

"Then I shall be alone," the one-armed girl said. And whether it was a promise or a prophecy even Great Alta herself could not say.

The Legend

In the town of New-Melting-by-Sea is a great house, called sometimes Journey's End and sometimes Aldenshame. On the wall, in the entrance hall, hung up like a banner, is a tattered remnant of cloth. Under the cloth is the following legend:

"Alta's Blanket," said to belong to the legendary one-armed queen Scillia. She brought it here at the end of the War of Succession, broken in health but not in spirit. She came on foot and alone, her great horse Shadow having been slain under her by her own brother, the tyrant Jemson. It was at the end of her thousand-mile Journey of Redemption around the kingdom, and this cloth was all that was between her and the cold. To show their respect, no one along the last quarter of her route looked at her, for to see her in nothing but stranger's weave, and it all tattered and worn through, would have been to shame her, and that her people would not do.

When she came at last to Journey's End, the sisters who owned the house let her in, and she lived with them till her death, seven years later. When she died, the sisters hung the cloth on the wall, and such was its power, cloth and wall have remained intact though the building has been rebuilt often in the years since.

The Story

The moon hung by a thread of cloud over the meadow. Below it a group of some thirty women spoke in uneasy whispers, clearly waiting for something, for someone. Their distress showed in the shadows beneath their eyes, in the angular hunch of their shoulders.

"Where *is* she?" a middle-aged woman asked, the moon writing runes across her forehead, deep grooves. "How can she be late in coming? The night is cold, and passion turns cold, too, with each hour."

"Hush, Manya," the woman by her side cautioned. They could have been twins, though one was dark-haired with streaks of gray, the other light. "She will come. She promised. And isn't it said, *Better late in the pan then never in the pot?"*

Two younger women, hardly more than girls, stood arm in arm, looking up at the moon, one of them with braids as light as that wintry moon, the other with plaits blue-black as sky. The cloud had become a fringe over the upper half of the moon so that it looked like a broken coin.

"The Moon!" the light-haired girl cried, pointing. Silently her sister pointed as well.

"If it clouds completely . . ." Manya warned. She did not have to say more. They all knew that once the moon disappeared, the dark sisters would go as well, back to their shadow world, and the mission this night would be so much more difficult.

"Where *is* she?" Now it was Manya's twin who gave the complaint.

"Hush, Sonya," Manya cautioned, and they both gave a single laugh at the reversal, a mirthless laugh, more like a sigh.

"I do not understand," another woman said, "why she dallies with those men. *They* are the enemy."

A mutter of agreement ran around the ragged circle.

"Not all." It was the girl with the light-colored braids. "Not all men." She spoke with feeling, but without proof. She was that kind of girl.

"All," said Manya. "Even the ones we like."

"Liked," corrected Sonya.

The girls turned away. They moved like dancers, completing each other's gestures. Shrugging, they rolled their eyes toward the sky. It was an old argument, after all, much older than they were, and there was no use fretting over it. The light-haired girl pulled the ties of her leather leggings tighter around her waist, a gesture having more to do with frustration than need, and the dark girl imitated her. Then they walked away from the circle toward the woods, as if that was their answer to the others.

The moon's fringe, like a curtain, had lowered even more, and the whisperings from the circle of women grew even more frantic.

Suddenly a drumming of hoofbeats signaled them. The girls turned back and called to the circle. "She is here!" they shouted. "She is come."

"Hush," the women called as one.

The moon disappeared into the cloud completely and a single rider on a single horse, black as the solid center of an eye, emerged from the woods as if the forest had spit them out.

The Song

One-Armed Queen

The one-armed queen came from the West,
In boots and cape and hood-o.
She brought her brothers to the test,
All in the hazel wood-o.

The one-armed queen came from the East
In boots and cape and hood-o.
She brought a war who wanted peace,
Out of the hazel wood-o.

So sing you one and all alone,
In boots and cape and hood-o,
And sing her back upon the throne
All in the hazel wood-o.

The Story

The remaining women greeted the rider, whose horse was rein-led by the light-haired girl. The horse was covered with sweat from its run, but when the rider got down, she was not sweating at all. In fact, she was shivering violently, for she was wearing only a thin cotton shirt, the one empty sleeve tied up with a bedraggled ribband to her shoulder, and leather leggings, and high soft leather boots run down at the heels. She had neither cape nor hood, and Manya shrugged out of her own cloak and offered it.

"Here, my queen," she said.

"Scillia," the woman answered back. "Until I am on my throne again, I am only Scillia."

"I cannot call you that, my . . ." Manya said.

"You *will* call me that," the woman—Scillia—ordered. Her voice was tired but hard. There was no doubting she was a queen.

"Yes, my . . . my Scillia." Manya stumbled over the name, but said it. "Take my cloak . . . Scillia. You have none."

"I gave mine to someone who needed it more than I," Scillia said, shrugging through the shivering. She accepted the proffered cloak.

"What news then?" the girl cried out. She still held the horse's reins.

Scillia turned toward her. "Ah, my horse girl. And what are you called, child?" she asked, holding out her one hand to take the reins back. "I need to know what to call you so we can speak properly. After all, you know mine. I will not be at a disadvantage."

"Marya, your . . . your . . ." the girl stuttered as she handed the reins back. "But I am called Seven."

"Seven." Scillia smiled. "And was that because you were seventh in your family?"

Seven laughed, and it was the first merry sound the meadow had heard. "No—Scillia. Seven because it took them seven years to get me. And then when they got me and I was only a girl, my father said: *A girl is less than no child at all.* My mother was so hurt by this, she took me in her arms and, still bleeding birthblood, walked the ten miles to old Selden Hame. And there she left me with the sisters."

"Ah," Scillia said, nodding. "Left you. But she did not stay herself?"

Seven shook her head. "Na. Na. Stayed only long enough to be cleaned up by the sisters. Then she walked back to her man, having named me Seven. 'Twas better so. She was not one to live with women. And I—well, they do say *Many mothers are best.* 'Sides—how else could I have gotten my dark sister? Hardly any but the sisters in Selden Hame know how 'tis done." She gestured to her side, though no one stood there.

A moment later, the cloud moved away from the moon, and Seven's sister appeared by her side. The one-armed Scillia smiled. "And you are . . . ?"

"Tween, your majesty," the girl said.

"Scillia," came the reminder.

"And I am Manya." The older woman shouldered the girls aside. "Do you wish to name us one by one by one, or should we be about our business? There is not too much more to this night."

"It never hurts to be named," Scillia said softly. She pulled the cloak even tighter about herself, as if getting the very last bits of warmth from it. "If we are to die together, best not to go unnamed into the dark."

"We will not die. We will win this fight," Manya said. The other women echoed her, all but Seven and Tween who were, unaccountably, silent.

"We all die sometime, my good Manya. Only Alta is forever." Scillia's voice was low and gentle, but the correction was nonetheless steely-made.

"And some of us will die in this fight. It is best that we understand that from the start." She dropped the reins and, whipping off the cloak, handed it back. The horse, as if made of stone, did not move.

The History

Female infanticide, so common before the reign of King Carum, has been long held to have disappeared completely with his ascendency. But new evidence disagrees with these old assumptions. According to population records discovered recently by Sir Elric Hanger and his wife, Lady Nan, in the ruins of the Northern Palace Grounds, a lingering misogyny in the rural south still led to an underground trade in girl babies. (See "Farm Babies and Baby Farming in the South Dales" by S. Cowan. Demographics Annual, Pasden University Press #79.)

So convincing are these records that they make clear the patterns of abandonment were subtly changing and incorporated into the so-called fostering laws, those laws concerning the rearing of children away from their natural homes. (See "Forgotten Fosters" by A. S. Carpenter-Ross, Psychological Abstracts, Conference on Daleian Research, 1997.)

Of course a foundling must needs first be lost! This simple fact has been overlooked for years in the studies done on the many fostering relationships, such as apprenticeships, oblation, even godparenting. And while there have been many scholarly studies done on fostering in the higher levels of society—for example, King Carum's own son was sent abroad to live as a royal hostage/fosterling at the palace of the Garunian king till he was sixteen and married to his foster-sister—foundlings at the low end of society's scale have been lost a second time, by the historians.

What is the difference between fostering and abandonment?

Ask the child.

The Story

Scillia turned to the girls. "I was a foundling myself, you know."

"I did not know, Majesty," Seven said.

"Scillia."

"I did not know, Scillia," the girl repeated.

"Queen Jenna was not your mother?"

"White Jenna was certainly my mother, but she did not give birth to me," Scillia said. She put her arm companionably around Seven's shoulder, touching Tween with her fingers. "She rescued me when my own mother died. And though the men of the South Dales may say *All history begins between a woman's legs,* I am not so convinced." She smiled. "Come, my friends, let us talk not of birth but of war."

"A man's war!" someone called out.

Scillia looked up, found the speaker. "Your name, sister."

"Greet," the woman answered.

"It is a woman's war as surely," Scillia said. "It is my war. The ones who thrust me so cruelly off my throne, who killed my brother Corrine who supported my claim, were men, yes. But behind my brother Jemson's claim, behind his iron fist, is his wife's small hand. Not only men can be cruel. And not all men. I would not have you say all."

Seven smiled at this, and Tween with her, but a number of the women were disturbed by Scillia's arguments, most especially Manya and her sister.

"I have no proof that men are anything but cruel," Manya said. "Doesn't it say in the texts *Man is wood, woman water?"*

"Water weights wood," Scillia said. "That is also in the texts. My brother Corrine is proof. He died under seventeen stones, still proclaiming my queenship. And with him died Old Piet, who had taught me the sword and had promised me one arm could still be better than none. My father, Carum, was always kind to me and generous and loving."

"And the man who raped me?" cried Greet. "What of him? I was neither handfasted nor married to him, but still he had me. And my own father called him 'brother' and told him to ride me more."

"And the man who cut my mother's throat in front of me," said Manya, "as if she were no more than a pig for the butchering."

Scillia shook her head. "We cannot go on countering man for man, tale for tale, and thus convince one another. I do not deny there is cruelty in the world. We have all borne its yoke. But in this thing you must trust me. There are some good men. There are some wicked women. But the throne will be won back because we are bound to one another by friendship and love, not separated by story and divided by history. Sisters, give me your hands." She thrust her one hand forward.

Seven and Tween grabbed her first, then the others, one by one by one. Manya and Sonya were near the last. Greet and her dark sister almost did not reach out, but at the last Scillia said, "Sisters, I have only one hand, else I would take you with the other. I have only one heart, and you have it all."

That did it. Greet and her dark twin put their hands on the top, though tentatively and with faces that showed they were not yet fully hers.

"I pledge to you," Scillia said, "all that I have, all that I am: my heart, my hand, my sword, my horse, the clothes I have on. I pledge to you my name. I ask your help, not to put me on the throne alone, but to put all of us there. My mother, Jenna, once told me of the Grenna, those green elves who live in Alta's woods. They rule not one above the rest, but in a circle. If I am returned to my throne, I will rule with a circle of those chosen by you, by all of you who ride in this war by my side. I have pledged this everywhere I have been, and so I pledge it to you, now."

"We follow, Scillia," said Tween.

"We follow," echoed Seven.

"And I," Manya said. Her voice was almost drowned out by the others. "And I. And I. And I."

Scillia pulled her hand out from the bottom of the pile, and straightened. "Then ride to Greener's Hollow. We gather there in three nights' time. Collect what weapons you can—sword, pike, knife, bow. If men think this is a man's war, they are mistaken. If women think they cannot fight, then in this they are wrong. There will be many at the Hollow before you. But I must ride now, for there are yet three more circles of women with whom I am pledged to meet." She turned and whistled for her horse, and the black came up to her. She placed her left foot in the wooden stirrup and pulled herself up with her left hand. There was nothing awkward in the movement.

"We will go with you, Scillia!" cried Seven and Tween together.

Scillia looked down at them. "I ride alone," she said. Then kicking the horse with her heels into a sudden canter, she was gone into the woods.

Above the clearing the moon was a full, bright promise. Seven cocked her head to one side. "She has no dark sister and only one hand. She needs us."

"Do not fancy yourself, girl," Manya said. "Many are singletons and she has been one-armed from the first. Perhaps a queen needs to be alone."

The Legend

About two hundred years ago, in Cannor's Crossing, the wife of the cobbler gave birth to twin girls who were joined at the hip and shoulder. The midwife took such a fright at the sight, she left before the birthing was done, making her way over the ford in a shallow boat and leaving the mother to die in a pool of her own blood.

What was the poor cobbler to do, never having seen such a thing? He took his knife and cut the girls apart, sewing up their wounds at hip and shoulder with the heavy black boot thread. Only the babes had but three arms between them, so one girl got two arms, the other just one.

They lived to an old age, those twins, and the one-armed girl got married, the other didn't. No accounting for a man's taste. The two-armed girl stayed with her father and learned his trade. But when the old man died, she died, as if he had been her twin and not the one-armed girl.

My grandmother told me this story, and as she was born herself in Cannor's Crossing, I have no reason to disbelieve it.

The Story

"I do not like it that she rides alone," Seven whispered to her dark sister. "Queen or not, no one should have to bear that kind of burden by herself. And she could use a bodyguard."

"Then . . . " Tween said slowly, "we must go after her."

Without a word to any of the others, they mounted their gray gelding, and kicked him into a trot. It was his fastest gait because he was too old for anything else with two of them riding. Once into the trees, however, Tween disappeared and, lightened, the gray went faster.

It was easy enough to follow the queen's trail, for her horse was large and uncaring of broken branches. Besides, Seven had learned well the art of tracking at Selden Hame under the guidance of the old singleton Marget.

"What we learn here," Marget had often said, "is not for war. Never for war. Only for game."

It was well, then, that she is long dead, Seven thought, for she had loved the old woman and would not have wanted to disappoint her. But the training would serve for war as well as game, and she said a small prayer to Marget's memory.

Seven had no idea how long she rode because the gray slowed to a ground-eating walk that swayed so continually, she fell asleep in the saddle and did not wake again until morning was already creeping through the lacings of leaves. Still, she trusted her horse. It had been trained at the same time she had been, and there was, also, only the one track anyway.

The path ahead was brilliant with sudden sunlight, and opened onto a meadow dappled with windblown leaves. There was the queen's own black and the queen herself—*Scillia,* she reminded herself—lying under the horse's belly, straddled by its four legs. *Fallen or asleep?* was Seven's instant thought and, not knowing which, she rode over and dismounted, even as the gray was stopping.

Before she reached the black horse, the one-armed queen was awake and on her feet on the far side of the horse in a single fluid motion, a long, sharp sword in her hand.

Breathing hard from the run, Seven said, "Not dead, then."

"Not even close," came the reply. And then a laugh. "Girl, I do not know who is more frightened."

"I am not frightened," Seven said. It was clear from her voice that this was no idle boast and that she was, truly, puzzled by Scillia's remark.

"Alta's hairs, child, you should be," Scillia said, sheathing the sword. "I might have spitted you, had it not been morning and your face shining in its innocence like a light." She stroked the horse's neck; under her fingers its flesh crawled with its fright. "Shade and I have racing hearts still, and look—both our skins move like worms."

"Truly, I did not mean to frighten . . ." Seven's voice trailed off.

Scillia came around the front of her horse. "Then why are you here?"

"To serve you," Seven said, starting to kneel.

"I thought I left you—all of you—behind."

"Tween and I thought you should not be left alone."

"Perhaps, child, I *like* being alone."

Seven looked crushed, as if this thought had never occurred to her.

"Besides, that old swayback gray of yours will never be able to keep up with my black."

"Nevertheless," Seven mumbled, looking down at her feet, "we are here."

"Nevertheless, you are indeed," Scillia said, looking at the girl's crestfallen face. "And I have to confess that in some ways I am glad of it. You can take both horses down to a stream over there." She motioned with her head toward the north end of the meadow. "I will find us something to eat."

"I have journeycake," Seven said. "We could share it."

"So have I. But we will save it for when nothing else can be found. There are many miles to go yet till night, and journeycake will not shorten the road, no matter what the songs say."

The Song

Journeycake, Ho!

Into the meadow and out of the woods
Carrying nothing but bartering goods,
Running so fast, there is nothing to take
But a skinful of wine and a good journeycake.
Journeycake, ho! Journeycake, ho!
Make it and take it wherever you go.
Traveling swiftly or traveling slow
It will keep you filled up in the morning.

This wasn't a trip I was planning to make
As I fled through the door with some good journeycake.
But my horse it was saddled, so off I did ride,
Thankful I still had my head and my hide.
Journeycake, ho! Journeycake, ho!
Make it and take it wherever you go.
Travel on water, on ice, or on snow,
It will keep you filled up till the morning.

The master was after me, likewise the noose,
I had to go quickly and lightly and loose,
So I grabbed what I could and I let the rest be;
I didn't have much—but I surely had me.
Journeycake, ho! Journeycake, ho!
Make it and take it wherever you go.
And if you've no money, you'll still have the dough
To keep you filled up in the morning.

The History

The War of Deeds and Succession is a rather large title for a very small period in our history. After the death—or rather the disappearance—of the aging and ill King Carum and his warrior queen Jenna, the country was split by three rival claimants to the throne: their two sons and their adopted daughter.

One son, Jemson Over-the-Water, had been educated and trained for kingship, but his training was unfortunately all overseas in the Garunian courts, where he had lived as a royal hostage. When he returned as a young man to the Dales, he spoke our language with a heavy accent and enjoyed the brutal Garun sports of bear- and bull-baiting, an affinity that seemed to have carried over to his relationships with people. However, he had the strong backing of the Garunians.

The second son, Corrine Lackland, had remained in his father's court. He was a young man of action, not thought. As a king he would probably have been a disaster, but as a hero and a martyr he was to have no peer in Daleian history. Indeed, much of what we know of this period comes from songs and stories about him—for example the "Ballad of Corinne Lackland," which ends this chapter, and the song-cycle St. Corinne of the Stones, at the back of the book. There are hundreds of other poems and songs recited or sung—in the Southern Dales especially—that refer to Corinne and his death. Badly corrupted by time and the passage from mouth to ear, they are still recognizable. A good example is the children's game-rhyme: "Stoneman, Stoneman, say your prayers/Brother Jemmy's on the stairs."

The popular favorite, of course, was Ancillia Virginia, who ascended to the throne twice, once on her parents' disappearance and once again after her foster brother's death. She was known as the One-Armed Queen because she lost her right arm in the horrific ten-day Battle of Cannor's Ford where—so the stories went—the waters ran red for a month after. The problem was that Ancillia Virginia was a queen at the time the land needed a king; gender was still an argument against such a ruler. Furthermore, she refused to marry or to bear a child.

Her death ten years later ushered in a hundred years of commoner kings, nearly one a year. The Connery Award for children's fiction, Year King, *details the life of one of these.*

Because of those disastrous rulers—because of Ancilla Virginia—the Daleian Circle of Seven was established and, in somewhat modified form, still runs the country to this day.

—from *A Short History of the Dales*
Grade level sixth form

The Story

Seven took up the reins and led both horses across the meadow. Scillia let out a deep relieved sigh. A sound answered her, and she listened for a moment before realizing it was just a song thrush. She forced herself to relax, but at the same time she listened a moment more. Just because it was daylight, that didn't make her safe. Or the girl. If anything, day could be the more dangerous. Her mother had always recited the caution: *You must set the trap before the rat passes, not after,* whenever Scillia or her brothers made mistakes in judgment. That warning was still part of Scillia's thinking, even more in wartime than in her mother's peace.

She looked around the meadow. It was awfully quiet, except for a lone squirrel busy at the near end of the field. Pacing under the trees, she found only an owl pellet, and it old and brittle, encasing a small shrew's skull. She made a face. Not much eating in shrews, even if she *could* catch one. They were ordinarily not worth the effort. This wood was a meager larder.

There were some ferns, but they were too dry to be palatable, and she did not dare chance a fire to boil them. But on a mossy rock face and path she spotted three different kinds of mushrooms, and that—at least—was promising. One kind had an inky top, and she knew it was especially good eating; the other two were chancy this time of year. Still there were enough of the blackcaps for a scant meal, possibly more farther along the path. She bent to collect them and heard a muffled yell and the high scream of her horse.

Without stopping to think, she straightened up and was running across the field in a single fluid motion, unsheathing her sword as she ran. When she came to the hillside leading to the stream, she saw there were two men in leather face masks—Garunian-made—more intent on having their way with the girl than killing her. Anger rather than fear steadied her, and she gripped the sword more tightly.

There was no sign of the gray horse, which meant the men probably didn't know there were two to their two, and her black was doing its own part in the battle, hammering at one man with its front hooves. But the other man was already on top of Seven, holding both her hands above her head with his one massive paw, loosening the leather strings on his pants with the other.

Scillia knew which one to tackle first. The more dangerous one was on his feet still; the other would be too busy for the moment. She half-ran, half-slid down the grassy slope, but silently, behind the standing man. Only the horse saw her, and he redoubled his efforts, one hoof striking a glancing blow to the masked head. As the man turned away in pain, he all but fell on Scillia's sword. She spitted him expertly, then using her foot to brace against his body, drew the sword out. She made a face. It was not the first man she had ever killed, but the sound of the sword in meat—and the smell of the blood—never got easier to take.

Quickly, she turned and threw herself atop the second man.

"Wait you turn, Brun—" he cried, thinking it his friend. He was dead before he could finish the name. Scillia pushed him off Seven, who was still screaming.

Throwing the sword to one side, Scillia gathered the girl to her breast. "There, hush, girl. They are both dead and will not hurt you." But Seven continued to scream, to push away, and it took Scillia a moment to understand.

"Three. There were three. One finished and went after my gray."

The sword was too far for her to reach, and besides, it was already too late, for someone had caught her hair up from behind, jerking her head back.

"Carnes!" came a man's voice, strained through a leather mask. It was the Garunian word for a female jackal.

Scillia let herself go slack against him, but made ready to fling herself forward and catch him off guard, when Seven screamed again, only this time it was a scream of fury, not terror. She flung Scillia's sword at the man's head, barely missing Scillia, and it struck point first between the eyes of the mask. It did not sink in very deep; the mask's leather was too stiff for that. But it was deep enough to kill him. He tumbled backward slowly, like a mountain falling. It was a moment longer before Scillia realized he was dead.

"Alta's Hairs!" she cried. "You could have killed me, child."

"No chance of that," Seven said. The words she spoke were brave ones, but the tremor in her voice and the tears running down her cheeks gave them the lie.

"Where did you learn that trick?" Scillia asked, painfully freeing her hair from the dead man's grip.

Seven took a deep breath, steadying herself. "Marget," she said. "From Old Marget. It's the Game."

"Game?"

"The Game of Wands."

At last Scillia understood. Her mother had talked of the Game of Wands, which the warrior women of the old Hames taught their children. But it was nothing she had ever learned from Queen Jenna. Her mother had insisted her children only be taught games of peace. *She should have taught me war,* Scillia thought, surprised at the bitterness she felt.

Well, it would be the child who would be her teacher now.

The Rhymes

Trot, trot to Selden
Trot o'er the lea,
They caught seven children,
But they never caught me.
—Ball-bouncing rhyme, South Dales

Hark, hark, the jackals bark,
The women have come to town;
Some in armor, some enamored,
Some with their arms thrown down.
—Skip-rope rhyme, Cannor's Ford

Ride a black horse,
Ride a gray mare,
Follow the lady
If only you dare.
—Toe and finger count-game, South Dales

The number of the Beast
Is three times seven,
All good children
Go to Heaven.
—Counting-out rhyme, North Dales

The Story

"I must get you back to Selden," Scillia said. "This is no place . . ."

"This is my *only* place," Seven said.

"Were you not hurt then?" Scillia asked. She was surprised at how awkward the girl made her feel.

"I was hurt," Seven said. "And I expect I will cry. But later. When there is time for crying. When my dark sister is here."

"I am your sister for now." Scillia put her arm around Seven and was only a little hurt at how rigid the girl's shoulder was beneath the touch.

Seven turned and looked at Scillia. "You are neither my sister nor my mother," she said. "You are my queen. You *must* be my queen for me to go on. You *must* be." For the first time there was a hint of tears in her eyes. She dashed an arm across her face. Whatever tears had dared show were gone.

Scillia pursed her lips. She knew she had just one turn to get this right, to make this remarkable girl hers for good. And Alta knew she had need of her. "Then, straighten your leggings, and a dash of cold water on your face, Marya Seven. I will have no one around me who cries. War is not for weeping, until long long after."

"They will make a story of this, my queen," Seven said.

"They will make *many* stories," Scillia answered. "Let us be sure that the ending they scribe is the right one."

"With Queen Scillia on her throne." The girl smiled tentatively.

"With the cold-hearted One-Armed Bitch where she belongs." Scillia mounted her horse. "Come behind me, girl. We have a mare to find."

The Myth

Then Great Alta took a child and set her next to the One-Armed Queen. "One of you is for war and one for peace," quoth Great Alta.

"But which is which?" asked the child.

The One-Armed Queen was silent.

Great Alta smiled. "The question is not which," she said, "but why." And she took them up and placed them together in the land that is called by the name of Dales.

While most of Sydney Long's mail comes addressed to Mr., she is a woman. She served as an officer in the U.S. Air Force for six years, reaching the rank of captain. Her eldest son is carrying on the family tradition, having graduated from the Air Force Academy. He now flies F-16s. Sydney herself is a graduate of the Clarion Science Fiction Writer's Workshop, and also does technical writing, including multi-million dollar proposals. She lives at present in central Ohio.

About "For the Right Reason" Sydney writes: "Most of us want to lead at some time in our lives. When the river meanders along, leading is easy. However, when the water leaps into a white froth and a wrong decision can lead to disaster, leading is difficult. But what is the right decision? And what if you have no way to find out? All the people and events in this story are strictly fictitious. Yet there are strange thematic parallels between Izzie's struggle and my own that I did not realize until after the story was finished."

—LMB

For the Right Reason

Sydney Long

The last temptation is the greatest treason:
To do the right deed for the wrong reason.
—T. S. Eliot

J-class spacer clearing jump point, Captain." The tech's voice betrayed his surprise.

Captain Isoura "Izzie" Antopolous looked up from her 4-D tactics exercise. The only surprises in this backwater eddy of a station were spawned by those on staff who practiced pranks as an art form, or religion. "ID?" she asked.

"None given. They aren't answering comm." Admin-two Scaparelli's voice wavered with a hint of nervousness.

Surely this was another of Dolph's antics, like the Andorian stickwalker in her bunk. Certainly more likely than an unscheduled ship. Izzie pulled up the log. "The log shows null, Scaparelli. Nothing's out there; nothing's coming in." She tried to refocus on the problem of deploying six vessels in the thirty classic formations with eighteen variations. Not that she'd ever use it except on her boards, but she needed a good score for any hope of promotion. And this year was her last shot. She might languish from boredom, but she couldn't make mistakes, not here, not if she followed procedures. The Keith Bauer Communications Station might be dull, but it was safe.

Scaparelli swallowed and looked convincing. "This is for real, Captain. The near beacon went out last shift."

The beacon had failed before, several times. So that part was feasible. Even the lack of notification regarding the beacon failure in the OOD report was like Dolph. He forgot all officers are brothers and remembered all officers compete. But an unscheduled spacer? Never. She pivoted in her command chair to face Sergeant Kuesza. "Any traffic in the area or scheduled in?"

"Same as usual. No traffic, nothing scheduled."

She studied each of their faces for any sign of suppressed amusement. Instead, she found tiny creases of real concern. Either they played it better than she imagined or they really had a situation. Her stomach fluttered just before her board chimed and scrolled to the procedures for UIS—unidentified incoming ships. Thankfully, Izzie scanned the steps, then reached across the workstation and pressed a button. Within a minute, a grumpy voice responded. "Gunthorpe here."

"Sir, unidentified spacer, J-class, inbound. I'm assuming it's the I.G. and thought you'd want to know as soon as possible."

"Yes, thank you. Notify me when they land. Meanwhile, wake all the officers and section heads. That'll give them a few extra hours to prepare." His voice paused longer between words, as if his mind was already shutting down to return to sleep.

Izzie knew she was pushing his patience. "Sir, if they continue refusing to identify themselves, regs call for a warning shot to their sensors."

"You're the OOD. What's your call?"

She'd wanted his confirmation, but he was placing the decision squarely back in her hands. She wanted to pause, to delay the moment when her words would be beyond recall, but she also needed to sound decisive. She took a breath and blurted out her choice. "Unless I have any evidence to the contrary, I'll follow procedures. Exactly."

"Carry on, Izzie."

She felt her stomach tighten again even as she logged the conversation. She wanted to be right, needed to be. His words had been evasive, reminding her it was her decision. And if she was wrong, it was her black mark. She glanced at the time to see how long before shift change. Too much.

Everyone in the room had turned back to their work and acted as if they hadn't been listening. "Follow standard procedures for unidentified incoming. Don't leave out a step unless you want another tour on this rock." Izzie hammered out the level-one wake-up call on her input board. The other officers would have at least some time to splash a semblance of order on their offices while she was stuck in her turn as duty officer. Of all the black-holed luck.

When her last screwup had landed her in the armpit of the known universe at the KB listening post, Izzie had taken solace in knowing she could no longer harm anyone except herself. Only now, she needed a promotion to avoid ending like her father: stuck down a gravity well when all he ever wanted was space.

Her earliest memory of her father was a time he had come home on leave. He and Mother had departed on vacation for what, to Izzie, was an impossibly long time. When they reappeared, he stayed for only a few short days before he rejoined his ship. He strode up the ramp to the restricted area, his hair curling beneath his cap, his arms reaching out to clasp his shipmates around their shoulders as she had wanted him to greet her.

The next time she saw him, Mother had died, so it was Granpa who went with her. Her father came slowly down the ramp, his spine stooped, his mouth clamped tight. "Why didn't you mind your own business and let me be?" He hurled his words at Granpa.

"She needs a parent. I thought you'd want this."

"You just didn't want the bother. I know your type. You showed me you got the pull, but it don't impress me none. Soon as I get a berth, I'm outta here." He limped past her, eyes focused on his next ship, not her.

The rest of her childhood she watched him hobble; his pain every minute, every day, worsened by the relentless pull of gravity. When she was finally grown and he was freed from parenting, his bones were too fragile to take the boost out of the gravity well. Going to space herself was the only way she knew to pay back both him and Granpa.

If the service forced her out now, she'd be just like him—shut off from the one thing she loved. And bitter. She'd rather be dead.

Through the doorway strode Captain Dolph, his uniform immaculate, despite the hour, with his confidence blazing like a nova. At least, thought Izzie, novas eventually burnt themselves into quiet dwarves. If only— She clamped down on that idea. The KB Station was too small a facility on too small a moon in a dead-end jump not to get along. And she had a job to get done.

He moved through the small room, clasping hands and sharing small jokes in the manner of a star athlete joining a lasertag team in the gym, before he sprawled at an empty comconsole. Izzie felt her cheeks warm. She tried to ignore him but found herself gauging everything she did by what Dolph would like. *Damn him, why did he have to come here and start me thinking twice about everything I do?*

Izzie listened as Scaparelli hailed the spacer once more. His words were patient, yet his tone hovered between frustration and anger. Everyone in the room was silent, too silent as they waited for the answer to his final verbal warning. Izzie's fingers punched search parameters on the ship's profile into her console but kept coming up with the same answer—J-class friendly. A wisp of a thought fought for her attention, then fled when Scaparelli's voice cracked. "Permission to fire warning shot, ma'am."

The silence deepened. She couldn't remember an inspector ever pushing the procedures this far. No choice but to follow the regs herself. That was what officers did, enforce the regulations. "Permission granted." She held her breath, her hand forming a tight fist. The comconsole flashed its acceptance of her voice and unlocked access to the laser cannon.

"Hold up, Scaparelli. Gunthorpe's got to verify that first," said Dolph.

Izzie stood, frozen until she became aware her mouth was hanging open. She closed it and glared at Dolph while she gathered words. "Flare out, Dolph." She spit out each word.

"I'm trying to keep you from making another mistake like your last time." He smiled that stupid, charming smile.

"What do you know about that?" She refused to be coddled.

"Word gets around. Word always gets around. Space is smaller than you might think. And I wonder what the I.G. will say about the shoddy maintenance. Beacon down, tug grounded."

She took a deep breath. She had no time for this, but if she didn't make the time . . . "Dolph, I'm the duty officer until relieved by the next shift, or the colonel's orders, which you don't have. The shoddy maintenance, as you call it, is a result of obsolete equipment and exceedingly long supply lines. At least the comm units are working. We'd hear the Hegemony sneaking by twenty parsecs away. Are you so confident of your own department, you have time to loll here?"

Dolph grinned and interlaced his fingers together behind his head.

"Scaparelli, commence low-power sensor shot," she said.

He hunched over his comconsole. "Locking in coordinates and vector, ma'am." His voice was shallow.

Izzie glared at Dolph.

"Ready to fire." Scaparelli's hand poised over the palm lock. He looked her way. This was her last chance to cancel. *It's all in the regs,* she reminded herself.

Izzie nodded and it was too late. She felt good; it was by the books.

Scaparelli was intent on his follow-up message. She turned back to the screen.

The image bothered her. Something was wrong, reminded her of . . . Approaching too fast. Her thoughts coalesced. On the display, bright lights pulsed from the incoming spacer.

"The beacon's totally gone. They blasted it," Kuesza's voice raised in disbelief. "Captain?" He swirled in his chair and looked at her expectantly. Before she could get a word out Klaxons blared and section doors hissed shut. Laser fire! Too late. Her sensor shot couldn't have, wouldn't have been responsible. The inspector wouldn't destroy the beacon or fire upon them, only simulate it, and this was no simulation. It had to be Hegemony.

"Laser fire in progress. This is not a drill. Emergency gear and battle stations now. Repeat, this is not a drill." Captain Dolph's baritone boomed over the comm.

"You got to be faster, sweetheart."

She ignored the term of endearment, which he used as a weapon. "This is not a quiz show. I suggest you get to your duty station, which since you're off shift is in the tunnels." Izzie turned to Sergeant Kuesza. "Status?"

"Shields up and holding. For the moment. All sections are sealed and airlocks enabled."

"Return their fire."

"Don't we need the colonel's authorization for that?"

"They're shooting at us. I can return hostile fire without prior permission." She wasn't going to have Dolph beat her here also. She met his gaze. "Any concerns, Dolph?"

He flashed that megasmile. "Couldn't have done better myself."

Izzie didn't take that as a compliment. "Then get to the tunnel." She turned back to her comconsole and pressed the button to contact Colonel Gunthorpe. "We're under attack, sir." Her voice trembled and she bit her lip in anger. She didn't want to be scared, but even more, she didn't want to show it.

"I'm on my way." Gunthorpe broke off the connection.

"Captain, primary lasers are malfunctioning," said Kuesza.

"And the secondaries?" Damn. Too much too fast. She needed time to think.

Scaparelli blurted out, "All comm is down. I can't reach anybody."

"Laser's down. Cannibalized for parts," came Kuesza's interrupted reply.

She fought against panic. *Think of something, anything. Just hold on until the colonel arrives.* But she had no magic tricks, not against an enemy who so obviously held the high ground. The KB mission, their reason for being stuck here, was to warn headquarters of any Hegemony action in this sector. And they had no comm.

Lights overhead and on the holo display dimmed as shields designed to stop a meteorite, not hostile fire, sucked up the available power. *This is it. Keep calm and breathe.* She groped among the boxes for her own emergency gear. *Just a few minutes. Hold just a few more minutes.*

The alarms screeched the shield's demise while she sealed her suit. Angry red hot spots erupted on the ceiling like a hideous rash. Laser shot. They were using laser shot—the randomly scattered grouping of filament-thin lasers—effective for maximum personal injury on essentially noncombatant personnel. Tears started down her cheeks. Now the war with the Hegemony had followed her, and she was going to make a wrong decision and get someone killed. Again.

In front of her, one thread of laser broke through the ceiling, stretched downward, and vaporized the case of her comconsole. Sparks flared. Izzie jumped.

Around the room, dispersed strings of light shot down and bored their way to the center of the moon. The magnitude of the destruction excited her. She felt caught up, emotions afire. The moment stretched and held her until Smith leaped out of his chair and away from a beam. Kuesza, slower, screamed when the light pierced his protective suit and traced a deep jagged line from his left shoulder down his chest. The smell of seared flesh turned her stomach. Flimsies fluttered from the rush of air upward and out the laser holes in the dome top. Izzie secured her faceplate and flipped her suit channel to command override. "Dome is breached. Seal up now, then check around you for wounded who need help. All personnel evacuate to tunnels per the drill. *Now.*" The screams lingered still in her memory.

At the other end of the room, a small mob surged in front of the cycling air-lock door to the tunnels, the people in front pounding on the closed doors. More people staggered in from the air lock to the sleeping quarters. Whatever fool had designed this facility had never imagined the log jam the air locks would become. She had to get most of these people out of here—before that pockmarked ceiling weakened, crashed down, and pinned them beneath.

She could have used Dolph's help here. *Be fair. You did order him to the tunnels, remember. Can't have it both ways.* She turned on her command comm. "Morris, Schiller, look at me."

Lieutenant Morris turned, his face, defiant and waiting, glared through the dp faceplate. Izzie threaded her way through the maze of laser lights and continued her commands. She let her voice grow in volume, but forced the tone low. "By the numbers, men. From this point back, go to the maintenance hangar. If it's breached, seal it. Salvage what you can. Understand?" Some of the men nodded. "Morris, you're in charge.

"The rest of you, spread out, watch the ceiling for new beams and wait your turn unless some bright boy has another idea." She waited. The air lock clicked open. "Those with wounded go first. Four only." She watched four enter the chamber. If they knew how her own knees wanted desperately to knock. *Am I making the right decisions? If only the colonel were here. He would know what to do. What's keeping him?* She continued. "Those remaining: if any body part warms, *move.* Two more cycles and we're all through."

Morris punched Schiller above the elbow and started his small band toward the hangar. The men glanced often at the ceiling.

The last group of techs pushed into the air lock and the door closed. Izzie rubbed her neck as best she could through the dp suit. She had to keep thinking clearly. While she waited for the air lock to cycle once more, she moved among the comconsoles and workstations. The wounded had been carried into the tunnels. Those left were dead. When Izzie turned around to walk back, she saw it.

A lighted screen glowed in the now airless room. Across the long-range holo crept a horde of blips, a massed invasion fleet by the size of it. Izzie stared at the images. *What are they doing here?* This attack was more than an isolated harassment, it was a calculated effort to knock out any warning capabilities and sneak a fleet into the soft underbelly of the Home Worlds Alliance. Somehow she had to get word to headquarters, but how?

"Captain." Rogers, the colonel's noncommissioned aide, stumbled through the doorway with Colonel Gunthorpe staggering beside him, one arm draped over Rogers's shoulder. His smile vanished when his gaze darted around the damaged, almost unpopulated room. "Laser strafed the colonel's chest. He needs the medic bad."

"Already in the tunnels with the wounded." The colonel's face looked pasty. "How's he hurt?" Izzie tried to keep the resentment out of her voice. Gunthorpe hadn't gotten wounded on purpose. He *had* been on his way to assume command. She just couldn't help feeling stuck, even betrayed.

"Chest. I slapped on a dressing. No bleeding, but I think he's in shock." Rogers started toward the tunnel air lock, his body braced to support the colonel.

Injured and only three months until retirement, thought Izzie as she grappled with her inappropriate anger. *He wanted to write a military history. Hannibal was one of his heroes. A tactical genius. Good with his troops.*

A new barrage of laser, thicker this time, sliced through the ceiling at an angle and began melting the air-lock hinge. It had to be blind luck, unless they somehow had a plan of the station.

Rogers stopped, his gaze fixed on their escape, now cut off. Tears tracked down his cheeks, visible through his faceplate. The strength in his body dwindled, and the colonel slumped against a desk, too wilted to do more than endure for another moment.

Izzie pushed herself into movement, away from the random probing of the laser. Her lips mumbled a prayer for the men in the air lock. She could do nothing for them from this end. The building itself groaned, a deep wrenching moan of moving metal. She glanced up into the pocked roof and hastened her pace.

"We gotta get a message to headquarters. Gotta move. This building may be unstable," she said.

"But the colonel—"

"Is going to have to make it. We can't do anything through his dp suit. It'll keep him warm. We stay here and we all buy it." She tugged at the colonel's sagging form. His suit was intact. Rogers must have gotten Gunthorpe into the suit after he had been injured. Izzie motioned for Rogers to support his other side. Through the faceplate, Gunthorpe's eyes betrayed his pain.

"Leave me," he whispered.

"No, sir. The Force doesn't abandon its wounded." *At least, not for convenience.* "Hang on, sir. Just hang on." The intensity of her words scared her. Earlier, she had wished for the colonel, but instead of relief, he was another burden.

They managed to get him propped up between them, her shoulder just under his right armpit. Rogers had to walk stooped over to match her height.

"Where are we headed?" asked Rogers.

"To the hangar, where I sent Morris and the others. Some of it is bunkered." She bit her lip. *Who am I explaining my actions to? The colonel's too absorbed in surviving. Am I justifying myself to Rogers?*

She braced the colonel against the wall to hold him up while Rogers unlocked the air lock between Ops and the offices.

They pulled and shifted the colonel into the air lock and manually cycled through. The colonel did what he could to help, thought Izzie. He stayed conscious when it would have been easier—and less painful—to just drift off. His office was immediately on their left as they stepped out. In front, the chief clerk's desk drooped in two pieces; its top contents had slid into the ravine that now divided the center. Its drawers peeked open where they had been sprung. In the corner a body sprawled facedown. A thin line of carving disappeared around his shoulder and neck where his head, only partially connected, canted oddly. So little blood, she thought, for so much damage. Lasers—deadly, but clean and sanitary. Delivered from orbit, they saved the enemy the psychic horror of facing his victim. Cold, calculated, detached. Now, she and the rest of KB were no more than ants scurrying away from the path of boiling water.

She remembered to check the oxygen level in her suit. Another half hour. She leaned over the colonel and checked his readout. Only twenty minutes left. She adjusted the oxygen level down as much as she dared, lowered him to the floor, and raised his legs. "I'm going to scavenge what oxygen canisters I can while you work on the next door," she told Rogers. He clasped the colonel briefly by one shoulder before he left.

Methodically, Izzie entered each tiny office stacked down the hall on either side like crates. She pulled out drawers and didn't bother closing them. She stopped only to snatch each small metal container wherever she found one nestled next to the occupant's emergency gear.

On one workstation, next to the controls, lay a right hand, its fingers gently curved. Short black hair scattered across the back. Who had been sitting there? She couldn't remember. Izzie ran to the air lock, holding her breath to avoid vomiting.

By the time she reached the air lock with her load of canisters, Rogers had the lock ready and the colonel stashed within. When they opened the other side of the air lock into the warehouse, they found the rows of ceiling-high shelves had buckled and twisted, dumping their contents in the aisles. "We can't carry the colonel through this," said Izzie.

"The only other route is outside. If that spacer's still there, they'll see us."

She studied Rogers's expression through his faceplate, not sure what other meanings he might have. He seemed lost, more uncertain without the colonel's active input. But then he'd always seemed reticent for an aide, even a noncommissioned one. Not like the extroverted rank-by-association types she'd met before. Gunthorpe had sheltered him from the worst of the KB pranks, and Rogers, in return, worshiped him. "Only if they're looking. So we've got two chances. Three if they don't care, if they feel they've inflicted enough damage. Let's go for it."

"Don't you think we should wait?"

"We're getting low on air."

"What about those?" Rogers waved at the spare canisters.

"We'll need every breath of them if the hangar isn't sealed. I sent Morris ahead with some others; they'll need refills too."

Izzie leaned against the hard frame of the air lock while she shifted her burden of canisters. "What was that?" She looked about, trying to pinpoint the source of the shudder and loud crack she had felt from the metal through her bones. Dust cascaded from the top levels of shelving.

"The building's about to fall. We got to get the colonel out of here."

Izzie pulled the warehouse door shut even while Rogers twirled the mechanical wheel to open the other side.

They dragged more than carried the colonel back through the office section, in and out of the next air lock, and back into Ops and the air lock that opened onto the apron.

She nodded to Rogers, who immediately pulled the door shut behind her.

She felt the structure quiver. "Quick."

Rogers strained with the wheel. "I . . . can't . . . budge . . . it. Too . . . late." He leaned against the wall and made as if to wipe the sweat from his masked brow.

How long could they last? A day with all their spare canisters? How long would it take for Rogers to wrench away her and even Gunthorpe's air in a feeble effort to survive another day with two accusing corpses? She sprang forward and grabbed one side of the wheel. "Push up on that side while I pull down." Her muscles strained; nothing moved. She readjusted her grip on the wheel and tried again.

"We are not going to be stuck here. I will not allow it." Her voice bellowed. "Put your back into it."

"We're getting you out, Colonel," said Rogers.

Izzie pulled and twisted and jerked until her arms burned. "I will not be stuck here. *Open up.*" She slammed her fist into the wall and motioned toward the wheel. "Once more."

She set her grip, waited while Rogers set his. "Give it all you have," she said through firmed lips. "Now." Rogers's body tensed with his effort. She jumped into the air and pulled down. The wheel moved. Again and again they tugged and prodded and pushed and pulled until the wheel turned and they could force the door far enough for Izzie to squeeze through. Next came the colonel, handed through the narrow opening, followed by Rogers.

"The spare canisters," said Izzie. "I left them in the air lock."

Rogers paused for a moment, his weariness showing in the downward curve of his shoulders before he clambered back inside. Moments later, his arm poked through and set down a canister, followed by another and another. Next he squeezed back out with several canisters clutched in each hand.

They were in an ell made where the protruding Ops on the right joined with the warehouse on the left. Beyond the warehouse and connected to it lay their destination, the hangar. They plodded along the concrete apron that extended the length of the building on this side. Izzie concentrated on placing one foot after the other.

Suddenly the apron hummed with the vibration of firing engines, and the chemical exhaust of the primer engines roiled beneath the shuttle. Their only chance of escape, of calling headquarters, was lifting off, gathering momentum faster and faster as it shrugged off the inconsequential gravity of the moon.

Anger hit her in the gut like an explosion. Either she or the colonel should have authorized that takeoff. Whoever had initiated that launch— One face came to mind with an innocent grin and the words "The on-scene commander has the right and obligation to act on his own initiative, based on local opportunities." But at what cost to the rest of the station, to the poor sods who would soon stare down that invasion fleet? She thumbed open the comm line and flipped through the channels, testing each. "Antopolous to Jonah. Antopolous to Jonah. Come in." Static taunted her. The Hegemony had hit their relay station and the beacon. No comm. No way to contact the shuttle, the tunnels, the Alliance.

A movement at the corner of her eye teased for her attention. She looked up and froze. The hangar roof, like a slow motion holo, slipped, caught, then smashed down on the men she had sent there.

How many have I sent to their death? "No!" The word screamed from her mouth. She slipped from under the colonel's shoulder and ran toward the hangar. She had closed half the distance when Rogers gripped her from behind. "You can't go in there."

"Someone is bound to be alive."

"You'll get yourself killed. And can't carry the colonel by myself."

"I need to look." Izzie tore herself free and dashed the twenty meters to the hangar air lock. She tugged on the manual controls. *If it's open on the inside, I'll never get through.* She bolted around the exterior, but the wall remained an unscalable barrier. She might as well be a thousand kilometers away.

With the hard back of her glove, she tapped against the wall. One, two, three . . . one, two, three . . . one, two, three. She leaned, helmet against the wall, and listened with every bone of her body . . . and heard nothing. If she had heard something . . . she didn't know what she would have done. Wept in frustration as she was doing now? Her mouth tasted of ashes, bitter ashes. Senseless damage. Izzie scanned the blackness of space above them, broken only by the splash of stars where planets whirled and life quickened and grew and danced and knew nothing of this desolation.

Low across the sky tumbled their shuttle, its once-familiar outline scarred and mutilated. *So quickly, not even time to break free. What good did you do, Dolph—or was this another empty-handed gesture?*

A high-pitched whine from her suit warned her she had ten minutes of oxygen left. She forced herself to walk calmly around the building to where she had left Rogers and the colonel and the extra canisters. If she was on warning, the colonel would now be out. She picked up her pace. An old saying claimed bad luck came in threes. *I must be going for a grand trine: three times three.* Her mind numbed and she focused only on her next step and then, the step after that. Don't think too far ahead. It would only crash down on her anyway.

When she neared Rogers, the whine had risen to an unbearable squeal. Izzie dropped to her knees and picked up a canister from the too-small pile. Her fingers felt thick as she fumbled the exchange. He retrieved the canister and efficiently inserted and twisted it into place. Izzie switched back on and gulped down the rich air.

"Captain." He plucked at her suit. "We should move on. The colonel . . ." Rogers seemed barely to have the strength to meet her gaze.

"I don't know." She twitched one hand—it was all the energy she had left, all the will—to indicate the destruction. "We need oxygen. The farm."

"If it isn't blown also," said Rogers.

"We'll need food eventually."

"Only if we live long enough." Rogers knelt to place his shoulder beneath the colonel's.

Eight minutes, oxygen; eight days, water; twenty-eight days, food. Or something like that.

"What's next?" asked Rogers.

Izzie had been wondering the same herself. She sat on the floor between vats of green peppers and rice. They had found the farm intact, but abandoned. Evidently, the ag workers had evacuated to the tunnels. Without comm there was no way to be certain. She didn't want to think about the alternative.

Farther down the shed, the colonel coughed. Nothing she could do for him except keep him resting. His chest wound was beyond the simple first aid kit she had found. *He deserved better after a career, a lifetime, of service to the Alliance.* "Gunthorpe needs fluids. I want you to scavenge IV packs, tubing, needles, synthblood, antibiotics. Anything that might do him good and you can wrangle back here."

"Sure. Anything else?"

"Remember that shuttle we saw launching earlier?" Izzie pleated the trouser material that loosely covered her thigh into smaller and smaller ridges.

"The one that hasn't come back?"

"Didn't you see it? The Hegemony clipped its wings and threw it right back. It crashed somewhere beyond the horizon while we were still outside."

"Probably laughed at us, they did." He squatted beside her.

She stared at nothing in particular, her mind stuck in a whirlpool of nothingness.

"So what do we do?"

"Huh?" She returned to the present. "Somehow, we have to get word to the Alliance."

"And how do we do that?"

"Find out if any equipment still works. The Hegemony had a reason for silencing us. I saw a whole damned fleet of blips on the screen after everyone had left. We can't give the enemy the six-week head start they'll have if we wait for our resupply ship. Also, I'll go wall-bouncing mad before then."

"No shuttle, no comm, and you want me to find working equipment after that barrage. Captain, you're already mad."

"It gets worse." She smiled and went to check on the colonel.

"What's that fool done now?" Izzie barely heard the words and even less believed she heard them. It was like hearing a ghost whisper, only ghosts didn't wrack and heave with congestion. Or spit pink phlegm into bowls.

"Hold easy, sir. I'm coming." She moved to the colonel's pallet against the wall where farming supplies—supplementary chemicals, baskets for harvest, and tools to repair the 'ponics tanks—had been stacked within easy reach.

She knelt on the floor beside him and held his hand. It was warm. *Don't be a fever.* "What can I do for you?" *Not much except rest and fluids. Not without the diagnostic equipment or the medic in the tunnel. Not without a whole damn rejuv.* War reduced the actions of men and women to inconsequential twitches.

"Where is everybody? What's the fool Dolph up to?"

Izzie sank back on her heels. She hadn't thought of Dolph as a fool, only as dashing, decisive—yes arrogant, even bratty. But a fool? "He's in the tunnels, I think." *Or in what was left of the shuttle.*

"Then why are we here?"

"The main air lock melted shut and others are buried under rubble. We're short on air cans and I haven't gone looking for an open entrance."

"We hurt bad?"

She nodded and summarized the events of the Hegemony attack and the blips on the screen. "It's my fault the men are dead. If I make it out of this, I'll resign my commission."

His hand gripped her fingers. "And leave the force to the likes of Dolph. I won't accept it."

"But I led my men to their death and abandoned them. I could have—"

"Done lots of stuff better. With hindsight, who needs a prophet? A leader leads, but the direction isn't always perfect. You got a moment?"

"Lots of them."

"I want to tell you a story," he said between coughs. He spat pink into a pail. "It's short. Water."

Izzie poured water into a mug left on a desk by an ag worker. The colonel sipped it, then lay back.

"Centuries ago, before space travel, there was an academy on Earth. . . . Very rigid discipline, much like the Space Academy. The cadets, as they were called even then, marched in formation to the cafeteria for every meal.

"One day, the cafeteria didn't open. The cadets stood outside, still in formation, waiting, until one cadet took command and marched them inside." Gunthorpe sipped water, and hawked phlegm. He lay back and continued.

"Still no one came. Another cadet convinced them to march back outside and wait in formation."

"So?"

"That's it. Except that both the cadet who marched the class into the cafeteria and the one who marched them back out both made general."

"And what you're trying to tell me is?"

"It isn't what you do, but why you do it. . . . Leadership isn't always doing the right thing; it's doing something, sometimes anything, for the right reason." The colonel grimaced. "You had to get the men moving, to disperse them. You picked a decent location and got them going. If they had stayed where they were, they would have been killed, in your estimate?"

Izzie nodded. "But they still got killed."

"Which the Hegemony is responsible for, among their other crimes. Your leadership was in the moving them."

Leadership. Izzie slumped against a 'ponics tank and studied the colonel's face. He was at the end of his career and still he exuded leadership. She had never questioned his judgment, not as she had questioned her own.

She thought back over the day's events. No one else had doubted her decisions either. Just herself.

So now she needed a way to send a message to headquarters. But how? *Think back to your military history courses. What would Hannibal have done?*

Izzie scrambled to her feet and paced up and down the length of the shed. Nothing came to mind. All comm from the moon went via the beacon, which relayed it through the jump to its sister beacon on the other side.

At the far end of the shed, she stopped and scooped a large rabbit out of its pen. She stroked its incredibly soft fur. *Don't play with your food, Izzie,* she told herself. Still, she wanted something soft and warm to hold and hug.

If she couldn't communicate to the beacon, she had to find another way. With the shuttle, she might have repaired the beacon. If she had the parts. If. If.

Hannibal crossed the Alps late in the season with elephants. The only elephant around here was the tug.

The rabbit's hind legs pushed against her side. She returned it to the pen and brushed stray rabbit hair from her tunic and trousers. Ships called home. If the beacon on this side of the jump hole wasn't working, they'd have to jump a ship through.

"What about the tug?" Izzie asked Rogers.

"That thing?"

"Will it launch? Will it jump?"

He stared at her as if he knew what she wanted, yet had to think everything through. "Launch, yes. Jump? No way to tell for sure until we try. She hasn't jumped in fifteen years. Been no need. For all I know her field generators are out of alignment and she'll disintegrate into hyperdust. But we can't repair the beacon, it's slagged."

"I've given up on the beacon."

"But what about calling headquarters?"

"Call, yes, but I've thought of another way. The tug can send a tightbeam message itself."

"Sure." Recognition sparked across his face. "Just jump and send a message to the nearest relay." He paused, his voice growing cautious. "Regulations require annual certifications. Since she'd been used in local space only, no one's bothered."

Izzie gazed at the ground a moment before she gathered the courage to speak. "I won't order anyone to go up in an uncertified ship. It's our only hope unless you can think of any other way." *Hannibal didn't follow regs when he crossed the Alps too late in the year, but he made it. A leader takes risks, at the right time and for the right reason.*

"I'm the only one available to volunteer."

"There's me," Izzie protested.

"How many jumps have you piloted?"

"Probably as many as you. None."

"At least I've sat near the pilot. The colonel, he always liked to sit in. And he kept me nearby. Sometimes I even ran the computer. That's what does all the real flying." Rogers paused. "It's important, isn't it?" he asked. He ran his fingers through his hair and down the back of his head to his neck.

"If the Hegemony sent an invasion fleet sneaking by our post, headquarters has to know. Wars have been lost for less. At the same time you can ask for an emergency med-evac. For Gunthorpe." *And I can prepare for my court-martial if you fail.*

"Yeah. I'll check out the tug."

Izzie handed him a pack of air canisters. "I'll join you after I check on the colonel."

She briefed him on what she had planned and left food and fresh water near his pallet. Then she tossed the last of the spare air canisters in an empty bag and climbed into her dp suit. If they had any luck, she and Rogers just might get that tug off the ground in time.

When she climbed up into the hatchway of the tug, Rogers's suit was already splotched with grease.

"We need to launch today to notify headquarters in time," Izzie said.

"There's so much left to do."

"What can I do?"

Rogers looked around. "Need to fuel it, but you can't handle that hose alone. Regs require two people."

She smiled. "I'll manage." And she would. This improvising was invigorating, almost heady.

Izzie trotted across the apron to where the hose trolley sat. She turned on the power and watched the hose play out behind her as the trolley chugged forward. That was the easy part.

Under normal conditions, two men would have coupled the hose to the tug fuel tank. She pulled the trolley as close to the tug as she dared. Then she scouted in the tool box for something to hold the hose to the top of the trolley.

When she was satisfied it would hold, Izzie clambered on top of the trolley, unfastened the hose end, and leaned out to insert it into the opening. Two, three, four times she tried to match the threads and failed. Too much time was passing and she was getting nothing done. She dared not pull Rogers off his task to help.

Once more. She leaned out again. Thump. She felt the bump through her gloves. Twist. No. She wanted to throw the hose down. Instead she forced herself to breath deeply. *Don't hurry. Take your time, but get it right.*

She leaned over and her arm muscles quivered. She dangled each arm in turn and shook it. Finally, she brought up the hose again and held it out, ignoring her protesting muscles until the hose connected. *Please be right.* She didn't think her arm would last for another try. Slowly, she turned the hose, and it slipped smoothly into the thread.

Izzie had never been so thoroughly exhausted. Her arm, back, leg, even her eye muscles ached from dragging that fuel hose, and everything else Rogers had asked her to fetch, hold, and carry. The nonstop work wore out her muscles but eased her mind. Doing something, anything, was therapeutic. And they had done it, she and Rogers. Her idea, her leadership, and not a regulation to back her up.

She shielded her eyes from the bright flame of the ignition chemicals and watched the ponderous mass of the tug hover for a minute before it gained momentum. Their message was prerecorded. *Jump and press the button. Jump and scream. Then worry about what might wait, or not, for you on the other side.*

She had done it knowingly this time, sent a man to his possible death. But she had faith in her reason. She had faced overwhelming odds and had not given up. Whether Rogers succeeded or not, whether his success mattered or not, she had finally accepted the risk. And she knew it was for the right reason.

Juanita Coulson is the multifaceted author of sixteen novels, including the science fiction series *Children of the Stars.* Other works include fantasy, young adult, historical novels, gothics, and even some old Ace Doubles. She is also a songwriter, plays guitar, and is a frequent and welcome guest singer at science fiction conventions. She's a longtime resident of Indiana.

About "A Matter of Faith" Juanita writes: "As a 'depression baby' and a 'war kid,' I spent my formative years in a world dominated by global conflict, where old rules were being jettisoned for the sake of survival. Cultures long at bitter odds with each other were forced to combine forces to defeat a dangerous mutual foe. From a child's uncomplicated viewpoint, these tactics seemed eminently sensible. Adults, freighted with the past, had far more difficulty adapting to the new situation. With obvious effort, my mother learned to call her nation's former political antagonists 'gallant allies.' Remembering her successful adjustment and the era that demanded such wrenching change continues to feed my imagination even today. Onetime enemies *can* declare truce; and along *some* timelines, at least, alliances of necessity may open doors to lasting friendship."

—LMB

A Matter of Faith

Juanita Coulson

The skiff bumped to a stop against the riverbank. For a few heartbeats, Nuzha scarcely dared to hope her ordeal was over. But finally the awful roiling in her belly quieted and she raised her head. A uniformed shore patrol looked on with disinterest as the boatman said, "This uz where I uz paid t'bring y', old woman." When his passenger moved too slowly to suit him, he pushed her roughly, yelling, "Out! I'll not wait till th' invaders attack again and mayhap take m'boat for booty . . ."

"We give you greeting, Goddess-Singer."

Startled, Nuzha's tormentor gaped at a crowd gathering on the bank. They seemed to materialize out of the mist, and the guards moved aside for them. Their leader pointedly shifted from Destre dialect to the barbaric local tongue, asking, "Priestess, shall we kill that unbeliever for you?"

She relished the boatman's fear. The soldiers were indifferent to his plight, and he cowered while dark-faced, well-armed men and women helped her to shore and fetched her belongings from the skiff. Nuzha let him stew in his terror for a time, then said, "No, send the mud-eater away unhurt. He *did* earn his pay and bring me here safely. And he is not worth making apologies to the general for his death."

Seizing his chance, he hastily launched his small vessel, rowing for deep water. Once there, he stopped to shout, "Devil worshippers! Bogotana's demons rot you and your hag of a priestess!"

Hag? Nuzha hoped she did not yet deserve that title, despite her nearly six-tens years!

A hail of sling stones answered his insults. Yielding to the "hag's" wishes, the Destre warriors did not use killing force but stung their target badly, nevertheless. Abandoning bravado, he rowed back upstream, out of range of their volleys and jeers and, finally, out of sight.

"Sorry we are that carrion troubled you," the chieftain said.

"I am sorry the Council of the Dedicated did not let me ride a roan instead of that wretched skiff." Nuzha sniffed and drew her rain-drenched cloak more snugly about her.

"'Twas the safest way to travel here, honored one, *if* you do not venture farther." He pointed eastward, where skeletons of wrecked boats littered the narrowing gorge. The enemy fortress above was veiled in mist, but Nuzha envisioned catapult crews hurling boulders from that crag on any who tried to run the blockade. "Our Clarique allies will not challenge the foe with a fleet again until we and the army clean out that invaders' nest," the young chieftain explained. "Westward, on the canyon road, ambushers constantly harass our supply trains and couriers. You would be in great danger along that route, Goddess-Singer."

"Hmph! Do not mistake me for a soft and pampered woman of the interior," she grumbled, laying hand on her dagger hilt. "Afoot or astride, I have accompanied the People many turns of the seasons, going where I was needed. Long before the fall of Deki, I drew the blood of our enemies, and I keep my hardiness still, I assure you." Inwardly, though, she conceded the prudence of water travel; she could have done the People no service had she been slain on the river road.

The priestess studied her rescuers' striped mantles, identifying their tribe. "At even, my thanks, warriors of Kalisarik. I am Nuzha, out of Ve Nya."

Their leader bowed. "Wurtak, son of Oruin of Inhij clan. We awaited your arrival eagerly. Our scouts summoned me as soon as they saw the boat."

She regarded her welcomer thoughtfully, for she had expected to rendezvous with his sire. Apparently Oruin had fallen in battle ere she arrived. His son's curly dark ring-beard did not hide his years, which could not be more than thirty. He must be burdened by filial grief as well as heavy responsibilities. With a concerned frown, he asked, "Has no acolyte accompanied you?"

"None could be spared," she answered curtly, irritable after her harrowing journey.

He did not take it amiss. "Then, by your favor, some of us will render that service at ritual." Tribesfolk, few of them older than their leader, clamored for the honor. As he chose among volunteers, she saw that many bore fresh wounds. Most were gaunt as well, but suffered from a greater hunger than empty bellies, for they devoured the priestess with their eyes; she was a visual feast representing Goddess and homeland. Deeply moved, Nuzha blessed them with the holy symbol. "Argan grant you Her smile, Inhij clan. Kalisarik, eh? You are a rarity—Destre people acquainted with rivers."

"Ai! River and mountain." Wurtak indicated the watercourse. "This area is very like that around our home villages. And though hereabouts are no true mountains, the invaders' crag much resembles terrain familiar to us . . ."

"Thus I was informed. That was why I was sent, as well. Not for knowledge of rivers, of course," and she shuddered, refusing to look back at the place of her ordeal. "But the land about Ve Nya is rugged. I was hardened to rock and height from girlhood, and do not forget those skills."

"Is it so? It is good to have one of the Dedicated who knows our ways . . ." The clan chief saw her smother a yawn and said, "Forgive me for wasting your strength with idle talk! We will guide you now to the army leader and show you to your quarters."

Surprise momentarily banished fatigue. "Am I not to stay in your camp?"

"We have nothing suitable for one of your rank." Patently ill at ease, he said, "It . . . it was deemed best for you to quarter with the lady who is Captain Veo's advisor. We . . . we have collected a few things you might need there." Tribesfolk showed her pallet, blanket, and drum stool—booty, perhaps, or a dead Destre's former property.

Nuzha nodded absently, disturbed by their leader's evasiveness. So, it was merely a matter of adequate accommodations? Why then was he edgy? Was the lady a mistress rather than advisor? *That* was no offense to Argan's laws. And anyway, such a liaison was unlikely, for Captain Veo was alleged to be one of those odd unbelievers who took no joy of women. But given Wurtak's reticence, she would get no more answers now. With a sigh, she said, "Let us be about it."

A handful of Destre acted as her escort, carrying the donated objects and trailing their chief, who himself toted Nuzha's small bundle. As they ascended, fog thickened, mingling with low-hanging smoke. Within that miasma, soldiers and irregulars bivouacked left of the winding path and Destre auxiliaries on the right. Segregation was typical even among troops who wholeheartedly embraced the Alliance, and the Clarique locals serving with Krantin's Royal Army had adopted its attitudes toward Nuzha's clans.

She formed an impression of a sprawling mass of fighters and materiel, half-girdling the mist-shrouded enemy citadel above. The priestess had served in a number of unfamiliar places since the long-prophesied Alliance of Krantin's disparate peoples had come into being a scant turn of the seasons ago. Battlegrounds differed, as forces of the Alliance drove the invaders eastward. But sights and sounds and smells of encampments did not vary much. By now, at times like this, she almost felt she were arriving at some new, temporary home village as she accompanied Destre fighters from one front to the next in their advance.

This bivouac, however, was much more grim than others she had known recently. An eerie sullenness lay over the scene, with little joking, gambling, or ribald singing. There were numerous signs of a hard-fought campaign: ill-fed and unkempt people, ramshackle lean-tos, a badly tattered healers' tent surrounded by an overflow of sick and wounded who had found no room inside. Camp followers were scarce. Pickets guarded a few bony horses and cart beasts, and there was little fodder for those. That last detail confirmed the All-Clan Ruler's wisdom in assigning Inhij tribe to this dismal ground; unlike other Plains People, they were used to fighting afoot.

Destre who had been unable to meet Nuzha at the river gathered along the path to attend her with respect. Army men also noted the new arrival. "*Another* one of those to feed?" a soldier said loudly as she and her escort went by.

His companion warned, "Shut your fool mouth. Can you not see who she is?"

"What matter? A servant for the devil's Daughter . . ."

"Who may bid her people cut your throat if you insult her," the wiser unbeliever admonished. "Great Sword-Wielding Desin grant she inspire them instead to fight harder, despite past setbacks!"

A timbered headquarters and its satellite tents and cabins sat on a rocky shelf at the top of the path. Guards allowed the chief and Nuzha, but not the rest, to enter the command post unchallenged. Within, amid clutter, officers stood around a trestle table, poring over maps. After several minutes of being ignored, Wurtak coughed and they at last looked up. Their square-faced, mustachioed captain cried, "Ah! This must be the Destre priestess they promised me!" He went on in rather crude Plains dialect, "My greetings! Mm, in what form do I address you, Lady?"

"I am styled as a Goddess-Singer. My name is Nuzha. And *you* are Captain Veo, conqueror of the upper river, who, with the help of our Inhij clan, will capture Fortress Jode-Lu for the Alliance."

He blinked a moment, taken aback by this recital of his record and her fluency in his tongue. "A Goddess-Singer, eh? Nuzha? Good! I will remember that." Wurtak took an empty box from a stack, dusted its top with his frayed sleeve, and invited the priestess to sit. Veo blushed. "Forgive my discourtesy! I should have realized you were tired. But I had expected . . ."

"Someone younger?" she retorted waspishly. How often she met false judgments from unbelievers who could not see beyond gray hair and a body no longer youthful! "Do not be deceived by appearances. I am only tired because of an unaccustomed mode of travel. Boats do not suit me. But years do not lessen my gifts. I still arouse battle fever. That *is* why you asked one of the Dedicated be sent here?"

"Indeed!" Subordinates seconded him, but not all concealed distaste. Their captain snarled, "You doubt our need for her talents? Surely, after the last assault, you have no illusions that we can take that stronghold *without* Destre help." He awaited debate, his jaw jutting. Wurtak grinned, at one with

Nuzha's opinion: this unbeliever refused to let bias hinder his pursuit of victory. When no officer voiced dissent, he nodded and said, "Bear you messages for me, priestess?"

She drew a packet from her vest. "Well that I did not carry this in my cloak, or it would have been ruined."

"Ai, miserable wet country, Clarique," he agreed, tearing open the topmost missive. His face fell as he read. "Bogotana's demons! No reserves or resupply! Everything is requisitioned for the attack on the capital: 'Vital we capture and secure the right wing, the road and waterway to Jode-Lu,' the general says, but cannot spare . . ."

"Our Goddess-Singer requires shelter, food, and rest, m'lord," Wurtak cut in.

"I *told* you: not 'Lord.' No noble birth rank *here.* Only a muchtried veteran with an impossible task to . . ." Veo belatedly absorbed the hint. "A thousand apologies!" He snapped an order to a junior. "Ask Lady Beqael to step in here."

The man hurried toward a curtained-off area but halted as that divider was thrown back. A tall blonde emerged from the alcove beyond, where it seemed yet more maps were under study. She pressed slender hands together in a graceful gesture and said in excellent, unaccented Krantin, "You require my services, Captain?" Her focus shifted to the Destre, immediately narrowing to the priestess alone.

Nuzha returned that scrutiny. Height and fairness marked the sophisticated-looking stranger as a Clarique native. By their alien standards, the young woman was quite handsome. Beqael dressed in the loosely draped tunic and long slashed skirt fashionable in this realm. But those details faded in the visual impact of her distinctive brown cloak. A *sorkra*'s cloak. Beqael was one of the wizard-kind!

Now Nuzha understood why Wurtak had been so evasive earlier.

The general's retinue included magicians, of course, but Argan's Dedicated usually saw those only from afar. The priestess had never dealt with any of them personally. Must she now?

Many disturbing tales about sorkra haunted the Plains villages. Training and experience had taught Nuzha to overcome most of her dread of these witches and warlocks. Other reasons, though, kept caution alive.

True, the Alliance was in debt to them; their Supreme Sorkra's witchcraft won the victory at the crucial battle outside Siank.

And yet . . .

Sorkra also served the enemy, those ruthless white-clad invaders from beyond the Great Eastern Sea.

Veo had been speaking to his "advisor" in a patois of Krantin and Clarique. Nuzha could translate only a few phrases: "See to her comfort" and "*must* engender killing frenzy before our next battle."

Lady Beqael came toward the older woman, who suppressed an atavistic urge to weave ancient signs of protection against unworldly menaces. Curtsying, the sorkra said, "Will you do me the honor to accompany me, holy one?"

Inappropriate use of that honorific blunted fear. How ignorant she was! Hiding a laugh, Nuzha followed her out, the Destre escort in their wake. A short walk brought them to a solidly built hut. Wurtak drew aside its blanket-door and placed the priestess's bundle within. Then he and the others hurriedly excused themselves.

The women rearranged the hut's cramped interior to accommodate two. Nuzha hung her cloak to dry near a small brazier and sat on the stool, allowing herself to relax. The place was clean and blessedly free of vermin. Perhaps housing with an alien would not be such a trial, after all.

Exquisitely polite, the sorkra knelt, poured water from a ewer into a basin, and presented her guest with a fine linen cloth. Murmuring thanks, the older woman cleansed away travel grime, wondering if Beqael knew that water thus given compelled truce, even amid the fiercest intertribal warfare.

As the sorkra offered small grain cakes and a leathern bottle of watered wine, she said, "Eat slowly." That was not Plains custom, but in this instance was good advice. The fare was luxurious compared to what seemed available elsewhere in camp. Apparently the captain's advisor merited special rations, or her superiors saw lavishly to her comfort before sending her on hazardous assignments. Nibbling the cakes, Nuzha warily eyed the young woman seated across from her.

"I also am uncertain concerning this encounter."

Startled, the priestess accused, "You have entered my mind."

"Oh no! I merely guessed that you shared my feelings."

"Is it so? There are so many . . . tales . . . of sorkra powers." Something in the other's expression made Nuzha ask, "Do you fear *me?* Many outclanners tremble at our reputation . . ."

Beqael chuckled and shook her head disdainfully. "I am not one of them. While working with Veo's Destre allies, I have learned much, but your people protect their religious secrets jealously from outsiders. Secrecy stimulates curiosity, especially when one overhears fantastic tales of Argan's priestesses 'becoming' your Goddess. If that effect does indeed happen, how is it done?" Nuzha eyed her with cynicism, sure the sorkra knew far more about the Dedicated than she pretended. Blithely unaware of her listener's reaction, Beqael went on, "How do you holy ones . . . ?"

Nuzha had been eating, and the second use of that blatantly inaccurate term made her choke on a bite. The Clarique patted her back until the older woman regained her breath and said, "A 'holy one' is divine . . . immortal. I am only a Goddess-Singer."

"But what does that *mean?*"

Annoyed by the game, Nuzha said sharply, "Have your mentors not already told you it is a Dedicated One who evokes Argan with song?" Such revelations were not forbidden. If they converted an unbeliever, it would be counted a triumph. Not that it was likely Beqael had any genuine interest in her guest's religion! She had profane goals.

"Ah! Then is it a summoning by magic?"

"Magic? You speak blasphemy."

Beqael apologized, her words lacking sincerity. The priestess glared, lingering apprehension about sorkra powers souring to bitter resentment. How dare this witch patronize her! Did she regard the Destre as quaint primitives, and their faith a subject for ridicule? Heedless of her guest's anger, the Clarique said, "But if it is *not* magic, how do you create the incredible illusions that . . ."

Her features became empty, her posture rigid. Alarmed, Nuzha set aside food and drink and leaned forward, ready to catch the younger woman if this were a prelude to the falling sickness. One of her own nieces had suffered that ailment, and the priestess had become expert in nursing its victims.

But this seizure—or whatever it was—did not mimic that affliction. The sorkra began to utter bizarre sounds, and superstitious dread was reborn full force in Nuzha's breast.

As suddenly as it started, odd behavior ceased. A nasty smile curved Beqael's mouth. She said contemptuously, "Did he think to catch me napping? He should not underestimate me merely because I am but recently come to this battlefront." Then she saw her guest's outstretched arms, with their tacit promise of aid. "How fortunate for me you were here! At times I injure myself during these probings. You may have saved me from painful harm." Abruptly, her tone shifted again, from gratitude to urgency: "I must notify Veo at once . . ."

The sorkra rose in a lissome motion Nuzha envied, and paused only long enough to say kindly, "Please finish your meal. And rest! I do not know how or when the captain will counter the foe's plans. If you are needed to . . . to sing to your Goddess, Wurtak will let you know."

Then she was gone, the blanket-door swaying back into place after her sudden departure.

Nerves jangling, Nuzha went outside and found no trace of Beqael there either. At headquarters, however, her message had already had an effect. Officers' aides rushed off on important errands. Troop-leaders of individual army units arrived to receive new orders. Below the command post, soldiers checked battle gear but without the banter Nuzha recalled from other military camps.

Wurtak, looking like a man with much on his mind, left the large building and came directly to hers. "The sorkra says the enemy will attack."

"When?"

"Tonight, at the least candlemark. They hope to take us off guard and break through. It grows desperate. This land is vital to the Alliance—and to the enemy. They seek not just to hold it, but to push us back across the border. We are short of supplies and able-bodied warriors, and . . . it is hard to fight so far from the plains."

Nuzha empathized with that desire for their villages, herds, and shrines. This Destre band was under such tremendous pressure, Wurtak more than most. He was young, surely not much older than Beqael, and only recently come to his slain father's rank. If Inhij clan were typical, factions within it must be questioning his ability and coveting his status. Forging restless tribesfolk into a living weapon was a task that often baffled chiefs older and richer in experience than he. The son of Oruin had done well to achieve so much. She put aside thoughts of scolding him for failing to warn her that she would house with a sorkra and said firmly, "When Deki city fell, we vowed to go to the ends of the world if need be to avenge her betrayal."

"Ai! We repaid it a thousandfold, shall *continue* to repay! Each whoreson invader slain is a blood-gift for Argan. But . . . so many are being cut down by the Death God in this accursed war, in this accursed rain-drenched realm . . ." He shook his fist at the dripping sky.

"Bogotana's Daughter is not limited by distance or alien lands' unnatural climates," Nuzha reminded him. "Even here, many days' ride from the plains, She still guides our blades and lances."

"Be it so, in the name of Her Holy Rule! Be it so!"

"Bring me to the ritual ground when it is within a candlemark of their attack."

"Ai! We will raise the sacred fire!" Wurtak cried with sudden enthusiasm. "The captain himself encourages this; he says it will confuse the enemy concerning our location."

As he hurried off to ready his fighters, Nuzha reentered the hut. She opened her bundle and took out the things she would need later. Then she considered. It was still day. Ritual would not begin till deep night. For now, fatigue was becoming overwhelming. Argan commanded her servants to yield to their mortality, and so the priestess wrapped herself in a blanket and lay down.

Though she closed her eyes, she remained wakeful, expecting the sorkra to return at any moment and destroy attempts to sleep. But time passed and that did not happen. It became more and more probable that Veo's advisor was immersed in her work. Was she casting spells with bones or powders or arcane potions?

No, Beqael did not use those methods described in the bards' scare tales. Instead, her ways were as mysterious as . . . as Argan's Holy Rule must be to unbelievers . . . unbelievers . . . un . . .

Nuzha could not remember dozing off. But when she opened her eyes and peeped out the blanket-door, it was full dark. An inner sense of candlemarks told her Wurtak soon would return.

She dressed with care. Tonight she would be the sole focus of attention, rather than part of the usual trio: no Law-Chanter priest to repeat the Rule and enthrall worshippers with divine words; no lovely Goddess-Dancer to sway sensuously across a fiery carpet as she was transformed into the Goddess. Only a stocky little Goddess-Singer to evoke Argan.

Water from the ewer swept away remaining traces of sleep. She at last felt completely recovered from the boat trip. After braiding and coiling her gray hair, she aligned her faith-jewel's chain, centering it precisely on her brow. She put on clean breeches and shirt, and as the silken fabric of her long tunic with its striking pictures of flames enfolded her body, Argan possessed her spirit.

When Wurtak and the acolytes arrived, bearing torches, they saw the profound change in the priestess and hailed her with reverence. Moving at a stately pace, she followed them to the ritual ground near the river. The faithful had reared a pyramid of stones circled by fire. Nuzha halted before the altar and let fall her cloak. When her unique, shimmering tunic was revealed, excited murmurs ran through the assembled worshippers. As one, warriors knelt and bared their heads. Volunteer acolytes positioned themselves in a line to either side of her, forming a crescent's arms, framing the pyramid.

Inhij clan celebrated Argan's presence with drums, and now the throb of their much-worn instruments quickened Nuzha's pulse. The rhythm underlined a rising chant of the Rule. Fervent prayers rang out on the night air: "Goddess, smile! Hear us! Lead us!" Acolytes drew belt knives and slashed their forearms, flinging droplets into the flames. They were more frugal of that life-strength than a priest might have been, for they soon must engage in mortal combat.

"Blood of sacrifice we give, Argan! Goddess, smile! Witness that we bind ourselves to You in honor! Guide us, if we die, through the portals of Keth the Dreadful . . . !"

Gradually, as the drumming quickened, tension became ecstacy, impossible to contain.

"Sing! Praise Argan!" the warriors cried.

Pent-up emotion burst melodiously from Nuzha's throat. Age was forgotten. In ritual, Argan's servants were unlimited by mortal burdens. She transformed her Dedicated Ones, as they in turn transformed the hearts and minds of her worshippers.

Nuzha's gift was not the eerie, inhumanly high vocal register of some. Instead, she commanded a full, sonorous middle range, its tones capable of creating shuddering exaltation in listeners. She loosed that gift now, affecting the People strongly with the power of Her song. Seized by Argan's mighty presence, they swore most bloody oaths.

"I dedicate my first kill tonight to my slain brother . . . !"

"Grant me courage, Goddess, to slay multitudes . . . !"

"Strength to take ten heads . . . !"

"Vengeance! Vengeance for Deki, for betrayal . . . !"

The priestess, protected by Divine Will, thrust her hands into the blaze and took no hurt. Inspired devotees plucked live coals from the bed surrounding the altar and, like Nuzha, felt no pain and suffered no burns.

There was an intrusion amid this joy: Beqael, almost hidden in shadow at the edge of the crowd, watched the ritual. Her eyes glittered, though not with faith.

Rage knotted Nuzha's belly, disturbing her concentration for the space of a breath. She quickly regained control and continued her song, but glared wrathfully at the bystander. That unbeliever! Scorning Argan's Rule! Attending the ceremony for her own selfish purposes!

A word, a single gesture from the priestess, and the People would tear this insolent young witch to pieces!

Suddenly, Beqael turned to the east, flung up her arms, and gesticulated. She must have sensed the enemy wizard sending his forces into battle. The night's deadly business was under way!

Nuzha's voice roughened and deepened, reaching into the very soul of the ritual. Wurtak's mentors had taught him well; he managed to hold his own killing lust at bay while he relayed orders amid the din of drums and song. One by one, eager, heavily armed clansfolk slipped out of the circle, seeking the foe.

Shrill yells and the sounds of clashing metal came from uphill, at the crag's foot. Wurtak and those Destre still remaining at the fire ran to join the fight.

Alone, the priestess completed her paean to Argan, then drew her dagger and waited. The Goddess willing, she too might have an opportunity to send a blood gift to the Divine One tonight.

Veo's forces were raising a loud shout. No match for Destre ululations, which could strike terror in enemy hearts!

For several moments, the night mists thinned, letting Nuzha see a raging battle at the midheights. Torches and fire arrows wavered and arced. Screams mingled with war cries. Some bodies fell from lower rocks, but more fortunate fighters clung precariously to outcrops, clashing and stabbing at attackers who tried to dislodge them.

Alliance forces were equal to the enemy's, though no greater. The result must be at least some breakthrough. The priestess inhaled slowly, gathering strength. She had promised Wurtak and Veo that she was not soft. If necessary, she would prove it.

Beqael, enmeshed in sorcery, wove nets of power with her long fingers. Sweat beaded the Clarique's brow and she shivered as she strove to shield the Alliance forces and fend off the enemy's magic.

Suddenly, she staggered, driven to hands and knees by an unseen blow. With a moan, the sorkra fought desperately to regain her feet and resume her spellcasting.

White-clad invaders emerged from the fog, running downslope toward her. Nuzha had seen their likes before—bewitched, suicidal assassins. They were arrows of flesh aimed at Beqael.

"Inhij clan! To us! Cut them down!" A handful of Destre were pursuing the foes. In vain! The assassins would reach Beqael first.

The priestess stepped between attackers and victim and hurled her voice, a spear of sound, stunning them—or rather he who controlled them—for a precious instant. They halted, motionless, gawking inanely, and she breathed a prayer of thanks.

Then, as if responding to a command from afar, the assassins' leader raised his sword. Yet he lacked a soul's fire, his action deliberate rather than deadly quick. His master had misjudged the threat, seeing, through his pawns' eyes, only a harmless old woman.

Other enemies had made the same error, and Nuzha knew how to use their disdain to her advantage. She ducked beneath the swordsman's shield and thrust her dagger at unarmored upper ribs, feeling him gasp in surprise and pain.

So! *These* soldiers were not potioned by pain-killing magic, as the foe had been in previous battles! That was good to know!

She had created sufficient delay. Another heartbeat, and the Destre warriors were upon the assassins. Unimpeded by the need to await a distant wizard's decisions, the Plains people dealt swiftly and lethally with the attackers.

Beqael shrieked in triumph. "Behold! Your puppets failed, foul one! I live! And I will defeat you!"

The outburst exhausted her strength. She collapsed in a pitiful heap. As Nuzha bent over her, Wurtak ran down the slope to join his clansfolk. He exhibited his heavy-bladed fighting knife, red to its hilt, and crowed, "They are retreating! You did most well! We killed a-many of them!" The others added their scores to the tally, pointing to the slain assassins. He saw blood on the priestess's tunic and asked anxiously, "Have you taken hurt?"

"None. It is that of the assassins' leader." She said with disgust, "I shall have to wash these stains in cold water before they set."

The warriors related how she had aided them, describing her as a true Plainswoman. Wurtak praised her courage but wondered, "How did they get so far past our lines?"

"Magic," Nuzha said. "They were bewitched to kill our sorkra, and the enemy wizard blinded you to their presence till it was almost too late." She brushed hair back from Beqael's face, which was contorted with pain even in her unconscious state. Her pulse and breathing were steady, but efforts to rouse her were futile. "We must convey her to her quarters," the priestess said, concerned. "One of you notify Captain Veo what occurred."

Bearing the young woman on a makeshift litter, they climbed into chaos. False dawn and numerous small fire-arrow–kindled blazes illuminated a scene from Bogotana's Depths. Invaders had driven deeply through Alliance lines before being hurled back. Dead and wounded were everywhere.

When the warriors had laid Beqael on her pallet and gone, Nuzha gently bathed the wan face and again checked her patient's pulse. She now seemed to be in a deep, recuperative sleep. Worry easing, the priestess sat back on her heels and tended to her bloodstained tunic. That homey chore touched memories, and she regarded the young woman with different eyes. Tall, blonde, and slim, nothing like Nuzha's own daughters, yet . . .

"Was your so-called web too busy to come to your aid?" she murmured, angry with those magicians who had left this pale child alone with only her own devices in such a perilous circumstance. It struck her, too, that Beqael suffered the same problems Wurtak did; both had assumed awesome responsibilities at an age when their contemporaries were still being forgiven mistakes. Instead, they carried full authority for numerous lives, with all the attendant uncertainties and guilt of those burdens. Wurtak at least was among his own people. But the sorkra . . .

With a sigh, Nuzha conceded there was little more she could do for Beqael at the moment. She tucked a blanket around her and went to the healers' tent to see if she might be of help there.

She could indeed. Though fighters bragged the enemy had taken worse hurt, the Alliance had many injured, and healers were grateful for any skilled assistance. Over the years Nuzha had nursed family and neighboring clansfolk through sickness and injury. She put that training to work now. Both Veo and Wurtak came to the tent to chat with the wounded and laud their bravery. Their visit had an immediate effect. Injured men and woman rallied, flattered to be remembered and called by name. Their leaders, Wurtak especially, gained considerable status by this thoughtfulness.

It was late afternoon before Nuzha returned to the hut. Not only had she nursed wounded, but she also had sung dying Destre to the Gates Beyond. Her mood was somber and tinged with a desire to repay those deaths personally. Such feelings were intensified by Peluva's golden orb shining dully through lowering clouds and the pall of smoke from funeral pyres. The priestess made her way past troops coming and going to the defense lines. An influx of refugees seeking safety with the army further confused traffic. The peasants' flight boded ill. She overheard them speak fearfully of the enemy wizard and his soldiers, who had begun some new and terrible method of warfare.

At the hut, she found the sorkra tossing about restlessly and bathed the young woman's forehead with cool water. Beqael wakened abruptly out of a nightmare; agitated, her eyes wide with panic, she stammered, "At . . . tack! To me! My web! Help! I ca . . . cannot fight him alone . . . but I *must!* H . . . help!"

The childlike cries wrenched at Nuzha's heart. She held the younger woman close until she came fully to herself, saying, "Shhh! The enemy is repulsed. Did you not hear Wurtak tell us so?"

Beqael shook her head. "I . . . I remember nothing from the moment when you saved me from the assassins."

"You spoke afterward—taunting the enemy wizard."

"Ah! Yes. A tactic to enrage and weaken him." The sorkra stared at her nurse. "You . . . you stabbed their leader. I did not dream that you were capable of . . ." Gradually, she regained her aplomb, making an attempt to tidy her hair and disarranged garments. Forcing a smile, she said, "You also are adept at tactics, it seems, tactics of enormous power. If we could leash and channel those, add them to . . ."

"The sorkra web." Her astonishment made Nuzha grin wryly. "Oh, I know that term. This is by no means the first time your network of magicians has attempted to enlist members of the Dedicated. Ever since the fall of Deki, when one of you learned about our gifts, you have persisted in thinking of us as merely untrained sorkra, ripe for recruiting."

"But you *are* sorkra! I have witnessed the proof of your arts: handling fire without hurt, creating battle frenzy, and the way you can stop the foe with your voice alone . . ."

Exasperated, the priestess snapped, "You are as stubborn as my youngest daughter, and as hard to convince of reality. Hear me: the Dedicated accomplish these things you mention through faith in Her will, not magic."

She could have been talking to air. Beqael enthused, "If we could somehow tap into your skills and employ them in our web . . ."

"Whether I give you permission to do so or not?"

That shocked the sorkra out of plan-spinning. Shamefaced, she amended, "Should . . . that become necessary. But I hope it will not. Please try to understand: the gods are legends, not actual entities. What you call holy gifts are in truth arcane weapons against evil."

Nuzha chuckled scornfully. Why, she was indeed but a child, for all her magic and sophistication! No gods? Was that what her mentors taught? The world would disabuse their students of such folly, to their grief, if they did not adapt and learn quickly.

"Evil? That is what unbelievers call us Destre, youngling. Those who dwell in our own land's interior and even the peoples of alien realms name us devil worshippers, though we are not. For us, evil is that which opposes Argan's Divine Will or imposes unbelievers' laws and ways upon the faithful. That is slavery, and we resist it to the death. The Goddess guides our fates, not sorkra arts."

"But you *must* . . ."

The hut's blanket-door swung open, cutting off the young woman's protest in midword. A junior officer peered in, saluted, and said, "My Lady Beqael, the captain demands . . . uh . . . requests your presence."

Uninvited, Nuzha followed him and the sorkra across a bivouac cluttered with frightened peasants and their beasts. The cacophony was awful, and army efforts to bring order out of the mess proved futile. Stench, bad before, all but overwhelmed the senses now.

Within headquarters, the noise, if not the smell, was worse. Wurtak and his best warriors exchanged heated words with Veo's lieutenants, who wrangled noisily among themselves as well. Fists hammered the table. People the priestess had not seen earlier joined the debate: a very muddy army courier and several locals—rivermen, to judge by the half-moon scars of that trade on their brows. A lone, hard-bitten peasant stood by, aloof and waiting.

Serious battle plans were under discussion, and Beqael hastily wove magic symbols with her hands. Nuzha suspected she was casting a spell of concealment, hiding from the enemy what was being done and said here. It was one of the most valued arts of her kind. But the strain of such sorcery was enormous, and she trembled from the effort.

"I have heard all of you out!" Veo roared, at last compelling silence. "None of it changes this." He rattled a missive just delivered by the courier. Freshly broken seals showered wax over the maps. "We have our orders. The heights *must* be taken at once, or the entire war shifts disastrously against the Alliance! You saw that flood of countryfolk fleeing to us for protection. The enemy's wizard is sending out his bespelled soldiers to slaughter them, just as he tried to kill our sorkra last night. And forces on that crag seem to be growing stronger, not weaker, even though they lose men in each skirmish."

"Your foe redoubles strength from blood," Beqael put in. They listened closely, respectful of her knowledge of arcane practices. "That is why he now seeks these innocent folk: their fear and deaths provide him with fresh power. Those he does not kill, he enslaves, freeing more of his troops for fighting."

Veo tugged at his mustache in angry frustration. "Unless he is destroyed, we can batter uselessly at that height forever!" He spat a terrible oath. "We were managing fairly well till *he* came to that citadel a scant moon ago!"

"You will manage only defeat, if he lives," the sorkra warned.

He shook himself like a wet and furious cat and beckoned the lone Clarique peasant to his side, gesturing to the map. "I am told you guerrillas have no love for him either. And I am told you have a way for us to get at him. Show us."

"Ae can no read y'map, sor. Na matter, 'cause th' trail's na on't. Only m'granther knew 'bout it, from far olden times. His granther's granther helped buil' th' big tower. Th' trail's been most forgot. But Ae c'n show yer fighters where 'tis."

Captain Veo scowled. "A hidden path up its eastern cliffs . . . going in blind . . . no chart . . ."

"Aye, but they's a weak spot in th'wall up there, sor. We c'n get in, we catch 'em looking west—at you 'n' yer army makin' a great noisy show, eh? Squeeze 'em atween us and kill 'em all."

"Can we trust him?" a junior officer asked. "If what he says is true, why has *he* not led his folk to breach the invaders' defenses?"

"Too few of them to pull it off." Veo eyed the guerrilla calculatingly.

"Aye, sor. Ye ha' said it true. Me 'n' m'men canna take tha' b'ourselves. Not a-fightin' th'magic."

"Hmph! There you have it, Lieutenant. Until the wizard came, these peasants trusted us no more than the enemy. They have little love for *any* outcountryman—or their own local lords, come to that. But now they see the Alliance as their only chance to survive. They need us, and we need them."

"The invaders butchered m'woman and m'babies," the Clarique cut in suddenly, his pale blue eyes bright with hate. "Like th'witch said, kilt 'em for their blood, t' feed his wicked power. I want th' murdering whoreson devil!"

"I will help you with that," Beqael vowed, her gaze as predatory as his.

"A witch to catch a warlock, eh? Gros-Donaq and Great Tyta Herself 'n' all the Gods help y' to it, so'long's *I* see 'im die."

The captain stabbed a finger at Wurtak. "You promised the All-Clans Ruler that your Inhij warriors would conquer that tor."

"We will." The chieftain's expression was grim. "From this man's words, that hidden trail is best climbed by a small party of our best fighters, volunteers every one."

"Granted. Our home country and your Goddess honor your names, if you succeed. If you do not . . . time is critical! Our general is locked in mortal struggle with the foe's main troops, farther north on the peninsula. His troops fight for their lives and he can spare us no reserves whatsoever. Now his spies have learned the invaders are sending a flotilla upstream to relieve that cursed fortress. As our guerrilla friend puts it, we are caught 'atween 'em.' We must take that stronghold *now!* We will have no better opportunity. The foe's numbers are depleted after that repulse . . ."

He took a deep breath, coming to a decision. Veo jerked a thumb at the rivermen. "Launch your fireboats tonight, everywhere along the narrows. Make those devils up there believe it is an all-out attempt to break the blockade. Meanwhile, we hit them landside with maximum effort. Lieutenant Dir, move our wounded and the refugees to the waterside, for hasty evacuation upstream, if need be. Small craft ready against that contingency. Our guerrilla ally will lead Wurtak's infiltrators and the Lady Beqael, disguised as peasants, around to the east. With luck the sorkra can mask their presence from the enemy."

"I will mask your true movements west and south of the height as well, Captain," the young woman vowed. "I shall further ensure that when we leave on our mission, none of you will remember our going—or what our aim is—until the moment when we actually confront the evil sorcerer."

Veo and his subordinates were glad to hear that, but Nuzha regarded the sorkra askance. So large a task! Would the girl's web of magicians assist her? The incident at the ritual ground showed they might be too busy elsewhere to help in a crisis. In this worsening conflict, timely rescue would be even less likely.

Shielding the movements of Wurtak's group, hiding Veo's allied forces, combating a dangerous and ruthless enemy wizard . . . too much for one young practitioner of sorcerous arts! She needed far more aid than she probably dared admit.

But it would not do to speak of this in front of the captain. That would hurt her pride. Few were so offended by kindly efforts to protect them as were the young! So Nuzha kept her own counsel.

Nor did she ask permission to accompany the infiltrators. If she did, Beqael would protest and Veo would fuss about the diplomatic consequences if a Destre priestess were killed in a military operation. How absurd! Saving everyone's time and breath, she simply made herself inconspicuous during the remainder of the conference and its aftermath of preparations.

As dusk approached, she turned her cloak to its shabbier side and followed Wurtak's party. Their route was circuitous, meandering northeastward around the heights. But she soon realized it was not particularly difficult. This twilight walk through brushy, rolling country reminded her of similar ones afoot near her home village, not more than six months before. This time, of course, she was not with kin, hunting night-roamers that preyed on the clan's herds. Tonight's quarry was two-footed, and much more deadly.

For a time, no one noticed her. The guerrilla leader hid the group's movements among fleeing peasants, albeit traveling in the opposite direction. One small gray-haired woman among so many drew no attention. Only when the party reached a treeless stretch of misty lowlands did they see the lone figure in their wake. They waited for her to catch up, and as she drew near, Wurtak asked in a hoarse whisper, "Priestess, why?"

She smiled approvingly. A wise young chieftain, this! No stupid unbeliever's reaction, such as ordering her to go back—for he knew she would not!

Beqael was conjuring tiny lights for the infiltrators' use in the rapidly descending darkness. Presumably that trick demanded yet more magic to shield these clever objects from the enemy warlock—yet more effort for an already badly overtaxed young sorkra. When she became aware of Nuzha's presence, her response was dazed, almost that of a sleepwalker. "Wh . . . what? N . . . no! You must return . . . " she exclaimed in a distraught voice.

"Shh, child. I am here to help you." The priestess kept her tone low, for they were in hostile territory now, and enemy patrols might be close by. She spoke softly to their guide and the Destre. "Look at her. Her work is essential to our success, yet she is distracted, working spells to protect us and the army. When we reach the upward trail . . ." Nuzha left that last to their imaginations and went on briskly, "Never mind. I will cosset her and free you to fight, else we fail."

A brief, murmuring consultation settled the matter in her favor.

"You must not!" Beqael wailed, and Wurtak hastily clapped a hand over her mouth. She blinked and nodded and he released her with a hissed warning. Barely audible now, she said, "But . . . but if she is slain . . ."

"I go to the Goddess with honor," the old woman said, amused.

"The danger, the . . ."

"You question my courage?" The warning note in that query made the Destre growl, ready to support Nuzha with blood against an insult.

"Not . . . not that." The young woman looked strange and fey, the hood of her cloak fallen back, her fair hair unbound and kinking in thickening fog. Droplets, iridescent in the eerie glow of her magic lights, beaded on her crown and lashes. "No, n . . . never that. Your courage saved my life," she gasped, laboring to speak. How much energy she was wasting in this pointless conversation, energy better applied to deceiving their foe! "B . . . but, this is too much to ask even of strength such as yours."

"It was not asked. I give, for the faithful and this mission. The Dedicated go where they are needed. I am needed here, to shield you while you shield these warriors. You are impressed by my skills? It is possible you will witness others tonight. Let us go."

"Must be kept safe from harm . . . ," Beqael mumbled.

Shaking her head, the older woman muttered, "To become a slave of your magicians' web?"

"N . . . not magic. Sorkra is lore . . . special . . . a gift . . ."

"I have gifts of my own, and my lore is faith," the priestess said with a tired chuckle at such stubborness. "I am untrue to that faith if I do not stand with my people at the line of blood. Come."

Beqael, heavily absorbed in sorcery, pleaded no further. Her gaze was wide and remote, apparently focused on things ordinary mortals could not know. Nuzha put an arm about her shoulders and steered her forward, motioning for their guide to lead on.

Without the guerrilla, they would have been hopelessly lost. The fog lay everywhere now, a damp blanket concealing them from the foe, and from each other. Mist was known on the plains, but not at *this* density! An arcane command from the sorkra converted the tiny magic lights into a glistening rope that connected the party, allowing their guide to lead them on with a minimum of stumbling and confusion.

Nuzha kept up with the rest without too much difficulty. Indeed, if she had not been forced to support the sorkra, this would be a rather pleasurable excursion. On water, out of her element, she was as a babe. Here her stamina was nearly equal to others'. At a run, short legs and age put her at a disadvantage. But, as she had been certain when she undertook this task, they were *not* advancing at a run. Far from it! Simple, well-honed endurance, now and later, on the promised path leading to the enemy's heart, would serve her very well.

The guerrilla was familiar with every knoll and copse, proceeding at a sure pace. Now and then they heard enemy patrols pass in the muffling fog. Beqael tightened her spells at such times, completing the illusion that no one but the enemy ventured into this section.

Twice, the guide made them stop and hunker down when a patrol came dangerously close. The silent watchers saw through swirling mist that the foe was not alone; manacled peasants were being herded like beasts toward the fortress. For a moment, the guerrilla forgot his mission and would have rushed to free his countryfolk. Wurtak's strongest warriors restrained him until he calmed himself, remembering that they hoped to free *all* the enemy's captives this night.

Whenever the infiltrators stopped to rest while their guide checked his bearings, insects swarmed and made certain the group did not linger overlong. There were other nuisances, too—burrs, thornbushes, and holes, made by burrowing creatures, which tripped unwary humans.

As they went on, other guerrillas, their guide's fellow-fighters, joined them. They were few and vengeance-driven, men with little left to lose but their lives, and willing to risk those in this daring, furtive attack. The Destre welcomed the addition to their numbers, small though it was. The guerrillas' crude weapons showed hard use, and they looked to be as bent on killing the foe as were Wurtak's clansfolk.

Nuzha estimated it was very near mid-night when their guide finally halted and said, " 'Tis here. Now we climb."

The Destre stared up at a dark, looming mass. They had been led in a wide arc around to the enemy's eastward flank. To their left rose massive fortifications, iron gates, and stone-girt terraces built into living rock. These not only protected the citadel's side, but connecting stoneworks stretched to the river, securing supply lines. The hulking defenses looked proof against anything but an overwhelming assult.

The way the guerrilla indicated, however, seemed merely a remaining natural part of the crag itself. When they peered closer they saw a faint animal track disappearing into overgrown brush, dense, tangled trees, vines, and thorngrass. Warriors ceased trying to tug burrs from breeches and shirts, knowing they soon would acquire a great many more on this trail.

"Will there be guards?" Wurtak asked, loosening his fighting knife in its sheath. The Clariques' leader nodded, spreading a hand to show the number. "Maybe Y'sorkra hide us fr' th'few till we slit throats."

"N . . . no." Beqael's voice was a squeak. "Do not kill them. H . . . he will notice life-forces disappearing and become suspicious. I . . . I will mask you, make you invisible. Go around them . . ."

Plainly, the warriors would have preferred simpler methods, but acceded to her wisdom in these matters.

Nuzha had been squinting at the "trail." Barely room for one. She would have to push or drag Beqael along. Taking a deep breath, she sought the Goddess and felt strength renewed. "Allow her to rest before we climb." The guerrilla leader saw the sorkra's condition and grunted. "Only a quarter candlemark," Nuzha assured him.

She made Beqael sit on a flat stone at the base of the path, eyeing her anxiously. Two Destre warrior women came to join her, and one said, "We will help, Priestess—carry her, if we must."

"Do you hear, child?" Nuzha whispered in Beqael's ear. A weak assenting murmur answered. The sorkra's eyes were wide as she muttered incantations. Here, all but touching the very fortress, the enemy wizard's power must be awesome.

The ascent was different from Nuzha's boat trip, but nearly as arduous. Often, the witch was a virtual dead weight. Priestess and warrior women indeed had to resort at times to hauling her along bodily. That was awkward and dangerous, particularly when maneuvering around turns in the steep, pebble-strewn path.

Scree layers of ancient building materials suggested this had been an access for the tower's workmen, generations ago. Nuzha envisioned the guerrilla's "granther" showing an impressionable lad the way up, telling him of past times when their family labored for some long-dead local lordling to rear this fortress.

Here and there, the trail became a sloping tunnel, a passageway roofed in the dangling roots of trees that grew precariously on the cliff sides. Minuscule sorkra lights were invaluable in negotiating those musty alleys.

And it was in those shadows that Beqael alarmed Nuzha most. Violent trembling made the Clarique difficult to hold, and her features contorted grotesquely. When she spoke ordinary words, she chilled her listeners. "Mu . . . must walk the webs farther . . . deeper . . . find the greatest sources . . . tools. No! Do not look down at those eyes . . . those awful, voracious eyes . . . !"

The priestess could not guess what was meant, nor did she want to. She gripped the shuddering sorkra more tightly and pressed on.

Upward, steadily upward. They were forced to stop several times to rest, especially after conquering the most treacherous sections of the trail. The three Destre women shepherding the sorkra needed these breathers more than the others. During one pause, Wurtak asked softly, "How is it with you, Priestess?"

Thanking Argan for yet another replenishment of energy, Nuzha smiled at him. "I endure. When our foes are slain, though, I may need as much help as our sorkra to get down this height again."

The Destre said they would gladly assist in that. Wurtak told her the slope was much easier on the western side; once Veo's troops secured that front and the wizard was defeated, it would be but a leisurely stroll back to the bivouac grounds. Another warrior spoke of potential booty, including food stores, within the enemy fortress. Fighters hefted weapons and gazed up the crooked path, anticipation in their faces. They encountered no guards on this upper level. All had left their posts. South and west of the looming citadel, brilliant fire now lit the night sky. Ferocious battle shouts were heard.

"The attack has begun," Wurtak said. "The wizard has withdrawn many guards to add to his defenses on the far sides. Grant he attend too closely to those flanks to see us with his magic while we complete our climb . . ."

Nuzha studied the sorkra and said, "I believe she continues to shield Captain Veo's true intent from the enemy, and will shield *us* as long as she can . . ." Beqael shook, as from a fierce chill and nodded emphatically. "Make haste," the priestess urged, "while she yet has strength."

They did. There was less need to be stealthy, but caution was still advised on the crumbling switchback. Tension gnawed at them. There were smothered growls as a climber unintentionally kicked scree on those behind or trod on another's hand. Edgy and impatient, all ached to reach their goal and begin the fight.

And then, all of a sudden it seemed, they were at the chink in the ancient wall. The guerrilla leader motioned for the rest to wait as he reconnoitered that dark slit in the masonry.

Grateful for the respite, Nuzha fussed over her young charge. Beqael was showing more signs of awareness now, her trembling under control—like that of a highly bred mare braced to win the race before her heart might burst asunder. Her lips peeled back in a taut grin. "My adversary has not detected us. We have achieved surprise," she gloated. Then she went on imperiously, "I must be in the forefront, to protect us from his spells when he at last realizes we are within the fortress." The fighters eyed her with doubt, concerned by her gasping and shivering.

"I will support her," Nuzha said firmly. "Go."

The guide led them through a twisting gap. Tiny magic lights barely showed the way, so dark was it. Nuzha feared that one particularly tight corner would prevent her from going on, but ignoring abrasions and rips, she pressed past sharp stones and dragged the taller and more slender sorkra after her.

One by one, the team emerged in a low-ceilinged, sloping hall almost as constricted as the entry passage. The dank ramp appeared to lead up from cellars to main levels of the citadel.

Wurtak exulted, weapons in hand. "Scatter. Kill them wherever we find them. Make them think their walls are breached ten times ten and that they are beset everywhere at once! Make them fear!"

Beqael's voice was an agitated croak. "Breaking down my shields . . . ! No!"

Vengeance-seeking guerrillas and Destre tore through the corridors like starved hunters seeking prey.

Beyond the walls, sounds of battering rams and battle cries rang ever louder and closer. As the infiltrators raced by defensive posts, light from Clarique fireboats shone through arrow loopholes and slit openings harboring the chains of huge catapult mechanisms. Enemies manning these positions forced empty-eyed, bespelled peasants to serve as shields and operate windlasses. The slaves collapsed with exhausted sighs when their overseers were slain. If the master wizard was indeed manipulating soldiers and pawns, he did not respond to losing these. Nuzha speculated that his attentions were too fully engaged by the worsening onslaught at the western wall.

Surprisingly, Beqael now broke into a run, the priestess at her heels. Ahead, alien yells of defiance ended in death shrieks. Again and again, rounding a corner in the wake of the warriors, Nuzha came upon bodies of slain defenders. Several of her own people had taken wounds but fought on bravely. Once, finding an Inhij clansman reeling from blood loss, she stopped long enough to bind his gash.

More and more foes cried the alarm, turning to protect themselves from this unexpected attack behind them. By this time their master could not but know that he had been fatally duped by his opponents.

The stronghold's gates began to yield to the battering rams. Nuzha yearned to sing of this magnificent victory. And so she would! Soon!

Where was Beqael?

In the turmoil, she had eluded the older woman and darted on. An unearthly light flickered across the threshold of the nearest portal. Misliking its glow, the priestess hesitated.

Then the sorkra screamed in pain, and Nuzha plunged forward.

Beqael had found the enemy wizard—or had he found her? He was a powerful, hairy man. But the worst of him was not seen, that horrible use of unholy things.

This chamber plainly was his sanctum, where he might make his stand until the fortress fell about him.

Unless he had unsuspected methods of escape . . .

Two victims had entered this place of arcane objects and evil presence. Apparently the guerrilla leader had come upon him first. But that fighter's blade was unbloodied, lying on the floor before him. He had not been able to take the vengeance he sought ere sorcery ensnared him.

Held fast against a stone pillar, the peasant writhed in agony, burned by coruscating blue-white bonds—some dread creation of the alien wizard.

Beqael fought to escape a similar arcane mesh. Every spell she cast to tear aside the encircling, scalding bands was countered by her foe, who laughed and wrapped her still more tightly.

"Monster! Thing of evil! You must die . . . !" she shouted.

Such courage! Worthy of one of the faithful!

The enemy wizard's tongue was incomprehensible, but the fury in his ugly face needed no translation. He blamed Beqael for his failure, knowing her for the linchpin of Veo's success.

Giggling obscenely, he wove ever more enchantments as she struggled to free herself from the torturing net.

From the corner of her eye, the sorkra saw Nuzha. "Flee!" she cried. "He must not have you as well! He will make magic with our blood sacrifice and elude the Alliance . . ."

"So that he may continue his evil elsewhere? That we will deny him, child."

How was it to be done? This was no mindless puppet she could outguess and stab. The wizard was proof against such blows, as the guerrilla's unused blade proved. She studied the chamber, noting an immense open hearth dominating its center.

Beqael had succeeded in stinging the foe, and he reeled, howling in rage. Recovering, he flung up a bestial hand, swatting aside her effort to repeat that small success.

With a careless gesture, his magic smashed Beqael to the floor. Then he advanced at an ominous pace. His feet were bare, and Nuzha saw with horror that his toes were tipped in demonic talons. He was going to rend Beqael with those claws!

"Argan, lend me your glory!" Her prayer was answered, Divine Will consumed her, making her a fleshly instrument of the Rule. Ecstatic, borne up by that Presence, the priestess tilted her head back and sang.

Until then, he had utterly disregarded her. Now he stared at this impertinent old woman. She increased her song's volume, making him wince. His evil little eyes bulged, and the cords of his thick neck stood out tautly in his anger.

As had his puppet at the ritual ground, the wizard raised his hand to strike, though not with spear, edged weapon, or cudgel.

"I have power as well, evil one, power beyond your fathoming," Nuzha said, serene with confidence. "Power you will never counterspell."

He gesticulated frantically, his expression darkening with bewilderment. Singing, ignoring his magic, Nuzha walked to the hearth. She plucked up handsful of fire, enjoying his stunned reaction. "Argan grants you a gift suited to your nature, man of evil. She gives you quick passage to Her Father's infernal realm. Here is what you shall enjoy there, forever," and she hurled gouts of flame directly at his head.

They became more than blazing embers, expanding, liquifying, bathing him in fire. His screams did not resemble anything human. Thrashing and wailing, he staggered about the room, instinctively trying to snuff out the blaze on the tapestries.

"Those will not burn, evil one," Nuzha told him, though he was beyond hearing mortal voices. "The gift is for you alone, your entry to Bogotana's Pit."

She did not wait for his dying moans before she knelt at the sorkra's side, relieved to find the young woman still lived. The Clarique guerrilla was in much worse shape but looked as though he too would survive.

By now, troops and their auxiliaries were finishing the last of the foe and ministering to slaves finally freed of ensorcellment. Roaming the corridors, the fighters discovered much-needed supplies and cheered loudly, their triumph complete. Wurtak found Nuzha in the sanctum, and after staring in pity for a moment at the victims he ran to fetch healers.

In the days that followed, the priestess spent much time tending the injured sorkra. Beqael's burns were painful, but injured pride and psychic scars would take far longer to fade. At first, she refused to unburden herself. Only when she could walk on her own once more did she broach a subject troubling her.

"What you did there . . . how? I *must* know. You were impervious to his spells, though he was one of the most powerful wizards my web had ever encountered!"

The women were strolling on the slope, where signs of battle had begun to fade. Morning sunlight had burned off fog, and wind had dispersed the pyres' smoke. The fortress, now manned by the guerrilla's people, stood cleansed of evil. Army and Destre were going on to join the main force. Enriched by captured arms and again well-fed, the Alliance would soon conquer the peninsula's sole remaining major city still held by invaders.

"Are . . . are you going to tell me what you did?" Beqael pleaded.

"I called upon the Goddess," the older woman said simply. "He was a plague, not to be tolerated. Argan used me to destroy him."

"Yes, but . . . You speak like women in my home village when their children are threatened." She paused, then went on. "Once you said I was as stubborn as your daughter. Then you have had children?"

"Of course!"

"It is not . . . forbidden?" The sorkra considered this revelation, fascinated. "It does not affect your gifts?"

The question first amazed Nuzha, then aroused her compassion. "Your sorkra web denies you that? Do they control you body, mind, and soul?"

The young woman managed a weak smile. "Oh, it is my own choice, to enhance my magic. The . . . things of the flesh can interfere with our walking of the webs. At least that is true when we are yet new to our skills. In time, when I am stronger in my arts, I hope that . . ."

She left the wish unfinished. Nuzha sighed and said, "I hope so too, child. To abstain from the pleasures of life . . . well, if that is your so-called lore, I will keep to freer Destre ways!"

Beqael eyed her with admiring awe. "Even during my worst pain, I sensed your strength. And yet you have not renounced the flesh for your gifts, and retain them still. You were with me, helping me, though not of the web . . ."

Chuckling, Nuzha shook her head. "What you felt was Argan. I evoked Her with song, and She helped me strike down that abomination." Beqael took a breath, but the priestess laid a hand on her cheek, bidding her listen. "Your magic is beyond my ken. It is not my gift. But should you wish to learn what I *do* have, become a devotee of Argan."

For a moment, Beqael did not see the twinkle in the other's eyes. When she did, she returned the smile. "You taught me how little I really know." Blushing, she added, "And you have lent me prestige, as well as saving my life. My web thinks I alone dealt with the monster. I . . . I have not confessed what you did, for if they knew . . ."

The priestess nodded gratefully. "If they knew, I should be harassed by other sorkra wanting me to join them. Thank you, child. You spared me much trouble. Keep your prestige with my blessing." They grinned at the trick Beqael had played on her superiors. "When you are strong enough to rejoin Veo's staff, perhaps we will work together again. The war is not finished. We can still help, each in our own way."

"I would like that," her patient agreed shyly, then said, "forgive me, please. I was wrong, trying to make you a sorkra."

"It is already forgiven, youngling. I knew that in time you would see that I too possess a web: Hers."

Beqael laughed aloud for the first time since her ordeal. Arm in arm, sorceress and Goddess-Singer walked down the hill, where newly sprouted grasses promised a brighter future for this land and the Alliance both women served.

Elizabeth Ann Scarborough is a Vietnam veteran and former army nurse whose Nebula-winning novel *The Healer's War* is based on her Vietnam experience. She has written fourteen solo novels, the latest of which, *The Godmother,* is about a fairy godmother assisting a social services worker in Seattle. For the last three years she has been traveling to County Wicklow in Ireland to collaborate with Anne McCaffrey on their novels *Powers That Be* and *Power Lines.* The rest of the year she lives in a small town on the Olympic Peninsula with her three cats, Mustard, Popsicle, and Dundee, and makes a hobby of folk music.

About this story Annie writes: " 'First Communion' is a tale of the early settlement of Petaybee, the planet Anne McCaffrey and I created for our series, based loosely on the Alaska that used to be my home. For nuts and bolts details of why things on Petaybee are as they are, read *Powers That Be.* Though I chose to use Consuelo and a South American war (with which I am more familiar) to be 'bought' by Intergal, I was thinking of Bosnia when I wrote this. Reading about the horrible situation and unable to think of a realistic solution to the suffering, I tried to think of a science fiction/fantasy salvation for the victims of that war. If feeding starving people can turn into a bloody war where the rescuers turn oppressors, it's interesting to imagine a situation where forced exile, given the right circumstances, might turn out to be rescue."

—LMB

First Communion

Elizabeth Ann Scarborough

The Blood River War, as the *Norteamericano* press called it, had been raging for fifteen years when the Intergalactic Corporation bought it, weapons, combatants, civilians, landmass, resources, and all.

Consuelo heard about it on the pirate radio station—the television stations had long ago been blown to hell by the rockets of the Juaristas. She carried the news to the hidden ones in the basement bunker of the dental clinic she used to work in.

"I don't understand," said Elena Cisneros who had been, at the start of the war, a street vendor; who had become a freedom fighter until every single person alongside whom she fought or whom she knew of had been wiped out by bombs, mines, or death squads. She would have kept fighting even then, but her legs were broken when she was blown across the road by a mine of her own devising. Then Consuelo found her and took her to the bunker, along with the two journalistas, the nun, the young mother, Joselita and her daughter, Iliana—both of whom had been unwilling Juarista whores—and the *professora,* who lacked eyelids and fingernails and whose husband and children had been murdered in front of her. "What does that mean? Who is this Intergal? How can they buy a war?" Joselita asked.

One of the journalists, the Anglo, Amanda Sloane, said, "Bloody vultures, that's who. I thought all they were doing was ruining scientific study on other planets and messing about in space. I didn't know they'd taken up slavery."

The Yanqui, an Amerasian named Suzanne Soo, had been sleeping, but propped herself up on one elbow long enough to yawn, "We're not exactly free now. Though I admit that when I used to cry into my pillow at night because I didn't have anyone to belong to, I had something else in mind altogether."

"Who sold it to them?" asked Iliana. Both she and her mother were big with child.

"The World Court, Simon Juarez and his coalition, and El Presidente."

"They got Juarez and El Presidente to agree on something?" the *professora*, Pilar Escobar, asked.

"They offered more money than the gross national product has been since before the war," Consuelo told her with a shrug.

"A bargain," Pilar Escobar snorted. "We have been worth nothing since the war began."

"It isn't us they want," Consuelo told them. "It's this land. Intergal maintains that war is an ecological crime, that the land the war destroys has become too valuable to be left in our irresponsible hands."

"We'll fight them," Joselita said.

But of course, they never got the chance. One moment they were hiding, talking, bickering among themselves like always; not noticing the change in the air, the way a breeze, after all this time, came to be haunting the bunker. The gas was colorless, odorless, and had only a slight aftertaste.

Consuelo didn't taste it, actually, until she came to in her coffin.

The first thing she thought was, how nice that she had been given a coffin. People had been left on the streets, or their bodies burned in piles or dumped into mass graves for as long as she could remember. A coffin was genteel and spoke of respect.

"Ah, here she is," a voice said. Others among the dead were here to welcome her. She hoped her family would be here among them. Her mama and papa had been killed when their apartment building was blown up in reprisal for something or other. She couldn't recall what the cause was supposed to have been. Maybe there wasn't a cause. One didn't seem to be required, or any lie would do. Her sisters and brothers and their husbands and wives and children had disappeared long before that, one at a time. Some of them, or parts of some of them, had been found eventually, but by then Consuelo was too far gone and too frightened to go see for herself. They trapped people that way, using their own dead like meat to lure a hungry predator, except a hungrier, more deadly predator waited.

And there was her lover Manuel, a soldier, of course; she didn't know which side. Who did anymore? But he was beautiful and still able to be ten-der to her, and he was one with whom *she* had chosen to share her body, before he disappeared. The baby had died soon after she bore it, alone and in bloody pain. She almost died herself then, but the pain was normal, the blood was normal, the same blood as that of the thousands of peasant women from whom she was descended, women who had borne their babies in the fields or on a mountain track and continued to work or to climb afterward.

Compared to living, this death she was having was easy. She hoped her mama and papa, when she met them again, wouldn't mind too much about Manuel.

Something warm and damp brushed her face and one of her eyelids was forced up, and she was blinded by a sudden intense beam of light. Oh, God. Was she not dead then? The sick weight of her disappointment made her think not. Was there an enemy behind that light? Had she been captured for torture?

But what did she know? What could she tell them? Her last memory was of being inside the bunker and that, and the existence of the other women, was her only secret.

Not that they needed an excuse. They hadn't been looking for information from the poor Professora Pilar. Not really. They only wanted to wound her until her brilliant mind was of no use to her, maimed by her grief as her face and body were maimed by their ministrations. They didn't even want her dead; she was a better object lesson alive: see how the mighty have fallen. Genius was no protection, nor was beauty, nor physical strength. Any of those could be conquered with the application of simple tools available almost everywhere: a penknife, a cigarette; bricks stacked and bound with ropes, suspended from body parts to bend bones and pull flesh from inner tissue.

Consuelo had no idea how her body would respond. Only the feel of the damp warmth on her face, the light piercing her eye, convinced her that she still had a body. But she told it to respond, to fight, to fly against them and make them kill her. Now. Before she had time to get so attached to life again that she would accept it under any condition.

She gathered her strength, called on her hands to make fists, her knees to bend, her shoulders to pump and her feet to kick, felt muscles tensing, straining, ready to . . .

"Shit, it's another fighter," said a weary male voice. "Get the needle ready."

"No. I'll go get Soo," said another voice, this one female. "She'll be more apt to accept her situation with someone she knows nearby."

"Yeah, maybe, but we don't even know if the people she was found with were even on the same side."

The woman's voice ignored the protest and switched to Spanish, saying, "Consuelo, listen to me. Open your eyes. We do know you're alive. Come on, open them. The doctor just needs to ask you a few questions."

Childish in her stubbornness, futile though it was, Consuelo squeezed her eyes shut more tightly.

Retreating footsteps, light, then the man's voice said, "You're not in Rio de Sangre any longer, Consuelo. You're not on Earth any longer. You're aboard an Intergal Company Corps troop carrier bound for a new life on a new world. Do you hear me?"

Consuelo shook her head, again like a child, but she heard, and she had to see, and she did open her eyes.

The man stood over her, and this alarmed her even more. He was bald-headed and had on a white laboratory coat over fatigues. He carried nothing more ominous than some kind of handheld computer, however.

"Why?" Consuelo asked.

"Why what?"

"Why am I bound for this new life, this new world? If the war has been stopped, why am I not being restored to my home?"

"How do you feel?" he asked, as if she hadn't spoken.

"Where are the others?"

She was sitting up now inside her coffin, which she saw was more like a little enclosed bed with a cover, like the glass coffin of Snow White in the ancient Disney film. No roses were strewn around her, however.

The nurse returned with Suzanne Soo. Suzanne did not seem to have been damaged in any way. In fact, she looked better than ever. But then, she was Americano.

She spoke softly, as she did when the bombs were not falling, in the stillness between firefights, softly as they all spoke in the quiet so their hiding place would not be discovered. "It's okay, Consuelo. We're safe."

"The others?"

"Joselita and Iliana still sleep. Their babies were taken from them some time after this trip began. They'll be allowed to choose whether to keep them, or have the children grow up in a Company Creche. Elena's still in deep sleep too, but the doctors have been working on her legs. Pilar is undergoing surgery to correct what the *bastardos* did to her. Sister Sienna was sent home to the States, and Amanda back to England."

"And you, Suzalita? What do you do here? Why are you not back in the States as well?"

Suzanne shrugged. "I'm covering the story."

Consuelo blinked, her eyes moving as sluggishly as her mind. "Story?" This seemed less like a story to her and more like part of a dream. Long ago, during peacetime, when she had begun working as a dental technician in the city, her present state might have been nightmarish. But she had been living a nightmare for so long that this was merely surreal and odd, like something she had seen in a film back when it was still safe to attend films.

Suzanne reached out and took her hand. Her brown eyes were more alive than Consuelo could ever remember seeing them—almost feverish with suppressed excitement. Some of the excitement must have come from being clean and bug free. Her shoulder-length obsidian hair, once matted and smelly, was miraculously shining and smooth again, and the angry red places on her face had faded. Consuelo reached up and touched her own hair and face. Her hair was still snarled and foul, though the itching in her scalp no longer troubled her, but her face was smooth and the sores on her arms had healed.

"Your story. Our story. Of the redistribution of the refugees and how money has ended a war, for a change, instead of created or prolonged one. A very important story. Intergal owns my network. They were looking for me. I was given the antidote to the gas almost at once. After they treated me, I've been allowed to talk to everyone, see the screening rooms, the holovid of the birth of Planet, Terraform B, or PTB as the crew calls it, the one where the people on our ship are to be settled, and filled in on some of the history of this project. It's fascinating, Consuelo!"

Before Consuelo could form more questions, the nurse returned to take her to the baths.

She couldn't shake the feeling that she was sleepwalking. Finally, she realized that the feeling persisted, not only because she had just awakened from a long sleep, but also because of the silence.

In the background she could hear a pleasant drone of engines, and over that the voices of the various crew members and passengers, the beeps and blips of computerized equipment, feet touching gratings and hands slapping safety rails, but it was all noise of the same level—no gunshots, no sudden thumps or cracklings, no explosions, no rattle of fire. And there was little to smell here as well. She could not smell herself, or Suzanne, or the nurse, or the room she was in. She did not smell fire or cordite, feces, urine, or decomposing flesh, odors that had been with her so long that the sudden lack of them was disorienting. It was as if her nose had been cut off. She checked it. No, it was still on her face.

She seemed to be the only newly awakened one, and the nurse beside her was patient as she guided Consuelo through the baffling intricacies of a shower that used no water, only sound waves that made no sound. Strange to stand naked while something that resembled static covered one's hair and body, to feel the slight buzz against one's hair and scalp. The cleansing was real, however. She untangled her hair with her fingers as the shower worked through it, and the nurse gave her a special shampoo that left it clean and shiny and free of the corpses of the lice and other pests that had died when she went into cryosleep.

Afterward, she dressed in a clean, faded aqua coverall several sizes too large.

"You'll be issued winter gear before we send you down to the surface," the nurse told her. "But this'll do you for now. Now then, I know you must be pretty bewildered by all of this, but if you'll just bear with me for a while longer, I have some questions to ask you. Then we'll try to answer any questions or concerns you might have."

Consuelo nodded dumbly. Over the years she had become desensitized to any shock the horrors of war had to offer, but her new situation numbed her with its calm and sterility, its order and purpose. She allowed herself to be processed like a cow to slaughter because there seemed to be no alternative. The war at least had been intensely personal, if random and senseless.

The nurse led her to a room where they sat opposite each other. There were no restraints, although a male corpsman stood near the door. He didn't look threatening, but he did stand between Consuelo and the rest of the ship.

The nurse reached over and took her hand, squeezing it in what was intended to be a reassuring gesture that Consuelo found too personal from someone she did not know, someone in control of her destiny. The nurse felt her flinch and withdrew her hand. The woman was young, younger than Consuelo by many years, perhaps not too much older than Iliana, Joselita Martinez's daughter. Her name tag said O'MALLEY. She had a long freckled face that was not flattered by an extremely short brush cut that made the color of her hair difficult to discern. Her eyes were brown, and weary, and wary, but perhaps there was kindness in them? The nurse had papers, a file, and she ran a short, blunt finger over the top document as she ticked off the questions. "What is your full name, Consuelo?"

"I thought you knew everything about me," Consuelo heard herself saying, the bitterness in her voice coming as a surprise to her. "Are you not the ones who bought the war and all of its people?"

The nurse sighed, and Consuelo saw her eyes flicker to the corpsman, felt him move in closer. "Of course Intergal didn't buy people. But we are responsible for relocation of the refugees and we're trying to do a responsible job. We want as much information as possible about each of you so we can place you where you will be able to forget old enmities and form new alliances and friendships. We also want to place you where your skills will be best put to use."

"I see," she said. "And if I do not tell you this, then what?"

The nurse shrugged. "Well, we don't torture people if that's what you mean. And if you don't wish to cooperate, I have no intention of coercing you. The purpose of asking these questions is to make sure we don't settle you in a community comprised totally of your former enemies. The company's aim here is to found a planet full of peaceful harmonious communities, not to provide a new battleground for your old wars."

Peace? Harmony? Strange words, twisted so often to justify one brutality or another. The brilliant Pilar had known that, and was mutilated and degraded for her insight. Consuelo was no heroine, she knew that. She had simply been lucky enough to escape challenge, escape notice and survive. She would have told anyone anything under the sort of torment Pilar had endured. So why not answer the questions of this woman who was not threatening her?

"Ask," she said.

"Your full name."

"Consuelo Margarita Meña Alvarado."

"Civilian jobs held?"

"Only one. I was a dental technician for eleven years until the bomb dropped on the clinic and put my doctor out of business—he and his family lived above the clinic. They were all killed."

"After that what did you do?"

Consuelo shrugged. "A little of this, a little of that. I looked for food, mostly."

"Here it says you had a child."

"Who told you that?" Consuelo demanded, blood rushing to her ears. It made her furious to think that any of the women she had sheltered would tell these purchasers of people anything.

O'Malley shrugged. "The computer. The company bought all of the files, all of the records, along with the real estate, equipment and personnel it acquired. We needed as complete a file as possible on every person to ensure the best possible placement."

"What was done with Juarez?" Consuelo asked. "What sort of a file did you have on him? And on Nuñez, the butcher?"

"We had fairly comprehensive records on the top-ranking officials of all of the factions and the most critical personnel, as there was more information available on them, due to press coverage and so forth over the years. Of course, much of that was disinformation as well, so the computer had to make educated guesses about many of the details. Unfortunately, it was pretty much wasted effort. Though we carefully segregated each faction onto separate ships headed for one of the better-developed resort colonies, a freak meteor storm destroyed both ships and all aboard them."

Consuelo smiled. "A great tragedy."

O'Malley nodded, no trace of humor lifting her lips as she said dryly, "Yes, you and the company board of directors are in perfect agreement on that. How ironic that even though amnesty for all war crimes was granted the passengers, they died on their way to the retirement their sale purchased for them."

Consuelo thought of it—two ships, each containing all of the high-level bastards from each side, exploding in space. It was too good to be true. Too good to be true. She froze, looked away from O'Malley's open face at her own clenched hands, fists that suddenly trembled.

"What?" O'Malley asked. Consuelo said nothing. "What is it?" O'Malley asked again.

Consuelo bit her lip and mumbled, "You tell too much for an interrogator."

"Excuse me?" O'Malley said.

She was tricky. Consuelo almost trusted her. The thought of how much Consuelo felt like confiding in this woman frightened her as she had not been frightened in all of her years of hiding, ducking, running, and hiding again. Surely it could not be. This was all some elaborate scheme to get her to reveal herself—a trick, a spell, a drug to deceive her into imagining this unimaginable situation. The war over, the generalissimos dead, her country the property of some incredibly wealthy organization, and herself on her way to a new world. It could not be. She raised her head and stared O'Malley straight in the face, saying, "You tell too much for someone who is to ask questions. You know too much for a simple soldier."

"Is that all? Well, for your information, honey, it so happens *I* have nothing to hide. And as for knowing too much for a simple soldier, don't you think some of us medical personnel were on the teams responsible for hauling your rears out of that hellhole you called home? Furthermore, this particular little soldier is not all that simple. I have a very high clearance because I have a more legitimate need than any high-ranking general or board member to know all about you and everybody else under my care on this ship—and all of you, every man, woman, and child, are the responsibility of the healthcare team. I'm here to get information from you if possible, it's true, but I'm also here to counsel and guide you and give you all the reassurance that your present situation, though in transition, is more stable and secure and desirable than the one you just came from. *Comprende?*"

Consuelo could detect no duplicity, no guile in her manner. She was either being totally frank or she was so good Consuelo had no hope of outwitting her. *"Sí,"* Consuelo said, with a shrug that matched O'Malley's. She leaned back in the chair and let her shoulders drop, feigning relaxation. "What else you need to know?"

"Well, I need to know what you did in the war, Mama, to paraphrase a popular question. Who are you? What side were you on?" Consuelo pondered which version of the truth or her most plausible lies to offer when O'Malley added, "And how did it happen that you, out of so many women, seemed to have been virtually unscathed yourself and even managed to rescue and successfully conceal several other women, supplying them with food and water and information at a time when the rest of the city was starving?"

Consuelo did not wish to speak of these things with this woman who wore a uniform and yet had most certainly never been shot at or chased or tortured or raped. This woman had never held her baby as the life drained from it or searched in vain for the bodies of her friends and loved ones. She had never huddled in the ruins of a building while bombs exploded all around her, or run a constant obstacle course of rotting bodies, land mines, snipers, death squads, and rape gangs as she slunk from one place to another. This woman knew nothing. Consuelo bared her teeth at O'Malley in an imitation of a smile, "I am a lucky person," she said.

O'Malley leaned forward, her face and voice suddenly so hard that Consuelo immediately revised her opinion of what the woman had seen and done. "Just how bloody lucky *are* you, *dear?*"

"For someone who has lost her family, her home, and her country, *very* lucky," Consuelo replied, not cautious now, not contemptuous, but feeling a fierce anger flame up inside of her, making her careless of her life as she had never dared to be in all these years.

"Yes, well," O'Malley's face softened somewhat and she sat back in her chair. "And who were these people you lost?"

Consuelo dutifully recited her lineage as she had learned it from her mother. Her, her father the ardent loyalist, and his people first, then the families of her brothers, two of whom were in the service of the established government, and her sisters, one of whom had died in the mountains with the guerrillas, two others murdered with their children on the same day by the rape gangs. She then spoke of Manuel and the baby, too young when he died to bear the burden of a name, and finally, her mother, and her mother's mother, back to the time when a distant great-grandmother lived in a village where it was commonly believed she could turn herself into a jaguar at will.

"So, is that how you survived?" O'Malley asked with a hint of a smile. "You turned yourself into a jaguar?"

"I might have tried if I thought it would help," Consuelo admitted. "But the two-legged beasts in the city would have made as easy prey of a jaguar as they did of tame animals and human beings."

"And yet you snatched some of the prey from their jaws, didn't you? You don't mean to tell me they wouldn't have killed any one of the women you sheltered and you as well if you'd been caught?"

Consuelo shrugged. "That depends on which 'they' you are talking about."

"And did you know which 'they' you were talking to?"

"Never. I trusted no one except those too weak to do me—and later, the others—harm. But after a while, one develops a sense for danger, I suppose."

"If that were any kind of an explanation, then many others would be alive as well," O'Malley said. Then she shook herself, "I'm getting off track here. I was just wondering if you were somehow—connected with some sort of an underground movement."

"Only the bunker," Consuelo said. "The dentist, he was connected. He knew the war would touch Rio de Sangre. One of our patients was José Maldonado, Juarez's right-hand man. He spoke of this to Dr. Mũnoz, and the doctor, a very serious man, believed him. He must have been collecting and storing food in the family cellar for many months. I found the cellar and the food when I tried to dig them out when the clinic was bombed. I told no one. That was how we survived."

"Oh." O'Malley sounded disappointed. After a few more questions concerning Consuelo's health and the health of her family before their health was no longer an issue, she stood, saying, "You were given a fairly thorough physical before you were put to sleep, but we need to do one more quick checkup and then you'll be free to eat. Are you hungry?"

Consuelo was amazed that, although she had not even thought about food since she awakened, she was now ravenous. O'Malley was as good as her word, though, and within a half hour Consuelo was wolfing down food no better than that she had endured during the war. She did find, however, that the absence of Rio de Sangre's rancid fragrance improved the flavor.

Although she ate several more times before landing on the new planet's surface, she slept as little as possible. It was not the smallness of her berth that bothered her—over the years she had come to appreciate sleeping in cramped holes. What she minded was that she was now catalogued, numbered, and accounted for, and those in authority knew where to find her when she slept. She was not the only one with this problem, apparently, judging from the way the ship's security force had to—very carefully and as gently as possible—extract her fellow refugees from the cargo hold, the ventilation shafts, and other places where passengers were unauthorized to trespass, much less sleep. The ship docked once to take on supplies and offload the more severely wounded, including Elena and Pilar, to the station's more sophisticated hospital. Of this, Consuelo was glad because she had found during her physical that she had developed a horror of doctors and clinical settings.

Even though she saw for herself the good work that had been done on the still-sleeping Elena and on the face and body of Pilar Escobar, Consuelo could not quite shut out the knowledge that in such places, as much damage as repair was sometimes done. And she was uneasy feeling the eyes of O'Malley watching her, even though she could not have said that she feared the nurse. Pilar, who had requested that her old friend be allowed to visit her, was more comfortable than Consuelo had ever seen her, and far easier to look at with her new eyelids, ears, and nose. The surgery was new, so you could still tell what had been done to her, but Pilar said she had been assured that the scars would fade, function improve, and she would be well enough to resume work in a very short time.

"Work?"

"I am to teach for the company," Pilar said. "Languages. Many of the company employees do not speak the languages of the refugees and vice versa. I am officially a teacher of communications."

"You won't be coming with us then?"

"Not right now. When I have paid for my surgery, perhaps. But I have signed a contract to go where they send me for the next five years."

"Ah well, that's good, then," Consuelo had said, hearing another pebble echo within the well of emptiness that filled her. She would miss the *profesora,* she had felt then. But when Pilar and the others left for the docking station, she found she was relieved. She did not wish to feel obliged to return to the portion of the ship containing the gleaming metal surfaces and scalpels, laser cones and medicinal smells so powerful they made the polluted mucous membranes of her nose tingle.

Time passed in watches, not in day or night, meaningless concepts on the ship, which was always lighted, and in her berth, which was always darkened. She slept five more times, exactly, before she and the others in her hold were instructed to rise, dress first in the thermal underwear provided for them, turtleneck top, tights, and a double-layered pair of socks. They were then herded to a shuttle bay and aboard a shuttle. As each of them boarded, they were issued a pack as large as a filled child-size body bag. A soldier mechanically repeated as she shoved the bags at each passenger. "This is your protective clothing. You are not to open the packs until instructed to do so. Proceed to the bow of the craft and take the first available seat."

Struggling with the awkward packs, the people dutifully shuffled forward, hushed voices occasionally growing shrill with quickly suppressed panic, and eyes wide with fear. Still, no one challenged the many soldiers who packed them aboard the craft. The people now were too used to soldiers, too conditioned to fly against them like a bird against a glass door, seeking escape. Even fearing, despite all that they had been told, that they were being sent to die, her people had no will or strength remaining to fight the uniformed ones. Even as she noticed this, she thought, "Not now. We must wait for another opportunity. Perhaps, for the alert, there will be a way later . . ."

She was surprised, once on board the shuttle, to see O'Malley strapping into a seat across from her. She stowed the clothing pack beneath her feet as the nurse had done and looked up to catch the other woman's glance.

"Here's to soft landings, Consuelo," O'Malley said as the shuttle left the bay.

Later, Consuelo asked, "Did they deport you too, O'Malley? Or are you just going to help resettle us 'refugees'?" She put a twist on the word. They were not refugees. They had been deported—from their own country.

"Neither," O'Malley said, "My family's been settled at Kilcoole Village, which is close enough to the base for a short shore leave."

This revelation was novel enough to break through Consuelo's self-preoccupation. "This is so? Your family also was in a war purchased by this company?"

She was being mildly sarcastic, but O'Malley nodded. "One of the longest in history."

"And were the *generalissimos* of both sides of your war also in an unfortunate meteor shower?"

"Nope. There were no *generalissimos*—at least not in Ireland. Nor a real war. Just generations of bitter poverty while our people went elsewhere to work, except for the few that stayed and waged a futile terrorist campaign as debilitating to their own people as to any enemy. The only people of rank involved are still on Earth—at least those who aren't here in space as members of the Intergal board of directors."

"You're a traitor then to your own cause? Working for the enemy."

"That's a bit harsh. Intergal is an intergalactic conglomerate, and they ended up employing people from both sides. Most of us who settled on Terraform B were bought out of our land actually—it's more of the immigration that's plagued Ireland for centuries. Since the foreclosures and the potato famine people have been leaving because they couldn't afford to live at home anymore. We've just gone a little farther than usual this time. My family's settling in pretty well."

"But not you."

"I'm still on active duty. Don't know if I could get used to an arctic world, and I like spacing. I must say, though, that my mammy seems happy enough. I'm going to meet my new stepdad now."

Consuelo said nothing, but there was no window to look out of and the people on either side of her were comforting the remnants of their families.

"He's Eskimo," O'Malley added, a bit anxiously, then said nothing more as she withdrew into her own thoughts.

The shuttle trip was not long, and during the last few minutes, the passengers were instructed to open their packs of winter gear and don their protective clothing. Pulling on the heavy sweater and snow pants with suspenders, the boots and the thermal liners and gauntlets, all in the same ugly slate blue of the Intergal uniforms, was confusing work to people used to only a single light layer of clothing. A crew member stood at either end of the passenger cabin demonstrating the proper way to wear the clothes, but it was still difficult to watch and fumble with fastenings at the same time. O'Malley rose from her own seat and assisted the children of the families on either side of Consuelo before slipping with experienced ease into her own gear. Consuelo watched how she arranged the garments and did likewise. The last item was a scarf to be wound around the neck and pulled up over the nose and portion of the ears not protected by the stocking cap before the hood was drawn up.

Consuelo was sweating heavily as she fumbled with padded fingers and a body made awkward by pounds of insulation to arrange the scarf. But no sooner had she done so than the shuttle docked and the door irised open.

A blast of icy air swept in and, despite the scarf and hat and hood, slammed against her like a cold iron plate.

A soldier at the door droned as another one drove the passengers out. "Hustle it up or you'll freeze to death. Come on, come on, *move.* Fasten those parkas. Pull up those hoods. Walk, do not run, into the processing center . . ."

He sounded more human than soldiers often sounded in Consuelo's experience. They usually did not care whether you froze to death or not and they usually did not tell you where you were going, simply that you made a left here, a right there, went uphill or down, blindfolded or gagged or bound . . .

But another soldier was stationed midway between on the long walk between the dock and the indicated door. Periodically, his or her (it was impossible to tell in this clothing) mitten would shoot out to halt a trotting figure and say, "Please do not run. The air is cold enough to freeze the condensation in your lungs and lacerate them with the resulting icicles. Ma'am, please remind your children not to run. Thank you. Please do not run . . ."

Consuelo shuffled forward with the rest, stunned by the cold and blinded by the whiteness all around her. She had, of course, seen pictures of snow, but it either fell in separate flakes from the sky or lay quietly on the ground in the pictures. This was snow as an atmosphere—the ground was white and all around them snow permeated the air, turning it white as well, sifting onto buildings in pale institutional colors bleached paler by the whiteness.

O'Malley's muffled voice said. "Well, well. At least the weather's good."

"Good?" Consuelo answered.

"No ice fog. We can see where we're going. Some days the exhaust just lies frozen in the air and you can't see your hand in front of your face. There's a bit of a breeze today, though."

She sounded cheerful enough, which helped Consuelo control the fear rising inside her to find herself in such a place. Hearing was difficult and she could see little and smell nothing. Indeed, despite the scarf and the hood drawn with a drawstring into a tight circle around her eyes, the hairs inside her nose froze and her face felt numb. Surely they had been sent here to die, not to live. How could anyone live in such a place? And yet O'Malley was happily shuffling past the others, as eager to join her family here as if she were attending some wonderful festival.

Inside the terminal, everyone was allowed to remove their hoods, lower their scarves, remove gloves and unfasten parkas while they were processed in and assigned to other transportation. Near a door somewhat removed from the omnipresent lines of people, O'Malley stood laughing and chatting with an older woman, two younger ones, and a man with hair like an Indio and slightly slanted black eyes. An Asian? No, this would be the Eskimo stepfather. O'Malley bent to lift one of the three children with the party.

Consuelo watched as the nurse and her family left. The emptiness in her deepened. The nurse had come to feel less like an interrogator and more—a little at least—like a friend. But about then, two parka-clad figures, both sweating like herself, their scarves heavily iced, turned toward her from the next line, and Iliana's voice cried. "Mamacita! It's Consuelo! Consuelo!"

The soldiers did not object as the women exchanged ponderous embraces. Later, when the questions were asked, they were directed to the same shuttlecraft—a large, saucer-shaped affair with jets at the rear and fins rather than wings on the sides, and, unlike the space shuttle, windows all around.

No one interfered when they sat together, and Consuelo feared the Company might be taking notes to see that they were split up. But in fact the passengers on their shuttle were all dropped at the same place, after a long tense flight over steaming open water studded with jagged mountainous chunks of raw ice and teeming with seals, otters, whales, dolphins, walruses, and other animals. These were pointed out by the door gunner, who seemed to double as a tour guide.

The shuttle touched down on a landing pad just long enough to disgorge the passengers, and lifted off again, leaving the small knot of people, a fraction of those who had been on the ship-to-surface shuttle, to shiver in the open, despite their layers of clothing.

The pad was set on a peninsula that now jutted into a sea of mist, while overhead two moons glowed in the sky, one of them blinking slightly; Consuelo wondered if it might be artificial. Underfoot all was white and sparkling in the light of the lanterns illuminating the landing pad. Far away the land showed its teeth as white mountains bit the sky. Groanings, creakings, rumblings came at them from the perimeter, along with the howls of wild beasts.

A single ramshackle building crouched beside the pad, smoke making a white plume from the raw silver chimney pipe to the sky. No human being peered through door or windows to greet or inspect the newcomers.

"Come," Consuelo said to the others, "there is a fire there, at least." They were lumbering toward the building when they heard the barkings of what seemed like hundreds of dogs.

Iliana spotted them first. "Look!" she cried, and pointed. The dogs resolved themselves into maybe fifty or sixty instead of hundreds, trotting toward the pad in streamers of six and eight, two by two, which seemed odd until they were close enough that Consuelo could see the harnesses and the sleds the dogs pulled and the drivers aboard the sleds whistling and calling to the animals. Also among them were horses and riders, and all of these people and animals bore down on the refugees.

Iliana cried out and hid behind Consuelo. Over the years they had come both to fear and covet dogs, since it was always a contest to see who would eat whom first. Once dogs and cats had been pets and gentle friends, but as the war escalated and more people were killed, more and more of the pets scrounged for food, singly or in packs. Wild dogs devoured the bodies in the streets. Hungry people devoured the dogs and any other source of protein or other nourishment they could find. Iliana was not old enough to remember when live dogs had been other than something to fear.

But the dogs halted a short distance away from the refugees, who could not even flee in their cumbersome clothing. The drivers and riders approached them on foot.

From behind them, a figure on a small and ancient machine, like a motor scooter on skis, skidded to a stop. This person—it was impossible to tell until he spoke that he was a man because of all of the layers of clothing—was a company soldier whose parka was Intergal blue, emblazoned with the Intergal insignia on the chest and sleeves.

The soldier made crude charades indicating that the refugees should go with the newcomers. Unlike the people on the ship and shuttle, he didn't attempt to speak Spanish or any of the Indio dialects, and he didn't attempt to find out if any of them spoke English, which some of them did. The dictator had pleased the *Norteamericanos* by making English a required language in the compulsory schools he set up with a small portion of their money. However, this soldier with nothing else to do out here in this frozen place was nevertheless too busy to ask. Consuelo wasn't surprised. The witless arrogance and impatience of soldiers was not new to her. At least this one did not seem actively hostile.

One of the bundled beings who had driven a team of dogs approached her and held out a mitten. *"Buenos,"* he said, in an astonishingly low voice, somewhat cracked by wind and cold, but surprising coming from a very short person. *"Yo soy Dorji."*

He said it slowly and carefully, but she appreciated the effort. Others in her party were being tucked into baskets behind the dogs or pulled up behind riders on the horses, and she allowed Dorji to tuck her in as well. Then there was no need for speech as the horses and dogs surged forward, carrying them all across the snow.

They rode for hours, stopping only to rest and feed the animals before making camp, and never once did the sun show any inclination to rise.

Bundled in her winter gear and the furred skins of animals, Consuelo tried to maintain the state of vigilance that had kept her and the others alive for many years. She found this difficult. This place was even more silent than the spaceship, though the whine of dogs replaced the while of engines, the cheep of birds replaced the beep of computers, and the whisper of the sled's runner's over the snow replaced the whisper of uniform fabric as crew members went about their duties. The only loud noises were the crackings and rumblings of the ice (as Dorji had explained) and the shouted commands of the drivers to their dogs. Much better than gunfire and screams.

The air she cautiously inhaled through the fur scarf the man had draped over her hood and the woolen one she held over her nose smelled only of ice: no smoke, no cordite, no stench except the occasional quick whiff of dog excrement before it froze, as it did almost before the dog expelled it.

Farther inland—south?—that shifting ice noise became less, and everything was almost eerily peaceful, as it sometimes had been when a large convoy of soldiers drove through the town and all was hushed while one waited to see what they wanted, for whom they had come.

At first the jingle of the harnesses and the dogs' elation as they ran downhill ahead of the sled to the whistling of the driver excited her also, but that soon faded. In time even her worry about where they were going and what would become of them became secondary to the need to sleep in this bundled, hushed, and at least temporarily safe space.

She awoke when she felt her shoulder jostled by a hand. Her eyes tried to open quickly, as they usually did after sleep, but it took some time because her eyelashes had acquired icicles and she needed to rub them with her mittens, also icy, to dislodge them. Dorji laughed at her, but when she was able to look at him, she saw that neither the laugh nor the frost-rimmed smile was cruel.

She started to climb out of the basket, but he said, his hand sweeping over the vast expanse of snow and ice broken only by low clouds at one end and craggy mountains in the distance at the other, "It is time to rest now. You may sleep either in the basket, or with the dogs."

She huddled back into the basket. "And where will you sleep?" she asked.

His smile this time had an edge of lechery, though not an open leer. In better times, she would have been amused by it, even attracted. But now, so completely out of her element and so much at the mercy of these new men who were not even her countrymen, it concerned her. Light banter could easily turn ugly. But he said, "For now, I do not sleep. I stand guard."

"Against what?" she asked.

"Bears, mostly. Wolf packs. As we cross the mountains, the great cats. Food is scarce out here."

"Where are we? Where are we going?"

"To our settlement. We call it Lhasa, after the lost sacred city of Tibet."

She shrugged. She had never heard of it.

"It's now called the Gong Li Industrial Park, I understand," he said. "Intergal bought it from China with the agreement that all of us still living in Tibet or on the Indian, Chinese, and Pakistani borders would be brought to this place, where we could plot against them no more."

"They brought *all* of you here?"

"Here and other places like it."

"How long have you been here?"

"For five years—or at least, for five summers—it's hard to tell on this planet, and we were left no computers, no watches, no instruments to measure."

"Have you not tried to escape?"

"No. For one thing, it would be impossible. They have all of the machinery, all of the technology. They control the shuttles and the ships. We have no one among us trained to control those things, although we understand that later our children will be given a chance to enlist in Intergal's company corps and learn these things and leave the planet. But our home is no longer there, so there is no point in escaping. Actually, this place greatly resembles the way our home used to look, according to old pictures and films. It's wilder, of course, as the terraforming has only recently stabilized sufficiently for colonies, but when there are more people here, in a couple of generations, we'll build cities too, I suppose."

"I see. Then you all have families?"

He looked at her meaningfully and said, "Not yet."

She dropped the subject and pretended to sleep. That night there was no incident, but the following night she was awakened by a terrible noise of growling and yelling and knelt in the sled in time to see a man fling a spear and a great white bear, almost indistinguishable from the snow, fall forward.

Dorji came to her then and said, "If you women would like some meat to eat, come along and learn how to butcher and dress out the bear. Our customs forbid us to do it, but I can show you how it is done."

"How about the killing?"

"That is also forbidden, but one makes exceptions. It is best if you learn to do this."

Certainly we all know enough about butchery, Consuelo thought grimly as she learned to dress out the bear without spilling its gall into the meat or touching its liver. They worked beside a fire, so the meat wouldn't freeze before the animal was inexpertly skinned and the animal cut into pieces. Dorji was approving. "The hide will make a warm bedcover—a few holes, of course, but if they are too large when it's been scraped and cured, it will still make boots or mittens for several of you."

"How kind," she said automatically. Probably he was not being kind. No doubt there was a motive of gain—to him and loss to her—but meanwhile, best to keep relations amiable. Whatever underlying motives the man had, he had not so far proven dangerous.

The next day the men came across several sets of tracks—snowshoes, horse and sled. The snowshoe tracks Consuelo saw pointed in the direction from which their party had come, although they had met no one. Someone else mentioned this and Dorji reminded him that the country was vast and the tracks could have been many days old, as there had been no snow for more than a week.

They traveled on four more days, and Consuelo slept more than she had dreamed she needed, lulled by the swaying of the sled (which only dumped her into the snow twice when the dogs took a turn rather too enthusiastically) and the need to bundle up against the cold. Much of the time the land was in darkness or twilight, but even during the day, the shifting of color and shape across the long vista of ice and snow was hypnotic—seldom were her surroundings merely white; sometimes the shadows were purple, sometimes the peaks were pink or tangerine. The shadow of a small bird could loom as large as that of an air shuttle at certain times of the day. Plumes of snow lifted on the wind to pirouette across the trail. Small animals scuttled fearfully away before the dogs and drivers, and once a herd of larger animals galloped ahead of them and the men stopped to hunt again, and gave the women a second lesson at dressing out a carcass.

So at night there was hot meat to fill her. And all day long and all night long, no one shot at her, no one so much as shouted at her. The men slept with their dogs every night, except for those who slept next to their horses, so it was actually a blessing that the cold air killed most odors. Every morning, before they started, Dorji and the other drivers sat cross-legged on the snow in front of their newly hitched dogs, apparently discussing the day's agenda with them. Oh well. She'd known lots of people who talked to their rifles. Talking to dogs made more sense, even if it was made somewhat difficult because the dogs, unlike the rifles, kept trying to lick the faces of the men talking to them.

So peaceful! One would have thought the cold sleep on the spaceship would have been enough for anyone, but she found she had developed an appetite for sleep. All through the nights and most of the days she slept deeply, mostly dreamlessly, but when she did dream, it was no longer of gunfire and death, but of flying, skimming over snow-covered mountains, and of great hunks of food and gentle hands soothing her—sometimes more. Good dreams, but the idea of sleeping so much made her somewhat uncomfortable. Had she avoided death for so long only to spend her life unconscious?

Four nights later, or perhaps five, as they set up camp, Iliana spotted two small faint lights in the distance. She said nothing to the men, carefully avoiding even looking at them, but to Consuelo and her mother the girl said, "I wonder why these men do not take us to that place. Have they enemies there?"

"Probably afraid the men there would take us away from them," Joselita said. Joselita was not an especially bright woman, and her ideas about her role in the world—any world—had been much shaded by her mistreatment at the hands of the soldiers. Before the war, she had been a cabaret singer, and Iliana, who sometimes crooned sad little tunes to herself, had quite a good voice. Now Joselita began coughing as she finished talking—she had been coughing a lot since they began this trip, Consuelo noticed.

Consuelo could see no harm in asking about the lights, so while Dorji unhitched the dogs, she pointed them out to him. "Who lives there? Would they not make a place for us for the night?"

"It's not a village, only a research station," Dorji answered without looking where she was pointing. "A company scientist lives there."

"Alone? Maybe he'd like company. Or some of the bear meat." Consuelo persisted, trying to sound innocent, not only because she wanted to know more about the scientist, but also because she ached to go indoors again, where it was warm. Despite all of the clothing, she had not been warm since arriving here. The thought of an enclosed room with a heat source made her yearn for the stifling climate of Rio do Sangre in a way she never would have believed she could yearn.

"The scientist is a woman and she likes only the artificial company food. She does not welcome visitors." Consuelo could well believe that. A horde of men such as these would be a danger to any lone woman, even an old one. Dorji's tone told her that approaching the scientist with offers of company and food had already been attempted.

Apparently this story was true, because Dorji and the men seemed as surprised as anyone to be awakened just at dawn by the dogs, who set up a howl to rival the screams of the dying. They were answered by excited howling and whining from other dogs in the distance, and the calling of drivers. Six—no, seven—teams were being driven toward them from the direction of the scientist's home.

They waited, the men half-defensive while the other dogs braked to a halt with a spray of snow and ice, and much sniffing, howling, and growling.

Dorji greeted the first driver in a tongue Consuelo didn't recognize, and apparently neither did the driver, who began speaking in a fast, feminine voice a language as incomprehensible as Dorji's.

Dorji, who seemed extremely well versed in languages, answered her at once in her own and she hopped off the sled runners to confer with him. Soon all the drivers were in a huddle, leaving their passengers to freeze while they engaged in an animated discussion.

The new sleds contained passengers as well. Curious and in need of a stretch, Consuelo climbed out of the basket and sauntered over to the sled of the woman who had first spoken to Dorji. The passenger in it pulled away the muffler concealing the lower half of his face.

"Buenos," she said.

To her surprise, he answered in the same language. These men must be more passengers from the ship then, brought on a different shuttle. But she didn't recognize him, she was sure. He was not old, and one parka sleeve was empty, tucked into the pocket. She could remember no disabled men of a soldiering age on the ship, when she stopped to think about it. His voice was not strong and she knelt as low as possible in her cumbersome pants and boots.

"Where are you from?" she asked, raising her voice against the wind.

"Lacrimas," he said, his eyes cynical and his voice husky as if his throat was sore.

"Lacrimas del Muerte? But that is where my father was born!" She started to say more, but just then the woman driver returned and, totally ignoring her, released the brakes from her sled and whistled to the dogs. Consuelo fell back in the snow to avoid being run over by the sled.

Dorji, who had turned away from the woman driver to sit in front of his lead dogs and conduct his morning conversation with them, broke off to watch as she slipped and slid to her feet. He did not try to help her but waited until she regained her balance and came to squat beside him. Then he excused himself to the dogs to ask her, "That man in the sled. Do you know him?"

"No, but he was from my father's village. That bitch tried to run me over before I could find out more."

"Yes, well, the women have been alone as long as we have." He let that freeze in the air between them for a moment before adding, "Which is why we invited them to stop at our village on the way back to theirs tonight."

"Do they live far?"

"Everything is far when you have only your feet, dogs, or horses," he said. "But speed is not necessarily a good thing. 'Tibet was free until the road was built,' is something my mother used to say when she wished me to slow down."

"It doesn't make much sense," Consuelo noted.

"It does when you know that in order to conquer Tibet, the Chinese first had to build a road through the mountains to bring their trucks and troops."

"I see. In our case, the same thing happened when the jungle was cleared to make roads and airstrips. We thought it was bringing prosperity. It did. To gunrunners."

He nodded. "I think everyone settled on this world has experienced something like that. So we are cautious of each other."

"O'Malley, a woman officer on the ship, said they asked us so many questions so we would not be settled in the same place with our enemies."

"That's right," Dorji said. "You never know. Still, it is good to speak one's own tongue with someone who does not know all of one's stories and songs, including which ones are lies." He grinned. "So we'll have a proper feast tonight. To welcome you to our village and for the Afghan women to welcome their new men."

"If you and they speak the same language and the men are from our area, why do we not all just live in the same village?"

"The company only provided so many houses, and there are times when the cold is so bad you cannot leave the houses without dying."

"You could build more."

"Not as warm."

"Ah, it's another form of trap then, to put us on a planet so cold that we can only survive with their help. Otherwise, if they were going to terraform a planet, why didn't they make it a warm one?"

"It just turned out that way, I was told. The only land masses that formed were at the poles. Even the scientists can't control everything."

"I suppose not."

He heaved himself to his feet, saying, "Back in the basket with you for now. We'll talk more tonight."

They ascended into the mountains through a young forest later that morning before dropping into a river valley. A short traverse up the frozen river brought them to the village, a cluster of ugly, boxy pastel-colored shacks, each with mysterious snow-covered mounds in yards studded by junk, frozen fish strung on lines, large frames holding hides, and extra sleds and parts—and doghouses.

The only thing stirring in the entire village was a welcoming committee composed of cats—about twenty of them, all orange-colored, they came swarming from between and on top of the houses, much to the agitation of the dogs, who began to wriggle and whine and call out their weird cries, half-howl and half-yip.

While some of the men unhitched all of the dogs, Dorji and three others herded their passengers to two houses at one end of the village. Though obviously as tired or tireder than the women, the men lit fires in the small, black stoves in the center of each house, opened sleeping bags onto the cots arranged near the stoves and tromped outside again, tracking the floors with snow which melted with the sudden warmth of the stove.

Joselita collapsed on one of the beds, but Iliana followed Consuelo as she trailed after the men. No one had explained anything so far, but she gathered these were to be their quarters.

The Afghan women and their teams began arriving. These competent females unloaded their passengers and unhitched and fed their dogs before helping the men in Dorji's party unload the bear and caribou meat. The meat was then added to other ingredients and set to simmering over open fires in what looked like metal cargo shells from the Intergal spaceship.

By this time, smoke curled from every chimney, sending forth a quick whiff of woodsy fragrance, a rare treat for Consuelo's frosted nostrils. Savory food smells soon crystallized in the air as well, and soon food was being carried from all over the village into three houses where ramshackle tables were heaped with unfamiliar delicacies.

People filed into the houses, making great piles as they shed their outer clothing near the doors. The houses were all small, with very little room for anything but bed, table, and stove, so people crowded shoulder to shoulder, jostling one another as they ate.

This was the first time Consuelo had seen any of the men in their party without their winter gear. They were as lean and hard as soldiers, with corded veins in their hands and forearms beneath the rolled-up sleeves of their shirts. Many of the Afghan women looked almost as tough, though one or two were round and merrier-looking than the bitch Consuelo had first encountered. They chattered happily with the Tibetan men of this village, and where language failed, used sign language both parties seemed to find hilarious. Consuelo ducked out of the house, looking for the one-armed man from Lacrimas.

She found him in the third house, shoveling bear stew into his mouth. His compatriots were there too. In this house, as in the ones assigned to her own party, several cots had been made up for the night. All but two of the men from the visiting party were there.

The one-armed man spotted her right away as well, and wiped his lips with his wrist as he watched her.

"So," she said. "You're from Lacrimas."

"Yes," he said. "And you are from Rio de Sangre. You are Consuelo?"

Fear, as familiar as her own pulse, rose in her. "You know me?" It came out in a whisper. The fear was by now an instinctive reaction. Being known in Rio de Sangre was seldom a good thing.

The man smiled, evidently amused by her discomfort. "I am Cesar Torres. Manuel Arrantes was my comrade. I saw him with you many times."

"Not so many," she corrected, for there had been all too few times, and seldom did they appear together in public. She felt less afraid, knowing that he had known Manuel. But still, he was glad to have this power over her. It showed in the tilt of his head, as insolent as a border guard's. Maybe not now, maybe not tomorrow, the attitude said, but I can have you if I want to and I can hurt you and there's not a damned thing you can do about it.

"Also, he carried a little picture of you," Cesar Torres continued, his eyes sweeping over her body in a way that almost made her wish she still wore her insulated outer layers. "A beautiful picture."

He didn't have to say that the photograph no longer matched the woman of whom it had been taken. She knew well enough that the years and the war had not been kind to her. It was just as well. Beauty attracted attention, not a good thing in times like those in which she had been living.

"It is good to see a comrade of Manuel's," she said, her mouth dry with more than a need for drink. Also, despite his demeanor, she said it to be polite to him, to comfort him, for it was clear from the man's lined eyes and his pale skin and the scars upon it that he had suffered much. "It will be good to have a *compañero* near." She lied for now. But perhaps there would come a time when she could say so sincerely. There were few enough people here who spoke her language or knew the shape of the mountains near her home.

"What makes you think I'll be near?" he asked, bitterness leaking through his hardass pose like blood leaking from under a scab. "Like you, I have been bought by this company. No good for work any longer," he held up his stump, "we few are to serve as studs for the Afghan mares." He nodded toward the woman talking with Dorji and the others. "I am sorry for you, Consuelo. I at least was a soldier. I had my time to fight. For you women it is a journey from one whoredom to another."

"Plenty of women fought in their own way, Cesar. Those who got the chance," she replied.

"Well, there'll be no more chances here! There's no escape! We're breeding stock for Intergal! Didn't you understand? They put us down here, away from our own kind so that we can't make trouble—make no mistake, this is the last you will see of me or any other *compañero.* This is nothing but a big cold prison camp and our keepers are these ugly foreign people who have ice water in their veins."

"Come now, my friend. Surely that's an absurd exaggeration. They're just beginning to settle this place, and it's true we're here against our will, but so far no one has offered us so much as an insult. Perhaps there's *something* to what you say, but . . ."

"There's no 'but' about it, *chica.* Last night, these women who came for us—we who have been shorn of hands, arms, legs—they took us with them to see the scientist, the Intergal woman. She does not like men, that one, but she knew the women. They've been here for years. They don't mind the cold and they can work like men. But they have no men, you see? When the company settled them here, they settled only the women in their village. They were waiting for us. We will have to depend on them for everything. The scientist looked at us and asked us questions. Her Spanish is good. So is her Afghan—the women are from Afghanistan. She asked us how we were hurt. She asked us about our families—if there had been insanity, which diseases. We all had medical examinations while we slept on the ship and treatment of our injuries, but these Afghan women want guarantees, so they took us to this genetic scientist woman to see if we were good enough to service them. Breeding stock, I tell you. All of us."

Consuelo laughed at the half-indignant, half-excited expression on his face. She felt a simultaneous flash of sympathy for him and maybe more for the Afghan women. "Congratulations, *amigo.* Sounds like a dream come true for you."

She didn't see Iliana's approach behind her until Cesar looked beyond her with freshly piqued interest. "Perhaps you are right," he said. "I hope you will enjoy it as well, breeding new soldiers for the company who bought your homeland."

She turned away in disgust and bumped into Iliana, who didn't so much as recoil from the collision. "What does he mean?" Iliana asked her. "Who will be breeding new soldiers?"

"You most certainly, *chiquita,*" the man said, his eyes sweeping her face and body. He was obviously delighted to have found a more plausible and gullible victim. "You'll be good for dozens."

"Shut up, you!" Consuelo told him, putting force in it despite her weariness. "You are not the only one the war has injured."

"I only speak the truth. You've gone from a hot hell to a cold one. This company didn't even have to kill us to take our women and . . ."

At that point the door flew open, blowing in a sudden flurry of fresh snow and cold air. Dorji, one of the other men, and three of the Afghan women entered laughing, as Iliana grabbed the coat she had just removed and ran out. Consuelo, deeply disturbed by Cesar's information, followed.

"You better ask your master if you can leave the room, Consuelo!" Cesar called after her in Spanish she hoped was too rapid for Dorji to understand.

Outside, she no longer saw Iliana. She stood without resuming her winter gear, allowing her anger to freeze on her face before she ducked into the next house. There were many people there, and some of them were eating, some singing. In a corner, one of the round Afghan women was showing Margarita Mendes what she was doing with a half-knitted sweater Consuelo guessed would look, when finished, like the soft gray and white one its maker wore.

She found the food, the bear now spiced and mixed with bits of the caribou, root vegetables, and some kind of tasty mess that might have been a moss.

There was an odd-tasting tea to drink as well, hot and soothing, and no sooner had she finished this than, despite the chatter and activity around her, she fell asleep sitting cross-legged in the corner.

She awoke in a bed, in the darkness, to a loud noise that ceased as soon as her eyes opened. Hearing Joselita's breathing, Consuelo thought she was still in the bunker, although there had been no proper beds there. Then she saw the reddish glow around the stove door and recalled where she was. As her eyes adjusted to the dark, she made out the other five bunks, four of which contained the outlines of bodies.

She rose and regarded the other people in the bunks. Joselita, Margarita, Lupe Morales from Marina Negro, and that other woman, the older one, Maria someone. She was from Rio de Sangre too, but Consuelo didn't know her except from the ship.

Iliana was not here. Perhaps she had been assigned to another house, but the empty bunk beside Joselita inclined Consuelo to think otherwise.

Just as Consuelo noticed Iliana's absence, the baying and whining and howling began, as if all of the dogs had suddenly gone mad.

The luck she had told O'Malley about alerted her then. It was the same luck that had caused her to show up at just the right moment to save Pilar Escobar from bleeding to death on the streets. The very same luck had propelled her onto the street at the right moment to snatch Joselita from the sidewalk after she had been discarded by one rape gang before another could pounce upon her. And Consuelo's luck had been with her again when, with directions babbled by a hysterical Joselita, she had found the house where Iliana was held prisoner at the time when the girl's tormentors had just exhausted themselves at her expense. Consuelo slipped in through a window, released the girl, and took her away while the bastards were smoking or dreaming of what fine men they were.

This night, her luck drove her through the door and into a wild gale of blowing snow before good sense convinced her to return to the house long enough to put on her winter clothing. Then she was outside again, where the snow swirled so heavily she could not see the adjoining houses. All around disembodied voices and shadows cried out to one another and raced among spangled draperies of snowflakes and grabbed at wriggling, jumping four-legged forms. At first she thought, "There's been a mortar attack, or a mine . . ." because of the running and chaos.

These shadows rushed by too quickly for her to ask anyone about Iliana. When she tried to shout, the wind carried her words away. She finally found the adjoining house, where the rest of the women from her party were lodged, but Iliana was not among them. Two of the women had been startled awake by the noise, but the others were still sleeping. The waking ones met her question with blank stares and shivered at the blast of cold air she had brought with her.

She plunged back into the snowstorm and stumbled across the houses where the party had taken place. Finding the first two empty, she banged open the door of the third.

Her countrymen struggled to get back to sleep, pulling their blankets over their heads, but Cesar Torres sat drinking something from a rough clay cup. He smirked slightly when he saw her.

"Where's Iliana?" she snapped at him. Just looking at him, she knew he knew what had happened to Iliana.

"Who?"

"The young, pretty one that came in after me when you were trying to frighten me."

His mouth twisted with contempt. "I wasn't trying to frighten you. Just a friendly warning. I'm surprised you're not in bed with one of them now."

"We have been treated with courtesy. We sleep as you do, together in one house."

"A convenient arrangement for a brothel."

"Enough! If you have been filling Iliana's head with more of your horror stories, when she has lived through so much already, I will personally remove your head with my own hands. Have you seen her?"

"Ah, sweet Consuelo, so fierce. It's a wonder you didn't win the war single-handed. I saw your little whore friend. One of the locals was trying to drag her into the house over there. She got away from him and ran in here, all wide eyes and heaving bosom—what I could see anyway, in all that heavy clothing. Naturally we offered her refuge, but she ungratefully ran away again. That was when the dogs began to howl. Diversionary tactic, I expect. Or does she know how to drive one of those teams?"

"She probably felt if she had to deal with dogs, she'd rather deal with four-legged ones. How could you let her go? Why did you not wake someone?"

"Me? A poor crippled war veteran? What was I supposed to do? Besides, once the dogs started howling, people were already awake."

The urge to smack him to the ground was conquered only by Consuelo's knowledge that she was not capable of dealing a hard-enough blow. If the bastard Cesar returned it and knocked her out, then who would find Iliana?

Instead she slammed the door against his sneers and returned to the cleanliness of the snowstorm. Snow-blurred forms of people and dogs still rushed madly about. Which one was Dorji she could not tell.

Still, the girl could not have gone far. She might have tried to hitch up the dogs if she was desperate enough, but she wouldn't know how to drive them. Even Consuelo was not sure she could do it, though she had watched many times.

She thought of returning to wake Joselita and the other women, but what could they do? Joselita would throw a fit and be of no help. She might even get herself lost as well. As for the others, they knew no more of this sort of weather than did she or Iliana.

She followed one shadowy figure after another, trying to catch one to see if she could find Dorji, but apparently he was out chasing dogs, with the others. The dogs seemed to think being untied was a bit of a holiday and made a game of eluding their masters.

One of the dogs bounded past her, and she grabbed for its rope, catching it in her mitten. It was a very strong dog and dragged her running after it until she fell, her wrist and leg tangling in the rope long enough for the dog to drag her, sliding across the snow on the slick fabric of her suit.

Finding it had a passenger, the dog jumped in circles around her, tangling her further before dragging her a short distance more. She was able to lose herself then while the silly dog ran ahead and was lost in the sheets of snow. She stood, a bit dizzy from the ride, and looked around her, seeing nothing but snow.

Surely the houses were not far. She hollered, "Where is everyone? Hey!" But she realized not only could she no longer see the houses for the snow, but that the snowfall had also muffled sounds. Finally, she heard a yip and someone shouting and she started off in the direction she thought that had come from, thinking the sound was coming from the village.

But she walked farther and farther, finding nothing but whiteness, the ground, the sky and air around her gauze bandaged in snow. She could see her hand before her face, but only through the ice crystals forming on her lashes. And she had nothing with her! No flashlight, no matches, no weapon, not even a knife. Now Iliana was not the only one lost.

She stood for a moment, recalling the conventional wisdom that when one was lost, one should stay in one place and wait to be found. But the rapidity with which she felt herself freezing made her realize that this would not be a good idea in her case.

So she continued walking, slow and clumsy in her unaccustomed clothing, groping with her hands, searching for the edges of a building she might miss with her eyes. Twice she stumbled and fell, her thick boots sinking into the new drifts of snow.

Surely, she thought, surely this storm will stop soon and someone will come looking for us. But she doubted anyone realized yet that they were missing, except Cesar, who was unlikely to tell anyone anything helpful.

Well acquainted with the ironies of life and death, she saw a certain grim humor in her present situation. How ridiculous to live through the war, to survive being frozen asleep for months while being shot into space and brought to another world, and to arrive in a new home after days of being bumped along a trackless waste of ice and snow, only to die the first night—no doubt within a few yards of her bed. And for the first time in years, she was not ready to die. Not until she found Iliana at least, and saw for herself if these people were the monsters Cesar Torres believed them to be.

O'Malley, at least, seemed to be a reasonable woman, so conscientious not to pair off enemies. In the end, what did it matter? Even those who had fought on the same side, such as Cesar and she and Manuel, could carelessly harm one another.

O'Malley would ask her where her famous luck was now. Well, where was it? Did it work only when bombs were dropping and sniper's bullets were to be dodged? Did it only work in the city, when it told her to take this street instead of the next one? Did it serve only to warn her away from places where death squads were harvesting their crop? Did it only prevent her from falling prey to the rape gangs wielding their worms of hatred, destroying life's flavor and nourishment for the women of their enemies as well as for their own sorry unborn children?

She had always known how to avoid *them,* but she had also known how to find the very few of their victims she could harbor. Perhaps it was not kind to try to save someone as scarred as Iliana, but because Consuelo had been led to the girl, she had to believe Iliana was salvageable. Only now they were both lost.

Still, even if she couldn't rescue herself, her luck should still help her find Iliana. Thinking of her luck somehow freed it from the ice closing over the rest of her mind and sent it beaming through the snow like a searchlight, like whalesong, while she listened with her mind for what it told her. She stopped thinking of anything at all and simply followed that sense.

And in time her numb feet stumbled over a pile of snow and she felt the snow stir weakly under her collapsing knees. She knew before her mittens wiped the snow away from the girl's face that she had found Iliana.

Having found her, she lay down beside her. At least neither of them would die alone, she thought, closing her eyes.

But a moment later, she opened them again as something large flopped down on top of her. Some animal had fallen over both of them as she had over Iliana, adding to her own body a little heat.

Stifling, smothering heat. The snow world had all been a dream, Consuelo thought, waking. Beside her Iliana snored, and all around her the other women breathed and sweated like animals, penned in the darkness of the bunker.

Then someone planted a hoof on her mitten.

She looked up, into a long mournful brown face. As her weight shifted, a small form wriggled out from beneath her left elbow, and the rabbit that had lodged itself there hopped three or four paces away. An orange cat was tucked next to Iliana's face, purring as if the girl were an open hearth. From across their feet, a fox lept to its paws and bounded off a short distance, then sat down and stared at them.

Consuelo raised up and the long-faced animal—moose, not a full-grown one or she would have been crushed—fell away from her, then struggled to its own feet and stood watching her reproachfully.

The snow had stopped, but the village was nowhere to be seen. Consuelo might have only imagined that it existed. They lay in a box canyon, surrounded by tall mountains. If Consuelo had kept walking the night before, she would have walked into the face of a cliff. Above them, the sky was now much brighter, a blurred slate gray, but neither sun nor moons nor stars shone down from the expanse cupped by the peaks.

Iliana sat up, blinking, looking slowly around at the moose, the fox, and the rabbit. The orange cat rose languorously, stretched itself, and inserted one calculated claw into the skin of Iliana's wrist where it showed between her cuff and her mitten.

The girl jumped and smacked the cat away. The cat, taking no offense, walked two or three paces then sat down and studied the two women for a moment. The animal was as unlike the collections of mangy fur, parasites, and bones that roamed the streets of Rio as it was from the moose. Sleek and well fed, like a small fire glowing in the snow, it gave its thickly furred paw a swipe with its tongue, shot one more glance at the women, then rose and sauntered off a few more steps before looking back over its shoulder.

It could not have said more clearly, even if it spoke not only the speech of humans but Spanish as well, that it wished them to follow it. "Come," Consuelo said, giving Iliana her hand. The girl tried to rise, but one leg would not work properly and she slid back into the snow.

"Did you hurt it when you fell?" Consuelo asked.

Iliana slowly nodded. Further damage had been done her that night, Consuelo saw. Her eyes were more vacant than they had been since first she came to the bunker, and wheezing sounds came with her breath. Finally, after two years in the bunker, Iliana had begun talking again, even crooning her little tunes, but now she had retreated back into the place inside herself even the rapists could not touch.

"You must try or we'll freeze to death here. Come," Consuelo told her and helped her hobble in the direction of the cat, which had stopped once more to watch them.

In response, Iliana sat back down and shook her head, moaning.

"Iliana, you must!" Consuelo urged. The girl sat. Consuelo turned to the cat and shrugged. The cat gave her a look of amused understanding, as if it was well acquainted with how difficult one's dependents could sometimes be. Then it rose and set off in a different direction than it had previously taken.

It walked straight into the face of the cliff, leaped on top of a large boulder, then down the other side, and disappeared.

"Please, Iliana, walk a few steps. We have to find shelter. Maybe you wish to die, but I do not, and I'm not going to leave you. Get up now."

And this time the girl cooperated. Consuelo's own strength had been drained by her wanderings and a night in the snow, despite, or perhaps because of, having a moose lie on top of her.

The two of them made it to the boulder just as the cat leaped back on top of it. Consuelo noticed then for the first time that the boulder was clean of snow. Perhaps it had blown away. And though drifts were piled high on either side of it, when she looked for a way around it, fearing that she could not climb upon it like the cat, she saw that there was a narrow space on one side, also perfectly dry and clean of snow.

She half-dragged, half-pushed Iliana into this space, followed, and then saw the fissure in the rock concealed by the large boulder. The cat leaped down once more and, with a flick of its tail disappeared into the widest part of the fissure, an area about two feet high and a foot and a half wide. The cat re-emerged, then slipped inside once more, twice, and finally came back out and sat down again.

"See if you can squeeze in there," Consuelo told Iliana. "Go on! If there were wild animals, the cat would have hesitated. Although it seems the wild animals are somewhat different in this place than they are at home . . ."

With a bit of prodding, Iliana crawled into the space, her length disappearing rapidly. So it was either a large space or else there *was* a wild animal gobbling the girl as fast as it could reel her into the hole.

"Iliana?" Consuelo asked after a while, dropping to her hands and knees to try to peer into the opening. Abruptly, a bare hand shot out of the hole and grabbed her arm, pulling.

She wriggled in after the arm and crawled headfirst down a steep incline beyond the narrow entrance. The passage was short and at the end was a grotto.

The first thing she noticed about it was the light. The interior of the grotto was, if anything, lighter than the sky outside, glowing with an iridescent golden light shot with veins of citrine, ruby, turquoise, sapphire, emerald, and peridot, the colors melting into one another in waves, vibrating around the chamber as if alive. In the center of the floor bubbled a steaming pool of water, reflecting the dancing colors on its surface and filling the room with a palpable warmth and humidity.

Iliana had already shed her mittens, boots, scarf, and coat and was peeling off her snowpants.

Beads of sweat coursed down Consuelo's face, and she felt as if she were baking inside her winter clothing. As she began stripping off layers, she noticed something else about the cave that was different: smell. In here you could smell things, the faintly sulfurous, tangy green and citrusy floral scent of the pool, and body odor. Consuelo was reminded that neither she nor Iliana had bathed since being on board the Intergal ship.

Iliana stepped into the pool without testing the waters first, then bobbed back up again, slicking back her hair. Since she didn't seem to be freezing, Consuelo joined her. The water was quite warm, but not uncomfortably so. It was clear, and she could follow the trail of bubbles to the bottom, where it disappeared down another long chute. On the pool's bottom, mosses grew and small, strangely shaped flowers bloomed.

She allowed herself to sink underneath the waters. The rising bubbles made a kind of music—almost a voice—far more distinct than such a sound should have been, playing a melody she could not quite catch and singing words she could not quite hear.

She had no idea how long the two of them lingered in the pool, listening to the bubbles, watching the colors move, smelling the fragrant waters, for she fell into a deep and blissful dreaming.

She dreamed first of the vastness of ice and rock, and she dreamed it was her own heart on which she traveled, totally alone. In this aloneness, she had lost nothing, for she had never had father or mother, lover or child, friend or companion. She was, in fact, mute, deaf, and blind. And then came the explosions, like those in the war, the quakings, the fires, fragments tearing into her body, ripping her skin, entering her blood.

Still sleeping, she wept.

But the dream went on and the explosions stopped and as she examined her wounds, flowers blossomed in them and birds flew out of them. During the terror of the violent time, she had given birth to new things and each of them was part of her. Her own sobs echoed in the howls of wolves roaming her thighs, and her curiosity about what had become of her was absorbed and explored by cats, large and small, who prowled over her breasts and shoulders on thickly furred paws. Her tears sent rivulets streaming down her body to water her memories, hopes, dreams, and fears, which became trees and plants, flowers and crawling and flying things to nourish them. Understanding the pattern, understanding what she shared with this world, all of the songs she remembered flew from her mouth with a flash of wings.

And the dream shifted until she saw a small version of herself, sitting in a cave, having a dream. Beside her in the water Iliana lolled, jewel-bright songbirds fluttering from her mouth, singing.

Like a bird herself, Consuelo soared beyond the cave and above it and saw, coming into the box canyon, a party of men and women and horses and dogs and one small orange cat, trotting ahead of the others as fast as its paws could carry it.

And then her eyes truly opened and she saw Iliana, no longer pale and trembling but rosy from the heat of the water, the last notes of a song dying on her lips, which settled into a smile. Consuelo felt the song and the smile rising in herself as fear had so often risen.

The two of them rose, dressed, and crawled out of the cave.

In the first sled, Dorji stamped on his brake, tore off his mask, and strode toward them. "Why did you run away? Are you both crazy? This is a very hard world."

Consuelo touched his cheek with her hand, still warm though unmittened. "Perhaps not so hard as you think. Come. We have something to show you."

One by one the others crawled back into the grotto after them, and without being told to, removed their clothing and waded into the pool. Cesar Torres was the last, his smirk melting from his face, as if with the warmth seeping up at them from the heart of their new homeworld. "I'll be damned," he muttered.

"Maybe," Consuelo said, "not."

Susan Booth is forty-something, British, lives near London, and says she usually writes longer—in the neighborhood of a hundred thousand words or so. We are pleased that she made this exception for us.

About this story Susan writes: " 'Edge of the Sword' began, like C. S. Lewis's *Narnia,* with a picture. The story behind the picture turned out to be surprisingly straightforward. However, it was also what I think of as a 'dangler': a story, incident, or idea that sits around for years sneering at me because I don't know where it fits. It was only recently, when my friend Pat Elrod bullied me into rewriting it, that I realized it belongs inside the dark, ambiguous mazes of a novel I'd always planned to write 'someday.' So forgive my heroine her moral simplicity. She, at least, is very young—and her certainties will be tested before she is very much older."

—LMB

Edge of the Sword

Susan Booth

Sunlight glances from the spearpoint peaks as I stand looking out over the Chunga range. The sky is blue glass. No life stirs, here above the summer snowline, and yet . . . do I hear a call, achingly lovely, blending with that of the cold wind that wails about me? It will bring snow, that wind, falling with the night.

No one, not even Quolin, my twin, understands why I had to come here, to this high mountain where I so nearly died.

Yet, here I am, knowing that as I stand between childhood and womanhood I stand also on the edge of a sword. I can go only forward or back: there is no way for me to step aside. This is the only fitting place for that choice.

An age, it seems, yet it was only ten days ago that I first came here. The educational visit to the Chunga mountains was nearly at an end. To me alone of all the party, it seemed, the high peaks called. I had resolved to climb Chanlun, the Ice Sword, and there was some anxiety among our instructors that one as young as I should attempt this alone. I was grateful when Luan, our instructor in the Way of Mihart and a man who knew mountains well, said he would accompany me.

We set off in a dawn that was like the birthing of the world, and it was as if I, too, were reborn on those cliffs of ice and stone. Their harshness challenged my spirit even as it stirred me with its beauty.

These were not thoughts I could share with Luan, for it would have seemed a betrayal of all that he had taught me, that I should feel glory in my duel with the mountain. Indeed, I was ashamed of my own emotions. The very night before, in our camp in one of the webs between Chanlun's fingers, we had spoken of the philosophy that all our world now follows.

The Way of Mihart teaches that only by looking into our own souls can we Miharteen find peace. There is no true beauty or wisdom except within ourselves, so only there will we find them. That is why the Temple genechangers have decreed that henceforth there shall only be New People, like myself, bred and trained to the cause of abandoning Mihart's warlike past forever.

Luan had argued that if a world is to be built on peace and union there could be no compromise: Mihart must end even those minimal defensive patrols it maintains and destroy all its spacecraft, or some Miharteen might be tempted to return to former foolishness. Certainly, it is true that voices are still raised in Council against our isolation from galactic affairs.

Something deep within me had rejected Luan's words and I was much troubled by this, for he was very wise, a true example of what the Miharteen must become. That I should disagree with him was unthinkable . . . and yet . . .

When we stood on the summit of Chanlun I felt triumph, the victor in my battle with the mountain. There was indeed glory here, above the land yet beneath the sky. It seemed alien . . . and, almost, I knew what it might be like to walk on another world. Our people seldom leave Mihart now, and it was most unlikely that I would ever see alien skies.

It was as we began our descent that I noticed a strange formation below us. It could almost have been an old meteorite crater: a deep, almost circular pit, the sharp line of its rim worn ragged by time and weather. I pointed it out to Luan, and we edged our way across the ice slope to investigate.

On the brim of the crater we paused, looking downward into wonder . . .

The legend of the Zhilyhka is as old as Mihart. Its winged figure has been the warrior's symbol for all our history. There is, it is said, only ever one Zhilyhka, and it spends its whole life soaring in the winds at the edges of the world. Every five hundred years it grows old and dies, crashing down into the mountains, where it lies in the ice until the egg it carried within its body hatches, and once more the Zhilyhka soars to the skies.

Strangely, I have found now that many worlds have a similar legend. On Terra, for example, the creature is called the Phoenix, but there it is a bird of fire, not of ice. To the Terrans, the Phoenix is a symbol of immortality as well as beauty, but the Zhilyhka stands for freedom. The Terrans believe the Phoenix to be myth and so, we had always been told, was the Zhilyhka.

Yet now Luan and I stood looking into a pit of rock and ice and snow. On the floor of that pit, the noonday sun sparkled on a huge skeleton. The bones were gossamer light, translucent, as if carved from crystal. The impression of plumes along the edge of the wings was etched into the rime. And, amid the bones, there was a shining ovoid, smooth and green, like glacier ice.

The walls of the pit were steep, but not impassable. As I started down, I heard Luan call for me to wait, but I did not heed him, or pause in my reckless descent.

Indeed, I did not stop until I stood before the egg, and then I halted in awe, almost unable to encompass the enchantment of what I saw within. High above my head the smooth shell rose, and behind its transparent ice green curtain lived a welter of color and movement. Veiled by pale green silk, quivering quicksilver plumes swirled and danced, glimmering in all the colors of ice: silver, indigo, jade, azure, turquoise, violet, white . . . and amid them all I saw the curve of a beak, the flash of an eye, the gleam of a talon.

Entranced, I laid my hand on the egg. It was cool and trembled under my touch, fiercely alive. Suddenly, I knew that the creature inside was trapped, unable to break free of its birthing cage and find its way home to the skies.

Hands closed hard about my arms, and I was jerked away.

I struggled against Luan's hold, crying: "We have to set it free!"

"No!" He turned me so I faced him and shook me brutally. "Don't be foolish, child. That is the Zhilyhka, the Soul of the Warriors of Mihart. Only a warrior can free it from the egg, and that must be done between the rising and the setting of the Midsummer sun or it will perish forever. Today is Midsummer Day, but there are no warriors of Mihart now. We will witness the death of the legend." He let me go, looking at his hands as if surprised at his own violence. I stood still, shocked that he should hurt me so.

He stared beyond me to the egg, hatred in his eyes. When he spoke it was not to me, but to himself. "Yet, even when it dies, if the people ever learned that it had existed at all, they might be tempted to return to the old ways. I must make sure that cannot happen . . ." He looked about him at the overhanging walls. "Of course, I can set avalanche trigger charges to bring down the rocks, bury it forever . . ."

Even as he spoke, I spun and ran back to the egg, knowing that I must free the glorious creature within even if it—or Luan—killed me. I reached it, battered it with my fists, kicked at it . . . but the shell was as impervious to my heavy climber's boots as the rock would have been.

Then I was wrenched aside and flung to the ground. Luan stood over me, his face flushed with rage. "Stupid child! I'll make sure that you don't interfere again."

Desperately, I rolled away from him, over and over in the snow, knowing that there was no escape. He was so much stronger and faster than I.

My left hand fell on one of the crystal bones of the skeleton wing. Time had worn its edge to a razor, but the rounded end joint fitted into my hand as if it had been shaped for it. Luan reached for me. I had never in my life used a weapon, had always been taught that it was terribly wrong—but Luan had not hesitated to use his greater strength against me. Was that not a weapon, too?

I struck out with the bone-blade. It pierced Luan's hand, and scarlet stained the snow. He cried out and reeled back. I scrambled to my feet and whirled toward the egg, the blade grasped in both hands and extended before me. I struck out with all the strength that I had.

The blade fragmented into rainbow shards of crystal. The eggshell cracked jaggedly upward, then shattered with a noise like a calving iceberg.

The Zhilyhka was free. It stretched upward, its wings glittering: emerald, sapphire, diamond, amethyst, beryl; a million facets sparkling in the sunbeams.

It screamed, and the mountain shook. I fell to my knees, unable to breathe for the beauty and wildness of that sound.

The fierce head bent forward toward me, its tongue a flicker of silver inside a beak of pearl. Something forced me to look up into those eyes which, it is said, see past, present, and future as one. Aquamarine, they were. Green and blue and deeper than the sea of Kamil. Color flooded the world.

And in it I saw the Temple of the Way . . . saw the flames leaping and a woman I knew to be Quolin, her face twisted in terror. I felt the loneliness of time. Strange stars danced in the Great Void. There were faces, not Mihart, human and alien. For a moment I knew them as I knew myself and loved them more. Then starships blazed before me and exploded into dust. A man and a woman passed by, fair and cold. I knew hate. They vanished into a dizzying whirlpool of worlds, some beautiful, some terrible, all wonderfully strange . . .

And over all laughter: chilling, mocking, alien laughter. And from it a voice, dark music in my mind.

So, here is a true child of Mihart. My thanks, warrior, who will be honored and cursed. The Miharteen will both die and live again before I return to the egg. Freedom is a twin-edged blade, warrior. You will save what is most important, destroy all who created you. Aye, you are a herald of destruction, warrior woman. Your name will be blazoned across the stars. Worlds will sing your name, but never Mihart. Truest of its children, it will renounce you, for you are my child too. Child of freedom, child of beauty . . . child of the stars.

I saw the Zhilyhka rise like a jeweled shadow in the blizzard the wind from its wings raised around me. The blast was as cold as space . . .

Darkness claimed me.

When I woke, it was to find my sister Quolin holding my hand as the aircar carrying us raced home. She told me that I had been lost in a storm on the Ice Sword. The rescue party had found me near the summit, unconscious, with Luan beside me, dead and frozen. It seemed he had been weakened through the loss of blood from a deep cut on his hand. The rescue party thought that he must have gashed it open on the ice. They say he must have been trying to save me, but I wonder . . .

It all seems a dream now. The visions are fading. I can no longer picture those I saw in those moments of prophecy. Even the man with the summer hair and winter eyes, whose face reminded me of the Zhilyhka in its arrogance and beauty, even he is gone. When we meet, I will not know him, save in some secret depth of memory. Soon, I think, even the splendor of the

Zhilyhka will live no more in my mind. As dream, it will dissolve, and my remaining memories will be as rain blown in the winds.

Yet, even if it was a dream, and I do not deny that it could well have been, I know that this remains true: I can no longer follow the Way of Mihart. When faced with the destruction of beauty and freedom, I fight. My hand cleaves to the sword in a way that should not be. Even Quolin does not understand, though until now we have been as one.

Mihart is no longer enough for me. I will walk under those alien skies. I will wield the sword again. I will find those promised comrades, promised enemies.

My heart leaps at the thought.

Destruction was also promised, but this I know, child though I am. Those who will not fight for freedom and beauty will always find destruction, as Luan found it. There is no place in this universe for freedom without daring, wisdom without truth, peace without strength, love without honor.

There are warriors of Mihart yet, Zhilyhka. While you ride the winds, there will be still.

After a life of gypsy city hopping, Gay Marshall now lives in rural Ohio. Her previous jobs have run the range from short-order cook to professional illustrator, and her side interests have varied from spelunking to the archaeology of Roman Britain to raising and showing pedigreed Persian cats. Like most writers, she is a devout bibliophile.

Of "The Heart of the Hydra" Gay writes: "What if the universe is not what we expect? What if, amid the tangle of human political intrigue, amid the cartels and the self-interest, Wordsworth's Happy Warrior should truly appear? What would be the impact of that honorable and generous spirit? The following pages sprang from that particular speculation."

—LMB

The Heart of the Hydra

Gay Marshall

Fire-blackened girders sprang up from devastation, imprisoning Aerot's fragile green sky in a twisted web of steel as her primary sun pushed over the horizon. Far off, her secondary star rode high and faint, ineffectual against the morning chill numbing Major General Dyrick Seidor's weather-seamed face. It reddened the fresh scar that marred his prominent nose, and he noticed Colonel Marney Keland carefully avert her eyes.

Shit, is it that bad? He repressed an urge to kick something. *When I'm back on Earth I'll hit Covert Ops for a new face—darken the hair, get rid of the blue eyes.* His jaw clenched. *Damn Allerdeck for transferring me halfway across the galaxy into this jerkwater war! Nothing's been stolen. All of ConFed's nasty experimental toys are still safe in Covert Ops' bag. I haven't turned up enough proscribed technology to activate a sodding alarm clock, and I'm no dumb-ass mud-slogger.*

Guilt scorched him, and he stole a glance at the colonel. She might be an anachronism, but she was a veteran, a comrade to have at your back when hell was in session, a pretty black woman before incessant war thinned her cheeks, tarnished her laugh.

She's here doing an honest job, Seidor admitted ruefully. *Not doing Allerdeck's dirty work for him.*

Sensing his irritation, Keland watched her feet, careful not to kick into the delicate pink snowbanks. The kids trying to hold formation behind them did the same. The festive birthday-party drifts covered yesterday's kill—the face of death still too fresh, too unsanitized, for recruits.

Lord, I'm tired. Seidor emitted a dry grunt that served as a laugh. *ConFed intervenes to protect the Ca'Cuy from Gredi aggression and we're not here six months be-*

fore the locals decide we're the bad guys and go begging the Gredi to toss us out. The whole damned thing's insane. After seven years there are no targets left to strike. We've even burned the sodding house-pets, and the slimeys still come at us.

Colonel Keland caught his cynical snort, and pointed ahead. "There's the pad. I reached ComNet. She's on her way down."

At a curt signal the battle-weary honor guard fell back, leaving the two officers to cross the pale pink expanse of snow alone. Lacelike bridges had collapsed over the sinuous canals of this once-graceful city; damming water converted to a thick chemical soup that refused even to freeze. Blackened steel sheets, tossed down to replace collapsed bridges, echoed hollowly underfoot as Seidor averted his gaze from what floated in that partially crystallized sludge.

It was a useless gesture. At the edge of the landing field a body, one of their own, lay partially swathed in a baby blanket of pink snow. The maimed flesh was silvery with the frostlike pattern of solentium burns, and Seidor's hand closed around the scanner in his pocket—the finest Covert Ops could provide. He fought an impulse to kneel, to run it over the base of the skull, to anticipate on its tiny screen the molecular signature of subatomic cell disruption. Undetectable to standard autopsy procedure, it was noiseless symptomless death, its victim easily targeted within a ten-mile radius—ConFed's newest and still untested little secret. God help them all if the Gredi had somehow obtained this latest bit of insanity.

The corners of the specialized scanner bit into Seidor's palm. *Blazing hell, I must be going mad. There isn't even a skull left to check. Can't use subatomic CD on a man without a head.*

Stifling hysterical laughter, he growled, "The cease-fire's been in effect ten hours. Why haven't our dead been collected?"

He more felt than saw Keland shoot him an appraising glance. "Sorry, sir. We've had a lot of cleanup. The Ca'Cuy northern offensive left us with high casualties, plus the rubble . . ." She paused, her dark eyes hard, then said hotly, "I don't see why those fat-assed ConFed bureaucrats are sending out more brass. You've held Aerot for the past five months, and with bloody little support! We don't need any alien bitch . . ."

"Colonel."

"Sorry, sir, but I don't see what an Eltanin Peace Mistress can accomplish here. We need troops, veterans—not these kiddy recruits or some sodding milksop alien expert! Shit! The Eltanin Matriarchy never even fought a war, and they sure the fucking hell never won one!"

Burning with indignation, she looked almost pretty. Seidor never cohabited with fellow officers, but he suspected the colonel harbored more than a passing regard for him. Well, she had a right to go after his buns—she'd pulled them out of the fire often enough.

He gave her a twisted smile, and said wryly, "They never lost one either, and it's a mistake to say they never fought a war. They don't indulge in gaudy aggressive campaigns, but there isn't a culture in this corner of the galaxy that hasn't taken a crack at them and been sent home bleeding for their trouble. The Matriarchy has been expanding at a snail's pace for millennia. They never surrender so much as a star system, and heaven pity the commander insane enough to infringe on their sectors."

Reaching the landing area, Seidor slapped snow from his tightly fitted dress tunic. It was the first time in months he had been out of battle fatigues, and he glanced at the colonel who appeared equally uncomfortable. Belligerence still showed on her features, and he warned, "Watch yourself. The Eltanin may look humanoid, but they're an old star culture, marsupials not mammals, and their thought patterns are as alien to ours as the Slimetails'."

Nodding dubiously, Keland glanced at the sky, fading to a paler green as the sun rose, and said idly, "I thought humanoid marsupials were extinct. I've seen their ruins and stuff on the Sen-Ease."

"Female-pocketers are gone. It's interesting—only male-pocketing races have survived."

"You mean the guys do the honors?"

"Twenty-two ConFed months' worth with Eltanin males."

Keland's grin exploded, her teeth startlingly white in her dark face. "The bitch at least has the home front organized. You've been boning up on these Eltanin, haven't you?"

"Just want to know what I'm saluting, Colonel." Seidor stamped impatiently, and bent to increase the temperature in the soles of his dress boots. "Where's that launch?"

"I'll check."

Colonel Keland chimed her combat mike, but Seidor tapped her arm, pointing upward. "Don't bother. We have company."

Silver coins, blinding in the morning glare, slipped across the darker green zenith, gained in size, and sank to rest on neograv columns like giant luminous bivalves. It was not one launch—it was a small flotilla. Ventral sections of the ships opened, throwing out cargo ramps, and Seidor saluted crisply as a party advanced to meet them.

The Eltanin Peace Mistress was not what he expected. She was a nondescript woman of medium build, her hips narrow, her breasts rudimentary and undeveloped. She was dressed in gray-green, with sturdy boots laced to the knee. Her shirt and pants, belted at the waist, were full enough for comfort, fitted enough not to hinder action; and her only concession to a uniform was a tailored jacket, one arm fitted like a coat, the other a cape flowing from shoulder to knee. The cloak's dove gray pile was broken by five bands of embroidery, each different, each wrought in magnificent jewel-bright colors, except a patch in the third row where the idle rubbing of the woman's fingers had worn through the pattern.

Seidor stepped forward, extending his hand, but his formal greeting was interrupted as the Eltanin said brusquely, "I am Lady TeaLa Raye Trynith, Peace Mistress of the Eltanin Matriarchy. I herewith assume command of

Aerot at behest of the ConFed Directorate. Am I addressing Major General Seidor?"

"Yes, ma'am." Seidor snapped into it, wondering why he was gawking like a first-year cadet.

"You command this theater of operation?"

"General Tormendez was killed five months back. A replacement was never sent. We currently have seven field armies on Aerot, three holding the southern hemisphere and four in the north. Our divisions are high on manpower, but low on technology. Under the Convocation on Sapient Responsibility Charter we can't employ military technology above a C.6 level when confronting the Slimetails." Seidor bit off his irritation, and added, "Tormendez and the joint chiefs were taken out five months back. A goddamned fluke, but I've got what's left. ConFed's been dragging its feet and we have a supply problem—they've been in no big hurry to reinforce us. Seems we're politically unpopular."

Seidor bit off the words, and added tersely, "This is Colonel Keland, commander of our divisions in this sector. My forces are holding their positions. We've been in a cease-fire situation less than ten hours."

"Are you currently secure?"

"For now."

The Eltanin nodded. Her dark hair was braided into a tight crown, and the silvery oval of a Compound Encyclopedia glistened at her temple, an inch-wide mercurylike bead feeding limitless information directly to her brain. She had a square face with eyes of expressionless gray slate. She was no beauty—nose too prominent, lips too thin, brows too heavy. Despite that it was an oddly compelling face, and Seidor thought, *By God, she's unsculptured—not a touch of the cosmetician's knife! Raw as when she sprang from the womb.*

The woman was obviously unorthodox by ConFed standards, and Seidor reappraised her cautiously. Indifferent to his scrutiny, she gestured to a tall woman accompanying her. "This is Rear Admiral The Lady Skana Glee Bydon. Admiral Bydon will coordinate our fleet assault operations."

The admiral was older, with threads of silver in her complex of gold braids, and Seidor suspected that, like the Peace Mistress, her aristocratic features were all her own. Bestowing a brisk salute, he said, "I doubt you'll find much to assault here, Admiral Bydon. We took out all targets of strategic value years ago." *And,* he thought, *a hell of a lot of nonstrategic value.* Suppressing habitual cynicism, he added, "Little can be done under a cease-fire in any case."

Without responding to his sally, the Peace Mistress shifted to her admiral. "Finish off-loading, Skana, and hold your fleet at strike alert. I will contact you with target coordinates."

Target coordinates? Seidor shot Colonel Keland an uneasy glance and said cautiously. "I admit to some astonishment at your presence here, Lady Trynith. I was expecting an officer of ConFed's Peacekeeping Force, or confirmation of my status, and I was unaware the Eltanin had interests in this sector."

"Aerot is disturbingly close to the Matriarchy's fringe of expansion, General, and the death toll is becoming an . . . embarrassment. Fears have been expressed that the Ca'Cuy—or the Slimetails, as you call them—might be victims of genocide."

"Genocide!" Seidor erupted. "The Slimeys are exterminating us as fast as we're exterminating them!"

"All the more reason to end this insanity. I will need an evaluation of your position, General. We must move quickly."

"I repeat, Mistress—we are under a three-hundred-hour cease-fire."

A dark brow arched sardonically. "I have noticed that ConFed's cease-fires awkwardly permit the Ca'Cuy to fall back and regroup."

The muscles along Seidor's jaw knotted. The woman could have lifted the observation out of his own skull, but he growled, "We can't advance without direct orders from Supreme Commander Traket and the ConFed Directorate." He drew a breath of icy air, laden with death. "I'll submit your request, but—"

"You will submit no requests, and you will initiate no communication with the Ca'Cuy."

"But . . . *a cease-fire is in effect!"* Seidor felt the pressure rising and restrained himself. "A cessation of hostilities has been agreed to under ConFed Articles of War."

"War is not a game but the most repugnant atrocity committed by sapient beings, and when indulged in it must be ended in the shortest conceivable span of time."

"Just what the sodding hell do you think we're doing here!" Seidor snarled. "Damn it, you're on Aerot to negotiate a peace, to make whatever concessions are necessary to end the killing!"

"No, General Seidor. I am here because this imbecility has crept too close to Matriarchal holdings."

"According to my orders you're on this planet under the auspices of the ConFed Directorate."

Trynith's thin lips stretched. "Your Directorate is greedy, General, and not about to endanger its lucrative Eltanin trade policy for a single backwater star system. And I am *not* here to patch together another ConFed no-win tissue-paper peace, to be followed by decades of atrocity." Her eyes turned a cold glacial gray. "I have been duly appointed supreme commander of all field armies on the planet Aerot during a state of war. Forget that, General Seidor, and I will have you shot."

Seidor heard Keland's sharp intake of breath. His own chest felt tight, but he snapped, "Understood, Peace Mistress Trynith."

"I am solely responsible for all actions taken on Aerot, and will note as much in my dispatches to your Directorate. Now where in this . . . disaster . . . is your command center?"

Seidor stared beyond the Peace Mistress to the supplies and troops off-loading from the flotilla. The Eltanin forces were veterans—well armed, disciplined, dangerous; and he said stiffly, "We're established in a Ca'Cuy temple. It's not far, but I'll send for a hovercar."

"We will walk, General. I want to see firsthand what I'm dealing with."

The night-black ovoid of the ConFed tactical sphere posed a macabre contrast to the battered magnificence of the Ca'Cuy temple. The sphere's myriad lights glinted off exquisite frescoes of alien gods while the muted pings of technology, the urgent undertone of voices, parodied the glorious music Seidor had heard here short months earlier.

"Your forces appear well deployed," the Peace Mistress conceded, interrupting his musing. "I find your failure to pacify this planet disconcerting."

Seidor stiffened. The Lady Trynith had said little this past hour, but he suspected she missed less. He felt a flush creep up from his collar, and Colonel Keland's generous mouth was hard. She was not the most diplomatic of his officers, and Seidor snapped hastily, "Our situation here is impossible, Mistress. Aerot is the linchpin of the Gredi expansion corridor. The entire planet is now involved, but under Convocation Charter we are limited to C.6 low-tech warfare. In spite of that we rolled over the Gredi-faction Slimetails months ago, didn't leave them the facilities to manufacture a pisspot, but here's our stumbling block."

Stepping to the tactical sphere, he refocused it on an adjacent star sector. "These are the Gredi systems. Their inhabitants are racially similar, and for generations they have endeavored to annex these planets. That's why we're here—to stop such aggression—but the Ca'Cuy are split into factions, with the majority now appealing for Gredi intervention. While we are not technically at war with the Gredi a constant flood of troops and supplies reinforce their Slimetail faction. Their fighters strafe our troops and burn out our orbital supply dumps, but the Directorate forbids hot pursuit in the interest of interstellar stability."

Stung by the Peace Mistress's cool appraisal, Seidor growled, "I'm not even permitted to strike the Gredi landing ports on Aerot. They have, quote, *privileged sanctuary*. How the sodding hell am I supposed to win a war where the enemy isn't the enemy? I'm forbidden to strike their supply bases for fear of starting another war that's daily killing more of my people! I'm fighting a damned hydra! Every time I chop off a head I can reach, two more take its place!"

Lady Trynith looked puzzled. The silvery oval on her temple pulsed, and she said, "Ah, a hydra—the nine-headed mythological beast slain by Terra's young Hercules. An apt simile, General Seidor, and perhaps like young Hercules, instead of lopping off heads, we should burn them with fire."

"Burn them?"

"Yes—burn them." Trynith swung, and snapped, "Tactical. Rephase. Aerot. Battle zones GQ four, GQ twelve, GQ twenty." The black sphere contorted and the star systems winked out, leaving the red grid of planetary surface. "A C.6 technical level entails highly effective transport capacity. The Gredi bases are concentrated here—near the equatorial zone, equidistant from both our southern and northern theaters of operations. That works to our advantage because I intend bottling up those fighter ports." She proceeded to outline the reallocation of troops, then finished briskly, "Colonel Keland's divisions will cover the Gredi infantry ports. I want our combat forces moving by twelve hundred hours, General Seidor."

"Twelve hundred hours? But any aggressive action must be cleared through ConFed, and the Ca'Cuy must be notified of renewed hostilities before . . ."

"Nothing will be *cleared* and no one will be *notified.*" Turning from the tactical sphere, Trynith scanned the puzzled faces around her and snapped, "Ladies and gentlemen, the rules have changed. I do not indulge in ConFed's games. I am here to cut out the heart of this hydra, and by twenty-four hundred hours I want this planet secured."

"Impossible!" Seidor erupted. *Shitting hell! The woman's insane!*

"Hardly. Move your forces effectively and we will retain the advantage of surprise." The silvery bubble of the Compound Encyclopedia pulsed. "I believe prespace Terrans had a word for it—*blitzkrieg,* lightning war. Only you are not to engage in it until Admiral Bydon is in position. Solar-Linkage DST artillery has been off-loaded and her fighters, armed with SL/DST strafing cannon, will provide air support."

Seidor felt color drain from his face. "Solar Linkage is proscribed technology, even at A.1 levels! By God, you'll burn off the planet! The death toll . . . !"

"Could not possibly rival ConFed's slaughter these past seven years." The Eltanin's scorn seared the room. "You, General Seidor, and officers like you, haven't left enough of the Ca'Cuy for a humble Peace Mistress to emulate your casualty lists." Her lips twisted in a wry smile. "I will, however, refrain from further burdening your souls with a planetary burnoff. Admiral Bydon is an artist—she only hits what she intends to hit, and what I intend to take out are those Gredi bases."

Seidor blinked. "But their landing ports have privileged sanctuary!"

"Privileged sanctuary is a myth. I do not indulge in skirmishes, or police actions, or whatever other euphemisms you mammals use to dignify this slaughter. I am not here to fight a war—I am here to end one."

The Peace Mistress's eyes were suddenly not cold at all, but fiery hot. She smiled, and a single dimple appeared high in her right cheek. It miraculously transformed her countenance, bestowing an air of recklessness, and Seidor, betrayed by months of smoldering discontent, fought an insane impulse to smile back.

"Aerot is mostly marshland and shallow seas," he offered, quelling the treacherous rush of adrenaline. "The Ca'Cuy are amphibians. They avoid mass confrontations and simply vanish into swamps where mechanized warfare is impractical."

"Excellent. That should lower their death rate."

"It won't do much for ours," Seidor shot back dryly.

Sparks of laughter flashed in Trynith's eyes. "I do not intend an extended campaign with incalculable casualties on both sides. Taking those marshes is hardly a strategic necessity. By jumping directly to the Gredi landing ports we'll cut their lines of support and leave the Ca'Cuy to shrivel in their swamps."

Fascinated despite his skepticism, Seidor growled, "So we employ Solar-Linkage DST and wipe out the landing ports. Then the Gredi move in with SL/DST of their own and this putrid cesspool of a war accelerates. What of the dead then, Peace Mistress?"

"The Gredi will not retaliate." Turning from the tactical display, Trynith said softly, for his ears alone, "Conflicts are not won on battlefields, General, but in boardrooms. ConFed has not allowed you to *win* this war. It is far too useful. It removes the surplus young who become restless and question the established order. More important, it creates a situation that generates fear, and by offering your people easy solutions that entail change, power is passed to the very beings who initiated the conflict, who finance the Gredi, the Ca'Cuy, and yourself. If you would fully . . ."

Trynith paused at a soft but piercing beep from her ComNet link and keyed her personal channel.

"Bydon here, Mistress. You wished to be informed. Your husband was transferred to the depocketing hall at ought-six-hundred ConFed standard. I have him standing by on interstellar boost. Frequency casement four."

The Peace Mistress stiffened, then said, "Thank you, Skana. One moment." She looked at Seidor. "General, prepare to move by twelve hundred hours."

Seidor saluted, grateful for the interruption, then paused as Colonel Keland growled in an undertone, "She's entitled to an interstellar boost frequency just because she knocked up her old man? Hell, there're a billion bleedin' brats born every hour!"

"Not Eltanin brats," Seidor said absently, his eyes on the retreating back of the Peace Mistress. "Evolved marsupials have internal pockets—they don't open until the child is ready to enter the world, and for millennia they had the worst infant-parent mortality rate going. It patterned their entire culture. Eltanin women took three or more husbands just to ensure offspring, and it's the reason their empire expanded so slowly—with population growth hanging by a thread, you employ your armies judiciously."

"Judicious, hell! The woman's a megalomaniac!" Keland nearly shook with tension, and hissed softly, "Shit, Dyrick, what are we going to do? We can't use Solar-Linkage. It's prohibited by Convocation Charter."

Seidor fingered his scar absently. "I don't think we have much choice. Did you see those Eltanin troops? Trynith has air strike support and could just as easily turn that DST artillery on us. And she's appointed by ConFed. It's her baby, so unless you're planning mutiny, you'd better move."

"If you say so, General. I just hope we aren't vaporized in the backlash." Her white teeth suddenly flashed. "But at least we'll get an honest crack at the bleeding Slimeys!"

Seidor watched her depart at a run, her combat mike already crackling. *We'll play this one cautious, baby, cover our asses each step of the way. And Mistress bloody Trynith is going to exonerate us in every one of her sodding dispatches because ConFed could be setting us up to take the fall for this debacle!*

Obsolete tholium lasers licked the mossy embankments, followed by explosions of earth as the Ca'Cuy assault was beaten back, leaving the area between the forward observation post and the Gredi landing port littered with charred debris. The Slimeys never learned the futility of charging entrenched positions, and Seidor noted that Colonel Keland, positioned far to the right of their observation post, was husbanding her resources, stoically holding fire as the Ca'Cuy retreated.

Refocusing his distance viewer, filtering out the early afternoon sun, Seidor felt dazed. It was less than ten hours since the Peace Mistress had disembarked, and already troops ringed Aerot's Gredi landing ports. Before him loomed their primary field, its starkly functional architecture so alien next to the graceful creations of the Ca'Cuy. Round-bellied transport ships squatted among barracks and warehouses. Lowering his angle of sight, he picked out troops scurrying like disturbed insects, the racially similar but heavier Gredi easily discernable among the native Slimetails.

A single Ca'Cuy officer paused, caught in the zoom lens, and Seidor felt the familiar catch of breath, captivated by the lithe grace of the splendid creature. Under five feet, it stood on two slender legs, its delicate forearms gripping an outdated repulse rod, its long tail flicking with nervous elegance, its spinal frill fully extended above its rounded head. Coral and gold scales glittered, competing with its magnificently impractical body armor, and its round emerald eyes caught the sun and filled with light.

Biting off a curse, Seidor snapped off the viewer. *Maybe that's why we call them Slimetails,* he thought bitterly. *We have to tear them down before we can bring ourselves to kill them.*

Turning, he rested against the low wall, rechecking his memory, making certain Keland had two companies dug in on either side of the port's only exit. Leaning beside him, her own viewer scanning the action, Trynith asked, "When did the firing begin?"

"Ten minutes before you arrived. Roughly half an hour now. The other bases?"

"Secure, with ConFed troops in position. What is Colonel Keland's situation?"

Chinning his combat mike, Seidor briskly demanded, "Fore-Star, this is Gravity-Well. What is your situation?"

"Tight and holding," Keland's voice crackled. "Caught them sitting on their privileged sanctuary with their fucking pants down. We've got them spooked, but if they get organized we'll never hold them. Where the hell is that air cover?"

Seidor sighed. Colonel Keland, contemptuous of their C.6 technology level, never gave diddly shit for com-link security, and routinely failed to utilize scrambling capability. He arched a brow at Trynith, who said without looking down, "Tell Fore-Star to hold. Support is on the way."

He relayed the message, then returned his attention to the port. He watched several minutes in silence, then said grimly, "They're recovering, and those are troop transports. The place is boiling with Gredi. We don't have sufficient ground support, and if Bydon doesn't show, this is one lost cause."

Seidor ground his teeth. The Peace Mistress had rushed this thing, moved too fast, and those were his troops down there in danger of being cut to pieces. He'd seen it before—at a C.6 level even an enlarged infantry division could be overrun by determined ground forces, and he glared at Trynith. Catching his glower, she responded with a wintry smile.

"Admiral Bydon will be here. I want the Gredi air-fighter ports taken out first, so we wait." Dropping the distance viewer, she rested against the wall. "And wars are not fought for *causes,* General, they are fought for profit."

"Profit be damned." Seidor gestured angrily at wreckage smoldering in the watery sunlight. "Look at the waste—this little donnybrook is costing ConFed trillions a day."

"It is costing *the people* of ConFed trillions a day, and where something costs, money is transferred from the public coffers to private individuals engaged in manufacturing this . . . equipment." Leaning back, she scanned the sky, then continued easily, "The Ca'Cuy are a sublight culture, General, barely into their atomic age. There's not a single munitions factory on the planet capable of producing sophisticated weaponry, and there's no way they or the Gredi have the capacity to sustain seven years of C.6 technological warfare, yet every hour your soldiers die—killed by ConFed's own outdated armament."

Trynith unsealed an inner pocket of the gray cape to pull forth a small lump of blasted steel. "I picked this up on the way down here, from the wreckage of an antiquated tholium laser. Its Ca'Cuy operator was still strapped into the jump seat, or what was left of the poor creature. Take a look." She tossed it to him. "Recognize the logo? In-Vec Technologies. A ConFed corporation, I believe, one of the biggest, but only one big fish owned by a bigger fish that is in turn owned by an even bigger fish." Her grin was wicked. "Your own people said it, General—be a good soldier. Keep on killing each other gloriously till we are as rich as we want to be."

Ice congealed on Seidor's spine as he looked at the warped logo, but he snapped defensively, "The private sector does not dictate ConFed policy. We have an elected Directorate . . ."

"Don't be naive, Seidor. The same monied interests who manufactured this military scrap *own* ConFed, control your economy, control your people. Who do you think pays for your spectacular so-called free elections? Buys the politicos who are candidates in them? These toys are only part of what wealth can buy, and the minor part at that. Gold also purchases souls, including those of Directorates, and when public monies run short and the people panic, your Directorate borrows wealth—at enormous interest rates—from the very cartel that put them into office and to whom the grossly inflated price of this military hardware is paid. Borrowed at rates so high that you, and your children, and your children's children, will still be paying it generations from now."

Trynith's smile vanished and the lines in her face deepened. "If you wish to know the true *cause* for which you are fighting, General Seidor, the true reason you have slaughtered millions under the guise of *protection from tyranny,* look to the beings who collect that interest."

Seidor felt a bead of sweat trickle from beneath his helm, and said slowly, "Without ConFed's intervention these people would have been enslaved years ago. We're here to protect the Ca'Cuy from Gredi aggression."

"Protect the Ca'Cuy? The quote Slimetails unquote don't appear overly delighted with your noble intentions. If seven percent more of them die they reach the extinction threshold. That is a problem my people understand. The Eltanin faced that threshold millennia before Terra boosted her first satellites into space." Embers of rage flickered beneath Trynith's icy contempt. "When ConFed is through *protecting* the Ca'Cuy, I fear they'll have few generations left in which to enjoy their liberty."

Flaming bloody hell, the woman's right! Seidor thought. *Every trooper out here suspects as much. And what of Covert Ops? Is it owned by these so-called monied interests too? Along with the subatomic CD potential?*

Targeted cell disruption was still experimental, had never actually been used, but it was only a matter of time, and in the wrong hands . . .

Seidor shuddered, then his grim speculations were cut off by the beep of Trynith's personal frequency mike. He studied the Peace Mistress as she engaged her privacy shield and turned away to listen. When she rejoined him her face was set, and her fingers again moved restlessly on the third band of her cloak's embroidery.

"How's the baby business?" he inquired casually. "The home front secure?"

"The depocketing progresses normally," she said distantly, "But Arnock is old to be having . . ."

Her voice faded, and Seidor caught a suspicious brightness in her eyes. Nodding toward the jacket, he said, "Five lines of trim, five husbands, right? Third husband under fire?"

Trynith's fingers dropped from the frayed patch as though it were white-hot. Turning away, she raised the distance viewer but admitted softly, "Yes, my third husband. He's . . ." She stiffened, her voice suddenly crisp. "They're moving. Alert Colonel Keland."

"Shit! They'll roll right over us!" Seidor chinned his mike. "Fore-Star this is Gravity-Well. They're coming out. Close ranks and hold."

"I'm on it, Gravity-Well." Keland's voice sounded tense. "But if the Eltanins don't show you can break out the body bags!"

As the connection closed Seidor could hear Keland mobilizing her troops, and he swung his distance viewer. The port's causeway swarmed with Ca'Cuy, intermixed with the heavier Gredi. They fanned out even as the air shivered under the warming hum of ConFed lasers. The sound crescendoed to a skull-jarring whine as Keland went into action, but most of the Ca'Cuy slithered easily into the marshy ponds, and Seidor bit off a cry when the first golden forms erupted among his troops. The dying had begun. Cursing in a soft monotonous undertone, he started angrily when Trynith's hand grasped his shoulder. Her slight smile became the genuine article, and she nodded upward. "Look."

Formations of silver coins scarred the zenith, swept to the horizon, and reversed to shoot across the Gredi port. The universe exploded. Dark rays neutralized the atoms of matter, absorbed the power released, recycled and redirected it in night-black beams of devastation. Structures, ships, living flesh, ceased to exist. Earth, water, rock, the very atmosphere, dematerialized, and the ground leaped beneath Seidor as air fell into the vacuum with a thunderclap that stunned the senses. He could hear the shriek of Bydon's first fighter wing veering off, circling for another pass, and huddled as the second barrage hit. His shoulder slammed against the wall, his helmet crashed into the unyielding plasticrete, and pain lanced through his neck. Tasting blood, he surrendered to a momentary darkness.

When he uncurled, Peace Mistress Trynith was on her feet. The coinlike ships had vanished. Seidor pressed a sleeve to his bleeding nostrils and, hunkering down, moved crabwise to join her. Hawking and spitting blood, he raised his distance viewer. All that was left of the landing port was a crater. Beyond it, the marsh swarmed with black dots as the remaining Ca'Cuy fled en masse, interspersed with the more cumbersome Gredi. He heard Trynith's voice as though through wads of cotton.

". . . advance your battalion by companies. You are to advance by companies. Acknowledge."

Colonel Keland's voice came back, thinned by static. "Fore-Star to Gravity-Well. Fore-Star to Gravity-Well. We cannot advance. I repeat—we cannot advance. We are approaching privileged sanctuary. I repeat—we are approaching privileged sanctuary. Do you copy?"

"I copy, Fore-Star. You are to advance in pursuit of the enemy. Mop up the remnant, Colonel. I want all Gredi resistance crushed. Refrain from killing Ca'Cuy—take prisoners where possible. I repeat—you are to advance in pursuit of the enemy. Acknowledge."

Incredulous silence followed the terse order, terminating in a strangled, "Acknowledged. Advance in pursuit of the enemy. Take prisoners where possible. Come on. Let's mop them up . . ."

The contact ended as Keland's voice was drowned out by a surge of rebel yells. Seidor, the air hot and fierce in his lungs, swung the distance viewer. ConFed forces surged forward in orderly ranks, supported by mobile artillery. They were met by sporadic bursts of solentium lasers. They did not split but rolled over the few resisting Ca'Cuy to plunge into the landing port's crater, vanishing under a smoking cloud of dust, fanning out as they emerged on the far side. Seidor was on his feet. Over the distance he could see the sudden shock of contact, like a mighty wave pounding into rock, as the fleeing Ca'Cuy and their Gredi allies turned.

"Dear God!" For once it was not profanity.

Trynith responded with a sardonic chuckle. "There was never any problem with ConFed's officers or troops. If permitted, they would have pacified this planet in a week."

Seidor couldn't answer. His throat ached, throbbed with trapped breath, then ConFed's burgundy and silver standard exploded from the interminable confusion. His pent-up cry escaped in an exultant bellow and somehow he was standing on top of the bunker, yelling, cheering, venting months of grief, of humiliation, of frustration, as the silver standard advanced, blinding and bright under Aerot's golden sun.

In nine hours a world fell. Three days after the strike on the Gredi landing ports ComNet relayed news of a ConFed/Ca'Cuy armistice. Four days after the strike a massive reconstruction effort was proposed, and five days after the strike the safe unpocketing of a son was reported to the Lady Trynith.

From the ConFed Directorate issued ominous silence, but a group of tight-lipped senior staff officers arrived to relieve Seidor, dispatched by Supreme Commander Trakct. Seidor said little. The Peace Mistress was leaving Aerot. He was to stay on long enough to oversee the change of command, but he could not grant her request for a quiet departure as the crowds turned out of their own accord. Even a pitiful remnant of Ca'Cuy watched from the broken arches of their resanctified temple, and she greeted her audience with the same equanimity she bestowed upon the war. Only when her personal-frequency mike beeped to report the safe unpocketing of a son did she appear incapable of grasping the situation. Seidor, laughing, repeated the message, then said briskly, "Congratulations, Mistress. Send my warmest regards to your husband . . ."

He stopped. The Lady TeaLa Raye Trynith didn't hear him. The warrior had fallen away, revealing the radiant features of a blissfully happy woman, eyes bright, a row of frayed embroidery crushed joyfully in her fist. Half-turning, he winked at Keland, and with a parsec-wide grin the colonel chinned a universal channel on her mike, and bellowed, "It's a boy!"

Cheering erupted, nearly obliterating a second announcement—the ratification of a ConFed/Gredi/Ca'Cuy nonintervention pact. The expressions of the senior staff officers remained carefully neutral, polite masks that revealed nothing. Seidor stepped nearer the Lady Trynith as they began the short walk to her ship, and asked in an undertone, "In God's name, Mistress, *how* was such a pact ever made acceptable to all factions? The Gredi should be coming at us with everything they've got. Everyone knows acceleration would open a second front."

"Everyone knows?" The Peace Mistress smiled sadly. "It's amazing how quick ConFed's keepers regained their sanity when galaxy-wide trade embargoes threatened to stem from their lucrative little peacekeeping action, and how quickly the Gredi grasped the implications of the Matriarch's Third Fleet circling their stratosphere." Her smile exploded like sunlight. "Merely visiting them on an interstellar tour of good will, you understand."

With a covert glance at the ConFed staff officers behind, more reminiscent of a prison escort than an honor guard, that single dimple reappeared high in Lady Trynith's cheek. Seidor felt his own expanding grin ease the lines from his face. As word of the pact spread, voice after voice joined in a single exuberant roar of joy. It went on and on. Hell had held sway for seven years—now they were going home, and Seidor fought an impulse to stop walking, to grab the Peace Mistress, to swing her in his arms. Instead he said, "Lady Trynith, I don't know how . . ."

He paused as her strong slender fingers tightened on his outstretched hand like a coconspirator, and with hard-won calm, he said, "It's ended. With help the Ca'Cuy will recover, and with the Gredi out of the picture we won't have to maintain a permanent peacekeeping force here." Pulling off his ceremonial helm, he forked back sweat-matted hair. "Thank god the killing's over! You've settled this to everyone's satisfaction."

"I doubt the interests backing your Directorate are too exultant at this moment. And it is my profound hope that this incident has not impeded your own career, Dyrick Seidor." A shadow wiped the dimple from the Peace Mistress's cheek and the years seemed to roll back over her. She gave a tired shrug, and said, "But that is not my concern. For now, I am going home to my husbands and my son." As if struggling to regain her happiness, she added, "I will name him Aerot. Aerot Arnock TeaLa Raye."

Seidor nodded. During the remainder of their walk to the landing pad the city's destruction was masked by bright ranks of humanity and Ca'Cuy, interspersed with an incongruous sprinkling of Gredi. They could not talk over the cheering, and with Colonel Keland at his shoulder Seidor fell back, respectfully letting the Peace Mistress proceed alone. Rear Admiral Bydon waited by her ship, her composed features eased by a smile, and they were ten paces from the entrance ramp when Seidor got his first inkling of trouble.

Trynith turned to speak, only to gasp as astonishment filled her clear gray eyes. She swayed, and a vertical frown line marred her brow. Springing forward, Seidor caught her. She fell. Her hand closed convulsively on his arm as her lips struggled to form words but released only gagging breath.

"Medics! Dear God! *Medics!*"

He cried out an unthinking plea for help. Bydon was beside him, her face waxen. From a great distance he heard Keland bellow, "Medics! We need a sustain-pod! Get over here! Move your fuc . . ."

The Colonel's shout faded before a vast internal silence. The Peace Mistress convulsed in Seidor's arms. Admiral Bydon, her mouth a thin gray line, pressed an injector to Trynith's throat. The woman's struggles only intensified. Bursts of sounds mocked speech. The dying was not easy. Trynith's eyes shrieked pain, shrieked supplication, then their light faded, draining off the soul, locking the once-animated features with appalling finality. Seconds later a trickle of crimson came from her nostrils and ears.

Seidor did not hear the uproar or feel the frantic medics lift the Peace Mistress from his arms. He could only gaze at the hard features of Supreme Commander Traket's personal advisor. The man stood ten feet away, his face a carefully controlled blank, and there was no surprise in his eyes.

They did not give up for hours. Within Bydon's ship they fought to repair the unrepairable while Seidor leaned against a wall in the sterile anteroom, clutching a jacket-cape of soft gray velvet, unaware of his bloodied fingers repeatedly rubbing a section of worn embroidery. He did not look at the doors of the operating theater, and in the bitter silence a terrible suspicion congealed, throbbed, and assumed life.

Across a dark chasm he felt Colonel Keland's strong warm fingers grip his arm. "It's over, Dyrick. There's nothing more to do." She appeared frail before such death, vulnerable and somehow childlike, and her voice thickened as she said, "The medics say it was a . . ."

"A brain hemorrhage," he finished flatly.

She frowned, her dark eyes bewildered. "Yes. Only how did you . . . did you . . . ?"

"Know?" Without further explanation, he pushed off the wall, his knuckles white as his fingers locked on the gray jacket. "What's happening?"

"T-They've left to make the announcement. We . . . we'd better make an appearance."

"You go ahead." His lips felt numb, as though he were drunk. "I'll come in a minute."

He waited as the door closed behind her. He was alone. Preternaturally calm, he entered the operating theater. A medicinal smell scarred the air. The bright overhead lights had been switched off, leaving the gurney in restful shadow, and his boots kicked wrappers that had missed the disposal chute as they were flung aside in frenzied haste. The body was draped, but the face—older, characterless in death—was exposed. The blood had been wiped away. A single overlooked smear profaned the gray flesh beneath the ear, and the silvery glow of the universal encyclopedia had faded, leaving it to cling like a decaying parasite to the temple.

Laying down the jacket, Seidor meticulously lifted the sheet and placed a lifeless white hand on the gray velvet's worn trim before pulling his Covert Ops scanner from his pocket. With rock-steady hands he ran it along the chest, up the neck, over the base of the skull. Almost imperceptibly it began to beep.

Twilight was fading and the evening's chill clamped Seidor in its damp embrace as he stepped from the ship. The bright crowds had dispersed, exposing desolation, leaving the landing pad empty except for a stony-faced Eltanin honor guard at the base of the ramp. Across from the open expanse rose the graceful spires of the Ca'Cuy temple. He could discern a thin ghost of their exquisite wailing music. He paused to listen. Perhaps in their own way, grateful for the ending of the war, they grieved, and he looked to the harsher lights around the newly installed command center.

The cell-disruption targeting panel . . . ? He stared at the dim distant lights with such intensity his eyes watered. *Hell, it could have been used from anywhere—the command center, a hovercar, even one of our ships. The thing's damned near small enough to carry around in your pocket, and wherever it was it's gone now—scattered into its component molecules, most likely. Covert Ops is nothing if not efficient.*

Seidor pivoted until his back was to the center. He stood, anger gnawing like a cancer. What had she said? *I doubt the interests backing your Directorate are too exultant at this moment.*

People awaited him, Keland and Admiral Bydon; but he circled the ship, weaving through the Eltanin flotilla to walk alone amid the ruined city. Collapsed buildings blocked the once-gracious canals, forcing him to detour, skirting water scummed over and black with the wastes of war. Pale and distant, Aerot's secondary star rose above the last sullen streaks of sunset, and dark scarlet clouds slashed the sky like bleeding wounds. Far off, Seidor watched a solitary Ca'Cuy kick through the rubble, the pink snow the color of clotted blood in the failing light.

Searching for food? For its dead? Its golden scales were dull, its sleek hide dry and broken by oozing cracks. The elegant tail dragged listlessly, while nearby a frail youngster keened, its thin persistent wail competing with the interminable beep of the scanner, both sounds lost under the vast indifferent sky.

Stars burned bright and clean above the sunset, and slowly, meticulously, Seidor picked out the brittle glitter of ConFed's myriad worlds—aloof, indifferent, immune to suffering. Dropping his eyes, his thumb slid over the icy surface of the scanner. On its tiny screen glowed the persistent image—a molecular signature of death stamped in the base of a once-living brain, severing the courage, the joy, and the potential.

Don't be naive, Seidor. The monied interests who manufactured this military scrap own ConFed, control your economy, control your people. Who do you think pays for your spectacular so-called free elections? Buys the politicos who are candidates in them?

With a shudder, Seidor looked again at the glowing scanner in his hand. *Dear God, my own people killed her. Covert Ops arranged the assassination, they're the only ones with the necessary knowledge, but who gave the order? Allerdeck? Supreme Commander Traket? The ConFed Directorate? And why? Because she intervened? As a warn-*

ing to others? To whom do you report treason if the very government itself is treasonous? And if Trynith's evaluation is correct, if Peacekeeping and Covert Ops are truly controlled by monied cartels, what am I doing on Aerot? What am I fighting for? Who am I fighting for?

Drawing a ragged breath, his gaze returned to the eternal stars as words echoed and reechoed in his skull, *Be a good soldier, General. Keep on killing one another gloriously till we are as rich as we want to be . . . till we are as rich as we want to be . . . till we are as rich as we want to be . . .*

Pat Beese lives in the Chicago area. Like many of us, she's on her second or third career. After graduating from Loyola University with a degree in English literature, her first job was as a teacher; later, when her passion for fine jewelry became too expensive, she went back to school and completed a second major in sculpture and small metals. She now makes one-of-a-kind pieces in a basement workshop. She also harbors passions for history, music, art, and archaeology and writes poetry, generally with a black and white Shih Tzu dust mop dog on her lap.

About her story Pat writes: "Like Venus rising from the foam, the idea for 'White Wings' arrived fully formed and ready to go into action. Also like Venus, it was demanding and self-centered. This story mandated immediate writing—at the expense of a novel that was in the works at the time. Nothing short of full attention would suffice. Only when it was satisfied could I sleep."

—LMB

White Wings

P. J. Beese

Little pigs, little pigs, let me come in."

"Punch in your code, soldier!" The crisp command issued from a small grid next to the black, shiny thumbprint lock. "Procedure!"

"Melissa, why don't you disable that asinine code lock and just use the thumbprint? The damn code's a waste of time."

Up in the cockpit, the commander slid down in her chair, throwing her head back to rest against the crash cushions in a weary gesture. "How many times do you have to be told? I'm feeling like a goddam baby-sitter! Under my command we do things in a military manner. Now, enter your code."

"Mel," Jon answered, "I'm not *in* the military. I'm only working for a living. This code is a damned nuisance. Can't you just let me in? It'll take one button for you to open the door."

"Nope. No can do. You know the regs as well as I do. Code."

Jon heaved an exaggerated sigh at her rigid attitude, and began punching in his twenty-two-digit code. "Regs!" he spat, under his breath. He continued in an undertone. "Sometimes, Commander, you're a royal pain in the ass!"

Melissa's voice spilled like acid out of the communicator. "What was that, mister? Did you have something more to say to me?"

"No." There was a long hesitation before Jon added, "Sir."

The mechanisms made only the smallest of whirring sounds as the door slid back from its seals. "I know," he said, shaking his head. "I can hear the commander saying now . . . 'We're a contact team, and this is a naval vessel.

The ship comes first. It must not be endangered. All sorts of situations could arise.' "

"That's right, Joni, they could," Mel said as she came along the narrow corridor, pushing thin wires back away from her face into her red-gold hair with long sweeps of her finely shaped fingers. "With that code, if you're compromised the ship will still be secure. No one could cut off your hand and use it to gain access. Or did you forget that seventeen crewmen had their throats cut on Telware Two Five Seven?"

"I remember. In fact, I can't forget. One angry juju man and a whole culture is knocked on its ear. How could some raw recruit, sensitive or not, realize he was trespassing on the magic man's personal preserve?" Jon closed his eyes and shook his head. "The mind-screams must have been terrible."

Melissa shrugged. "And you can't figure out why I insist on doing things by the book? You guys are very dangerous if something goes wrong. You make a cultural misstep like Telware, or worse yet, lose yourselves completely in a foreign psyche. The results are disastrous. Whole worlds lost to us. We *will* continue to follow regulations on this ship."

"Okay, okay. It's just that I can't figure out who the hell is going to compromise me or this ship on this godforsaken hunk of rock!"

He pointedly turned his back on her, then made his way to his quarters, sealed and locked the door behind him, then leaned heavily against it. Unfathomable tears sprang to his eyes. He looked around the tiny room through a rainbow shimmer. The length of his bunk and only wide enough for the bunk plus a shower stall and a chair, the room had been his home for over two years now, if you included the trip out from Ambrose Station. "No," he said aloud, his voice shaking. "It's been forever. More than twenty years, hometime."

Then, like the clap of thunder that announces the unexpected storm, it hit him, and he dropped his head and let the tears flow freely. *Too long. I've been away from home too long.* When the emotional cyclone ran itself down a little, Jonathan White Sky Feathers pushed himself off the wall and stumbled to his bunk. He dropped down on the edge of it and plunged his face into his hands. He sat that way for a time, allowing his eyelashes to dry and his shoulders to stop shaking, then he stood and went into his tiny shower stall-bathroom to wash his face. He ran the coldest water he could get out of the tap, and splashed it up liberally. He toweled off, then placed his hands on the rim of the sink.

"So what are you going to do now, Jonathan, old boy? The medicine man told you not to go." He ran one hand over his smooth, almost hairless face.

The soft tap at the door sounded like the clang of a gigantic bell to Jon, so ragged were his emotions.

"Go away, Dars," he called, his voice cracking.

"I've got Mel with me."

"As if it could be anybody else. Go away."

"No, Joni. I'm not going away. Now, let me in," Darius returned determinedly.

Jon sighed heavily, already knowing he'd lose this round. "Then at least send Mel away. She's too much for me to handle right now. You know I'm always strung out after I've been in the field. I can't cope with her untrained mind. Her stray thoughts alone would drown me."

"Joni, she's your C.O. . . . " Dar ventured, in spite of knowing that Jon would be actively sending and receiving for hours yet.

"And the love of my life, and if she comes in here right now she'll drive me into insanity!" he screamed. "Now get her away or the door stays locked!" He knew that as his commissioned commanding officer Mel could unlock any door on the ship. He also knew she would try to respect her delicate sensitives' absolute need for privacy.

After a moment Darius called, "Mel's headed back to command, Joni. I'm alone. Now let me in."

Jon opened the door and quickly and politely moved back to the bunk to avoid any physical contact with the other sensitive. No reason to actively share his pain. He sat on the edge of the bed and dropped his head over his clasped hands. "What do you want?"

"Come on, Joni," Dar replied. "I'm as sensitive as you are or I wouldn't be here. In fact, I'm more so. I outscored you on every test. Now you're throwing off enough violent psychic energy to rock this little world off its axis. Why the hell are you having so much trouble shifting gears?"

Jon ran his hand through his thick, black mane before he let it fall over his eyes again. "I don't know, Dars. I really don't know." He sighed as he ran his forefinger over the bridge of his hawkish nose. "I can only tell you two things. I'm fed up with trying to talk to a bunch of rocks, and before I left home the tribal medicine man told me not to come."

"But, Joni," Dar started brightly, "these aren't rocks. These are intelligent, living beings with incredibly long life spans. There's a hell of a lot we could learn from them. All we have to do is communicate."

"They look like rocks. They smell like rocks. They taste like rocks. I've spent the last four months trying to communicate. There's been no response of any kind. They're rocks."

"Joni, that's just not true. You know yourself there was a considerable ripple of excitement when we first flew in."

"Yeah," he answered cynically. "On a human scale of one to ten that excitement would have registered a minus three."

"Rather a lot for a rock, I'd say," Dar ventured, turning up one corner of his broad-lipped mouth. Then the smile vanished. "But that's not really what's bothering you, is it, Joni?"

Jon shook his head wearily. "No, I guess not."

"So what is it?"

"Something you wouldn't understand."

"Try me."

"Something . . . religious."

"Like what?"

Jon closed his eyes, shook his head again, then opened his haunted black eyes to meet Dar's for the first time. "You're about the best friend anyone could have, Dars, and I've appreciated your help on any number of occasions. But you're just not going to grasp this one." He took a deep breath, filling his broad chest, and exhaled slowly. "I've been away from home too long."

Dar cocked his head, and a puzzled expression crinkled his dark eyes. "You've been away from home longer than this, Joni. I know you have. We were together on that long haul out the galactic arm. You didn't have any trouble that time."

"But that time I wasn't supposed to be home taking care of the rituals. My dad was still alive."

Understanding stamped itself on Dars's mobile features. "Ahhh. I see."

"What do you see? Some textbook theory about guilt and Oedipus complexes?" Joni snapped. "You can forget that shit! I'm the head of my family now, and this is an important ritual time back home. Without my help, my entire family may be unprotected. And something about that is ripping me apart."

"I understand," Dars said, nodding.

Joni leaped off the bed, throwing himself at the opposite wall, smashing two huge dents into the metal doors that concealed his lockers. "What the hell can a mongrel like you understand about dissatisfied spirits and unprotected souls?" Joni ranted as he turned on Dars.

"Plenty, man. Plenty," Dars answered coolly. "You ever hear of a little thing called voodoo?"

"Shit! That's nothing but crap they feed the tourists."

"You think so, man?" Darius asked as he stood, the angry blood rising to his face, turning his toffee-colored skin darker. "Then you've never been brushed by the death angel's wings. I have. It wasn't pleasant. And someone very dear to me didn't survive."

Jon went pale and he took a step back. "Maybe you do understand," he said quietly.

"Yeah. Maybe I do," Dar responded bitterly. He sat down again, and forced a mantle of calm over himself. "Now. What are you going to do about what's going on inside you, Joni? You're a long way from home and on a quick slide to cracking up."

"I don't know, Dars. But I'll try to figure something out. In the meantime, keep Mel away. She's a wild river of emotions for me, positive and negative, and I just can't handle it right now."

"I'll do my best, but like it or not, she is the boss. Is there anything else I can do for you?"

"No. I don't think so. But watch out for yourself. I'm not certain I'll be able to control everything that comes along, and I don't want to hurt you, physically or mentally."

"I'll take care. I promise. But there's one more thing you've got to add to your equation, Joni."

"What's that?"

"Your job here is to make contact with the Roks."

He groaned. "Yeah. And neither one of us has done a very good job of that, have we?"

Dar smiled a rather sad and lopsided smile. "No, I don't guess we have. But I'm not ready to throw in the towel yet. There's mentality there. I've felt it. We both have. We just have to figure out how to reach it." He stood to leave. "Call me if you need me," he said, pointing into his ear with his thumb and at his temple with his forefinger. "Either way." He closed the door softly behind him.

Jon sat in the chair Dar vacated and looked around again. Through force of habit groomed on many contact expeditions the room looked almost sterile. All his personal belongings were stowed in the lockers in order to avoid collisions with floating souvenirs during passage. Suddenly he knew what he wanted, needed. He reached across to open the locker nearest to him, and pulled open the bottom drawer. There, carefully wrapped in transport can't-break packing, was a special piece of home.

Cautiously slitting the seal with his thumbnail, he waited for the green light on the top of the can't-break. When it flashed, he slowly peeled back the lid. Beneath it, resting on its perfectly conforming piece of shock-absorbent gel, was his mandella, its white, loosely tethered feathers glistening against the dark blue night sky and stylized pattern of snow owls on the shield itself. Freedom, strength, journeys of body and mind, joy, and unfathomed mysteries. All this he held in his hands.

The moment he lifted it from the box he felt better. "So," he murmured quietly, "you *do* hold a piece of my soul." He sat there for a time, staring at the mandella, absorbing it, arranging its dangling feathers, moving the beads on their cords till he felt the shield was as beautiful and as strong as it could be. Slowly he became aware that much of the anger, the frustration he'd been feeling had slipped away from him. He even managed to close his eyes without seeing the whirling tornados of pain that had plagued him. He drew a deep and quiet breath.

The door to his quarters opened. The mandella flew from his hand, pulled by something unseen, something stronger than his own astonishment, to land roughly on his bunk. Whatever peace he'd managed to find flew away with it.

"Am I disturbing you?" Mel stood half-in and half-out of the doorway, her hand still on the handle. The wires no longer dangled from her head. "The door wasn't locked anymore. I hoped that was an invitation. I've been worried about you."

Jon covered his eyes as he was racked with a headache of terrible proportions. "There's been some reason for worry, I guess. I was hoping Dars had asked you to stay away."

"He did. But since when did that ever stop me? It's my duty to keep an eye on you." She smiled slightly.

Normally welcome, Jon now felt her desire for him like slithering cold snakes crawling over his body in a scum of rotting filth. Her anger over a little disorder, a few bent regs, beat at him like hundreds of tiny pinching devils. Her worry was so sickly sweet that it stuck in his throat, almost closing it, and he gagged.

She came all the way into the room. "Joni, I'm concerned about you."

He shivered as he choked again. "Mel, please get out. You're causing me great pain."

She stepped closer, reaching out to touch his hair. "Joni, I don't want to hurt you."

"Then get the hell out of here!" he howled, his hands shaking with the restraint necessary to keep from beating her into senselessness so she would no longer torture him with her useless, rude, raw emotion.

Her voice tightly controlled, she answered, "I'm the commander on this run. Even if you're not in the military, this *is* a military mission. It's my job to take care of you sensitives because you guys get so wound up in your emotions you can't tell up from down. You need a calm, rational woman to keep an eye on you. And I intend to keep a close eye on both of you." She turned and left.

Shaking now, disconcerted again, almost beyond control of his own angers, he reached blindly for the mandella. Just the touch of it gave him some peace. He grasped it as a drowning man would a bit of flotsam. Staggering upright, he knew he had to get off the ship, away from the manufactured things of man, and find a contact with his soul.

The overbright light from the too-near star stabbed at his tired, strained eyes, and Jon squinted against it. He searched the horizon for the nearest high point of land, wanting to be as near the sky as possible, as close to the faraway spirits as this landfall permitted. As far as he could see in any direction the landscape was a barren mass of rocks. How many of them were sentient Roks he could only guess. The ship's nose pointed toward the group they'd been trying to communicate with, and that way, too, just beyond the grouping of Roks, was the nearest hill. Clutching the mandella to his chest, he trudged off down the path the three of them had worked into the rocky ground by kicking aside bigger stones and trampling down such lichens and mosses as managed to find a toehold. A short distance from the ship Jon began to feel a little stronger. He tucked the mandella under his arm and ran the zipper of his jumpsuit all the way down to his right ankle, liberating that leg. Pulling his left leg free from the knit binding that held the fabric close to his skin, he dropped the flapping suit to the stony path. Jon walked away from it without looking back, and, without stopping, peeled off his undershirt. Continuing forward haphazardly, he hopped along as he removed his boots and then his socks. His watch-com and dog tags rattled into the larger stones alongside the path.

By the time he reached the Roks he was garbed only in his skin, the mandella still clutched firmly under his arm. It felt warm there, comforting. Trying not to step on the Roks, Jon looked down, and it was as if he were seeing them for the first time. Unlike the black, basaltic rocks around them, these Roks had a faint greenish tinge under their basic dark tone, the result of a high copper content, and they glistened in the bright sun like mica, though Jon had detected no obvious flakes of the compound. They were different sizes and shapes, apparently random, many with sheer faces that looked as if they'd been fractured off of some larger mass. The entire group of them filled a little hummock in the bedrock of the rise, a "tribe" of perhaps two hundred fifty individuals. Carefully picking a path between them, Jon moved forward.

"This place is as good as any." He was away from the ship, surrounded by life. It was alien, but it was life. He held up the mandella. Concentrating on its symbols, he invoked his totem owl. The owl was his freedom. It permitted him to go anywhere, anytime. It was his connection to his people and his past. Actuated, his totem let his spirit fly toward his distant home.

"What the hell!" he exclaimed. Alerted by a slight hissing sound behind him, he pulled himself back into his body with a snap. His skin prickled and a shiver danced coldly down his spine. Except for human-made noise and a few reptilian slithers, he'd never heard anything on this world. The Roks were the only life-forms they'd detected, except for a few lichens and mosses, and the occasional lizard or bug. And he was fairly certain Darius and Melissa were still inside the ship.

His eyes popped wide open. "Son of a bitch! You're moving!" he said excitedly to the Roks as he realized the path behind him had closed. "I've been here four months, talking to you day after day, and this is the first time I've seen you move!" Warm excitement flooded over him, almost exultation, for the moment, at least, burying his internal woes.

Suddenly there was movement everywhere. Roks were sliding forward, first one face, then another, creating the hissing by friction with the gravel beneath. Little sparks of static discharge jumped around the ground like short-lived lightning bugs. Some of the larger Roks rolled like petrified tumbleweed. In moments, Jon was completely surrounded. There were even several Roks between his feet.

"Ayaaaaaaahahahah!" He raised the mandella above his head and let out an enthusiastic whoop, shaking the shield so the feathers danced like the white birds they represented. "I'll be damned!" he cried. "Maybe we haven't been wasting our time here after all!"

Gently pushing some of the Roks aside with his feet, he created a space large enough to sit in. He dropped down cross-legged, placing the mandella carefully over his knees, adjusting the feather streamers so they hung down in front of his legs. A tremendous stirring rippled through the Roks. Brief flashes of nonsensical images filled his mind, and he closed his eyes to try to capture them.

"Birds. High, high above," he whispered as one image finally coalesced, pulled from his own strong childhood remembrances. A new vision filled his mind. "A flash of white. Pure. Hard." It made no sense, but it was strong, filling his mind for several heartbeats. Then he recalled the violent cloudburst he'd been lost in until his grandfather found him, huddled in one of the Old Ones' stone houses, shivering. "Storm. Flashes of lightning."

Suddenly the images were running wild again, one superimposed upon another till they became painfully blazing colors, sharp-edged, tearing, pulling apart his memories. Joni opened his eyes and fought to push them away. To his amazement, some time had apparently passed. The sun-star had moved from over his right shoulder to over his left. Close about his knees, along his legs, up against his back, Roks were pressed. The white feathers of the shield were completely obscured, every centimeter of their fluff covered by Roks.

I've got to tell Dars about this. And the commander. This is the breakthrough we've been waiting for! There's a contact here now. His thoughts surged with new understanding. *They want to know about birds. No. Flight. They're reacting to my totem! They want to soar above the ground like the birds, like me. It's not much, but it's a beginning!*

He tried to stand, but he was so crowded in that it was hard to shift. "Move back, boys," he said, carefully nudging a few of the Roks away from his legs. As soon as there was a gap, another Rok filled it, as if they all wanted to touch him. "Come on, fellas. Give a guy a break," Jon said as he tried to find some clear place to put his hand for some leverage.

As he began to put some weight on his outstretched arm, a Rok, moving more swiftly than he would have thought possible, rammed his wrist near the heel of his hand. "Arrrrrrr!" He lost his balance, falling across the congregated Roks. Immediately they were upon him, Roks of all sizes and shapes rolling and bumping over each other, causing sharp static electric shocks to jab at his skin. Forming ragged ramps of sorts, filling every open space, weighing down his legs, lunging for his face, they buried his bare chest.

"Nooooo!" he screamed, lost in a panic, grabbing for the mandella, fearing he'd be unable to breathe, crushed by the Roks' combined weight. He clutched the shield convulsively to his chest. A rush of warmth covered him. Though he was unable to tell if it originated in his mind and worked its way out, or came from the outside in, it was strong enough and comforting enough that most of the panic lifted.

Forcing himself to be still, he emptied his mind as thoroughly as possible, waiting for anything more the Roks would tell him, waiting to discover what they wanted. He still grasped the shield tightly. He could feel the Roks gathering above him, aware that every breath was becoming more shallow, but somehow there was no room for fear in him.

Two very small softly rounded Roks worked their way down through the crowd of their brothers to rest themselves one on each of Jon's eyes. They were not heavy, but the pressure was not comfortable.

"Age. There's great age in these two," he mumbled, "and knowledge. Like the medicine man," he whispered, wasting his withering breath but relishing the human sound he created. "These two are very old!" A flash of understanding filled him. "Of course! The older they are, the smaller they are! They wear away!"

A field of white filled his mind, blinding and painful in its purity. "Take it away!" he screamed, then realized, to his dismay, that he'd once more wasted a great deal of breathing room. Again the warmth flooded through him, this time amplified with a feeling of caring coming directly from the two resting on his eyes.

A new vision replaced the blinding white field, this one of graceful, silent, winging birds. As Jon watched, he was overcome with the feeling that these birds were more than mere avians. More than his totem. They were the spirit, the soul, the uplifting embodiment of the grounded Roks. He understood, too, that they had not recognized the stylized pattern on his mandella. There was no way they possibly could. This planet had no flying life-forms. The Roks had reacted to the feeling of flight, the freedom flight embodies. They needed a way to soar, and now they'd found it. They'd reached out through Jon himself. A part of his soul touched a part of theirs.

"Maybe if I make peace with their spirits, I'll talk to mine as well."

He lay quietly among them, sending his mind, open, out to them, and they flowed in.

Darius felt his throat constrict. His breath was trapped in his chest, and he knew Mel was furious even before he turned to see her bearing down on him.

"Where the hell is he, Dars?" Mel asked, icicles stabbing through her voice. Melissa's face was as red as her hair, her anger a burning presence.

"I told you," Dar answered, his voice a little ragged. "When I left him he was in his cabin, and fairly calm. You apparently saw him after I did, even though I asked you to leave him the hell alone."

She put her hands on her hips. "Well, this is getting us no place. It's a cinch he's not aboard. He's probably gone out to do his Indian sensitive thing. Get naked and fly. And there's nowhere to go except to the Roks. Come on," she said, starting for the air lock but grabbing something as she passed the weapons locker.

Dar stared at her, hard.

Her face became the unlined mask of a military mannequin. "Dars, we don't know what kind of shape he's in. If he gets violent . . ." She let the thought hang in the air. "I don't like it either," she said, answering his unspoken disapproval, "but the hard choices are mine. Have been ever since I took command of this tub."

They left the ship and started down the path. Before long they found Jon's discarded jumpsuit.

"Oh, brother," Dar said, running a hand through his short curly hair. "I hope his spirits left something of him for us humans." Thoughts of death angels and avenging spirits swirled through his mind like wind-blown trash.

"What are you talking about?" Mel asked as she strained her eyes to look farther up the path.

"Never mind. We'll know soon enough."

They found his boots and his socks, and even the watch and the dog tags glittering among the rocks.

"Well, he's close to God now," Dar said, bouncing the dog tags in his palm. "There's not a whole lot of man-made stuff left."

They rounded the last little bend in the path.

"What in heaven's name is that?" Dar asked as he stopped dead in his tracks.

"I don't know," Mel answered slowly. Carefully she approached the pyramidal grouping of stones that filled the Roks' hummock. "Did they build this themselves? It's taller than I am! I've never seen anything in your reports that said they could move."

"They had to," Dar replied. "There's nothing else alive on this planet. Nothing but . . . Joni."

"Dars, what if he . . ."

"Shut up, Mel," Dar snapped, risking her anger, as he lowered himself to a sitting position.

"But, Dars . . ."

"Shut up! Give me a chance!" Darius closed his eyes, utilizing all his training to try to drop the inhibiting screens that all people keep around them in order to stay sane. "Mel, back away. And pull yourself in as much as possible," he ordered. Opening himself up to the things around him, Dars searched for those feelings that meant "Joni."

It was several moments before he spoke again. "He's here, Mel."

"Where, Dars? I can't see him."

"There's only one place he can be. Inside the pyramid."

Her eyes widened in horror. "Is he alive? Can he be, under all that?"

Dar shrugged his shoulders. "I only know he's here. I'm not clairvoyant."

"Come on, Dars. We've got to get him out of there," Mel said as she started to dig, pulling the Roks away one at a time.

"I'm not certain that's a good idea, Mel. We don't know why they built the pyramid."

"I don't care why they built the damned thing, Dars! Dig, soldier!

Dar followed her lead and began pulling down the mound.

Both Mel's and Dar's hands were torn and bloody by the time they caught sight of Jon. Frantically Mel pulled the Roks away from his face, brushing small bits of dirt off his eyes and mouth and nose while Dar worked to free his chest.

"Joni! Joni, can you hear me?" Mel's voice was trembling with weariness and anxiety.

Jon's eyes fluttered open. "Mel, is that you?" he asked weakly.

She put her ear next to his face in order to hear.

"I've been home. Tell Dars my family is protected now." His eyelids dropped again.

"Help me, Dars. Let's get him out of here."

Darius picked up the mandella, tied two of its streamers together fashioning a sling, and tossed the shield over his back. Then, straining, he lifted Jon's shoulders. Mel took his feet. Struggling, panting, and sweating, the two of them managed to get Jon back to the ship and into his bunk. They made him as comfortable as possible, then, exhausted, set automatic monitors on him.

Darius dropped the mandella on the floor beneath the dented locker door. "I'm going to shower and take a breather. You could stand some downtime yourself, sir," he said to Mel.

"I'll stay with Joni. He doesn't look good. He's too pale. And I'm not sure he's breathing right in spite of what the monitors say."

"Okay. I'll relieve you as soon as I'm on the good side of exhaustion."

"Thanks, Dars," Mel said to his retreating back.

"Mel, wake up." There was an edge to Dar's harsh whisper. "Wake up, dammit! You've been here for ten hours!"

"What!" Melissa responded loudly, then dropped her voice as she remembered where she was. "Where've you been all that time?"

"Out of it, just like you."

She sat up, rubbing the sleep out of her eyes. "Is Joni all right?" she asked as she turned her head toward his bunk. "I don't usually sleep that deeply!" She spoke groggily, brushing away the hand that was still roughly shaking her shoulder.

Dar moved to stand over Jon's bunk. "It's Joni who woke me. There's something wrong with him. Psychically, I mean. It's like he's hungry. I think it's time we get off this rock and find us a real doctor. And maybe a good magician, too."

"Okay. I think I can still lay in a course," Mel said as she tried to rub more thick sleep out of her eyes and staggered toward command. "Can't understand why I don't want to wake up! Is it something to do with those Roks, Dars?" Without waiting for an answer she continued. "Give me a hand with the prelaunch. This time you're not just along for the ride."

"Yes, sir, Commander," Dar answered as he followed her down the narrow passageway.

"There. That's got it," Mel announced a little later. "Hit ignition while I plug myself in."

"Which one?"

"That red one, there. Just press it and hold for a second."

Dar reached across the console and hit the indicated switch while Mel fitted long, thin control wires into jacks in her scalp. There was the whining roar of the fuel along the sides of the ship, but nothing more, no "pop" of ignition, no push of acceleration.

"What happened?" Darius asked, concerned.

"I don't know. Hit it again."

Another long, winding whine was followed by nothing.

Dar started unplugging the wires connecting Mel to the console. "Something's wrong here, Commander. I suggest you fix it."

"Smart ass," Mel mumbled as she pulled studded contact gloves off and stowed them away. "Are you at least going to give me a hand?"

"Do I have a choice?"

"Of course not. Come on."

The first thing they checked were the fuel lines. They turned up nothing.

"I give up. I'm gonna run a diagnostic," Mel said as she pulled her head out of another dusty access. "Should have known better than to start this. Fuel leak would've been too simple." She paused as she wiped her face. "You can't really help with that. Tell ya what. Check on Joni. See if there's any change. Then listen to him, if you know what I mean. If there's anything to be done, do it. If not, take ten. Just don't get too far away. I may need you if I turn up something."

"Right."

The lights were way down in Jon's room, and the monitors cast an eerie, sickly green across his face. Darius turned up the cabin lights long enough to confirm that the color was the result of the electronics, not Jon's real shade, then dampened them again. He checked the readouts, but nothing substantial had changed since they'd left him. He "listened," but there was nothing new there, either. Just a roaring spiritual hunger. Jon was breathing a little easier, but if that was through his own strength or the oxygen that was being pumped into him, Dar couldn't begin to guess.

"I'm gonna get you back to the medics, buddy," Dar whispered as he checked everything one more time. "You hang in there. When we get back you can introduce me to that medicine man of yours. If he's still alive."

Dar left Jon's quarters, closing the door softly behind him. *Too wound up to rest anymore. Slept too much already. Think I'll get some fresh air while I can. Bottled stuff gets stale pretty quick.* He opened the hatch and stepped out into a soft twilight. *What a place for romance.* He sighed as he stretched. *All you need is a front porch and a swing.*

He started to walk toward the rear fins. Something in his path caused him to stumble slightly. Looking down, he realized it was a small Rok. He ducked under a strut, and tripped over another Rok.

"Holy shit!" he exclaimed as he walked around the aft stabilizer fin. "Mel's gotta see this." He went back to the hatch at a run.

When he dragged her outside, Mel was as surprised as Dar had been.

"Where did they come from?" she asked as she stepped around the edge of the huge pile of Roks that surrounded the ship's stern.

"Damned if I know. The only thing I'm getting from them is that they're alive, but they've been singing that tune since day one."

"Look. They're piled so high they're way up over the engine cowling."

"Is that why this tub won't start?"

"Probably."

"So, Commander, what'cha gonna do about it?"

"Knock 'em down, I guess," Mel answered as she started to climb up the engine rings.

When she was atop, Mel began throwing down Roks. "Pull them down from the sides, Dars. Maybe we can get them to tumble," she called. "But don't get caught in a rockslide. It's going to be a long trip home as it is."

"Yes, sir," he called back, tossing off an irreverent salute before beginning to pluck at the Roks.

After some time Mel shouted down, "Dars, is it just my imagination or are we getting nowhere?"

Dars looked up at the pile of Roks he'd been dismantling and grunted. "I don't think it's your imagination, Commander. I think the damned things are filling in behind themselves."

She sat down, looking both thoroughly discouraged and very tired. "What're we gonna do?" she asked as she rubbed her lacerated, dirty hand over her face. "These engines will never ignite with these Roks filling the drums."

"Right now," Darius replied, "I think we ought to get some food and some rest. We're both used up. And it's not all physical. I know I need rest. Mel?"

"Yes?"

"Do you realize that's the first time you've ever asked me for advice?"

"Yeah. Well, don't enjoy it too much."

Darius smiled. "Cross my heart."

"Okay," she said, sliding down much more quickly than she climbed up, "something to eat is a good idea. But first I'm going to sit with Joni awhile. I know it's not your duty, but rustle us up some chow. I'll eat with him."

When she first looked in the door, Mel thought Jon had stopped breathing. When his chest rose to the accompaniment of a rasping gasp, she was relieved. She moved closer and took his hand.

"How ya doin', Joni? You're gonna have to hold on a little longer. It seems we can't get rid of your pet Roks."

Jon drew another labored breath and licked his lips. His eyes flickered part way open. "Water," he croaked, his voice barely strong enough to carry over the hum of the monitors.

Mel quickly jumped up to get the water, and held his head so he could drink. "Just a sip now," she cautioned.

He ran his tongue over his dry lips again. "Give them the mandella," he managed to say.

"What? Joni, what's a mandella?"

"Dars," was all Jon replied before he closed his eyes again.

She replaced his head gently, then ran from Jon's quarters toward the mess. "Dars! Dars!" she yelled. "What's a mandella?"

Darius looked up from his cooking. "A mandella is an Amerindian religious artifact that represents strength and the ability to unify the various parts of the soul. It's usually a decorated shield full of symbols. I carried Joni's back from the hummock this afternoon. Why?"

"He told me to give it to the Roks."

"What! He's delirious."

"Dars, he also told me when we first found him that he'd been home. That his family was protected. Does that make sense to you?"

"In a way. He might have gone home in spirit. I know he's been worried about his family being unprotected."

"Dars, give the mandella to the Roks."

"What for?"

"Because they're going to keep a piece of Joni if we don't."

"Commander, you can't be serious. That mandella is a part of Joni's spiritual life. We can't just give it away."

"Dars, if we don't give it to them, they're going to bury us so it stays here. Think about it! When did the Roks get excited? When Joni went out to do his macho Indian flying thing. He flies in his soul. You fly in your mind. I can only fly in this ship, but by God I still fly. What can the Roks do? Nothing. They think at each other—very slowly. How exciting can that be? Then along comes Joni baring his soul, reaching out to a planet light-years away. Freedom! Excitement! Joy! Instantaneous gratification! What more could an aeons-old Rok desire? You said yourself they're long-lived. How long will it be before the ship erodes away? Four hundred years? Five? That's the blink of an eye for the Roks. And the mandella's strengths will stay here forever. Unfortunately, so will we."

"Shit, Mel," Dars answered reluctantly. "I'll do it. But you're the one who's going to have to face Joni when he asks what happened to his mandella."

He tiptoed into Jon's quarters and picked up the mandella. As he crept out, he untied the lacings he'd fastened together and cleaned as much of the debris as possible from the shield's face. The feathers were no longer pristine white, and the elaborate symbols on the face were scratched. "But I don't think that's gonna make a whole lotta difference to the Roks."

Dars walked to the back of the ship carrying the shield in front of him for all the Roks to "see." He carried it a fair distance past the ship's back end, then placed it on top of a large boulder which, at first glance, did not appear to be a Rok.

"Have fun, boys," he called as he walked back to the ship. "Party down real hard. But let us get the hell off your world."

After he punched his code into the keypad and allowed the ship to read his print, the door slid aside. Dar took a huge step backward in surprise. The doorway was filled with Jon, his monitor cords dangling loosely, his skin rent and torn from the Roks, his legs barely holding him upright.

"Joni! We gotta get you back to bed! How the hell did you get here?"

"It's no good, Dars. The mandella's not strong enough without me. I've got to stay," Jon croaked as he tried to climb down.

"No way, man. Mel's gonna have my hide just 'cause I found you outta bed. Now back you go."

Darius stepped up into the hatchway. As he did so, Joni pulled forward with all the strength remaining to him, and fell out the door. When Darius tried to get out to pick him up, several medium-sized Roks rushed together with a grinding crash exactly where his foot would have been if he hadn't seen a movement and drawn back at the last moment.

"Man, they would've crushed my ankle!" He raised Mel on the com and explained the situation. "Joni says he has to stay."

"No!" The metallic shriek filled the corridors of the ship and rang through Dar's head.

Mel was at Dar's side at the open hatch in a matter of moments, but she was already too late. Roks had been gathering by the hundreds, and they'd already formed a shallow mound over Jon.

"Oh, my God!" Mel's hand flew to her mouth in dismay. "Is he still alive in there?"

"I don't know. I can't feel a thing. It's like my mind is wrapped in cotton. They're blocking me." He watched her eyes narrow as Melissa focused on her choices.

"Projectile weapons are ludicrous. What good would it do to shoot at a rock?" She paced in a tight little circle, ticking items off on her fingers. "Energy armament of any kind is out. We'd fry Joni as well as the Roks, and maybe ourselves." Another finger pushed aside. "A repulsor this close would scatter parts of Joni all over the valley. That's out, too." She chewed her lower lip. "If we had that new robotic rover . . . but we don't. Damn those R & D boys anyway! They promised us that thing more than three solar years ago." She looked at Dar beseechingly. "Can't we just go out there ourselves?"

Dar shrugged. "Not if you want to come back."

Shaking, Mel looked piercingly at Dar. "Then we're getting out of here. Now," she said as tears broke, flowing down her cheeks.

"What are you saying? We can't leave Joni! He's probably alive under there!"

"Don't you think I know that?" Her voice was a ragged knife in the planet's stillness. "But he's out there, and I can't get to him. You're in here, and you're next. We're getting out of here before that mound gets so tall it'll shear off the fin during takeoff. Now get up to command. I'm sealing this hatch."

In the command seats, Dar found the nerve to ask, "What makes you think this truck'll start now?"

"Those Roks. Most of the first ones to cover Joni came from the back of the ship. I hope enough of them have moved so we can get ignition. If we get even one engine to catch, we're outta here. Hit it," she said indicating the ignition switch, her hands still flying around her own connections. She pulled a deep breath, steeling herself. "I told you the hard choices were mine."

There was an extended rumble, but something in the stern finally came to life. Without any grace, lumbering like a grounded seabird, the ship rose. As it turned away toward the correct flight path, Darius caught a glimpse of the blue and white mandella, and near it a growing Tower of Babel, reaching for God in the nighttime sky. In the distance the hills crawled and rippled, swarming with writhing Roks surging forward to get to Jon.

Mel worked the controls, but her hands shook and tears ran down her face. "Joni said to tell you, Dars, that he'd been home," she said disjointedly, her breath hitching in her throat. "It was important to him, even in that terrible state. His people were protected. I guess that includes us."

Adrienne Martine-Barnes is a novelist and artist, and a recent emigré to Oregon, which she regards as God's Country. She has published a number of books, the most recent of which is *Sword of Fire and Shadow,* with Diana Paxson, which is the last volume in their collaboration about Fionn Mac Cumhal, the Irish folk hero. When she is not writing, she makes masks, quilts, dolls, and does watercolors and paper vessels. She also arranges felines, to which end she has published a monograph, *Neko-Bana: Or Zen and the Art of Cat Arrangement.*

About "Flambeaux" Adrienne writes: "I come from a family of servicepeople. My grandfather David Martinez served in the Great War, and was decorated by 'Black Jack' Pershing himself in 1918. When I was born, my father and uncles were getting ready to go 'over there' and served in both the European and Pacific theaters. For as long as I can remember, I have believed that war should be an equal-opportunity employer, that gender should never be an excuse to exclude one from serving in combat. My philosophical position is pretty simple—a daughter is not more precious than a son, and if one is expected to be willing to die among strangers, the other should have that right as well.

" 'Flambeaux' arose from my lifelong fascination with the custom of hanging a device—flag, star, ribband—in the window to indicate that one's offspring was a combatant. It also grew out of the conflict between mothers and daughters about a woman's place: her role in war and peace, power and authority."

—LMB

FLAMBEAUX

Adrienne Martine-Barnes

Companier Major Sarah Solomon stood in the Disembarkation Room and waited for the lock doors to open. Matteo, her personal clerk, stood nearby, his stubby fingers encased in delicate equipment, watching the data scroll across his display. The numbers and codes meant nothing to her without an access shunt, and as an officer she was denied such augmentation. Her troopers were not numbers, but flesh and blood people who were all too mortal. For her, this was the worst part of being an officer—the waiting to discover who had survived and who had not.

Beyond the enormous door that separated Disembarkation from the outer lock Sarah knew there was a kind of controlled chaos. It was a chaos she had to imagine, that she was not permitted to view, lest she begin to become reluctant to send her troopers into combat. That, at least, was the rationale she had been taught at Command School. She suspected it went deeper than that. Technology had not managed to eliminate actual people, had not been able to replace them with mindless machines, or even smart ones. And an officer still had the duty of sending the troops out to die among strangers.

The major was well aware that one reason she and the other officers were barred from the outer lock was to prevent them from seeing the Gracieres giving their swift mercy to those judged too severely wounded for treatment. Command insisted it was the only practical thing, that they lacked the resources to treat the worst wounded. If their wounds did not kill them, alien infection would. Perhaps, but Sarah knew of no evidence that the accursed things they called the Outers could infect a human. It was a policy she questioned silently, for it seemed to her neither humane nor conducive to morale. She was simply grateful she was an infantry officer and not in Medicorps like her brother, David. The suicide rate among the Gracieres was enormous.

She risked a glance at the Medicorps commander, Jomo Ngamo. He held a slate stiffly against his sternum, his bronzy skin gleaming with sweat, his eyes focused on the display. Sarah could guess nothing from his expression, but then she never could. She tensed further, throat muscles straining against the unyielding fabric of her collar. *How many this time?*

The doors began to part at last, clanking and protesting, and the smell of decontaminant, sweat, blood, and body waste swelled into Disembarkation. The air exchangers sped up, but the stench persisted, making her swallow hard. There were no dead or wounded to be seen, only the suited figures of those who were ambulatory, the survivors among the Combatants Inferior and Superior who had gone to fight the Outer hours before. They were too many to count, all moving through the opening, pulling off gauntlets and helms, talking in hoarse, loud voices.

"Report," she said stiffly to Matteo, trying not to crane her neck to look for a particular, beloved face.

"Seventy below, one hundred sixteen unrecoverable, fourteen medivaced, Major." Matteo's fine tenor showed no emotion, but Sarah knew he was upset. A quarter of the troops either dead or out of action. It was a moderate casualty count, almost low in the present campaign. But the number called "unrecoverable" were those who had been graced, those who had not died among strangers. Their bodies were already being cremated, whisked away before their loss could be registered by their fellow fighters. She felt the familiar sense of failure tear at her heart and wondered if she had the stuff to continue as an officer.

A figure broke out of the mob swirling around her, and a helm whipped off with grand flamboyance. The movement stilled the silent terror that Sarah had held at bay by will alone.

Major Solomon was looking up into the sweat-shimmering face of the Ugenia Clemency ten Boora. She grinned at Sarah, stuffed a nicostim between her lips, and dragged deeply. Sarah took in the fine-boned face, the depilitated forebrow studded with metallic inputs for the helm shunts, the flare of crisp, curling russet hair that rose from the back of the head like a minor bonfire. Agate green eyes danced with delight, and the hooky nose of her people looked too large in her slender face. None could mistake her for other than a Ugene, that strange and almost legendary group of humans from the L-5 colony called Delfheim. Sarah found her beautiful and desirable, even stinking of sweat and decontam and the smell of the crematory ovens, a burnt odor at once nauseating and familiar.

"Those things will kill you, Clem," Sarah said more jocularly than she felt.

"Aye. If the Outers or the Graciers do not get me first." She drew on the nicostim again, and a cloud of vapor belled out as she exhaled. "We all must die sometime, Sar." Her accents, the lengthened vowels of a Ugene, set her apart as much as her remarkable appearance. "I cannot wait to get cleaned up."

Major Solomon became aware that Matteo was waiting at her elbow, that his slate was spilling flimsies from its port, that she must put her duty before her delight.

"Fine. I'll see you in the mess, then."

"To hear is to obey, Companier Major," Clemency answered mockingly, crossing her breast in a salute. Sarah knew that by the time she returned to her quarters, Clemency would be clean and asleep, sprawled in the middle of the bed, naked and utterly oblivious to the bustle of the ship. Reluctantly, the major turned away and gave her full attention to the business at hand.

Clemency's head rested against Sarah's breast, the rather wiry tendrils of russet hair tickling her chin. They had joined eagerly, touching, tasting, grasping, breaths mingling, legs entwined, laughing and loving and forgetting the terrors of combat. Now they rested in their usual languor, sated and relaxed. Sarah gazed down at the metal-studded forebrow and nearly wept with delight.

"So, are you coming with me?"

Clemency's question startled her, and Sarah's sense of well-being vanished. She went tense, her jaw muscles straining. "I don't think that would be wise, Clem."

"Wise? Wise! What does that have to do with anything—Oh, Solomon!"

"In the first place," Sarah began with as much sweet reason as she could muster, "your people are not famous for welcoming us mere planetaries. What would your family think?"

"Family? There is only Mother, and she will not be pleased to see me, alone or companioned. She regards me as a disobedient child, and something of a freak. 'Ugenes do not engage in combat,' " Clem intoned deeply, "as if half the windows on our lane did not have flames waving in them. She actually believes that the Ugenes have bred aggression out, that we have realized the Founder's damn dream of a pacific society. My mother is a fool living in a fool's paradise." There was no mistaking the quiet bitterness in her voice. "She does not even know we are fighting for her, and all those like her, who keep their white hands clean of blood."

They had had this discussion before, several times. "Yes, yes, I know. Still,

I am no Ugene, and I will just make things worse. I will stick out like a sore toe."

"Sarah, you are such a snob. The Ugenes are not *Homo superior,* no matter how we pretend to be. We are just people who have been bred for certain characteristics of somatotype and phenotype, and who have decided that makes them better than the rest of humanity. You know that if you were not my commanding officer, I would companion you in a moment. I love you, Sarah. You have taken me to your home, have presented me to your people. It is only fair that I introduce you to mine—however wretched that will be."

Sarah sighed, remembering their previous *arandar,* in Hebron, her mother and aunts and sisters trying not to stare at Clemency's height and features, the result of generations of careful selection and ruthless culling. Her father had been cordial and curious, her uncle Reuben distant. Clemency's infectious laughter had charmed them all at the end. Most of all she remembered the wistful, hungry look in Clem's eyes as she looked at the two flambeaux in the front window of the stucco house, one for her and one for David, her brother.

That had been a year before, and Sarah ached for the sights, sounds, and smells of the Hebron Valley. Especially the smells of foods prepared by the strong, brown hands of her mother, her two sisters, her aunts and her nieces. She wanted to pluck a sun-warmed apricot from the great tree in the orchard, the tree planted by Isaac Solomon's own hands nearly two hundred years before, planted on the very day when real peace had been made between her people and their Arab neighbors. Isaac had been one of the architects of that peace, and the heavy-limbed apricot tree was a living tribute to his diplomacy and sheer stubbornness. To taste the sweetness of its fruits, to put the warm, firm flesh into her mouth, was to feed a hunger both physical and spiritual. Sarah was torn between longing for home and her passion for the tall woman beside her. Love was so terrible.

Fair was fair, she supposed, but that did not mean she had to like it. She was curious actually to see the Ugene colony. It was a tightly restricted community, and few were admitted into it who had not been bred there. The Founder, as everyone called Paul vander Delf, had been a man of vision and violent prejudice. He had despised most of humankind, and when he financed the creation of his space colony, he had excluded all who did not meet his rigorous racial standards. That meant he wanted neither Jews nor Arabs, Orientals nor Africans, nor anyone not of the purest old European bloodlines. The standard biography of vander Delf, *The Last Aryan,* drew a picture of a man of enormous complexity, great intelligence, and bigotries that were nearly incomprehensible to her. As a Jew she understood heritage and bloodlines, of course, but Sarah knew too, that she had ancestors from almost every race of Old Earth. Her family tree had Sephardim and Ashkenazim, Yemenites and Ethiopians, and even some genes from the Tewa tribe of old New Mexico. Like most of the descendents of those who had managed to survive the Bio-Wars of the early twenty-first century, she was a mixture of bloodlines, not all of them perfectly documented.

Clemency was as opposite as she could be. Like all Ugenes she was the product of a very small gene pool. The Founder had chosen ten thousand men and women he judged to be sufficiently perfect for his dream of *Homo superior,* and more than a third of those had been culled during the first two generations of the colony. Sarah had read the nonstandard biography of vander Delf, *The Man Who Would Be God,* which painted a very different and unflattering picture of the man. The Ugenes had tried to use their considerable political and economic influence to have the work suppressed and failed while the book became one of the most widely read works in the Solar System.

"Clem, your people don't think mine are human."

Clemency gave a mild snort, and the breath tickled Sarah's skin. "I know. It shames me. The Ugenes are very full of themselves. And my mother will be horrified to have you in her home, though she will not show it even for a moment. Well-bred humans do not display strong emotions, and my mother thinks she is very well bred. Three of her progens came from the Founder. But, I really want to see her again, and I may not have another chance."

Sarah chilled at these words. "I wish you could transfer to the officers program."

"I do not. I would go crazy. I cannot tell you what it is like, Sarah, to put on my suit and go down to the surface and fight. I am never more alive than when I do battle. I swear I can smell the blood of the Outers when I make a kill. It makes me whole in a way nothing else does."

"But, Clem, what will you do when we beat them?"

"Sar, we do not even know where they come from, or why they are invading the system. All we have learned in forty years is how to fight them—and we nearly did not manage that. If vander Grif had had her way, we might not be having this conversation at all. I do not believe we will defeat the Outers in my lifetime, unless we develop a star drive and discover where they come from. And if we do that, I want to be on the front lines when we hit their homeworld."

Sarah had heard this sort of argument before, mostly from raw recruits who had not seen much action yet. It still had the power to surprise her, to disturb her, and to fill her with an immense pride in the men and women who served under her. She had never experienced battle directly, and would not so long as Command continued its present policy. At the same time, Clemency could not transfer from the infantry into the officer corps without pulling a great many strings and using the power of her heritage. She could not be promoted from the infantry, as she might have in previous times.

A hundred years before, when promotion from the ranks was still possible, a charismatic young officer named Rodger Montoya had refused to accept the peace made at the end of the Second Belter War. He had led his troops in an assault on the domed city of New Benares on Ganymede and slaughtered the civilian population.

The Confederation Worlds had been shocked and outraged. There had been boards of inquiry and commissions and committees. When the dust settled, blame was fixed on a hazily defined quality called "blood-lust." The result was that combatants could no longer command, and commanders could no longer engage in combat. A Peace Party, headed by the Ugenia Violetta vander Grif, was formed with the aim of eliminating all military structures from the Confederation. Even community police forces were scrutinized and threatened.

The arrival of the Outers had stopped the dismantling of the military, though Violetta's daughter Eunice, the then-Secretary General of the Confederation of Humanity, had argued for diplomacy and delayed rearmament for several years. But diplomacy demanded communication. If the creatures had a language, no human had ever discovered it. Doubt existed in some quarters as to whether the aliens were even intelligent as mankind measured such things.

After three generations, the Confederacy knew little more about their enemy than when they had first encountered them. No human had ever experienced direct contact and lived to tell the tale. The infantry fought them wearing powered armor that isolated the combatants within layers of protection, armed with fearsome weapons of destruction and guided by computerized systems. So great was the fear that some combatant would go mad with blood-lust that access to the combat suits was even more difficult to obtain than access into Delfheim.

It did not matter whether the Outers were alien invaders or some homegrown monstrosity. All the Confederacy had managed so far was a holding action against them. The military machinery ground reluctantly forward, inventing new weapons, killing its own people out of perceived necessity, separating fighters from their officers. Sometimes, in the ward rooms, Sarah could almost smell the despair, and she knew she was not being overimaginative, nor was she alone in her sense of hopelessness.

As usual, she tried to ignore the feelings, to swallow the emotions. "Very well. I will come with you to Delfheim, even though I still think it is a terrible idea."

"Oh, Sar!" A strong arm clasped her so hard her breath was knocked away. "I am glad!"

Clemency insisted on wearing her dress grays when they debarked at Delfheim, and on Sarah getting into her most formal blacks. "I didn't come on *arandar* to wear a uniform, Clem," Sarah had protested weakly. Clemency had worn Sarah down, in the end, so they stood together, one tall pale woman and one short dark one, encased in breathless, unyielding fabrics while the locks cycled through. The high collar, with its enameled flames blazing against the dark cloth, pressed against her constricted throat, and she could feel sweat trickling down her sides despite the coolness of the air around her. Sarah's mouth was dry, and there was a maddening itch between her shoulder blades where she could never quite reach. She wished she had not come. She wished she could resist Clem, but she never seemed to be able to. She supposed she should be grateful her lover had no taste for reckless adventure, for mountain climbing or deep-sea diving. The way her heart was thudding now, entering the very restricted precincts of the Ugene colony was as much high adventure as Sarah could stand.

The doors slid open soundlessly. She caught her breath, glad her stiff collar prevented her jaw from sagging when she had her first view of the interior of Delfheim. Sarah had been prepared for something glass and metal, something gleaming and pristine. Instead she stood at the bottom of a lane lined with neat fences bounding tidy flower gardens before whitewashed houses with deep thatched roofs, spouting great stone chimneys adorned with enormous nests. There were birds in the nests, great white storks, feeding young, moulting long feathers, and splattering droppings as they flew about.

The street was cobbled, strewn with straw and droppings. Whiteclad women, aproned and linen-coiffed, appeared with buckets and brooms to sweep the debris away, and scrub at the cobbles. All around was the sound of squealing pigs, complaining goats and sheep, and geese honking and hissing. The smell was incredible—a mixture of animals, decaying straw, blooming roses and boiled cabbage so overpowering she nearly gagged.

Clemency appeared not to notice that they had stepped back in time. Some of the women gave them curious glances, and a few nodded a greeting, but for the most part they advanced up the lane as if they were utterly invisible. Sarah found that more disquieting than the actual environment. There were streets in Hebron as old-fashioned, and smells as pungent after the sterile atmosphere of a troop ship, but no stranger could have gone ten paces without attracting a curious following of round-eyed children, begging, pestering, questioning, and giggling as they pointed small, grubby fingers.

"Quaint, is it not?" Clemency asked cheerfully.

"It certainly isn't what I imagined—nor anything like the few photos that have been published."

"No. Everyone believes the Ugenes live in glass hives full of robots, but the Founder said we had to live simply in order to remain strong. There are some robots, of course, but they are used only in the vats and the creches. The creches *are* glass hives, but the Ugenes do not live in them, not after they are eight."

"I see, I suppose. This village is a very well-kept secret."

"Our security is superb," Clemency answered without pride. "We do not permit any holo-cams or snoopy mediavolk."

Sarah took in the absence of young children and the lack of visible males as well, and wondered where the men were. She was about to ask when they entered a square, surrounded by a few neat shops, and a small eating place, smelling of rich coffee and sweet pastries. There, disposed at their ease, were several dozen tall men, sipping cups and puffing away on long clay pipes while they chatted. There were a handsome lot, but so uniform in looks and dress she could not have identified any individual without prolonged study. They looked too much alike, and she felt her skin roughen. None of the men looked up as they passed, and Sarah began to wonder if they sat there all day while the women scrubbed the cobbles, cooked the food, and tended the bright gardens.

"It looks rather . . . charming."

"Dull, Sarah."

"Dull?"

"The Founder was not fond of intellectual pursuits, and he did not approve of commerce—too competitive—so there is not much to do, unless you manage to become an Improver. For that, you need influence, brains, and the ruthlessness to cull without emotion. So, most of the Improvers are from a few First Families, while the rest of the population moulders in rustic purity."

"You sound like you are being a little sarcastic."

"Yes, I am. You cannot conceive of how stifling it is to live here. Every day is just like every other, and all things are arranged according to the writings of the Founder."

Sarah found her mind reeling at the contrast between her preconceptions and the actuality, and she didn't like the feeling. "But, Clem, how have the Ugenes gotten so much influence in the Confederacy—from this?"

"First we convinced all the planetaries we were superior to them—then we started believing it ourselves. The public only sees the part of Delfheim where the Guilden attend the university or create even more perfect Ugenes. No one guesses that the Guilden spend long hours memorizing the writings of the Founder, or realizes how incredibly ignorant we actually are. We have great wealth, from the gene patents and other technologies we invented when we were beginning. We have influence everywhere. It suffices."

Sarah felt a shiver of dread crawl up her spine. "Clem—why did you really bring me here?"

"I could not bear any longer the look of awe when you embrace me. I needed you to discover that there is nothing so remarkable about me except that I was bred to appear magnificant and heroic—some Brunhilde out of grand opera. I wished you to know me for what I am—human—and not for what you imagined me to be. I wanted you to love me, not as a goddess, but as a real person."

Sarah held back a flinch of pain at the ache of longing she heard in Clem's voice, the hunger to be *someone,* not just a genetic oddity. More, she was embarrassed at her own secret pride in the nature of her beloved, her pleasure in Clemency's beauty and sheer physical perfection. It shamed her to realize she had worshipped her friend, had spun about her gossamer veils of magic, instead of seeing her humanity.

She was suddenly almost too weary to continue, overwhelmed by the strain of the long, hopeless campaign, and by a gibbering host of ghostly feelings, emotions full of ambivalence instead of clarity. Sarah wished they could pause and enter the inn, stop and drink coffee and smoke a nicostim and spend an hour staring at the fat pigeons paddling across the square under an artificial sun. More, she wanted to be in Hebron, to ask her mother what she should do while she spooned rich stew into her mouth, and chewed loaves of flat Arab bread, where muezzin called and the shofar sounded, and perfection was God's handiwork, and not man's tinkering.

The walk was long enough to make Sarah's feet hurt in the handsome but toe-pinching boots. At last they arrived at a wide lane flanked by enormous houses set well back from the road. The way was swept clear of every particle of debris, and the gardens were more formal, with knot-mazes of low-growing shrubs and hedges pruned to an unnatural precision. No pigs squealed, no sheep bleated, but she could hear a few birds singing softly amidst the scent of roses and boxwood.

Clemency was more and more anxious, her stride widening so that Sarah was paces behind her, her shorter legs no match for her tall companion. Finally she stepped into an opening in the hedge, and all Sarah could see was her flaming hair and shaven head above the greenery. She scurried to catch up, a little frightened of getting lost in this strange place.

She found Clem standing on a stone pathway, staring hungrily at the shining panes of wide windows across the front of a veritable mansion, stone below and wood above. Lace curtains concealed the rooms within, but Sarah knew her lover was not looking at them but was hoping to glimpse a shape-shifting flame hanging there. Clem gave a sigh, a shrug, a look of disappointment, then straightened her wide shoulders grimly and marched up to the formidable front door. She did not knock but turned the knob and walked inside. Sarah followed, her mouth aching with dryness.

Clemency's gray boots made a hollow echo on the floor of the foyer. Sarah saw a black-and-white tile floor, dark wooden paneling, a vast carved table with an arrangement of flowers, and felt cool air swirl around her. The house, however beautiful, was cold and seemed empty and lifeless. Then a door opened somewhere out of sight, and she heard faint footfalls coming toward them.

Sarah's first sight of the Ugenia Grace ten Boora was of a tall figure in white against the shadows of the hall. A white lace cap concealed still-red hair surrounding a face that might have been thirty or a hundred. She was garbed in a plain linen dress that fell to the floor, with an apron pinned to it at the shoulders and tied at the waist. Her hands were covered in lace mitts, so only the slight pink of her fingers lent any color below, and her face was so pale she seemed more ghost than human. Green eyes, emerald clear and hard, marred the perfect whiteness, for her eyebrows had been depilitated or plucked, and her lips were pinched and colorless.

For a long moment mother and daughter stood in silent confrontation, and Sarah wanted to be almost anywhere but watching. Then Grace ten Boora swept forward and clasped Clemency against her, and the hard, green eyes squeezed shut, holding back tears. The long pink fingers closed around

Clem's upper arms, lace against gray durcloth, a gesture of affection as unmistakable as it was universal, and the pinched lips pressed upon Clemency's cheeks.

"Child!" The voice was low and husky, surprisingly vibrant in such a blanched woman.

"Mother." Clem hugged her back, awkward and tense, then stepped away a little. "I have brought my dear friend, Companier Major Sarah Solomon of the Seventh Brigade, and Hebron Below, with me."

Hostile green eyes examined Sarah while she tried to puzzle out the meaning of Clem's words. What was this Hebron Below stuff? The Ugenia extended a mitted hand, and surprisingly warm fingers touched her palm. "Welcome to Delfheim, Major Solomon. It is, to be sure, some honor to meet you. Clemency-child has written of you in her rare missives, and I have never before encountered a Sabre, to be sure."

"It is a privilege to come into your domicile, Ugenia, and to meet you." She returned the handshake firmly while she tried to shake the sensation she was lost in Wonderland. *Sabre?* Sarah felt like some exotic in a zoo—a giraffe, perhaps, or a Venerian air jelly—until she realized that the Ugenia was corrupting the word *sabra,* the old name for those born in Israel after the Return. It was not a reference to her military occupation, even though it sounded like one. She longed for a large Marsport whiskey and soda to cool her tongue. "Clemency has often spoken to me of you."

"None of it favorable, I should wager," the Ugenia replied tartly, giving her daughter a glance. Sarah felt her cheeks heat with blush. "At her age, I was none too kind to my mother, though I was always obedient to her wishes. I never went against her. Curious, is it not, that we can determine how the very stars were born, yet we cannot understand why mothers and daughters are always at odds. But, come. There is tea ready in the parlor, and I have prepared a few of Clemency's favorite treats. I hope you enjoy chocolate." She released her grip on Sarah's hand as if suddenly conscious she had held it overlong.

"I never ate it before I knew Clemency, but now I enjoy it very much." This was a polite half-truth, for she found chocolate more sweet than she liked while Clem was positively greedy for the stuff.

"Never ate it? Is it a forbidden food?"

"No, Ugenia, merely uncommon." Sarah could feel Clem watching her, measuring the warmth of that first encounter warily. They followed their hostess down the dim corridor and into a huge chamber filled with patterned rugs, upholstered furniture, and what seemed to be dozens of large paintings in ornate frames upon the dull white walls.

There was too much color, too much pattern, Sarah decided as she wondered where she was supposed to sit. The room was chilly too, after her brisk walk. The sweat could not evaporate under the breathless textile of her uniform, leaving her body clammy and grubby-feeling, longing for the chance to wash her hands and face and get into something less constricting than her uniform. She gazed at the furnishings. It seemed to her as if the room was an attempt to warm an environment made cold by the icy character of Clemency's mother.

Sarah decided she was being overimaginative, and she picked a large chair, then glanced at Clem for a clue as to what was proper manners. Her lover folded into a small settee, stark gray against a rich brocade of rose and turquoise. The mother was already seated across from the daughter, as if they were adversaries, fussing with cups and small china plates and vessels of tea and coffee and hot chocolate. There was food spread on the table between them; an excess of food, like the room itself. She sat down and looked at the platters of dainty cakes, cookies, shaped sandwiches, trembling jellies, and wondered who else was coming.

The Ugenia picked up a cup and looked at Sarah. "Do you prefer coffee, tea, or chocolate, Major Solomon?"

"Coffee would be wonderful, thank you." The smell of it tantalized her taste buds, bringing with it memories of demitasse cups brimming with steaming *café au Turc* in the souks of Jerusalem during her student days. Homesickness rose in her throat, a yearning for the sounds of children laughing and camels braying and merchants chanting their wares beneath a blazing sun. They served simple cakes, made of honey and flour and ground walnuts, with the thick coffee, or fragrant mint tea. The canvas walls of the booths smelled of spices and dust. *I am more tired than I thought.*

Sarah took her coffee, tasted it, and found it delicious after months of shipboard brew. Clem accepted steaming chocolate, mild greed gleaming in her green eyes, and the Ugenia poured herself a cup of pungent tea, primming her lips above the rim of a porcelain cup so thin the light shone through it. The three women drank in strained silence. Plates of tiny sandwiches were passed, the crusts of the bread trimmed away. The fillings were fish or ham, and Sarah let herself taste it, eating slowly. After months of eating in the mess, her tongue was nearly in ecstasy.

"Tell me, Major, just why you have chosen such an unnatural career?"

Concealing her startlement at the suddenness and bluntness of the question, Sarah nearly choked on her mouthful. "Unnatural, Ugenia?" Clem looked at her over the rim of her cup, and Sarah could see her eyes were alight with some unknown mischief. Suddenly she felt like a mouse between two cats, both of them wanting to bat her with clawed paws.

"Certainly. It is entirely unnatural for a female to engage in matters martial, and, I would have thought, even more so for one of your people. Everyone knows the Hebrews were never good fighters."

Sarah blinked at this remarkable generalization, and wondered if the Ugenia was being rude deliberately, or was just too insular to realize what she had said. She studied her adversary, measuring her, refusing to be rushed into a hasty reply. "Our history is one of conflict, Ugenia, and we have fought for thousands of years. We have our military heroes, and our heroines as well, from Judith and Shoshona to General Miriam bat Judah during the Second Bio-War. It is part of my heritage."

The Ugenia frowned, a deep crease furrowing the hairless brow above the hard, green eyes. The agelessness of her appearance vanished, and she looked decades older in a moment. It was clear she had not anticipated argument, that she was used to having her pronouncements accepted without question.

"But, surely, a woman's place is in the home, not dashing around with her head shaved and full of . . . things." A white-mitted hand gestured at the helmet inputs that gleamed on Clemency's foreskull, a speaking motion of genuine distress and a certain bewilderment. It made her seem less imposing and more human, though Sarah could see it infuriated Clemency.

"That is a matter of culture, Ugenia, not one of gender," she answered, as if she were speaking to one of her teachers. "We are an aggressive species, and while we have tried any number of experiments over the centuries to eliminate that trait, it persists in spite of everything. One is forced to conclude that as we are created in the likeness of the Lord, such behaviors must be inherent in our Maker as well." She struggled to keep her voice even and her words as objective as possible while she raged silently for her lover's sake.

"I believe you must be mistaken. Gender has everything to do with it. No natural mother wishes anything but that her daughters become mothers themselves. You, of course, must bear them . . . but you are a planetary and cannot help such things." The Ugenia shuddered slightly, as if she had said something obscene. "If the women go off and fight in battles, what will happen to the next generation?"

"It will muddle along, I suppose, the way it always has."

"Muddle along!" The Ugenia was outraged. "That is the most ridiculous thing I have ever heard. We cannot permit things to muddle . . . what a dreadful word. Control must be maintained at all times. Otherwise there will be disorder—chaos!" Grace ten Boora gripped the thin saucer between her fingers tightly, her voice rising almost hysterically while Clemency stared in dismay. There was a sharp snapping sound. The delicate porcelain cracked, and the edges cut into the pale pink fingers. Drops of blood followed a spill of tea that cascaded down onto the shining whiteness of the Ugenia's aproned lap. She released a cry of pain that seemed to slip down the dreadful whiteness of the dull walls.

The Ugenia rose, hitting one of her knees against the edge of the table and sending pots falling and dishes cascading onto the floor. Her apron dripped tea and her fingers dripped bright blood onto the beautiful carpet, while she glared at her daughter. "This is your fault, you wretched, willful child! I hope you are proud of yourself!" Then she whipped out of the room, her bleeding fingers bound in her ruined apron, her long white skirts fluttering. There was a moment of stunned silence, and then Clemency began to weep.

It was a terrible crying, a lost child's crying, and Sarah set her cup aside and moved over to the settee beside her lover. She had never seen Clem cry before, not for comrades fallen in battle or slain in the outer chambers because they were too injured. The weeping, hopeless and broken-hearted, frightened her as she drew Clem's head across her breast, as she stroked the crisp, curling red hair across the back of Clem's skull. She tried to comfort her beloved, and felt helpless. After a second she realized she could do nothing but rock a heartbroken woman nearly a foot taller than herself, an awkward bundle of anguish and grief.

After a time, a long and timeless time, the storm abated, and Clem groped a long-fingered hand toward the wreck of the tea table, snagging a fine, linen napkin between them and blowing her long nose deeply. "Why can't she let me be who I am?" Then she was off again, sobbing deep in her chest, clutching Sarah so tightly that breathing was difficult, raging and crying all at the same time. Incoherent phrases tumbled out between fresh downpours, reducing Sarah to feeble "There, theres" while her heart ached.

Clemency lifted her head away from Sarah's shoulder, flung away the sodden mass of napkin in her hand, and reached for another. "All I ever wanted was for her to be proud of me for who I was, and to hang a flambeau in the window. Is that so much?"

"It is not very much to ask, Clem, but it may be more than your mother can give." Clem leaned back, slid down ungracefully, and rested her head against Sarah's shoulder. Sarah put an arm around her gently.

"You sound like you are on her side," Clemency complained, her voice husky with tears.

"Side? No, I am not taking anyone's side. I just see there are two viewpoints—at least—in here."

"I really, really hate it when you are all logical!"

"I know, beloved. And I am only logical to irritate you. I lie awake nights, planning things to be logical about, because I know how annoying it is."

"You do not! You ravish me and sleep like the dead, if the dead snore like pigs."

"All a façade. The snoring covers the sound of my brains being logical."

Clemency laughed, then sighed profoundly. "I never could be what she wanted. I always got dirt on my aprons and tore my mitts. I never wore my corsets, or I laced them so loosely it hardly mattered."

"Corsets? You wore corsets?"

"Of course. It is all set down in the Rule."

"The Rule?" Sarah had a sense of the surreal, as if she had moved into a dreamscape without warning. She didn't remember any mention of any Rule in her previous conversations with Clemency.

"The Founder set it down—how a woman has to dress, right down to the knickers, and how many skirts she can possess, where her kerchief has to rest along her brow—everything is in the Rule."

"And here I thought we Jews had a corner on that sort of thing."

"No one discusses it, and we do not dress like that outside the hamlets, but the hamlets are most of the colony. It is supposed to keep us properly humble until the Winnowing. The Founder believed a tightly laced corset kept a woman's natural lasciviousness in check."

Sarah held back a grin with difficulty. "I can see how it might—what with not being able to breathe and all. I just don't quite understand the why of it, I guess."

"Sex and aggression have one and the same cause," Clem answered matter-of-factly.

"Now I am really lost," Sarah replied, stretching her legs and wishing she could get out of her uniform and boots. To hell with corsets—the Founder never knew about service uniforms!

"The desire for sex makes men aggressive and women lustful. Celibacy is the only possible way to avoid that. But, since you have to have children to continue the breeding program, the Founder invented the vats and creches. Ovum and sperm are frozen and crossed and a bunch of stuff they told me in school that I did not pay any attention to and do not really understand. The vats did not stop the early colonists from being a pretty horny lot, though—they had come up here to create supermen, after all—so the Founder just made celibacy mandatory, and wrote the Rule to enforce it."

Sarah took a minute to digest these revelations. "If I were of a legalistic bent, I'd say that was a great, big human rights violation under the Confederation Charter, Clem." She did not add that it sounded totally crazy and impossible to enforce, remembering she was a guest.

"Probably, but since Delfheim is closed to outsiders, who is to know? Besides, it is voluntary."

"Huh? If there is this Rule, how can it be voluntary?"

"Now you are being logical again! We voluntarily accept mandatory celibacy—see?" Clem sounded positively gleeful as she spoke.

Sarah sat in stunned silence for a moment. "That is a piece of hairsplitting worthy of a rabbinical court. Did you go into the service to get out of . . ."

"Oh, no. I knew about the Outers, and all I have ever wanted to do was fight them. Since I was seven or eight, at least. I am smart enough to have gone to the university, but you know I am not what you would call scholarly, like your uncle Benjamin or your cousin Miriam. I never wanted to be an Improver or an Enhancer."

"But, surely your university has more than eugenics to offer." The more she heard the more confused Sarah was becoming.

"It has an excellent department of political studies, I believe, and some physics classes."

"But, what about art and music and literature, history and religion and . . ."

"All those subjects were too sexy for the Founder, Sarah. Name me three Ugene artists of any kind. Go ahead."

Sarah thought and could not name even one. She had just never thought about it before—who thought about art when the species was under siege? "All this?" She gestured at the paintings on the walls.

"All pre-twentieth century and all covered in the Rule."

"Let me see if I understand this," Sarah said slowly. "You aren't allowed to have sex, so you won't be aggressive, so you won't go to war or compete. You don't create art or music because those might arouse strong emotions, but you can get involved in Confederacy politics to the extent of nearly persuading us not to defend itself against the Outers, to risk wiping out the species."

"Well, not the species, Sarah. Just those who are not Ugenes."

"That is completely insane."

"You do not believe me?" Clem stiffened under her touch.

"No, I do believe you, and it will likely haunt me until I die. Everyone in the Solar System thinks the Ugenes are morally and intellectually superior to all us planetary sorts, and no one would believe me if I said otherwise."

"I told you we had a good political studies department at the university," Clem answered, as if that explained everything. Sarah let the tension begin to leave her body, now that Clemency was calm and her usual playful self. To her surprise, she also found she was a little disappointed. She had thought the Ugenes were special, and instead they turned out to be just another human culture with strange customs. The Founder might have set out to create a model society, but it sounded as if all he had done was make a terribly oppressive one.

"Clem, your mother is a product of her upbringing, and you cannot really expect her to be a rebel just because you are."

"I know that, and I know she cares for me as much as she can. But I want her to see that fighting for what is important to me is not unnatural or even rebellious. She does not seem to be able to understand that this is not about being a woman, or being a Ugene, but about doing what I believe is right. I want her to respect what I am doing, and to hang out a flambeau for me."

"And if she can't?"

"Then I just have to try harder to make her understand."

"Sometimes, Clem, trying harder doesn't make any difference." She wanted to protect her lover from what she believed was an inevitable disappointment.

Clem rolled her head over against Sarah's breast. "I know, but I just want it so much." Behind her, Sarah heard a faint rustle of cloth and wondered how long the listener had been there. Then Clemency started crying again, softly now, and she heard the careful withdrawal of the eavesdropper, and knew they were alone once again.

The three women sat down together for the evening meal. The Ugenia wore a fresh white dress and apron, new mitts. Two fingers were hidden in a bandage. She presided over a table nearly moaning at the weight of the food and polished silver adornments it bore. There were branching candelabra without candles, vases of flowers, plates of roasted meats, several types of vegetables, rice, potatoes, and some sort of pancake. The meal began with a heavy soup, which Sarah thought would have been sufficient in itself, and ended with rich coffee and several desserts. When had the Ugenia found time to prepare it—or were there servants hidden in the back of the house? Did the Ugenes have servants? Sarah was exhausted from the questions.

Clemency had decided to sulk, and her mother to pretend that nothing of the sort was occurring, so the weight of conversation fell on Sarah's unwilling if capable shoulders. She tried to introduce several neutral topics, only to be balked by stubborn pouting from Clem, and a studied indifference from the Ugenia.

At last her patience wore thin, and she said, "Don't think this isn't a delightful dinner, because it isn't!" Two pairs of green eyes looked at her, astonished. "Food is sacred, and to consume it like this, with bad feelings, is very disrespectful." She swallowed a grin, hearing her own mother speaking through her, words she never thought to hear herself say.

"Sacred? What a curious thing to say," the Ugenia answered, interested in spite of herself. "It is merely calories, energy to live on."

"Not to me. Among my people, food is a gift to be honored."

"Honored? How can you honor a potato?"

"The same way you honor any living thing—by giving attention and realizing what you are doing. And by talking and even laughing occasionally."

"What a quaint notion," Grace ten Boora replied.

Clemency came out of her silence suddenly, perking up and leaning her shaven head forward like some strange terrapin. "There was this dinner we had while I was in training, where we could not figure out what the meat was. It was awful, tough and funny-tasting, and we all got into trying to think of the most outrageous animal it might be. One guy said it was defrosted mammoth, and Martin Ibote—you remember him, Sarah—said octopus marinated in pickle brine, but Dawn Simpkin bested us. She cut off this tiny piece, chewed it for about five minutes, until we were all just transfixed, staring at her, and then said, 'Belter.' We all thought she had lost her mind. Then she nodded and added, 'Yes, definitely Belter, probably Hidalgan, born in forty-seven on the south slopes, during a meteor shower. The toughest Belters are born during meteor showers.' By this time even the Belter recruits were laughing too hard to start a food fight—though I never ate anything that more deserved to be flung instead of eaten in my life."

Sarah laughed, and the Ugenia seemed to unbend just a fraction. Then she remembered herself and said repressively, "I find laughing about cannibalism in extremely poor taste, Clemency-child."

"My dear mother, this stuff was beyond bad taste, and we had to eat it, or our sergeant would have disciplined us."

"Disciplined you? You mean he would have . . . struck you, a Ugene?" She was plainly shocked at the idea.

"No. I mean *she* would have made us take a second helping."

The Ugenia laughed at that, looked quite startled, and hid her mouth quickly behind her napkin. Clem pretended not to have heard her but gave Sarah a glance of amusement and affection as she reached for another pancake. Sarah chewed some rather overcooked carrots and watched her hostess's struggle from beneath her long, dark lashes. She guessed that laughter wasn't encouraged at Ugene tables, or anywhere else. Maybe it was against the Rule, or just uncomfortable in a corset.

Recovering her dignity, the Ugenia lowered her napkin and said, "We do not indulge in foolishness here. I will thank you to remember that."

Clemency gave a groan, a comic groan, accompanied by a rolling of eyes that nearly overset Sarah completely. "How can I forget? I was never serious enough for you, or any of my teachers. You would think, after all we have learned about genetics, that the Improvers would at least have discovered where the humor chromosome was, and taken it out or something. The thing has gotten me into trouble all my life—much of it very enjoyable, which, of course, is not at all proper."

"Life is a very serious business," the Ugenia replied, though she sounded less than convinced.

"Yes, but why does serious come out meaning stuffy and pompous and just plain no fun at all?"

"The Founder . . ."

"Spare me the maunderings of the Founder. He is dead. He has been dead for decades. He was not God, even if he wished he were, and we can't go on trying to believe his nonsense as if it were Holy Writ. The rest of the system is evolving and leaving us—"

"What the rest of the Solar System is about has nothing to do with Delfheim."

"Mother, do you actually believe that, or are you saying it because you think you ought?"

"Do not behave provocatively, Clemency-child!" The Ugenia turned to Sarah. "She always says outrageous things when she desires attention. You must ignore her, for it just encourages her to behave badly if you notice." It was the appeal of one adult to another, as if Clem were six, not thirty-six.

"And you always infantilize me, so you will not have to listen to what I say." Clemency was angry, but in control of herself. Sarah held back a shudder—she hated this sort of thing.

"When you have a daughter of your own, you may understand more fully."

"Mother, dear, I am not going to have a daughter, or a son, or a pink kitten. You must realize that. Not here, not in Delfheim. The Improvers would be terrified that my plasm could contaminate the fucking vats!"

The Ugenia looked prim and pained. "There is no need to be vulgar." She drew herself a little straighter. "I am not without a certain influence. Your actions, your behavior, has been a youthful indiscretion, a small aberration, which will be overlooked when you come back."

"Mother, I hardly think that sixteen years of service in the Confederate Infantry can be termed a youthful indiscretion—even if you possessed the influence of a vander Grif."

"You must have children. What are you without them?"

"Culled," Clemency answered coldly, her merriment gone.

"Our line—"

"Will not be there in the Final Days. I never believed that, even when I was young and stupid."

The Ugenia looked stricken, old and bone weary. "Why are you so cruel to me? Why can you not be good and dutiful like other daughters? Why are you not here, at home, doing your proper duties?"

"I am doing my duty—serving humanity, not this elite, suffocating backwater of fools who imagine they are superior." Clem was savage now.

The Ugenia ignored her, rushing on earnestly. "The Outers are the Winnowing promised by the Founder. They are here to sort everything out, that we might begin anew, without the dreadful impediment of the planetary races." Sarah had never felt more invisible in her life, and it made her seethe.

"Try believing that when the buggers start ripping the locks away and swarming through the hamlets. I have seen them, Mother, and they are totally indifferent to whether I am a Ugene or a planetary. We cannot communicate with them, know almost nothing about them except they are hostile and aggressive and seem bent on sending humankind into oblivion. I am fighting to defend you, damn you, and all the rest of the people in this tin can we call Delfheim. Why is it so hard for you to understand that?"

"You are the one who does not understand, Clemency. We have no need to be defended. We are superior. You are acting very regressively, like the willful child you always were. Aggression solves nothing. War solves nothing. I am so ashamed of you sometimes. I cannot even leave the house. What must the neighbors think?"

"I saw a flambeau in the de Groots' window, so I imagine they would think I was doing the right thing. And in the Rickenstats' window I saw another. You act as if I am the only Ugene in the service."

"Clemency-child, their children are not fighting. They are officers or medics or . . ."

"Dirck Rickenstat was in the Third Brigade as a Cominf the last time I saw him. That was on Io, I think, at Mukeerji's Salon and Chai House."

"Cominf?" The Ugenia was totally lost.

"A Combatant Inferior, which is the same as Clemency," Sarah answered before her lover could explode.

"You must be mistaken. I am certain Ugenia Rickenstat told me he was some sort of officer."

"The Cominf heads a troop of from ten to twenty combatants, but is not an officer. They have no command authority," Sarah continued more calmly than she felt, "but only the task of overseeing the positioning, if any, of the members of their team. Against the Outers, positioning is of little use. They do not have any consistent form of combat against which we can plan. We just don't understand how they function. Confederation Command is divided as to whether they have individual intelligence, or a hive mind. There are even some who hold we are not fighting an intelligent species at all, but something more like a virus. All we are certain of, after these decades, is that they are hostile to any life-form they encounter, animal or vegetable. They will attack a grove of Mars gum trees with the same singleness of purpose as a town of humans, Ugenia."

The older woman looked very uncomfortable. "You must be mistaken."

"No," Sarah answered.

"Mother, why is it so difficult for you to believe that someone other than a Ugene can know up from down?"

The Ugenia stiffened once more. "I believe only that the Founder was correct, that we are chosen, superior, and that the planetary populations are corrupt and must be entirely removed for the good of humanity." The major was chilled by these words, spoken as if she could not hear them or understand them.

"What arrogance!" Clemency blazed with fury, and Sarah warmed as she spoke. "I cannot believe that every time I suit up and go out the lock I am defending anyone so self-righteous and just damn stupid as you are!" With that she stood up, slapped her napkin down on the linen-clad table, and stormed out of the dining room, her boots ringing against the floor.

The Ugenia sat, silent, still, and a little woebegone, her mitted hands folded in her aproned lap. "Why cannot she see that she is wrong?" she asked Sarah after a time.

"What if she is correct?"

"Then my entire life has been a lie, Major Solomon." The proud head bent a little, a human movement with nothing superior about it. "I do not know if I can bear that."

The hush in Disembarkation was disquieting. The major could not remember ever hearing the room so still at the close of an engagement, the clerks so white-faced beneath the greenish gleam of the lights. There was a continuous chitinous clicking of small keyboards, the ragged intake of anxious breaths as data was displayed and absorbed, the occasional scrape of boot against metal floor, but nothing of the usual quiet banter.

The major knew things were going very badly. She had gotten reports from officers on other ships all afternoon, and they were all offering up frightening numbers of casualties, both on the ground and in the locks. They had assaulted a huge complex of Outer nests in the tunnels beneath the remains of what had once been the bustling commercial city of Europolis, six Companies against an unknown number of aliens. It was the largest battle in nearly a decade, with more troops pouring in as fast as Command could bring them.

On the viewscreens, laserlight made the rubble below almost as bright as day as thousands of Combatants had burned their way into the arena. The heat had fused the solid rock into glass in the tunnels, making the footing treacherous for even the oldest and best-equipped fighters. The tunnels collapsed in places, killing trooper and foe without regard. And still Command sent in fresh fighters.

Sarah ignored her dry mouth, the stink of nervous sweat that swirled out from everyone waiting for the locks to cycle through, and the faint subvocalization of clerks muttering into their implanted headsets. She refused to imagine what was occurring on the other side of the heavy metal doors. Instead, she prayed, silently and fervently, to a god she had not petitioned in a very long time. She did not ask that Clemency be returned to her unharmed, but only that her troopers be safe. She knew she was dissembling, but she hoped that any listening deity would forgive her. The collar of her combat grays was a noose about her throat, and the shoulders of her uniform seemed suddenly to shrunk several sizes, so she felt constricted and suffocated.

The doors rolled away at last, and the stench of decontaminant bellied into the chamber. Beneath it was the smell of blood and bowel and singed flesh, and the hot, red scent of the crematory ovens. Clusters of shaven heads unhelmed, gleaming with implant nodes. They surged and swirled into the enormous chamber, the faces sickly pale. The major swept her eyes across the arrivals, seeing how few they were. The absence of one particular combatant, one beloved face, one tall, slender body made the breath still in her chest for a moment. Then the doors crashed closed again.

"Report," she told her clerk without looking at him.

"Ground casualties thirty one percent, Companier, and another twenty percent were graced." Matteo's voice was choked with a rage she had never heard in it before, and she gave him a glance. He tugged a flimsy out of his slate, his stubby fingers trembling. She could see he was blinking back tears, and she wished she could join him. "Command sends congratulations on a successful mission. Our companies have distinguished themselves, and the enemy has been cleared from the arena." He extended the sheet of flim toward her, struggling to keep his control.

"Very good, Matteo. The Combatants must be exhausted. Sound the dismissal to quarters."

"Yes, Companier Major," he answered as she accepted the rustling page. He crossed his heart with one hand in a salute, then struck the key that sounded the soft chimes of discharge.

Sarah just stood, holding the flim, and listened to the ringing tone. Somehow she had never before noticed how closely the sound resembled the tolling of a bell. She watched the troopers stagger away and wondered how they felt, if they experienced any sense of having distinguished themselves, or whether they were only tired and despaired of their fallen comrades.

Knowing she was delaying the inevitable, Sarah held up the flim, scanning first the list of those wounded who had been taken to Medivac. The brevity of that list, more than anything else, informed her of the losses, and the name she sought was not there. Then she looked at the names of those who had perished in the tunnels, facing the Outers, whose corpses lay mingled with dead foes piled among them, to mummify in the cold between the worlds.

Finally she made herself look at the names of those whose ashes already rested in modest Service-issue containers, metal boxes emblazoned with a dancing flame and graven with a plaque. There would be shelves of them in the mortuary, awaiting transport to grieving families millions of miles away. The words *ten Boora* seemed to jump out at her, and she closed her eyes against the pain. Then she opened them again, and read the entire list of those who had tasted the swift mercy of the Graciers' thrust. If one name was a personal loss, there were still two hundred others to mourn, men and women she had eaten with, drunk with, and grieved with after other campaigns. She saw the name of Matteo's lover among the graced, and turned to express her condolence.

Before she could speak, the little clerk said, "We should bury our dead, not burn them. It is bad enough we kill them ourselves!" He ground his teeth and looked at her in defiance. "I really do not give a flying fuck if you put me on report for criticizing Command policy, Major. I had to say it!"

"Did you say something, Matteo?" she asked blandly. "I really cannot hear myself think in all this racket." The room was nearly silent except for the rumble of the ship's engines and the strained voices of the several clerks and officers who remained.

"No, not a thing, Major." He saluted again, more smartly this time, and turned away.

"Major?"

Sarah turned and found herself facing Companier Stratigique Cecil Monrovia, her immediate superior. "Yes, sir!" How comforting it was to have the structures of duty to fall back upon.

"I picked up this bottle of real single malt on my last *arandar,* and I would be honored if you'd help me to dispose of it before it goes off." His skin was ebony, sheened with sweat, and the sclera of his eyes gleamed like the ivory of the elephants that had once walked the plains of his homeland. He had the stilted accents of the Africanier, but his deep voice bespoke the sympathy that custom prevented him from speaking on duty or off.

Sarah wished no more than to be alone with her pain, to mourn Clemency until she was empty. More, she wanted to sit *shivah* for her lover, and she knew that was a luxury the Service would neither grant her, nor approve of. So, she must take her comfort where she could. They would get drunk together, and no names would pass their lips. On the morrow they would send more troopers out, would repeat the whole, sad routine again. She could not bear to think of tomorrow.

"It would be a crime to let a single malt go to waste, sir, so I accept with pleasure," she said, lying and knowing it.

The major, dressed in her regimentals, stepped through the lock doors of Delfheim and into the village where she and Clemency had passed but a few months before. She was surprised to find herself there, and even more surprised that Clemency had arranged for her to be able to enter the restricted colony. It gave her the feeling she had not known her lover at all.

She carried the little metal box emblazoned with a flickering flame under one arm, her duffle slung over the other shoulder, and she was tired to the bone. Sarah did not want to be there, but she didn't want to be anywhere, not even home in Hebron. She still carried out her duties efficiently, saw to her troopers as if nothing had happened, but inside she felt so hollow that sometimes she wanted to scream her throat raw. How she had gotten through the last few months she didn't know, and now, here she was, in the last place in the system she had ever thought to be, returning to Delfheim with the ashes of her beloved.

The swept cobbles were uneven beneath her feet, and the smells of pigs and plants and manure swirled in the light breeze that brushed her cheeks. Sarah got curious glances as she passed, from white-kerchiefed women and men idling over their long pipes and cups of coffee, curious and even hostile. She ignored them as much as she could.

The journey from the lock to the ten Boora house was both too long and too brief. Sarah did not really want to see the Ugenia again. She wanted, she realized, to see instead her own mother, her aunts and uncles, sisters and nieces. Most of all she wished she could see her brother, David. He always understood how she felt, even when she didn't herself.

She stood at the heavy wooden door for several minutes, listening to the sounds of the birds and smelling the sharp, spicy odor of carnations blooming beneath the wide windows across the front of the house. Finally she knocked, and the door swung open so quickly she knew that Clemency's mother had been standing in the foyer, waiting, listening.

The Ugenia, white garbed and straight-backed, looked down at her. She seemed unchanged from the previous encounter, remote and confined within the Rule. Sarah felt a rage knot her belly, but she swallowed it, remembering she was still a guest, a stranger in a strange land. The long reach of the Ugenes had been powerful enough to bring her here, and she did not want to discover what else they could do in her life.

"I've brought Clemency home," she announced brutally, her voice sounding like a crow's rough caw in her ears.

"Yes." The Ugenia turned away and moved across the entry, leading Sarah once again into the over-colored parlor. The table was set out with silver and fine porcelain, and the chill room smelled of coffee and chocolate. There were not quite so many dishes as before, but otherwise it seemed the same. Perhaps the Rule prevented change.

Taking a seat, the major let the silence remain between them while the Ugenia poured coffee without asking. They were entirely strangers now that Clemency was gone, and Sarah wondered how she was going to endure the time she would be there. Why had Clem arranged matters so that Sarah not only had to take her ashes personally, but bring them back to Delfheim? If she was so adept at arrangement, why couldn't she have managed not to get so injured that she had to die by the Graciers' knife? Why did she have to return to this chill house and this woman of ice pouring coffee into fragile vessels of clay?

"When she was a girl, refusing to wear her corsets and soiling her mitts, I never imagined outliving my daughter, Major."

The Ugenia's words startled Sarah out of her futile musings and brought her back to the present. "I suppose no parent ever guesses how their children's lives will turn out, Ugenia. They just think that the children will have happy lives and give them grandchildren to dote upon someday."

"Are you going to give your mother a grandchild?"

"I have two sisters, and I have left that to them, and to my brother, David. My nieces and one nephew are already in their teens."

"But, surely, as a woman, you must desire a child of your own!"

Sarah stirred her coffee, listening to the click of metal on porcelain. "I cannot recall ever having had that yearning."

"I see. You are willful, like Clemency."

"Wilful? I don't think so." Once more she had the sensation of being adrift in some Wonderland, of not understanding half of what was being said. "My parents did not expect me to live their lives, only my own, so long as I did it as well as I am able. My choice not to have children does not trouble them so far as I know."

"You must be mistaken. Your mother has four children—a shocking number, to be sure—so she must expect you to follow in her footsteps and do rightly. Clemency would be alive now if she had done rightly instead of being disobedient and willful."

"My mother has the wisdom to know I am not her, Ugenia!" Sarah wanted to shake the other woman, to make her see something she had no words for.

"Why are you not?" The sudden venom in the words was utterly shocking, as if some control had slipped away.

Sarah stared at Grace ten Boora and saw the struggle for breath beneath the encasing garments. She saw the tremor of hands and the flush of rose across the sculptured cheekbones. "I am myself, not another."

"Yes. For a moment I forgot you only happened, that you are only a planetary. But Clemency was not like you. She was planned. She was selected. She was supposed to be like me, just like me, in every detail. But she never was. Clemency was never good."

"Clem was possibly the finest person I have ever known," Sarah almost shouted. "She was brave and loyal and loving. She performed her duties with distinction, and her comrades in arms respected and admired her. New recruits took her as a model, and more experienced troopers gave her exemplary marks." *And I loved her as much as life itself, you old witch!*

"Pah! She robbed me of a daughter, of a child, and she ended our line. She disgraced me!"

"That is the most selfish and narcissistic thing I have ever heard," Sarah answered viciously, no longer caring if she was rude.

"She was all I had!"

Sarah closed her eyes against her own pain. *Clem was all I had too,* she wanted to say. *I don't know how I will bear it without her joy in life. Damn you, Clem, for making me come here. We cannot communicate, your mother and I. We are too far apart. Why did you make me come here? Damn the Founder and damn all the Ugenes for a bunch of regressive idiots. I'd rather be talking to a Hassid!* This last thought, arising without warning, made her laugh a little in spite of herself.

"You still have yourself, and, I assume, Clemency's father." Somehow this man had never been mentioned, but Sarah had assumed it was some Ugene custom and never asked.

The Ugenia reared back, and Sarah was certain she had violated some taboo. "Valiant?" Grace ten Boora laughed without merriment, a cold, bitter laugh tinged with ancient rage. "Oh, to be sure, I have Valiant von Blitzenburg!" She jabbed a mitted hand toward the fireplace, pointed a shaking finger at a plain white jar between two charming porcelain figures. "He fell at the Second Battle of Titania and returned in a box identical to the one beside you. He had no right! Neither of them had any right to fight, or to leave me!"

Sarah lifted her heavy eyebrows, widened her eyes in surprise. "Did Clemency know that?" It would explain so many things that Sarah still found puzzling.

"Certainly not!" The Ugenia made a moue of distaste, then sipped at her cup, sitting, if possible, even straighter in her chair. "I never spoke of it, and it is not known by anyone besides myself and the Board of Improvers. They were very reluctant to allow me a child at all—such shame I have borne—and only awarded me a daughter because of my own wealth of Founder genes."

"Oh, I see." She didn't see at all, and felt more lost with each fresh revelation. So she drank some coffee and wondered how the Ugenia managed to sustain her stubborn ignorance, how she failed to realize that Clemency's willfulness was as much from her as from any other source. This woman was strong, fierce, and quite unyielding—a fighter in a war with war. She was an idealist, Sarah decided, and felt a sickening empathy, for even in her wrongheadedness, she was rather magnificant. The grudging admiration she felt annoyed her more than she liked. "I am truly sorry you lost your daughter as well as your spouse, Ugenia, but that is how human history often works itself out."

"I care nothing for history, human or otherwise, Major Solomon. It has always seemed to me a mere justification for repeating the mistakes of the past."

Sarah gave a little laugh, and was rewarded with a fierce glare. "You and Clemency are very alike."

"She was nothing like me, else she would be alive and properly dressed, instead of coming back to me in a box. How can I love a heap of ashes? What good are those?"

Sarah drew a long breath. "You are alike in that you are both utterly selfish and entirely devoted to what you believe in." The words cost her more than she could measure, but she knew she was right.

The Ugenia began to reply angrily, then picked up a cookie and dunked it into her tea. "Selfish?" She said the word slowly, after she finished chewing, as if she had never heard it before. "No one has told me that since Valiant—and that was almost half a century ago. Perhaps I am. Perhaps I have had to be, to survive. You cannot know what it is like to be alone, to endure empty days and years with an absent husband and a daughter who despised me."

"Clem didn't despise you. But I think you were too much alike to get along easily. We always dislike in others what is worst in ourselves, don't you think?"

"Umm." She reached for another cookie. "Why could Clemency not have been like you? I do not know you well, but I think you are a good sort of daughter."

"But, Ugenia, Clemency could only be like herself. We can only be ourselves. There is a story we have, about a rabbi in Warsaw or Cracow, centuries ago. One morning this rabbi—I have forgotten his name, so I will call him Avram—came rushing down to his students. He had had a marvelous dream, he said. He had dreamed he died and stood before the Throne of the Lord, ready to be judged and found wanting."

"Why wanting?" The Ugenia dunked her cookie, curious in spite of herself, unbending by slow degrees.

"We Jews are perfectionists, and we always think we are not quite good enough. It is our curse and our saving grace. So, Rabbi Avram waited there, ready to hear that he had failed because he had not been enough like Moses or Joshua or someone. Very anxious he was, for he was a decent, humble man and he loved the Lord with all his being. When the Lord spoke, he was most gentle and only asked why the rabbi had not been more his own self, more Avram, not more like Moses."

The Ugenia picked up a little sandwich and nibbled at it thoughtfully. "Why?"

Sarah sighed, wondering if she could ever bridge the enormous cultural gulf that stood between them. "The Lord made him to be Avram, not Moses."

"We Ugenes are made to be like the Founder."

"But that is impossible."

"Impossible?"

"The Founder is dead a long time, and you can only guess how he would be today. He was a man, from a time and a place in the past—a historic person. He did not escape history by creating Delfheim. And the Ugenes remain enmeshed in history, no matter how they struggle to escape it. It will not go away because you wish it. Clemency knew that, not intellectually, but in her bones. And she did not want history to end. So she fought. She loved it. It gave her great delight to face the Outers, directly; made her feel alive, she said. She cared passionately for what she was defending—which in the end was always you, Ugenia." Sarah was so weary now, aching with repressed sorrow, heartsick for Clem, for herself, and for the bewildered woman across from her.

The Ugenia put her cup down and pleated the edge of her apron with restless fingers. "I see. I do wish you were my daughter—well, not precisely. But I see things when you speak that I have never seen before. Disturbing things. I find them interesting. And something else. You do not make me feel mean and ugly. Clemency-child did, somehow. If only you were a Ugene!"

Sarah laughed, in spite of her exhaustion. "Now, there is a thought that would make your Founder rotate in his tomb, Ugenia."

Her hostess broke into a wide smile that rose all the way to her green eyes. In that moment, her likeness to Clemency was so great the major nearly wept. She had loved Clem's smile. "Yes, Sarah-child, it would. How wicked of me—and how delightful to be wicked!"

The endearment caught her completely off guard, and she found the tears she had held back since Clemency's death streaming down her cheeks, cold against her skin. There was a flutter of fine cloth, a waft of lavendar, and she was crushed in a fierce embrace, pressed against starched fabric, and rocked tenderly. She sobbed against the corset-shielded breast of the Ugenia and felt the stroke of hands upon her dark hair.

When, at last, the first storm of grief was past, Sarah found herself reflecting rather wryly that there were always tears at the tea table here. It was probably forbidden somewhere in the Rule. She wiped her cheeks with her fingers, and snuffled noisily.

The Ugenia handed her a rather crumbled square of linen edged with lace. "Could you find it in your heart to be my child now, just a little? It would mean such a great deal."

The major caught her breath, blew her nose, and nodded helplessly. Fresh tears prevented her from speaking, and after a moment, she stopped trying. It was not fair that she should receive what Clemency had longed for and been denied, but it was somehow just. She leaned upon the sodden chest of Grace ten Boora and took what comfort she was able. It would have to suffice.

The weeping was done, the farewells spoken, the leave at an end. The major turned for one last look at the big, cold house before she stepped into the lane. The windows were cloaked in their lace, the eyes of the house hidden. A slight movement caught her eye.

Between the sweeps of lace, a mitted hand appeared. Trembling fingers pressed a flambeau against the glass, inverted for those who had perished. The hologram danced in the light, and Sarah gave a weak smile. "Well, Clem-darling, you finally got what you wanted. Damn shame you had to die to do it." She could not quite keep the bitterness from her voice.

As she began to leave, she saw the hand again. Another flambeau appeared, its point upright. Sarah was moved, touched, outraged, and somehow unsurprised. The Ugenia did nothing by halves. Swallowing the knot of conflicting and painful emotions, the major walked into the lane.

I have occasionally been bemused by a particularly fuggheaded argument about gender and combat which observes that only a handful of women's names appear on the long black wall of the Vietnam War Memorial in Washington, D.C., as if this made their sacrifice somehow less than the men's. These people conveniently forget the tens of thousands of *Vietnamese* women who died in that war. In any case lives do not add as integers, but as infinities.

Margaret Ball lives in Austin, Texas, where, she says, when not writing she makes quilts and raises children at her home in her spare time. Publications include the fantasy novels *Flameweaver* and *Changeweaver,* and more recently *No Earthly Sunne.* She claims no military background whatsoever: neither do the women in this story.

"Notes During a Time of Civil War" requires no comment, only your full attention.

—LMB

Notes During a Time of Civil War

For the Muslim women of Bosnia

Margaret Ball

The week after the shelling started again, we heard that the U.N. wasn't going to send peacekeeping forces in. They still recognized Washington as the only official government in what used to be the United States, and if Washington said this was a police action or an ethnic redistribution or whatever, nobody outside the continent was going to argue with them.

But it sure looked like war from where we were, right on the border of the Occupied Zone. And it happened too fast for any of us to comprehend. One day we heard They had taken Dallas, and the next day They were coming down our street with their light tanks and Their ugly muddy-green uniforms. Nobody was prepared. How can you be prepared for a thing like that?

They herded us together, the women who were at home on the block, yelling and hitting us with the butts of their rifles if we didn't clear out fast enough. I saw Diane Crenshaw pushed out the front door of her house. Her forehead was bleeding and the boy behind her was yelling something about the penalty for looting. She had tried to get a coat and some food to take with her, I think. Actually I don't know what she was trying to get; a coat and food would have been the best things to have, but we didn't know that then. We were dazed, I suppose; some of us barefoot and in housedresses, some of us crying.

Tom was at work. I haven't seen him since. The children, most of them, were at school. We haven't been allowed to see them either. They tell us they are being well taken care of, but who knows?

We heard a shot inside Rachel and Mark's house, and Rachel screaming. She's not screaming now. She doesn't talk at all. And Bobby Lee isn't with her. Bobby Lee, who was too young to start kindergarten this fall, and so shy that he always had a handful of Rachel's skirt clutched in his fingers. We used to tease her that by the time she got Bobby Lee ready for school, every garment she wore would be hand-printed in Kool-Aid and pizza sauce.

There's red on her skirt now, but I can't see if it's a handprint. It doesn't look like Kool-Aid.

Jim Saunders was home. They killed him in front of Sarah. She keeps forgetting what happened, asking where Jim is; then she starts to cry, wipes her eyes and says, "Thank God Sally's away at UT Denton. Denton's not a strategic location, is it? They wouldn't take Denton?" I think, if they've got Dallas and Austin, what are the odds they *didn't* take Denton? Best not to say anything, though. Not to flaunt my luck. Emily was home from school with a cold, so I've got her with me. At least I know she's safe.

I hope Tom escaped when they came through the business district. Some of the younger men were talking about going up in the hills, maybe he went with them, maybe he's not lying dead on a downtown street—I heard they were marching the men out and shooting them in groups, tipping the bodies into the middle of Congress Avenue to be cleared away by bulldozers. Not Tom, though, surely some of them got away in time. Maybe maybe maybe . . . Who am I kidding? At least Emily is too young and I'm too old to interest them, they took all the pretty young women like Diane Crenshaw somewhere else, you know what for.

We're at the supermarket on Balcones, all of the women they didn't take somewhere else. All of the ones from our block, maybe from three or four streets; I don't know everyone. They told us to get to work, loading canned goods and frozen goods onto dollies, wheeling them out to the trucks. Where is all the food to go? Don't ask. One woman said something and the guard hit her across the mouth with his rifle and she fell down bleeding in the frozen foods aisle. We had to step around her to continue work. After a few minutes she got up, slowly, and took her place in the line. Emily stays very close to me, very quiet. Thank God, at ten she is old enough to know when to keep quiet. Perhaps if we do exactly what they say and don't make them angry it will be all right.

I keep saying "the guard," as if pretending he was a stranger would make it better. Actually it's Joe Whatsisname, the assistant manager. The man who sold me a book of stamps last week. Funny, I guess I always knew he was one of Them, but I never thought anything of it. We've been living side by side in peace for so long; if I had thought about it, I would have said we didn't have those kind of problems here; we're all human beings, we know how to get along with one another.

I guess Joe Whatsisname didn't feel that way about it.

All yesterday we loaded cans and cartons of food and they never gave us anything to eat, though they did let us go to the water fountain and the rest room at the back of the store. One at a time, with a guard. Today Emily whispers that she's hungry. We're working in fruits and vegetables today, not so fresh after last night with the refrigeration units turned off and all these bodies huddled on the floor, heating up the room. I slip her the broken bits and pieces I find: a cabbage leaf, a broccoli floret, a whole handful of grapes. Keep one of the grapes for myself. It bursts between my teeth, sweet and succulent and moist. A mistake; now I know how hungry I am. I'm dizzy with it.

Soon all the women here are following my example. Sarah Saunders is careless—she crunches a half carrot where the guard can hear her, can't pretend *not* to notice. He shouts and points his gun at her. For a frozen moment I think she's going to be killed, then Joe comes running over and tells the boy to put up his pistol. It's going to be all right, I think. Joe is telling him that they are civilized, they don't shoot women. Noncombatants. Prisoners. But he goes on. Rules must be obeyed. Lessons must be learned.

Joe is calm, giving his orders. I can't believe what he's saying. The fluorescent lights overhead flash on his gold-rimmed glasses. Two of the boys in their green uniforms force Sarah to the floor, one kneeling on her shoulders, one holding her ankles apart. I hold Emily close, pushing her face into my stomach, trying to cover her ears as Sarah screams in outrage, shock, and then raw pain. Five of them, *five* of them, and none of the rest of us did anything to stop it! We're cowards. I hate us. But what could we have done?

The first few nights I thought I would never be able to sleep on the cold floor. I hadn't thought of myself as old, hardly even middle-aged; but in the mornings my bones ache and I feel like an ancient crone crippled with rheumatism. By now, though, we've just about cleared the store, and at night I am so tired I can sleep anywhere, in any position, as long as I feel Emily's soft hair under my hand and hear her regular breathing. Emily is safe. They do feed us now, not enough, never enough, and it's half-spoiled, but I pick out the best bits for her. I may not survive this but she will. She must. One of us has to live for all of us. I lie under the bare shelves and read the signs until I fall asleep, COFFEE TEA SOFT DRINKS SCHOOL SUPPLIES. We should start a school, there are a few other children, all girls, but we're so tired at night.

Now, since last week, they come back into the store every night after we've finished with the rice bucket. They point at women, two, three, five of us, and take the women away. The same women night after night for a while, then one night it's a new group and we never know who or why. Rachel was in the first group. In the morning when she came back she wouldn't meet my eyes. We all know now why they take the women, but we don't talk about it. But I was wrong—we are not too old for them.

I wonder what happened to Diane Crenshaw and the other young women?

They took me tonight. The office building behind the supermarket—they're using that for a barracks, and one floor is just for the women. They locked me into an office alone, took the other women farther down the hall.

Now someone's unlocking the door. Oh, good, it was all a mistake, they never meant to—

I can't look at his face. Oh, it hurts more than I thought it would. I'm dry and scared and his hands are clenched tight on my shoulders and he's battering his way into me. I wish I could faint.

It's getting better now. If I stare at the spots on the ceiling I feel nothing. Not the other women, not my own bruised slack body. Nothing. It's as if they had opened a hole inside me and I'm bleeding away through it. Four so far tonight. Don't count, don't think, just get through the night. The key in the lock. The key in the lock. And again. How long until dawn? I feel nothing. I could fly away through the window, all my insides have leaked out and leave me light as air, but I must go back for Emily. They haven't broken me yet. There it is again: the key in the lock. It means nothing. You cannot rape *nothing.*

My week is over: now they're taking other women. Emily was scared but she stayed by Rachel at night, she says, and she knew I'd be back. She knew I wouldn't leave her. No, I promise. I will never leave you.

Sarah Saunders was in an earlier crew. It broke her. Poor Sarah, she didn't have an Emily to stay sane for. She claims she is pregnant by Them—at her age!

Last night, in the dark, she pried a jagged strip of metal off the edge of a shelf and tried to abort herself. I think she has punctured something; she bleeds and bleeds. Trying to kill a fetus that could never exist, alone in the dark with the pain. "You should have used it on Them," I tell her. They would have punished her, of course, probably killed her, but could it have been worse than dying like this? Green pus oozing out of her body now, we have nothing to wipe it with, and the fever going higher and higher. At least she is warm, somebody says.

It happened before dawn. They took all our watches, so I will never know what time Sarah Saunders died, but it was before dawn. Four days of the fever and pain, and then she shivered all over and died. Lucky Sarah.

Tonight, when They come in, one of Them points at Emily. No. No, there's some mistake. They can't take her. She is such a little girl. My baby. I scream and they pry my hands loose from her wrist. She's crying that I hurt her, holding so tight. Something slams into my head. Blackness, stars. I stagger toward the door. No, no, I cry, take me, not Emily, she's just a baby. I tear my blouse open, shove sagging breasts at them, grimace in a parody of lust. Take me, I'll show you a good time, she doesn't know what to do but I'll do anything you want, I know tricks you never dreamed of . . .

Emily's eyes wide and dark, staring at me, staring through me, the last thing I see, such a darkness you could fall into and drown. Of course They don't take me instead. Am I such a fool that I still think this is about lust? It's about destroying. Breaking us.

An old woman slaps me, tells me to shut up and stop wailing, they'll bring her back in the morning.

I crouch in a corner, with her in my mind, every step, the doors, the elevator, the long row of offices, the lonely waiting. Now she is hearing the key in the lock.

Emily.

In the morning she comes back, walking stiffly, a little block of ice to be warmed in my arms. I hold her and sing baby lullabies, feed her sips of the cold rice gruel, beg her to live, to come back to me. She breathes but does not talk. Her eyes are an accusation: you did not protect me.

They come again in the evening and take her; and this time I do not fight or cry. This time I save my strength for what good it may do. For my daughter, whom I cannot protect.

Emily. Emily. Emily.

Sarah Saunders was not having delusions after all. We are all pregnant, the healthy ones, the sick ones, the ones who thought they'd gone through the Change years ago, the little girls. Even Emily is high and round with—what? Too sick, too malnourished, too old, too young, what can we be carrying but death and hatred? No babies can come out of this.

Emily has not spoken for weeks now.

Rachel has miscarried. It killed her. The *thing* ripped its way out of her body, the monster, the thing that never was, never could have been a baby. Sharp blades, knives with jagged edges poking out of her stomach. It was a nightmare construct of murder, but a weak little one. Somebody stamped on it, reduced it to a crumpled mass of sharp edges that leaked pink fluid. We hid it in the night bucket, pulled Rachel's skirt back over her poor torn body, told Them she died of a fever like Sarah Saunders. All this with no discussion, no argument. We know that They must not find out, though we don't yet know why.

I can feel it moving in my body. And I know now that it wasn't just the miscarriage that killed Rachel; these things kill in being born. Already the growing blades have cut the taut skin of my belly in places, I wake and find new pink stains on my clothes. It is worth it; one last pain, and then I can sleep knowing that I have given birth to Death. We think they will all be born on the same night; we are all growing at the same rate. Death will be born into the world, and we will die. And so will They. We will all die then.

Except Emily. Last night I watched the sharp edges moving and pressing under her smooth young skin as she slept. Then I put my hand over her mouth and nose and leaned down, hard, while her legs kicked. Until they stopped twitching. It was the last thing I could do for her, the last love in me. After all, I had promised: *I will never leave you.*

Pat Elrod lives in Fort Worth, Texas, with her spouse, Mark, and dogs, Mighty Mite and Jake Speed. She is the author of a fantasy-mystery series, *The Vampire Files,* and a historical fantasy series beginning with *Red Death* and continuing with *Death and the Maiden* and *Death Masque.* She is a costume-maker of note, and when not writing may be found hunched over a sewing machine. She says she's been a science fiction fan since first watching "Space Angel" on Saturday morning TV as a kid.

About "Fugitives" Pat writes: "It was both exciting and terrifying to be asked to contribute to this anthology. My past work has been on the hard-boiled-supernatural side, or on the historical-supernatural side, or on the let's-have-fun-and-see-what-other-genres-can-be-mixed-in side. Now it occurred to me I'd have to come up with a dose of unmixed science fiction. *Sans* vampiric sleuthing or eighteenth-century finery I bulled ahead on this one, and by golly it was fun too! 'Fugitives' may turn into a novel, as soon as my other characters release me."

—LMB

FUGITIVES

P. N. Elrod

Kella's eyes were burned by the cold wind as she inched up to the crest of the hillock to look for hunting parties in her wake. Gray and brown vegetation covered thousands of identical hillocks in every direction as far as the horizon. The sky was empty of movement, but that meant little enough when a flier could cross the distance in seconds. She and her companion were confined to a walk.

She scrambled down to where Faron was curled up on the lee side in an attempt to escape the wind. His head rested on one crooked arm and he was sound asleep. Once again she was tempted to leave him where he lay, but the man's skills were her only insurance against an unknown future. He was not wanted, but necessary. If they were lucky they had at least one more day left to reach their goal—*her* goal; Faron was still too doped to think straight. If they hurried, one day might just be enough. After that, what was left of the authorities at Riganth Prison would certainly have reorganized and begun tracking down escapees.

Faron protested the hard shake and subsequent pull to his feet, but docilely followed as she threaded between the higher bits of drab landscape. The sunlight was intermittent, but enough to give her a direction. Except for the cough Faron had picked up in prison, the only sounds in the primal world were their footsteps and the endless susurrating wind bearing them away to infinity. When the watery sun dropped from sight there was just enough time to cower in the questionable shelter at the foot of yet another hillock before the starless dark closed on them like the lid of a coffin.

Kella knew the delay was impossible to avoid and tried not to chafe, but she couldn't help resenting it. They might still stumble forward, but in the twists and turns needed to negotiate around the rough terrain, they'd soon lose their way. It was just too dark to move. They had one chance, maybe, with temporary safety and a remote possibility to make a real escape. She wasn't going to blow it by giving into impatience.

It was cold. They huddled together to share body warmth. Faron coughed twice, moaning in his sleep. Kella envied his easy surrender to the physical. Her own body craved rest, but her mind wouldn't settle enough to allow it and continued to race in useless speculation about the future. Useless, since it was unlikely they had any. Options for escaped prisoners from Riganth were dismally limited to a return to their cells or death. Freedom was a fool's hope. Kella gave an inward shrug. Fool or not, she would die before going back to her cage.

She filled the time scanning the utterly black sky for the telltale lights of a flier. Five uncomfortable hours crawled by before she was able to discern shapes again in the faint dawn. Cold dew was on everything. Shivering, Kella stood and tried to stretch warmth back into her stiffened limbs.

"It's time, Faron."

He mumbled, coughed, and tried to roll away into the peace of his folded arms.

"Come on." She nudged him with her foot.

He shoved it away.

"Get up, unless you want to die."

He struggled briefly with his eyelids and lost. "There's no difference between buying it here or anywhere else," he mumbled. "One way or another we're dead. Yours is just a lot more work before they catch us. I'd rather save myself the trouble and wait for it."

Kella might have given up on him but for the fact that his speech was lucid. Some parts of his brain had slept off the drugs during the short night; the rest of him just hadn't realized it yet. All he really needed was a little push to get moving. "Would you really? If you're that tired of living I can fix things for you."

"You'd be doing me a favor."

With a smile she bent and closed both hands firmly around Faron's throat and squeezed. She did it slowly, enjoying it. His petulance changed to panic and he struggled, then actively began to fight. He broke her hold and twisted away, gasping and coughing. She kept her distance and tried to hide her own sudden fatigue.

Faron was fully awake now, free of the drugs, on his feet, and glaring. "You rotten—you were really going to do it!"

Her teeth were showing. "Who says I've stopped?"

"I do, I was just joking."

"Your humor could be the death of you."

"Only with you in the audience. All right, you got me up, let's get going." He gestured for her to assume the lead, obviously reluctant to have her or her hands out of his sight.

Kella took a bearing from the swiftly rising sun and struck off, but their pace was slow over the uneven ground. She was tired down to the bone, hollow with hunger, and terribly thirsty. As they walked she plucked occasional fronds and lapped dew from the leaves. She speculated on the edibility of the plants, but knew better than to risk it.

The planet had a short day; three hours after their start the sun was directly overhead and the air was as warm as it would ever become, which wasn't warm. Faron called for a stop; Kella ignored him and plowed on, right into a low solid object that cracked her shins as she fell onto it.

"Hey, didn't you see that? I tried to warn you."

It was a circle of metal and plascrete, less than a meter across sprouting from the earth like some new strain of mushroom. It was colored to blend with the surrounding land. Kella stared at it, trying to recall what it was and why it was important.

"What's the matter with you?" Faron demanded.

"Nothing," she snapped. She ran her hands over the smooth metal.

"Well, are we going to use it?"

She just managed not to ask him what he meant and stood back, favoring her bruises. "You first."

He made a face. "Of course, always me." He examined a thick plastic housing attached to it. "Locked," he pronounced, "and probably for a good reason. This isn't part of the prison, is it?"

Her memory flickered. "No, of course not."

It was a . . . the correct word escaped her. A door then, she impatiently told herself. The one she'd been looking for, though not at all the one she'd been visualizing. Her expectations had conjured up something more mundane. And vertical. With a building attached. All right, so the building was underground, shelter was shelter, and this was the way in. "Open it."

He grimaced. "With what? I need specialized tools."

"What kind of tools?"

"A cutter and circuit probe would be helpful, and maybe a magnetic bypass with a program override."

"Then I suggest you improvise."

"With what, leaves and dirt? Without the right tools you'd need a battering ram to open that."

"I might just try one, providing the impact element is your head."

The look on her face was evidently inspiring. He broke the plastic housing with the heel of his boot and peered at what was left of the circuitry.

"This is more along your line," he stepped back. "Have a go."

Her fingers began trembling as she probed the mess, then her heart started racing and sweat suddenly popped out on her forehead. Her hands dropped of their own accord, and she had to break off before Faron noticed.

"Anything wrong?"

"No, and this is hardly my line. You're the specialist, you do it."

Faron swallowed his puzzlement and had another turn. "I'm not sure what you mean. I'm expert enough with the right tools, but these multi-binary probability codes are a bit over my head—I could spend the rest of my life doing this."

"That is entirely possible," she said, with meaning.

"Still, I could try a more direct approach. This tech is just old enough for us to get away with . . . there, press that down and hold it."

Kella had to concentrate to keep from shaking as he touched a bare wire against a contact. Sparks flew and her hand jerked back.

"Wants to bite," he remarked, sucking his own stinging fingers. He tore a ragged hem from his shirt for insulation. "Use this and hold it down hard."

There were more fireworks and slow smoke from melted plastic.

"I heard something give that time." He grasped a crank that Kella had taken for a decorative sculpture and gave it a turn. It was stiff, but worked; deep within, metal grated against metal.

The lid came up with a rush of warm air.

"Smells all right," he said hopefully, then collapsed into a coughing fit from the exertion. "Oh damn, I hope I can rest at the end of this."

"Rest is for the dead."

"That's what I like about you, Kella, you're always such cheery company."

She said nothing, peering down into a narrow circular shaft. A metal ladder clung to one section of the wall and disappeared into blackness. She couldn't see any sign of there being a bottom to the thing.

"Not sure I like the look of that," Faron commented, after his own study. "Isn't there an easier way in?"

"Probably. If you want to go looking for it."

He glanced once at the landscape: endless hillocks, cold wind, no food. To a man used to the finished walls and readily available comforts of an automated culture, running about unprotected on an open planet was the next closest thing to hell. Objections forgotten, Faron swung his legs down, his feet tapping against and finding solid footing on the ladder. He shifted his weight and descended. Kella copied him carefully but paused just as her head came level with the ground. There was no way she could pull the hatch cover back again. The angle was wrong for her to reach the crank. There had to be a way to open and close it from this side.

She spotted the control box, saw its simple diagram. Even the most illiterate, untrained grunt would be able to figure out that pressing *this* button would move the cover in some way. Kella read the stuff, understood it, but could not bring herself to act upon it. Even the *idea* of doing anything made her hands go slick with sweat. Bad move, when she needed them to grip the ladder rungs.

When her sight started to blur, she looked away from the control and that made her feel better.

The hell with it. The Riganth authorities would probably come here first, anyway. One open hatch more or less wouldn't make much difference to them. At least, that's what Kella told herself. But that was the fool in her talking, bleating, making up little lies to keep her from facing the big ones, the ones that promised survival and escape despite the odds.

Before the burgeoning fear could take over, she raised a mental image of slamming a door in its face. There. It could claw and beat all it liked now. She would keep it contained, leaving herself free to concentrate on the task at hand, which was getting down this damned ladder without slipping and killing them both.

Two rungs below the top she found the manual crank that would close the cover.

Her face went hot with embarrassment. *I should have known this would be here.* She worked it off, awkwardly turning the thing until her muscles burned. Slowly the lid lowered into place until it completely eclipsed her last sight of the sky, sealing them into the pressing darkness.

Blind, but feeling safer than before, she felt her way along, carefully, one rung at a time. No need to hurry so much. There was enough shielding above them now to foil the most sophisticated scanners. Any searchers would gather only negative information for the moment; they'd eventually come back for a closer look and find the broken lock, but by then it might be too late.

If things worked out. *If* her fool's luck continued.

Eventually, Faron puffed out that he'd touched ground. He was too winded to do anything but stagger out of her way and lean against a rough plascrete wall. Coughing again.

They were in the angle of two intersecting service passages. Small lights at long intervals emphasized the darkness. Faron muttered something not meant to be intelligible but managing to express his unease at the lack of real lighting.

"Better than nothing," she responded.

"Not by much. Which branch do you fancy, left or right?"

"The right." She had no real idea where it led, but knew she had to sound decisive.

"Think anything's living down here? And hungry?"

"You'll be the first to know." She gestured ahead with an open hand.

"Thanks very much. I suppose it hardly matters, I'm so starved now I wouldn't make a good meal anyway. At least it's out of the wind."

The pace was faster on the level floor. Kella counted steps; at a thousand seven hundred forty-eight they reached a door in the left-hand wall.

"I suppose you want me to open it?" he asked without enthusiasm.

She moved back to give him room.

"There's no art doing it this way, I hate it."

"As long as it works."

He removed his boot and smashed the lock, then rearranged the circuits. The door hissed partway open, enough for Kella to wedge a foot inside. She pushed and Faron pulled and the thing reluctantly ground back into its wall slot.

"I think we broke it." He was panting hard and momentarily gave in to his cough.

She raised her head, as though sniffing the air. "This must be the service hall to the power plant, feel the warmth and vibration?"

He nodded, still catching his breath. "How old is this place?"

"Why do you ask?"

"Radiation. Sometimes older complexes don't have a lot of shielding, especially down in the basement."

It was a legitimate worry, but then Faron *liked* to worry. "This is the attic," she reminded him.

"Oh, wonderful, that has to make a difference."

"I'm glad you approve. Put your boot back on, you look unbalanced."

"So it's finally starting to show after all this time. Who would have thought it?"

"Come on."

"To where?" He hopped, struggling into his boot, and caught up. "Is there an end to all this?"

"When we find it. The maintenance crew had to live somewhere when they weren't working."

"Are they gone? I mean, *is* this place empty?"

"Yes."

"Seems odd to build something this big then move out. Was it System?"

"Who else would have the resources?"

"That means this is System military?"

"Yes. One of their groundside bases."

"But the soldiers—" His brows began to climb well up into his high forehead.

"They're all gone, now," she told him in a firm tone. She'd overheard quite a lot from the prison guards on the subject.

"If it's empty, why is the reactor still on-line?"

"Everyone was pulled out during the war. Losses were too high to make manning this base practical immediately afterward, but they meant to return someday, that's why they left some of the automatics running."

"I just hope no one stayed behind. Why are *we* here?"

"To look for a way out."

"That makes sense, since we just got in."

They approached a heavy door set in the right wall with a thick transparent panel and various garish-colored warning notices.

Faron halted, crossing his arms. "That's the reactor section and I'm telling you flat out, I'm not going in there."

Kella peered inside. There wasn't much to see, just the entry room and another door on the opposite wall bearing even more warnings. The door was partly open.

She stopped breathing for a moment.

"You think the soldiers might come back?" he asked, shifting unhappily from foot to foot.

That open door was a faint indication that they'd already returned. She had, in fact, been counting on it, but it seemed wise not to burden Faron with the knowledge. She tried the entry door, but it was solidly locked, as it should be. She cupped her hands around her face and pressed against the glass for a better look within.

All that she could see through the second door was a slice of another innocuous corridor, this one stark white. The lighting was still dim though. If the System had begun a reactivation of the base, the techs would have started here first to bring all the power up on-line, including plenty of light to work by.

"What d'you see?" Faron asked when she backed away.

"Nothing." The lack of lights had reassured her. She swiped at the smear her face had made on the glass until it was gone. Only now did a wave of fatigue wash over her, causing her to realize how fast her heart had been beating.

"There's another opening ahead," Kella announced.

"I'll get my boot off then."

They drew closer. "You needn't trouble yourself—it's unlocked."

"Fine with me."

She hesitated, studying it. One open door, especially in the reactor section was suspicious enough, but two . . . "I don't like this, it's not right."

"Someone just forgot to secure it, is all."

At times the man could be as dense as a neutron star. "Or someone else was recently here instead."

That put a whole new face on it for him. "We can always go back."

"Not a chance."

They cautiously entered a long gray passage lined with more doors. The service lights were more closely placed and the walls were finished. Faron looked inside one of the empty rooms.

"I think we've found the living quarters. All those wall cots remind me of the Riganth cells. Now if we can just find the mess hall."

"There's a map at the intersection."

They looked both ways before venturing out but saw only similar empty corridors. The map was a patchwork of colored blocks, showing hundreds of sections, but the code key and other labeling had been removed. Kella rested a tentative finger on one spot.

"We're here, this is the only intersection of this type off the reactor area."

"If that red part is the reactor and not just a big lavatory."

"It's the reactor." There was an unnecessary edge to her tone. Faron had only been joking, she told herself. *Get a grip. Don't let him see you sweat.*

But Faron had been too distracted to notice, busy tracing pathways on the map with one hand. "All right, then light blue is barracks, yellow is for halls, the access and service ducts are green, and dark blue is . . . ?"

"Let's find out."

"I was afraid you'd say that."

Ignoring the side passages, they went straight to the dark blue sector, suddenly finding themselves in a large, carpeted room. It was well furnished with chairs, gaming tables, entertainment screens, and other comforts.

"It must be the officer's lounge," she said.

"Decadence at last," Faron sighed and made straight for a long wall lined with food dispensers. He punched hopefully at their buttons, but nothing happened. He punched again; the panels remained dark, the servers empty. Slamming a hand against the unit in frustration, he dropped into a chair, finally overcome with dejection and fatigue. Even his cough sounded disappointed and depressed.

Kella smothered her own black feelings and abruptly forgot them at the sight of a control panel on the other side of the room. The labeling was intact; she had only to turn on the power to eat.

Sudden cold sweat ran down her flanks and her hands shook as they hovered over the buttons. She had to turn away or be sick.

What did they do *to me?*

Faron was looking over with open curiosity. She pretended an interest in another corridor and left the room.

Damn them. Damn them for doing this. She balled both hands into fists but managed not to beat them against the nearest wall. Not that she hadn't done it before, but the noise would only bring Faron and might lead to questions she couldn't answer, and, by not answering, undermine any illusion of authority she'd taken onto herself. If he once realized just how dependent she was upon him, that it wasn't the other way around, then he might not be so cooperative. She needed his cooperation, his—she regarded the word with distaste—trust.

That's a good one for you, Kella. Needing trust when you can't give it. She knew herself well enough to understand she had a serious problem when it came to that particular facet of human behavior. It had never bothered her much before. Its lack had, in fact, helped her to survive this long, but until now she had been supremely self-sufficient.

Was *still* self-sufficient. They may have jumbled some of her neurons, but the rest of her could get around that. *Stop wasting time on something you can't help and* move.

Heart beating normally again, she resumed exploration. It was definitely officer country. Though the living quarters had been stripped of personal effects, the basic furnishings were still in place, all fairly high quality. If they had to starve to death at least it would be in comfortable surroundings.

Kella located a bath and found the water still running, which was something to celebrate. She scooped and gulped from the tap, splashing it over her face and neck, reveling in the luxury of abundance and time. In Riganth she'd been allowed exactly fifteen seconds in the showers to conduct daily cleaning.

After a time she stopped the flow of water and regarded the gaunt and wary face looking out from the mirror. It was less of a shock than anticipated, since she'd roughly gauged her own appearance from Faron's. Neither of them had been allowed the benefit of grooming supplies. Prisoners were paraded into the barber's but once a year to have their heads shaved and beards (if any) removed. Depending on the season, prisoners were readily identified, which made the guard's job easier. Her dark hair was longer than usual, a rough untidy mess, and she heartily hated it. She had a few premature gray strands at her temples and along her brow; there were new lines and deep circles under her eyes and a harder set to her expression—nothing unexpected after what she'd been through.

Faron was moving again and making clattering sounds. Drawn by them, she found him busily trotting between a food dispenser and a table, setting out steaming plates and gingerly grabbing at samples along the way.

"I've got it working, come on," he urged.

"It's not going anywhere."

"Thank goodness for that." He piled more plates on the table.

"You needn't overdo it . . ."

"Or I'll make myself sick? I'm looking forward to it." He sat and began stuffing food into his mouth.

"I was thinking you'd deplete the nutrient tanks in one go."

"Not a bit of it, I checked." He gestured at the control panel with a bread cube. "They're full up or nearly so, there's enough to last us for years."

"What a dismal prospect."

"You're right, what we need now is some friendly company. The next girl that comes in will have her golden opportunity with me, providing she's pretty. On second thought, I don't care what she looks like."

"Let's hope she feels the same about you."

It amused Kella that Faron still regarded her as a work companion and nothing more. Not, she sensed, that either of them wanted more. Neither appealed to the other in that way and both were content to leave it—and each other—alone.

He'd been a civilian tech on board at the wrong time when a System dreadnaught had caught up with their ship and turned half the crew into freeze-dried corpses on the first attack. With the bridge fragged and internal communications gone, no organized defense had been possible. The remaining survivors had been easily mopped up by a boarding party. Kella had tried to escape; she'd arranged to have a modified shuttle pod standing by for just such an emergency. It had enough shielding to sneak her safely past the dreadnaught's sensors, but she never got a chance to use it. She'd taken a knock on the head that had flattened her for hours, waking up in the dreadnaught's infirmary long after the fuss was over.

There'd been the initial questioning and her current cover had not been good enough. The ship's computer had picked up that something was amiss on her identity and tagged her for special interrogation, which meant immediate transport to Riganth Prison. Faron, too, along with half-a-dozen others that the computer hadn't liked.

And what had happened to them? Dead or drugged to the eyeballs, she thought. It hardly mattered now. Whatever information they'd possessed had been scraped or sucked from their heads long ago. The only consolation she had about her own unwilling betrayal was that much of her data had been obsolete. Had the attack come a week later when she'd been scheduled by her Resistance cell for a new assignment . . .

Kella forced herself to eat slowly and remembered just in time to use utensils. Faron had either grown used to the prison rule of fingers only or had forgotten about such civilized niceties in his haste to acquire indigestion.

"Why didn't you finish it?" he asked, slurping down a drink.

"Finish what?" She thought he was talking about her leftover soup, which had been too salty.

"You found the power panel; what was so important to keep you from starting things up?"

She shook her head. "Nothing, I was too tired to think."

"That must have been a first for you. I'd about given up. Good thing I had a look."

"Yes, I'm quite delirious with joy."

"I can tell."

"*Must* you dribble like that?"

"Look who's talking. How'd you get so damp?"

"The water's running, as soon as I'm done with this I'm bathing."

"Right, s'wonderful thought, I'll join you."

She gave him a look.

He choked on his latest swallow. "Uh—I mean—just leave some hot water for my turn."

"Gladly."

He eventually staggered away toward the private quarters, probably to collapse onto the first bed he found. Kella remained at the table, glaring at the control panel, her hands knotted into hard fists again.

The System interrogators at Riganth had ended the more obvious and painful forms of questioning months ago. When she'd physically recovered, they'd switched to subtler methods that robbed her of sleep and left blank patches in her memory. On the last occasion it'd taken her a full morning of concentrated and miserable experimentation before she remembered how to pull on her clothes. At the time it seemed unimportant, but when the drug-induced chaos in her head cleared the implications of the lapse frightened her as few other things could. Her mind was still intact, meaning that the System still had a use for her, favoring punishment over a clean execution. It might have been better to have been killed instead of captured.

But whatever they'd been planning had been cut short by the confusion and fighting of the prison break. Then she'd picked out the familiar face and form of Faron among the drug-dazed convicts. His usefulness balanced out his liabilities; she grabbed his arm and led him unresisting through the melee and into the wastes. Providing he was still willing to be led, it had been a good decision; she needed his hands and undamaged mind to manage the technical problems that certainly lay ahead.

The place was utterly silent and Kella became aware of the massive unnerving emptiness around her. The walls were too far away for comfort; there was sanctuary in the private quarters and distraction. The smaller rooms somehow made it easier to breathe, and she spent a hedonistic hour tending to the outer care of her body.

It was an illusion only, but after a lengthy shower, she felt as though the abuses of the last few months had been scoured and washed away by the almost painfully hot water. She emerged, pink, puckered, and a little unsteady from the glorious heat. No towel, though, only a drying mechanism with buttons that she studiously ignored. Leaving wet footprints on the floor, she quit the room to look for something to wear. Her prison clothes were disgusting. No amount of cleaning would ever remove the stink of the place from them. She kept only the boots, which had come from a guard she'd particularly enjoyed killing, and left the old coverings where they lay like a discarded skin on the floor.

She checked once on Faron, who was sprawled on his face across a broad bed, oblivious to cares for an indefinite period. He coughed in his sleep and his hands twitched from some deep dream. He'd be out for hours. Naked, but not feeling especially vulnerable, she returned to the lounge-mess area and a line of clothing dispensers along one wall. They appeared to be stocked with the usual packets of generic wearables. The stuff was cheap, stored small, and was easy to recycle when it wore out or got too dirty for normal cleaning: a quartermaster's dream.

The only thing between her and the satisfaction of new garb was another damned power switch.

Before the usual symptoms took over, Kella hit it fast and the control board lit up. It was like the one for the mess, but with fewer buttons to push since military personnel required more variety in their diet than in their wardrobe. Her hand hovered uncertainly over the selectors. Her mouth went dry. The buttons blurred and vibrated, mocking her hesitation. She licked her lips, focused hard on a button before shutting her eyes, and stabbed at it with an inner scream.

She opened her eyes, still trembling. But . . . nothing terrible had happened to her. Gulping air, she slumped a little, feeling enormously relieved. Maybe she'd be able to beat this, after all.

The wall unit beeped and out popped a packet with the sleep garment she'd ordered, but not quite the one she'd expected. Tearing it open, she found it was not only much too short for warmth, but semi-transparent, perfumed, and heavily edged with lace ruffles. She gaped at it, baffled, then the first genuine laugh she'd had in years escaped to assault the air.

Morning came when she woke.

The laughter brought on by the absurd results of her first effort at button pushing had had a relaxing effect on her, and now she was able to repeat the action in a quick and random way. As long as she didn't have to think about it, it wasn't so bad. Of the many things that popped out she chose a System officer's black combat fatigues, which afforded good freedom of movement. It was almost too loose-fitting. She'd lost weight and muscle tone at Riganth.

In the mess she managed to make some food choices without too much mental anguish and ate in solitude if not complete silence. Faron was coughing harder and more frequently than before and trying to muffle it. It wasn't like him to miss a meal; she punched up a cup of hot liquid and took it along as she went to investigate.

His room lights were turned way down, but the spillover from the ones in the hall were enough to see by. He was tightly wrapped in the bedclothes and looked far more miserable than when they'd slept in the open. His cough was rough with congestion.

"Good morning," she said.

He looked up dully, flashed his eyes wide then relaxed. "What a start you gave me. I thought you were one of them. Where'd you get the clothes?"

"Uniform," she corrected.

"I can see that, but have you noticed it's not in Resistance colors?"

"Are you ready for breakfast?"

"Dunno, let me wake up first."

She offered him the hot drink. "Here, you need the protein."

"Thanks." He took the cup in both hands. They were trembling badly.

She turned up the lights now and saw the sweaty yellow tinge of his skin, the kind one got from serious illness and not forced confinement. "What's wrong with you?"

"Nothing, I'm just tired, a little rest and I'll—"

"Fever?"

"What?"

"Don't lie, Faron, you're not good at it. Have you a fever?"

"I think so, everything hurts."

"Do you know what it is?"

He shook his head. "Something that was making the rounds in our block."

"What treatment did they give for it?"

"Nothing. You either got better or you didn't."

"*Was* there a treatment?"

"For the guards; the rest of us just got more pacifying drugs, so no one really cared what happened. Three of my cellmates died; I suppose it's my turn now." He said it in a matter-of-fact tone, expecting no sympathy or reassurances and getting none.

Kella was not a happy woman. "I suppose there's a better-than-even chance that I'm infected by now."

"Probably."

She felt her expression go more sour than usual. "I'm going to have a look round. Try not to overtax yourself."

"When you coming back?"

"Stay in this area."

"Kella—!" He broke off, suddenly doubled over by his cough.

She walked out.

Damn, damn, damn, damn, damn.

The sound of her boot heels echoed along the empty corridors. She stopped only at critical intersections to study maps and kept the pace quick, but found only a lot of locked doors. A few looked worth investigating, but none appeared to lead to a medical facility. There were many basic aid boxes on the walls at strategic points next to the fire extinguishing equipment, but their contents were, as was to be expected, basic. They had bandages, painkillers, stimulants, and respirators; the latter might be useful to help Faron breathe, but the kind of antiviral medicines they needed were elsewhere. A complex of this size had to have a med-unit though; it was only a matter of time before she found it.

She circled and cross-sectioned the wing she was in, then took a connecting hall into the next area. At the far end, where it turned into what might be the hangar bay service passage, she came upon the bloodstain.

Not more than two days old, it covered a substantial portion of the floor. The red had dried to a rusty brown, but time had not mitigated its disturbing nature. She picked out three sets of footprints that had tracked through the stuff. Two of them led in the direction she'd been going, another started back where she'd come, but branched off along another corridor before fading. There was no sign of the body, the weapon that had dispatched it, or the person wielding the weapon.

Her heart was thundering loud enough to echo off the walls, or so it seemed for the first few seconds.

Those two open doors. She should have paid more attention to them, to what they signified. She should have been doing anything but lazing around the officers' mess stuffing her face and—

Never mind that.

She forced her scrambled thoughts into order.

All right, the System techs were already here. She'd been expecting that from listening to the gossip among the Riganth guards. It had been just another bit of useless information to her until that Resister assault group had dropped in on the prison and blown everything wide open. Too far away from the break to make contact with them, she'd seized a less likely route out by coming to the base. A risky move, but official attention would be focused on the fleeing Resisters, not on a long-expected incoming tech crew.

And the techs would have their own *ship*, not just a small, short-range shuttle.

A ship full of equipment and the kind of automatics that would allow even someone like Faron to navigate them clean away safely.

Its accompanying techs would be no problem for Kella; she still retained her unarmed-combat abilities. The ease and speed with which she'd killed the Riganth guard had been proof enough of that. Her plan had been to stay low and take out the crew one by one, until she could secure the ship.

But the bloodstain changed everything.

Were the techs feuding amongst themselves? That hardly seemed likely. Had some other prisoner gotten inside the base as well? For all she knew Riganth was probably full of bright specialists like herself, each one with access to the same guard's gossip and also hell-bent on escape.

Competition was the last thing she wanted. Now the System techs were most certainly on the alert, their blasters charged and ready, clogging the comm channels with calls for help.

But the stain . . . was at least two days old. Something should have happened by now. Riganth would have at least sent a guard party to look things over. She and Faron hadn't exactly been cautious. A quick check of the base computer would reveal their power consumption and thus their location. What had happened to delay their ignominious capture?

She briefly thought of running back to warn Faron, but dismissed it as a waste of time. Better to keep moving and try to find out what was going on.

The single line of bloody footprints that branched off were tempting, but she opted for the double set. Much as it grated her to leave her back vulnerable, they were more likely to lead to the ship she wanted, the ship she absolutely had to take.

Faron tried to find a comfortable position for rest and failed. His limbs twitched, his joints ached, and coughing had become painful from almost constant repetition. The muscles along his chest and stomach felt like he'd been in a sparring match with a couple of bricks and lost. After waiting more than an hour for Kella to return he gave up trying to sleep and tottered into the mess, sat at the dispensing controls, and started a line of hopeful research. If the thing could produce liquids there had to be a way of introducing more than a few alcohol molecules into the final formula. At least the experimentation would take his mind off the wretched state of his body. It might even do him some good; alcohol killed germs and disinfecting things from the inside out had a certain logical appeal to him. He didn't want to think about dying; it was too damned depressing.

Either his luck had improved or the computer had taken in many similar requests in the past; the dispensers soon produced several samples. He tried them all and chose a smooth-tasting blue liquid with a subtle kick. It picked him up enough to get him back to bed and he settled in for some serious therapy. His cough was no better, but the stuff did seem to ease the aches. He drifted into a doze, kept awake only by the sudden, involuntary contractions of his diaphragm.

It was a shock—a thoroughly unpleasant one—when the man walked into his room. Faron looked at the blue stuff in his glass and wondered at the ingredients. He was mildly drunk, but nowhere near the hallucination stage yet.

The stranger was average in height, with dark, curly hair, walking with the alert, controlled movements of a fighter. He wore a System uniform and carried a standard issue full-auto blaster. Unhappily, it was pointed at Faron. He squinted to get a clear look at the man through his swimming vision.

"Who're you?" he asked groggily.

"Stay where you are."

"Be glad to, I'm really quite harmless, but don't come too close."

The man remained on guard. "Why not?"

"Just don't, I'm sick with something dangerous and you wouldn't want to catch it. I dunno what it is, but it makes you feel so rotten that dying would be an improvement. Are you a doctor, by any chance?

A head shake.

"Never hurts to ask. How did you get here?"

"Walked. Where did you come from?"

"The outside, up there." Faron pointed vaguely at the ceiling.

"You're from the prison."

"No, just a misplaced traveler—"

"Wearing prison fatigues and a beard?"

"It's the latest style off-world."

The man almost smiled, which was encouraging, but the gun didn't waver, which was not.

Faron shrugged. "Well, I had to try, didn't I?"

"Where's your friend gone?"

"What friend?"

"The one who doesn't clear away plates." His head jerked toward the mess hall.

"Look, it's a bit awkward like this, why not have a seat and introduce yourself? My name's Faron, what's yours?"

"Alard," he snapped, ignoring a convenient chair.

"How do you do?"

"Where's your friend?" He adjusted the weapon. "Lie to me again and I'll blow your foot off."

Faron's toes curled in response to the threat. "She's gone away, I don't know where she is, I really don't."

"Why did she leave?"

"Well, I'm sick aren't I? Maybe she went to look for some medicine. Not for me, mind, but because she might get sick herself. She's like that."

"Why did you come to this complex?"

"To hide, I suppose." His throat dried up, and he gave in to a coughing fit that left him too exhausted to move.

Alard put a little more distance between them. "You came here to hide? A military base?"

"Thought it was deserted," Faron whispered, out of breath.

"What are you two after?"

"I just want to get better. I don't know what she's looking for."

"But you have an idea."

Faron managed a swallow of his drink. "I've lots of ideas, but no one is ever inclined to appreciate them."

"I'm listening."

"She's probably looking for a way to get off this planet. If there is one, she'll find it. What're your lot doing here?"

"This base is about to be reactivated, we were sent to check out and prepare the systems."

Faron finished the connection. If Kella had learned about a group of technicians working here she'd be after their ship.

"Must be very interesting," he commented aloud.

"How did you escape the prison?"

"I didn't really, she did, and took me along. There was some kind of big raid, some Resisters trying to free a new group of political prisoners that had just come in. They cut the power reactors and cracked the place wide open. The prisoners that weren't too far gone on drugs turned on the guards as soon as the automatics failed. Kella fought her way clear of maximum security to take the easy route out through my section and happened to see me. We know each other, so she grabbed my arm and got us away."

"You're old friends?"

"She'd never admit it . . . for that matter, neither would I."

"Then why take you?"

"I have my uses. I'm very good at opening doors, for one thing. You know, you should have something done about the security systems here. They're terrible."

"You said her name's Kella? How long has she been gone?"

"More than an hour. Is there an infirmary in this place? Or maybe you've got a doctor with your ship—"

"Stay where you are," Alard repeated.

As with Kella, Faron watched helplessly as the man walked out, protests ignored. The bastard probably wouldn't return either.

Something odd about that, Faron thought. Alard may have worn the black uniform with all the proper equipment and trimmings, but his behavior was decidedly atypical for a System soldier. His first duty should have been to arrest Faron, then notify his commander. He'd had a comm-unit on his wrist, after all. Why hadn't he used it?

Unless he wasn't what he'd appeared to be.

That particular idea gave Faron a shiver that had nothing to do with his illness.

"You're getting feverish, old lad," he said, his voice sounding thin and small against the stark bare walls of the room.

It was too much to hope for that Alard might possibly be an ally. It was quite likely that he'd taken off to do bodily harm or worse to Kella if he found her. But if so, then why hadn't he shot Faron?

"Not that I'm complaining," he mumbled. "But it *is* untidy."

Faron went over his limited alternatives and decided that lying around drunk and waiting to die was the least attractive of the lot. Things were happening out there, somewhere, and if he didn't shift himself he might get left behind for good.

With a groan he got untangled from the covers. Holding his chest tight, he stumbled after Alard.

Pressed flat against the wall, Kella edged sideways, being quiet, taking her time. At least two people were ahead of her; their distorted voices had been bouncing off hard surfaces a moment ago. There was a very large chamber not far ahead that had to be one of the base hangar bays. She could almost smell the ship. She crept another step closer . . .

And set off a motion sensor alarm.

It was a standard security item stuck to the wall less than thirty meters away and anything but subtle in appearance. She'd simply not recognized it. She started to tear back down the hall, but a stocky man in a System uniform was suddenly in the middle of it with his blaster at ready. He burned a shot into the floor at her feet as a warning and sharply swung the muzzle up to chest level.

Kella stopped short, her hands out. Behind her a tall woman with fair hair trotted up, her weapon also held ready to fire. She shut the alarm off and stared. Kella was evidently not what they'd anticipated.

"On the floor," the woman ordered. "Spread your arms."

There was no room for choice. She lay flat and a heavy boot came down on the back of her neck.

"Search her, Tanig."

He slapped and prodded. "She's clean."

"Roll on your back and stay there."

Well, she'd finally found them: the System techs she'd planned on killing in order to take their ship. With considerable disgust, Kella turned over, propping herself on her elbows.

"All right, who are you?" The fair-haired one was a lieutenant and apparently the leader of the two, though she did not give the impression of being overly experienced.

"My name is Mavic," Kella answered. "Captain Mavic from Riganth Prison. Your zeal is commendable, but not necessary. You can let me up."

"You're a convict?" Her tone was disdainful.

Kella looked pained. "Obviously not. I'm one of the officers attached to the maximum security section. There was an escape a few days ago and I've been doing some hunting."

"Alone?"

"The rest of my unit is up there, groundside."

"Without weapons?"

"We're not allowed any. Drop your guard for half a second and a prisoner could steal it from you. Anyway, the man I'm after is unarmed and sick. I thought I'd finally found him in this maze until you two jumped me."

"Where'd you get those clothes?"

"The supply dispensers worked, so I borrowed some. Mine were in less-than-perfect condition after chasing him all over the moors up there. I can show them to you if you like."

"And your identification as well?"

"Yes," Kella put some exasperation into her voice. "What are you doing here, anyway? I heard a rumor that the System was going to reactivate the base. Is that it?"

"You don't really need to know, do you?"

She smiled. "I suppose not. Will you let me up now?"

The lieutenant smiled back unpleasantly. "No, I don't think so."

"If you don't believe me, then contact Warden Sena. I'm Captain Ven Mavic. You can tell her one of the escapees is somewhere in this complex and I want to report—"

Her boot smashed into Kella's side.

Tanig jumped. "Eily, what are you doing?"

"Shut up and look at her, do you think that's a regulation haircut?"

"But what she said?"

"Her answers were too smooth. I don't trust that kind of glib attitude, it means she's too smart for our own good. Get her back to the hangar while I reset the alarm, or did you forget that Alard's still out there?"

Faron paused and tried to force air into his starved lungs. Breathing was becoming more and more of a conscious effort as he walked, and it frightened him. He'd seen too many others slowly drown in their own congestion and now it was happening to him.

Damn Kella, anyway. Elitist bitch. Always doing what's best for herself and the hell with everyone else. It was just like her to run off and leave him to die, just like on the ship when the System dreadnaught had surprised them. She'd been doing her damnedest to get into one of the shuttle pods and get away. Fat lot of good it would have done her had she made it. The other ship would have either yanked her back in with its tractors or blown her up, depending on the mood of its captain. Good thing he'd been around to tap her behind the ear just hard enough to save her from herself.

Of course, after her time in Riganth, she might not thank him for his favor.

That had been a surprise, seeing her tagged for interrogation. It only happened when you were not what you seemed and the computers found you out. How was he to know that she was some kind of agent? Probably Special Ops or something even more secret and nasty. He thought she'd just been another tech-grunt like himself. He'd been taken away from the rest because he hadn't been military and they wanted to know why. Probably disappointed to find he wasn't a spy, only hired help; they'd simply shuffled him away with the other mundane prisoners. To be forgotten.

Until the break . . . when *she* had plucked him from the milling herd.

Why? It couldn't have been out of friendship or camaraderie; Kella wasn't the sentimental sort. Ops agents were supposed to be the best, trained to specialize in everything. That was their legend: to be inhumanly self-sufficient, ready for any emergency. Then why in hell had she taken him with her? Maybe she'd figured out who had tapped her and had dragged him away for the satisfaction of watching him die. If so, then she was missing out on the best part of the show.

Good thing that other fellow had turned up, even if he was System. At least he seemed to know his way around. Faron would have lost himself several times over had he struck out on his own. He'd only just managed to keep up with him, though, and if he didn't start moving soon, that would change. It'd be pretty stupid to wear himself out coming this far only to lose Alard and any possible chance for help.

He gulped back a cough and plodded on, the rusty patch at his feet going unnoticed.

"Is it on?" Tanig called out.

"Yes," came the reply.

Kella was sitting on her hands. Literally. They'd no ready means to tie her up, and Tanig had an unexpected turn of imagination. She was on the hangar floor with her back to a packing case. Tanig was three meters away next to the shield door that led to the rest of the complex. His blaster was still level with Kella's chest. He was haggard, unkempt, and nervy. In deference to this, Kella kept very still and studied what she could see of the hangar and its contents.

The ship wasn't anything special, only a standard courier vessel large enough for a few people and a moderate cargo. Some of the present consignment littered the area in a haphazard way. Several monitoring units had been unpacked and jury-rigged together, their screens displaying empty corridors. Presumably, it was part of Eily's defense against Alard, whoever that might be. One unit in particular held her attention. It had been badly gutted by a blaster charge or something similar. A few undamaged plastic and metal pieces lay scattered over a worktable along with a variety of repair tools and replacement parts. Because of her impairment, Kella couldn't be certain, but it might have been part of a communication panel.

Eily slipped past the shield door, shut it, and sighed. She looked like a woman with too many headaches, with Kella accounting for at least five or six of them.

She checked the screens at length before turning her attention back to her prisoner. "How long have you been hiding here?"

Kella thought it over and decided to answer; the truth would do well enough this time. Besides, her side still hurt. "Eight or ten hours."

Tanig glanced at Eily. The time meant something to them, though Eily wasn't giving anything away. Kella had no idea how long she'd slept but had made a conservative estimate in case Eily wanted to try linking her with the two-day-old bloodstains in the outer hall.

"Where have you been hiding?"

"The officers' wing, presumably. There weren't any signs posted, but the food was good and the beds were comfortable."

Eily tapped a few buttons below a screen and brought up a simple overview of the base with a dot making their own location. "Show me. You may use one hand. The left, I think."

Kella flexed her fingers and pointed. "About there."

"And why did you venture into this area?"

"I wanted to be sure I was alone."

"Are you?"

"Not anymore." It seemed prudent to be vague on that point.

"How did you get inside?"

"I found a surface hatch. The lock wasn't that difficult."

"Evidently, but they don't put mere lock-breakers in Riganth. Why were you really there?"

"Something political. You wouldn't find it too interesting."

"Treason?"

Kella shrugged with one shoulder. "Depends on your point of view, doesn't it?"

Tanig scowled, shifting on his feet to express his revulsion. Apparently he was too well trained to spit. Treason was the worst crime you could commit, as far as the System was concerned, and he looked as if he believed in the System.

"Trace the route you took from the officers' wing," said Eily, pointing at the map.

"If you want to know if I saw the bloodstain, the answer is yes. Was it this Alard's work?"

Eily was amused, Tanig was not. "I knew you were smart."

"Who is he?"

"A fellow officer until he went brainwarp and started trying to kill us."

And succeeding, if these two were all that was left of the crew. "Whose blood?"

"Our captain's."

"How did it happen?"

Eily ignored that one. "The bastard's loose somewhere in this complex, probably not very far away. You're lucky we found you first. At least you're still alive."

Kella's gratitude was thin at best. "Oh, yes. I'm so happy."

"Or have you met him already?"

"Obviously not. What caused this brainwarp?"

"Who knows?"

Kella watched Tanig as though he made her uneasy, but her chief interest was to observe his reaction to what Eily was saying. She was clearly lying about Alard's brainwarp; the glint in his eyes said as much.

"Why haven't you called for help?" Kella asked.

His eyes flicked once at Eily, worried.

"We have, it's on the way."

Another lie.

"Perhaps you should notify Riganth you've found me," Kella suggested.

"Anxious to return?"

"My cell is preferable to being randomly murdered by a brainwarped lunatic. Call them, they'll be glad to lend you some aid."

"First we secure Alard. No need to have civilians on the base and getting in the way."

Kella had trouble keeping her face straight; Eily's quick and ridiculous answer only confirmed that they had no outside communications. She was careful not to let her gaze stray to the scattered pieces of the comm-panel.

There was a very decided and practical method to Alard's madness. He'd effectively isolated the crew from any immediate help; that's what she would have done. Her own next move would have been to take out the leader. Alard had apparently accomplished that as well, though rather clumsily to judge by the mess he'd left behind. As she'd feared, the survivors were very much on the alert.

"Put your hand back where it was," Tanig ordered.

"What happened to your captain?" Kella asked, obeying.

"Why do you want to know?"

She shrugged. "There was so much blood, I wondered what kind of weapon would do that much damage."

He lifted his gun. "One exactly like this, the blast just happened to hit the neck artery."

She shook her head, as if in sympathy. "A bad way to go. What about the rest of the crew?"

He hesitated; Eily tardily stepped in to fill the void. "They're out looking for Alard."

More likely they either never existed or were in cold storage on the ship with their deceased captain, Kella thought. Right. Two of them, both with combat training, but Tanig was the only real threat. Eily was too distracted by the business with Alard to keep her guard up all the time. She'd holstered her hand weapon and forgotten it. A very bad move. Now if Tanig's attention could be drawn away just long enough . . .

Eily was watching one of the screens intently. "You said you were alone. Who the hell's that?"

Faron's unsteady figure staggered into view. The idiot.

"He's a convict—one of your friends?"

"I wouldn't put it quite that way," Kella growled.

"What's the matter with him? He looks drunk. Tanig, take the back way round again and bring him in, but careful, it might be an act, there could be more of them. Don't risk yourself if you can help it."

He left with a brisk nod. Eily brought her own gun up to cover Kella. Better odds, but she was too far away to risk anything yet.

On the screen Faron took one step too many and tripped the motion sensor alarm. He froze, looked down the hall he'd come from, and saw Tanig step out.

"Hallo." He coughed pitifully. "D'ye mind if I give myself up?"

"Face the wall, put your arms out, and lean on them."

"If I can," he mumbled. He turned and raised them, groaning. Tanig darted close enough to kick his feet apart.

"All right, I've got him," he called into the monitor.

Eily motioned for Kella to stand and go out with her hands on her head. Once in the hall she cut off the alarm again and covered them both while Tanig searched Faron for weapons.

He was looking deathly. "I don't feel at all well," he murmured in a subdued tone.

"Probably a hangover," Kella said acidly. She could smell his breath even at that distance.

"No, I mean I really don't. Who're these two? They with that other fellow?"

"You've met Alard?"

"Friendly sort. I think. No. I'm not sure. It's kind of fuzzy . . ."

"Where'd you see him?" Eily demanded.

"Back there." Faron halfheartedly indicated the way he'd come. "Only I thought he was ahead of me. Thought sure he was. Must have taken a wrong turning somewhere."

Or, he let you get ahead to act as a decoy. Kella and Eily must have shared the same thought; as one, they looked back down the corridor, but it was empty.

"We're out of here," said Eily. "Move it."

"Give us a hand," Faron gasped out, his voice gone thin. "I don't feel well. Don't . . . don't . . ." His head drooped against the wall and his legs caved in. He slipped to the floor with a solid thud. Tanig jumped back in surprise, ready to trigger his blaster.

"What's the matter with him?" Eily snapped.

Kella knelt and felt for a neck pulse. "He's fainted." Her eyes caught a peripheral movement at the first corner at the far end of the hall. She had a brief impression of a crouching shape pointing something at them.

Alard.

She dropped flat just in time.

Tanig yelled and spun as a blast struck hard into his side. Diving against the wall, Eily sent a half-dozen wild shots into the ceiling. She was a technician, not a soldier. Kella took advantage of the confusion to crawl to the cover of the shield door and roll through, then was up and bolting for the ship. Eily shouted after her and sent two more blasts in her direction. Kella had just made it up the ramp to the open side hatch when something heavy buffeted her arm, the force of the blow pushing her inside.

She stumbled, recovered her feet, and raced forward to the bridge. Eily was aboard in seconds, but by then Kella had ducked through the last door and had it locked.

Then she suddenly went hot-cold sick and felt ready to drop in her tracks like Faron. Her right arm hung useless and numb; blood dribbled down its length, spattering the scuffed deck with bright color. She listed away from the door, dizzy and with her stomach going upside down. Behind her there was a loud snap and a hole appeared where her head had been.

"Eily!" she bellowed.

Another shot, lower. She must have been crazy, blasting away inside the ship like that. Crazy or made shit-scared by Alard's killings.

"Eily—do that again and I'll set off the ship's weaponry!"

That bought a little time. Kella glanced at the controls, but the stress of the present situation brought on the old pattern again. Lights and buttons merged and danced, there was no time to sort them out; finding the right one was impossible for now. Discarding that option, she looked for weapons. Nothing obvious offered itself, only a basic aid box and another fire extinguisher. She tore the box down and fumbled out a pressure bandage for her arm.

"Come out," Eily called through the door. "I know you've been hit, I don't want to have to hurt you again."

"I'm not that hurt," she lied, trying to ignore the terrible mess she was leaving all over the deck.

"You've nowhere to go."

"Exactly, but you do. Get off this ship or I'll destroy it. I've had the training; I know how to access the firing controls. One blast in the hangar bay and we're all cooked."

"You're not that desperate."

"Eily, think hard on this: I've spent the last year in a System political prison with only System interrogators for entertainment. I'm never going back to that, so believe me when I tell you *I am that desperate!*"

Eily paused, hopefully put off by the convincingly shrill pitch in Kella's voice. Not all of it was bluff. Kella was thoroughly shit-scared herself. No time to conjure up fancy mind games to keep the fear locked away, all she could do was shove it to one side and hope it didn't rush over again and trip her.

She got the bandage on, more or less. The blood soaked right through the dressing before the thing tightened slightly around her arm and slowed the worst of it. The loose end dangled. Had to trim it before it caught on something. Wasn't there anything in this damned box with a sharp edge?

"All right," Eily called. "I'm backing off. Just take it easy."

A blunt nosed cutter with a safety blade. Great for slicing away bandaging, lousy as a weapon. Kella dropped it back in the box and grabbed up a packet of stimulant patches. She ripped it open with her blood-slicked fingers and slapped one on her throat. It'd take a minute to act . . .

"Listen to me," said Eily. "We need to help each other. Alard's outside, you know. You're better off with me than facing a homicidal brainwarp case. Together we might be able to stop him from killing us."

The tone and inflection were uneven as Eily moved around. She was doing *something.* What the hell was she up to?

"He got Tanig, he's probably got your friend as well. We *have* to cooperate on this!"

Kella took the small fire extinguisher from the wall and held it ready. Compared to Eily's blaster it was next to useless, but she had to have some kind of weapon in her hand. The iron-hard plastic and solid weight of the chemicals inside provided a kind of visceral comfort to her. She checked the ship's controls again. They weren't dancing so much. In fact, they were in very sharp focus now. She hoped she hadn't overdone it with the stimulant.

"We've got to pool our resources in order to stay alive." Eily's voice was unnaturally loud, the words were running together. She wasn't thinking about what she was saying, yet there was a purpose to it . . .

Kella's arm was starting to burn. She was ready to fall down. Damn it all. Even if she got control of Eily and thus the ship, then what? She could force the woman to play pilot for only as long as the stimulants held her up. It wouldn't be long, either, not with this arm, not in the shape she was in.

From outside the door came more nonsense as Eily preached about their common enemy. Yes, she was a proper little System robot, mouthing fatuous nonsense . . .

That almost covered the faint hissing . . .

Gas.

Kella made a frantic grab for the aid box. She'd caught only the first whiff of the stuff—something pungent—then stopped breathing. Heart pumping painfully, she clawed for a respirator mask, hastily fitting it over her nose and mouth, thumbing the flow valve open only just in time. The seal wasn't perfect; as she sucked at the bottled air, some of what was flooding the bridge seeped in, adding to her dizziness. She left the valve wide open and slowed her intake. That helped. Now air was escaping from the mask, reducing the chance of contamination.

What was that crap, anyway? Not tri-crynide or she'd be dead by now except for some reflex twitching. Somo, maybe? No matter, as long as she could still move and think . . . which wouldn't be for long given the circumstances.

She put her back to a wall and sank to the floor. Bad move, that. Too tempting. She might shut her eyes and not ever open them again.

But she'd have to do just that. Only for a minute or two, or however long it took . . .

She jerked her head up, shaking it hard, blinking hard. The mask slipped a bit. Somo gas it was, then. Must be part of the bridge intruder defense control. Just the thing to subdue a dangerous Resistance terrorist; just the thing so the poor misguided creature could be humanely captured and ultimately rehabilitated into something more to the System's liking.

Not this one, she thought, *not today, not ever.* She found another stimulant patch and slapped it against the other side of her neck. It wasn't the recommended thing to do according to the basic aid instructions, except for emergencies. Surely this more than qualified, what with somo gas filling every corner of the compartment.

Her heart raced faster; blood hit the top of her skull and pounded there, burning for a moment before dispersing throughout the rest of her body. Tremors ran up and down her wounded arm. No need to worry about dropping off to sleep now; her nerves were all but galloping from the stim.

The next time her head jerked it was in response to a minute change in the hissing. She stared at an air vent as though she could actually see the flow of gas. Any more patches like the last one and she just might. No need to look, though, she knew that Eily was flushing the place clean, preparatory to coming in.

Kella waited until the last second—when she actually heard Eily using the manual to crank the door open—before taking away the mask and shoving it out of sight behind her. She bowed forward, protectively cradling the extinguisher in her good arm, hiding it with her body. Then came the hard part: sitting absolutely still.

"All right, you." Eily's voice was thin, wavering, whether with relief or fear was hard to tell. She was just inside the door. Two slow, soft steps and she was standing right over Kella's apparently unconscious form. The still-warm muzzle of a blaster nudged into an exposed part of her neck. Kella settled more firmly against the wall. The muzzle withdrew. Now a hand touched her shoulder. Pushing. Kella's slow topple away from her looked natural . . . right up to the last instant . . . when the extinguisher nozzle was clear and Kella made a convulsive move with her good hand.

The high-pressure spray hit Eily square in the face. She spasmed away, blind, choking. She triggered one wild shot. Kella gave her no time for a second, and slammed the cylinder into Eily's skull with all her strength. The shock went up her hand, her arm, instantly transmitting the sickening knowledge that it had been enough. More than enough.

Kella was shaking, badly; the stim and her own adrenaline were playing hell inside her, but it was better than being dead. *Her or me*, she thought. *Better her than me.* She stared at Eily, at the bloodied depression in her temple, at her last, graceless collapse. No regrets for this enemy. She couldn't afford them and stay sane.

Where the hell is her blaster?

Eily was lying on top of it. Kella pulled it out. It was awkward in her left hand, but she'd be able to use it, if necessary.

And how soon would that be? Alard had been right out there. Had Eily remembered to lock the shield door? Better assume she'd forgotten. Assume that Alard was in the hangar and intending to board the ship.

A dull sound, more felt than heard, came through the deck.

Assume that he's actually boarding the ship.

Kella shoved the blaster into her belt for the moment, bent, and snaked an arm around Eily's waist. It should have been harder to lift her, but the drugs racing through her veins were doing their job. A wrench, a heave, and then Eily's body was in one of the command chairs. Kella unlocked the swivel mechanism and turned it so Eily was facing away from the door, then she backed off, wedging herself flat against the right aft wall. She pulled the blaster out again and checked to be certain that it was charged and that the safety disengaged.

And not before time. She heard Alard's cautious progress toward the bridge—first footsteps, then his muted breathing. He paused just outside the open door. From there he could see the mess on the deck: blood, scattered extinguisher spray. The stench of the latter was sharp in the air, like fresh vomit. He was taking his time. Kella breathed shallowly through her mouth and hoped that he couldn't hear her pounding heart.

He wouldn't be able to see anything more unless he came forward. It was a fifty-fifty chance who he'd spot first, Kella or Eily, depending on whether he looked left or right coming through the door.

Left, she willed at him. *Look left.*

Then he was in.

Fast bastard, she thought, having the time to think.

He'd looked left.

And his attention had been caught and held by Eily for the critical instant that Kella needed. He must have realized it, too. He tensed as though to spin, then aborted the movement. It came out as a small jump throughout his whole body. Then he went very still.

"Smart of you not to risk it," she said. She liked how her voice sounded. Cold. Measured. In control. Quite the opposite of how she felt inside. "Put the blaster down, then put your hands behind your neck. Take your time."

He obeyed.

"You're Alard?"

He nodded once.

"You got brainwarp, Alard?"

"Is that what they told you?"

"They said you were killing everyone. You got a reason for that?"

He slowly turned, looking her up and down, his eyes resting briefly on her wounded arm and then on the twin stim-patches on her neck. "They're System. That's reason enough for me." There was plenty of contempt in his tone.

Chances were his conscience wasn't troubling him much over those deaths.

"Resistance?"

"Mercenary."

"What outfit?"

"I'm an independent. They had a contract open so I took it."

The Resistance had no qualms about bringing in outside help, especially if the price was right. "Entailing what?"

His eyes darted from her face to the muzzle of her weapon and back. "I was hired to slip some extra programming into the base computers."

"What kind of programming?"

"Nothing elaborate, but if and when it receives the proper signal, it'll set the reactor to go critical."

One of her brows went up. If Alard was telling the truth, then the Resistance had made one hell of a bargain on the deal. For the price of a little forgery to get him assigned to the tech crew and one minor spacecraft they could remove the Riganth base as a threat anytime they wanted. Of course, the bang would take out Riganth Prison as well and too bad for all the prisoners there. Maybe that was the reason behind the Resister raid. Free as many as they could, divert attention from the base . . . she liked the planning behind it. Hell, it was just the sort of thing she might have come up with herself.

But it took a lot of talent and training to command the kind of computer expertise needed to get past a reactor's safeguards. "Special Ops?"

He shook his head. "No. They only gave me the program and instructions on how to put it in."

"And you botched it."

"I did not," he protested. "I completed the job."

"You left a pile of bodies all over the place."

"When the captain found out what I was doing I had to shut him down. So?"

"So as soon as the next next ship comes in, the first thing they'll do is check the computers for tampering."

"I'd have cleaned everything up before leaving."

Kella's mouth twitched.

"It's the truth!" he added sharply, his eyes again darting from her face to the muzzle of her weapon.

"But you can't really prove any of it, can you?"

"No, but . . ."

"Go on."

"I could have shut you and your friend down at any time since you broke into the base, but didn't."

"Or maybe you were hoping we'd provide a distraction you could exploit—and we did."

"Your friend's still alive, though. Tanig's not. I can show you."

Moving very cautiously, he backed toward the main communication panel and, one-fingered, pressed a few buttons. A monitor came alive. It was linked to the same remotes as the monitors Eily had jury-rigged in the hangar. The image hopped as he keyed in the code for the corridor pickup. Kella saw two bodies on the floor there. One was Tanig's. There was a vast wash of blood around him and he wasn't moving. The other man was Faron, lying exactly where he'd fainted.

Alard played with a dial and the remote focused on Faron. Numbers began to flow across the bottom of the screen.

"There's his heart rate, respiration, and temp," he said, pointing.

"All it means is that you were in too much of a hurry to waste time shooting an unconscious man."

"He could have been faking. If you were me, would you have taken that chance?"

Kella knew that she would not. But that still wasn't proof and given the circumstances, there was no way the man could offer any. The sensible thing to do at this point was to kill him, thus eliminating a liability she couldn't afford. Her stim wouldn't last all that long. There was also the System to consider. If Eily had been unable to make routine reports for the last couple of days, they'd be wondering why and sending someone out to investigate her silence.

Liability, logic insisted, and just as insistently, her instincts whispered *asset.*

"You said you were getting this ship?" she asked.

"As my payment. I'm a damn good pilot-navigator."

That was definitely one for the asset column. Until she got the neurons in her head unscrambled for good, she'd need someone in better shape than Faron to handle tech problems for her. She could run the rest herself, providing her instincts were still functioning and not jumbled up by the stim and wishful thinking.

No. They'd knocked things around a bit inside, but she wasn't that far gone. She would beat it. She'd beat *them.*

Had beaten them. So far.

How about just a little farther?

Why not?

Her stomach fluttered. Damned drugs.

A movement on the monitor distracted her. Faron was coughing again. The numbers at the bottom reacted, some rising, some dipping adversely.

"He's having trouble breathing," Alard informed her. "You want to do something about it before he stops altogether?"

Very well. Decision time. But when it came down to it, she really had none to make. Without help, she'd sooner or later collapse just like Faron, then either Alard, the System, or some goon from Riganth Prison would finish her off. It was just a question of who got to her first. At least with Alard there was the chance he might be telling the truth. A chance for her to return to her unit, a chance to get some crucial deprogramming, a chance to feel in *control* again, to turn the illusion she was projecting into reality.

There was a subtle shift in her. Alard went a fraction more alert, but she did nothing more than nod at the floor where she'd left the respirator. "Get that out to him. I'm sure he'll find it useful, too." She moved her gun muzzle away from him.

After a very slight pause, Alard picked the stuff up. He turned the mask over, watching her. "Why did you need it?"

She gestured at Eily. "She was clever, but never really wanted to kill, not if she had to think about it first. She flooded the bridge with somo gas to take me alive. If she'd had any sense, she'd have used tri-crynide instead. It's faster and more final."

Alard shook his head. "Not Eily. I knew her. She wasn't enough of a bitch to do it."

Kella looked him up and down in turn. She was almost smiling. Now was as good a time as any to make sure he fully understood her. "So very few of us are."

Pauline Griffin is a longtime resident of Brooklyn. She has contributed novels to the *Witch World: The Turning* series, is coauthor with Andre Norton of *Redline the Stars* and *Firehand,* and is the author of the *Star Commandos* series. By day she works in product development and computer support for The McGraw-Hill Companies; by night she is owned by three cats, Starlight, Cougar, and Snowflake, who is the model for the cat in this story. She is the winner of the Cat Writer's Association Muse Award for best short fiction for a tale titled "Partners" that appeared in *Catfantastic III.*

About "Lizard" Pauline writes: "When I was invited to become part of *Women at War,* I seized the chance to develop a woman who was an instructor of explorers rather than a professional soldier. It was fascinating to work with my teacher, Lizard, as she used her considerable skills first to survive and then to assume an increasingly more active role in combating the raiders whose sudden attack thrust her into the violence and terror of war."

—LMB

LIZARD

P. M. Griffin

Lizard—Ranger-Sergeant Liza Morrigan—scowled as she studied the face of the cliff. It was perfectly vertical, or close enough to it. Any slight deviation from the perpendicular it might actually have was irrelevant to one faced with the task of scaling the thing.

It would make a great test piece, she thought sourly. If this miserable hole of a planet were located closer to Deneva, she would definitely have slated the site for a field trip. She still might, assuming she managed to live through her present visit.

That was a decidedly open question. In the normal course of things, she imparted the survival theory, her students put it into practice, and she monitored their efforts from a comfortable flier. Now there was no eager class of cadet Rangers gathered around her, no equipment, and her transport was a well-charred wreck at the bottom of the bay. If she did not want to wind up keeping it company, she would have to move before the rapidly rising tide dragged her out again. The only way to go was up.

If any of her young charges had proposed trying this solo, much less free-souling—ascending without even basic protection—she would have saved him the trouble and broken his fool neck herself. That was class work. Real life was sadly different. When one had no gear and no choice, one had to go with that.

The Ranger mapped out in her mind what appeared to be her best route.

The climb would be a difficult one and would challenge her, but it was not beyond her capabilities. She should also be able to accomplish it well within the hours of light. Once among the jumbled rocks marking the final twenty or thirty feet to the crest, she could rest. She might stop there for a time instead of pushing directly to the top, giving herself a chance to recover her strength and allowing the raiders a little more time in which to finish up their looting and decamp from this part of the planet. Her business was to report the disaster, not to commit heroic suicide by trying to tangle with them. It was those subbiotics that she wanted dead, not herself.

Her hands tightened by her sides. The raiders struck suddenly, exploding out of space shortly before dawn, spreading destruction to Tybault's small spaceport and death to the unfortunates working or planeted there. Liza had just reached the rim of the planeting field after having spent several hours observing the colony planet's limited but interesting wildlife and had saved herself by turning tail and speeding back in the direction from which she had come.

Her lips pulled into a hard, unpleasant line. She had saved herself and left the rest of the populace to their fate.

She quelled that thought. Even a Regular, a Patrol agent trained to battle the ultrasystem's human vermin and outfitted with a vehicle designed to help him do it, would have done no better. He might have taken one or a couple of the invaders' fliers out with him, but that was all. She would not have been able to accomplish even that much in her unarmed and unshielded observation transport.

That she had eluded the two pirates on her own fins for as long as she had was in itself a near miracle to her way of thinking. Flying with a skill and daring born of sheer desperation, Morrigan had managed to bring her badly burning vehicle out over the bay and had leaped from it scant seconds before it had flared into a fireball and crashed into the water perilously close to her. Once her pursuers had at last departed, she swam shoreward and followed the line of the coast until she had found this minute spit of a beach.

Lizard was not satisfied merely to have preserved her life. Her expression was determined as she faced the cliff. She had her plans, and they did not stop at securing her own safety and rendering assistance to any survivors she managed to locate as she explored the ravaged colony. There was a vast debt to be collected for what had occurred on Tybault of Alor, and Liza Morrigan intended to have a part, however indirect, in securing its payment. Police work might not be her specialty, but she was a trained observer, and she had witnessed the initial assault. Under deep recall, she should be able to provide clues and maybe direct evidence that would identify the raiders and eventually seal them in an execution chamber.

The first step to accomplishing that goal was to get herself out of this place. Carefully, the sergeant settled her utility belt into the best possible balance and checked that each of the pouches was securely fastened. She had little enough with her and did not want to risk losing any of that.

From the first aid kit Patrol discipline required her to carry even on a supposed pleasure jaunt, she took a bandage dispenser and carefully covered the backs of her hands and knuckles, attaching the plastitape loosely enough so that it did not restrict motion or circulation.

Time to start. Lizard licked her dry lips. She could feel the hammering of her heart, the tightening of her stomach. Her eyes closed.

She fought to grip herself. She was facing death, and she was afraid. That was hardly unreasonable, but she would die if she remained where she was, more slowly but very much more assuredly. Go up, and she had a better than even chance of surviving. Surviving and avenging both her flight and this battered colony.

The crack she chose for her road was broad at its base, a chimney, although it did not remain so for long. Morrigan set her back against one side of it, then raised her feet and braced them against the other. Shells crunched beneath her soles. She did not like them, although they provided added purchase for her feet, and she was relieved when she finally pushed up beyond them.

The slit narrowed perceptibly. Morrigan got in an arm bar, gaining leverage with the back of her arm and her hand. Slowly, she forced her way up. She maneuvered her feet into the narrower place and was able to stack them.

She gave a sigh of relief and stopped to allow her muscles time to recover. That was more like it. Her legs would now be able to take the bulk of her weight. Arms tired quickly, and she had been anxious to get the pressure off them as soon as possible.

Although she was high enough that a fall would have serious consequences, Lizard pushed on with a lighter spirit. A good crack meant security, and this one was shrinking with every inch she managed to ascend. If she could not protect mechanically, a well-jammed fist or, later, hand gave support and augmented balance.

Under less deadly circumstances, Morrigan's heart would have been singing with the exhilaration of her effort. She knew she was climbing superbly, and even with the weight of disaster and ever-present danger on her, she wished her students were here to see her.

Tension started to build in her again, and to help ease it, Liza forced her mind to seize on thoughts of her normal life.

Her exemplary performance on the cliff probably would not have surprised her charges. Lizards were supposed to be able to hold onto a wall. That was what they called her, class after class of them, supposing, of course, that she was oblivious enough not to be aware of the fact.

Well, she thought sourly, she had never asked to be a popular teacher, and she was not. She was far too stern and exacting for that. Her reward was not that numbers of students returned at a later date to thank her. It was that so many of them did return, even in these troubled times when Rangers were ever more frequently called upon to face challenges that went well beyond the study of planets and their ecosystems, which was supposed to be the task of the Stellar Patrol's Exploratory Force.

The sergeant carefully thrust her fist into the crack and felt for the best placement before expanding it as much as possible to secure herself. Her feet fitted readily into the space below, and she raised herself.

The next spot proved too small to take her fist, and she inserted her hand. The hold she found was good, and her feet were well placed on a couple of constructions that were almost miniature ledges.

It was a good climb so far, but Morrigan did not feel encouraged. Conditions were going to get a lot worse in the much-too-near future.

Her hands were slender and small, and she was able to use them to full effect longer than a man would have been able to, but in the end, the split along which she was moving would only accept her fingers. She sighed, then twisted the digits of her left hand around one another to gain a solid fit and went for the next hold.

Lizard knew she could count herself lucky. The stone bordering the split was rough, irregular, and gave good purchase to the edge of her boots. It was more essential than ever that her legs and feet bear the bulk of her weight, and it was essential that she keep her center of gravity directly above them.

She reached up and then froze in place for several seconds until she found a satisfactory site for a finger lock space, this was bad, and it was no comfort to realize that she would soon be looking back at this time as a veritable session in paradise. The crack was beginning to turn. Another few feet, and she would have to venture out onto the open face, bereft of even this minimal security.

The Ranger swore bitterly. She did not enjoy taking chances, not even those encountered in the normal course of studying and opening up a recently discovered planet. That was why she had given up exploration for teaching in the first place . . .

Only a terrifyingly thin, nearly horizontal line remained above her. Morrigan placed one hand and then the other. Her right leg raised and angled to find its next purchase.

Suddenly, without a breath's forewarning, her left foot fired off its hold.

Desperately, her fingers clamped and tightened, and for one awful, awesome moment, she dangled by their pain-wracked support alone.

In the next instant, her right foot had found its place, and the treacherous left was braced against a second ripple in the stone.

A sob shuddered through the woman's body as she pressed herself to the rock, but she knew she could not remain there, and she took hold of herself with an iron grip of will she had not realized was hers to summon.

She had to be in command of herself. She could not continue otherwise. Every move had to be planned, not merely the next in the sequence but far in advance, right to the top. A face climber had to go with the holds, and she had damn well better be certain there would be others to follow the first ones she chose.

Her hand reached for a minute razor of a ledge. Only the tips of her fingers could claw onto it, but her boot smeared onto a bulge in the stone, relieving the pressure on them.

Lizard made herself relax. She kept her advance to a steady, reasoned pace, carefully scanning and evaluating the rock ahead of her. She made progress, slow but perceptible, and eventually the final visible hurdle was before her.

The ledge, which had appeared so formidable a roof from a distance, proved less perpendicular and less deep upon closer examination, and its surface was gratifyingly well corrugated. It remained the crux of the ascent, aye, but with those holds, getting over it would be more technical exercise than nightmare. What she would find once she surmounted it was now the matter of greater concern.

The Ranger-sergeant inched her way toward it, her fingers grasping small but usually sound irregularities, her feet edging onto them in turn.

She reached the roof, the bottom of the ledge. This would take all her strength, however fine the holds, and she went for it before full appreciation of the finality of the move destroyed her courage and weakened her resolve.

Long minutes of struggle brought her at last to the lip and the crisis of the climb. Placing her palm squarely on the stone, she pressed against it with all the force she could summon, literally pushing herself up and over.

As she rose, her left hand lifted to grab a new hold. That was essential and the great danger of this maneuver. Once a climber pressed into a mantle, she had to keep moving. If there was nothing for her to grasp above, the only way to go was down, and it would be in a rapid and permanent return to the base of the cliff.

Her fingers closed over a big knob. She used it to haul herself up, then sank to her knees, her breath coming in great gasps. It was over. The ledge was blessedly large, three times as wide above as it was below, and it sloped reassuringly inward, toward the wall. She still had a good twenty feet or more to ascend, but that did not trouble her. As she had reasoned and hoped, that would be no more than a scramble among well-secured boulders and natural steps at an angle which, though brutally steep, was anything but vertical.

Her heart lurched as a low, deep growl sounded seemingly within inches of her ear.

Morrigan turned her head slowly. She found herself face-to-face with a small creature, white by nature but now well begrimed with the red-orange dirt of the place, even as she was herself. Its ears were flattened against its head. The green eyes were slitted. The muscular body was in a crouch, tensed to spring or to lash out with the claws on its front paws.

Lizard rocked back on her heels. "All right, cat," she said softly. "Power down. You were here first, but the ledge is plenty big enough for us both."

She kept her voice low, her tone conversational. She did not fancy trying to fend it off on this narrow perch if it attacked, yet the idea of blasting it or just casting it down revolted her. The poor thing was terrified and looked as if it had been here since those subbiotics had struck this morning. That was a long while to have been out under Alor's unscreened rays.

The animal grew quieter as she continued to make no move toward or against it. Morrigan carefully removed a tube from one of the supply pouches on her belt and flipped open the lid with the broken nail of her thumb. Almost in slow motion, she raised it to her lips. She, too, was feeling the effects of the long hours she had spent under the sun-star's desiccating rays.

Her eyes closed with pleasure as the nourishing gel dispelled the parched feeling from her mouth and lips.

A low, plaintive meow caused them to open again. The cat was sitting up, its eyes fixed intently on the tube, whose purpose it quite apparently recognized.

"Are you hungry, too, little survivor?" she asked. "I don't have lots, but there's enough here to share with someone your size."

Rather gingerly, she held out the tube. The white cat came to her. It sniffed the gel extruded from the tip and licked a few drops of it, then to the woman's complete astonishment, it rolled over onto her lap, back down, and began sucking, even as a baby would its bottle.

Tears welled in Liza Morrigan's eyes. This cat had been the heart's delight of some child or woman or man. Now the Spirit of Space only knew where that caregiver was, and this poor little beast had been through half the Federation's hells.

She stroked the dirty fur, her fingers gently breaking up the larger clods and brushing away as much of the debris as possible. As she did so, she probed for open or less apparent injuries but found no sign of anything amiss.

The cat, a female, purred softly. When she finally finished with the emptied tube, she released it and caught hold of the woman's hand. She began to lick it with short, brisk strokes of her rough, pink tongue.

Lizard gave a sigh of contentment. She could feel the tension melt from her. This was why the medics so strongly urged that cats, or a single cat, at least, be part of every starship crew, over and above their inestimable value in the area of pest control. They helped fill some pretty basic human needs.

The Ranger's head snapped up, her sense of security vanishing as if it had never been. Had she heard something?

There it was again! It was not much, the rattle of a displaced pebble, the crackling swish of disturbed brush, but it was enough to tell her that something or someone was above.

She could feel, even hear, the uncomfortable, rapid thud of her heart. What should she do? The angle of the cliff and the shadow it cast made it almost a certainty that she could not be seen, not unless someone actually came down to check out the ledge. If that happened, though, she was in a bad position, even if there was but one intruder and they were fairly evenly matched in firepower. He would have the advantage of height and would probably spot her first.

Morrigan glanced apprehensively at the cat. Survivor was on the alert as well. Her ears were pointed forward, listening, and her head was raised, facing the invisible world beyond the edge of the cliff above them, but she showed no sign of actual fear.

The woman felt better, but only marginally so. A well-treated pet was likely to be friendly, as this little creature had already proven herself to be even with a total stranger. How could she be expected to recognize those who had come spitting fire and death from the sky?

Lizard came to her feet. She did not have to announce her presence if the odds were against her, but on the whole, she preferred to know precisely what she faced. There was an even chance that it was no enemy at all but a fellow survivor, someone who could help her or who was in need of help.

She froze at a sudden clatter of rapidly disturbed gravel and the snap of thin branches. A thud and gasp followed, then a man's voice, tight with pain, biting out a sharp curse.

The sergeant drew a long, relieved breath. That familiar, blunt phrase had been uttered in the unmistakable heavy accent of a Tybaultan settler.

Steeling herself, she began to climb. It would have been a stiff scramble under any circumstances, and now she was going to have to do it in silence. It seemed that she was dealing with another refugee, but until she confirmed that fact, she was taking no chances.

Survivor started off as well. The broken ground was less of a challenge for her than it was for the human, and she soon outdistanced her companion.

Morrigan licked her lips. The little animal made no sound at all, but what would she do when she reached the top? It would be best if she stayed hidden. If she did not, she would serve as an admirable distraction, but she might get herself killed in the process. The locals were bound to be blaster happy in the wake of the attack.

To her relief, the cat remained under cover, watchful but apparently not eager to press on into any further adventures for the moment.

Lizard lay concealed herself when she reached the crest. It took but a few seconds to get her bearings and to spot the one she sought. He was only a few feet from her, closer than she had imagined from the sounds that had betrayed him. The man was clad in the ubiquitous gray coveralls of Tybault's agrarian laborers, now in as bad a state as her own uniform. He looked to be in even worse shape himself. The Tybaultan was sitting on the ground, holding his left ankle with both his hands. His face, what she could see of it through its mask of dirt and dried blood, was white and contorted in a grimace of pain. She judged he was in his late middle years.

Her blaster was already in her hands, set to stun with the safety off. Now she raised it. "Stellar Patrol. Don't make any sudden moves."

He started, looked quickly at her, and swallowed hard. "I'm not going anyplace."

"Are you badly hurt?" she asked more gently.

"A prize sprain, I think. It doesn't seem broken."

"You from here?"

He started to shake his head but winced and stopped. "The next hold over. Ken Eddy's place. They're all dead there, and I decided to make for the ledge below and sit tight for a while in case those sons of Scythian apes came back again . . . The name's Lem. Lemmuel Tubbit."

"Ranger-Sergeant Liza Morrigan."

The settler scowled as she bent to examine his leg. "You folks weren't much use," he commented bitterly.

"Not folks. Just me. I'm only on layover here waiting for the *Altair Rose* to take me back to Deneva." Lizard made herself answer evenly. The man had to be carrying a weight of anger in the wake of the pirate assault, anger and fear and pain that could not be vented against any legitimate target. She could quell her pride enough to keep her mouth shut in the face of it. Besides, the Stellar Patrol had won itself a powerful reputation throughout the ultrasystem. Even isolationists like those who had settled Tybault of Alor expected its agents, Regular and Ranger, to come through in a tight situation and deflect danger from those they were sworn to defend. Spirit of Space, she expected it herself. However illogically, she was deeply ashamed that she had run instead of fighting and by some miracle driven off that raider fleet.

Liza examined Tubbit's injuries and administered what aid she could, given her limited supplies. "Well," she said in the end, "the ankle will heal on its own. I'm more concerned about that gash in your head. It's clean, but it's deep. I'll feel better once you go under a renewer." She paused. "It's not a blaster or laser burn."

"No. Eddy and I were moving irrigation pipes out in the farmyard when those vermin hit. I got a wallop from one of them." His expression hardened. "The blast blew me and a lot of debris right into the brush fencing the yard. That must be what saved me. I guess the sons didn't want to scramble through all that rubble to check me out when they came back."

"Came back?" the Ranger-sergeant asked sharply. "The pirates returned?"

"Yes. I'd just come to when they arrived. Alor had shifted enough to show that I'd been out for some time. Lucky for me, I was groggy enough to keep still. If I'd moved, I'd be real quiet now . . . Ken was out in the open where we'd been working, still sort of alive though there was blood all over him. They burned him, then looked at me. I must have seemed pretty gone because they didn't bother coming over. There was a shot in what was left of the house—that was when they finished off Suki, the oldest Eddy girl. After that, I heard one of them say they'd accounted for everyone, and they piled back into their flier and left."

"You were wise to take cover, Mr. Tubbit," Lizard agreed gravely, successfully masking the sudden, ugly alarm his comment had sounded in her mind. "I'll help you down to the ledge and leave you most of my supplies. That'll hold you for three days if you go easy on them, more if you ration."

"Where're you going?"

"To the spaceport. If I find help on the way, I'll send someone for you. Otherwise, I'll come back as soon as I can. I have to make certain that a report of this disaster gets out as quickly as possible."

"It's only a few hours' walk to the port, even if you have to keep an eye open for pirates," he pointed out sourly.

"The whole facility was taking a beating when I left there. If I can't find an operable interstellar transceiver, I'll have to wait for the *Altair Rose* to arrive. She's not due until late tomorrow night at the earliest. There may also be people in need of immediate care. Your injuries aren't life-threatening, but that might not be the case elsewhere."

"What am I supposed to do if you're not back in the three days?" the Tybaultan demanded.

"Either wait a little longer or set out on your own."

"On this leg?"

"Scramble up on your hands and knees the way we brought you down and use your knife to cut a cane or crutch. A lot of these bushes have stems long and sturdy enough to serve as one or the other. I'd do it for you, but the stump would be a flare for anyone hunting you."

Morrigan settled Tubbit as comfortably as she could. After reassuring him once more of her intention to return, she took her leave of him.

Her expression was dark. She had schooled herself to speak and act naturally with the man, but in truth, she was worried. His story portended major trouble to come for them and for any other survivors.

Lem had told her that the Davids' house, that belonging to the homesteader owning this land, was close by and had detailed how to get there. Time was at a premium if her newborn concern was well founded, but she would sacrifice some of it to check out the dwelling. What had happened at the Eddy place might have been an isolated incident . . .

Lizard had traveled only a few yards before a white streak flashed out of the undercover and sat down directly in her path. A rush of pleasure surprising in its intensity filled her at the cat's return, although she had seen all too clearly the problems the presence of an animal could create in a time of crisis. She had become far more attached to Survivor than she would have believed possible considering the short time they had been together.

Shame followed fast upon delight, shame and no little fear. It was much to her discredit that she had forgotten the poor beast so completely, and it was a damn dangerous lapse. If she was going to have to function like a commando, she had bloody well better start acting like one and keep her wits about her, or she, Lem Tubbit, and probably a number of other innocent people, not to mention the cat, were all likely to meet highly unpleasant deaths in the near future.

The sergeant straightened. She had a long walk ahead of her.

Survivor looked up at her and meowed sharply. Liza smiled. "You want me to carry you, I suppose? —All right, freebooter, come on up." She extended her arms in a welcoming gesture, certain the animal would know what she meant. Spacers frequently carried their cats on their shoulders, and a great many planet-huggers trained their pets to ride that way as well in imitation of them. She felt sure from Survivor's behavior that she was likely to be familiar with that mode of travel.

Sure enough, the white leaped into her arms and moved of her own accord from there to drape herself around Morrigan's neck.

They had traveled about a quarter of a mile when they came upon the smoldering remains of a homestead, one of the cluster of farms the settlers had established in this area. It had been a small operation, poor in even basic comforts, devoid of civilization's frills, as was to be expected on a first-ship colony started by rabid isolationists. Now it was nothing. Its present and future alike had been annihilated in a few moments of intense, human-generated violence.

Something, a child's body, lay not far from them. Survivor leaped down and ran to it. She began to knead a still arm with her front paws but stopped suddenly with a wail that made the hairs rise on Lizard's neck. Spirit of Space! Did that cry come from an animal or from a sentient soul in anguish?

She scooped the cat into her arms although she did not know if she would turn on her in her distress. Survivor remained quiet, and she held the little creature close. "She's gone, baby. That's nothing but a shell."

Morrigan's expression was hard as she knelt beside the corpse. This had been a fairly big little girl, and she had been uncommonly pretty.

In the end, she gave a sigh of relief. There was no evidence of the abuse she had expected to find. The clothes were undisturbed, and the only mark of violence on the child was the ghastly wound that had seared her life away.

Her eyes darkened. This girl had apparently died well after the initial attack. It looked as if she had run toward her killers, as if she had expected help, not death, from them.

The Ranger-sergeant rose slowly, frowning deeply. She examined the rest of the ruined hold, discovering five more bodies, all apparently slain in the attack that had destroyed their home. She uncovered a few sound packets of concentrates as well. She appropriated those to augment her supplies. Little else remained to be observed by one lacking forensic training.

Morrigan was troubled by what she had seen and more so by what she had not. The sense of mystery and urgency whipping her deepened and darkened the more she pondered the manner in which the raid had been conducted. It was wrong. All wrong. Space pirates simply did not behave this way.

It was not the probable extent of the violence that was driving her. That the devastation had to be widespread, probably planetwide, was all but a certainty. Raiders invariably wanted ample time to finish their business when they hit a planet. That usually meant knocking out all ability to resist or retaliate anywhere on-world, and Tybault, though sparsely populated, was—or had been—settled over much of her north temperate zone. It was unlikely that many of her people would have survived the attack.

At first glance, what had happened on Tybault of Alor appeared to be a repetition of the massacre on Tatarina, but everything inside her rejected that explanation, at least as the total solution. There were other factors at work here.

The question of motive was one of them. Her black eyes hardened. Tatarina had supported a relatively dense population that had mined and worked with vast volumes of gold. The armada raiding her wiped out a large part of the former to get at as much as possible of the latter in the shortest span of time. The butchers who had attacked Tybault seemed to have come only to kill, and they apparently had the knowledge to make a proper job of it. They had known where to hit and whom, or at least how many to get when they struck, and they had returned after their initial sweep to do a body count and mop up any survivors.

She was certain of that last with the murder of that poor child to corroborate Lem Tubbit's story. If the raiders had come back for some other purpose, she could not imagine what it was. As sure as space is black, they had not done any looting worth mentioning. There had been no perceptible rummaging through the shattered holding she had examined, and several of the victims still had minor pieces of jewelry and small amounts of specie on them.

Why? Why bother with a small, poor first-ship colony at all? She gave her head a sharp shake. Her superiors, Ranger and Regular alike, would be asking the same questions. What they needed was to get their hands on a few of those vermin and maybe on the log from one of their ships as well. That would supply at least some of the answers.

Under normal circumstances, that would be an optimist's dream. No pirate would be scramble-circuited enough to stick around this long after a raid, but in this case, she was not so sure.

Cold gripped the Ranger's heart. No, gut level, she was sure. The bulk of the fleet would be long gone, aye, but one starship or perhaps two would still be on-world. Their crews would have to stay until their work was complete.

Her brows drew together. That mop-up visit was the key. Those subbiotics had not merely wanted to cripple the planet while they robbed and ran. They wanted to account for every settler, at least in the vicinity of the spaceport and capital. Despite their efforts, both she and Lem Tubbit had survived. A handful of others probably had done so as well. Pirates were not fools. They would be aware of the possibility that some of their victims might still be alive, albeit most likely heavily injured, and that some few of them would be able to hold on until help arrived from the stars. Something more was needed to make sure of their bloody work and earn the commission that had sent them hurtling down on Tybault of Alor.

Fire would accomplish that. Just incinerate the capital, port, and the ruined homesteads and adjacent fields where their victims had fallen. Their artillery-class lasers would be sufficient to take out the latter. The fuel stored at the spaceport would help them account for the more densely populated areas. It was readily accessible. The settlers had planned to sever contact with off-world society once they were well enough established to be self-supporting, and they had not devoted a lot of effort or limited funds to the planeting facility. It simply consisted of the broad saucer where the starships set down fringed by standard prefab structures. Two of them, set apart from the other buildings for safety's sake, housed the volatile fuel. The pirates need only take it.

That, Lizard reasoned, was their intention. Hers was to see to it that they did not carry it out.

The Ranger stopped twice on her march to eat and rest for a few minutes, but she allowed herself no major delay, not even when she passed the ruins of two other farmhouses. If she was right, she would have to reach her destination and act within the next few hours, or it would be too late.

It was already fully dark when Morrigan at last reached the populated area on the outskirts of the spaceport. Stopping there for a final break, Liza hastily swallowed her share of the concentrates she had allotted for this meal and gave the remainder to Survivor. She then divided their ration of water, carefully mixing a trace of soporific powder from her first aid kit in her companion's portion. She was going into danger now. She would not inflict that on the animal, nor would she risk having the cat betray her.

Soon Survivor was asleep. Lizard lined a comfortable-looking niche in the rubble with scraps of a blanket she had salvaged from the Davids' shattered home. That done, she opened a concentrate tube and poured some water into a convenient hollow in the stone. Chemicals aside, the cat was tired, or she should be, and felines were notorious for their love of sleep. The issue should be settled by the time she awoke again. If not, with a supply of food and drink on hand, she might well wait a while for the Ranger's return. Should she choose to go, assuming Liza succeeded in averting the burning, she would probably be able to make her own way by hunting Tybault's wildlife and utilizing natural sources of water.

That would be a pity. The little cat loved company and petting . . .

Morrigan stroked her soft fur and, swallowing hard, strode quickly away.

Some part of the port lights still functioned, and a glow marked the site of the still-concealed planeting field.

Lizard slowed her pace. Better approach it carefully on the off chance that someone in the area might have lived through the disaster. Her intentions might be friendly, but survivors would not know that, and if any were around and armed, they would be likely to fire at anything that moved.

She traveled cautiously, taking advantage of the cover provided by the shattered ruins and debris. When she came so close to the facility that she feared sky lining herself against the light, she dropped to her knees.

Her progress was slow from that point, and the watch she had to keep on her surroundings and on her own movements made it slower still. She dared not relax, not with so little of the way to go. Fear was a tight knot inside her. What would she find when she finally got a sight of the field—destruction and death only or those she dreaded and believed would still be there? If the last, how many of them would she have to face? She was counting on one ship, the single small fighter that would be sufficient to complete the final annihilation of Tybault's colony. The tentative plans she had been considering were based upon that. If she were wrong and there were several vessels or a large one waiting there, then she was jumping straight out of a star's heart into the center of a black hole.

There was the field! Her pulse hammering in her ears, Morrigan inched her way forward until she lay at the very rim of the paved saucer where the few craft having business on the infant colony set down.

Three vessels were there, one living ship and two burned husks, as well as a couple of intact surplanetary transport fliers. No corpses were visible, but that was hardly surprising. They would have made unpleasant companions after a couple of days under Alor's hot rays, and the pirates had probably been quick to remove them from the areas where they knew they would be working.

The sound starship was a needle-nose, beautiful and as deadly as she looked. Small, fast, and heavily armed, these fighters were the terror of the outer starlanes.

Her crew, the standard three for a vessel of her class, were standing beside a flier resting in the cargo door of the larger of the two prefab warehouses storing the spaceport's fuel supply. Both buildings were completely unscathed and had obviously been intentionally spared. Either the raiders were about to begin loading the craft or had already done so.

Lizard studied the tableau somberly. Well, she had her targets. Now what in all space was she going to do with them? They were closely bunched together, but that did her no good at this distance. They were well out of stun range, broad beam or narrow.

The Ranger frowned. A single, slender slaying shot would make it, right enough, but she could not bring herself to loose the bolt, to burn down an unsuspecting man or woman, however greatly he or she merited death. Besides, she would still have to contend with the other two. Also, she would much prefer to take live, information-packed, talking prisoners.

A bluff might work. She had an infinitesimally slight hope of succeeding completely, but she could provoke her opponents into making a move that would bring them into stun range. On the other hand, she would be pinpointing her own position and could drive them completely out of sight.

"Stellar Patrol!" her voice snapped suddenly from out of the night. "Grab the moon, you sons!"

The pirates' reaction was almost instantaneous. Scarcely had she finished speaking than they dropped and rolled, each scrambling to reach cover. The Ranger fired. She clipped one woman, who managed to twist under the flier before falling still. The other two gained the interior of the warehouse even more quickly.

Morrigan swore bitterly as she rolled away from the spot from which her voice had originated. She had blown it. The remaining renegades had the next move, and she was sure it would come soon. They would be extremely anxious to avoid a pitched battle while they were inside that building with its store of highly volatile fuel.

Lizard gasped and instinctively clutched at the cold stone beneath her as a stream of furious energy seared the place where she had been lying not many moments before.

The third pirate! Damn her! She must not have been badly hit after all, if she had been hit. She had gained the flier and was sweeping the perimeter of the field with its powerful nose laser.

Desperately, the Ranger squirmed backward, trying to get out of range before . . .

Her body jerked straight, then writhed in agony as a slender, searing line of furious energy whipped across her right hip.

Morrigan retained her grasp on her weapon. Somehow she kept shock at bay so that it did not paralyze her mind and reflexes. Even as the first rush of pain hit her, she rolled over to face her attacker.

The firing ceased. Had the renegade seen her? Was she preparing to finish her off or merely trying to estimate the extent of any damage she might have wrought? It made little difference. She would soon fire again, and her next sweep would almost certainly succeed.

If she got the chance to shoot, it would. The afterglow of the fierce light still dazzling her eyes gave Morrigan her target. She carefully touched her weapon, releasing a long, narrow bolt.

She might not be proving to be much of a fighter, but she could shoot. Straight through the laser's discharge aperture her bolt went, penetrating the heart of the weapon in the moment the pirate activated it once more.

There was a flash of pure light, a brightness like the heart of an impossibly tiny star, then an eruption of sound and grosser fire as the fuel stored on the vehicle detonated in response, spewing gouts of flame in every direction.

The Ranger cringed. This was only the beginning . . .

A louder explosion shattered the night. Fire roared through the open door of the warehouse itself, one great tongue of the inferno now raging within.

She tore her eyes away and closed them to hasten their recovery from the excess of light, then twisted around to take stock of her own injury. Even with the light from the blazing building, it was too dark to properly examine the wound itself, but she could see the charred stripe the laser had torn in her trousers.

She was not badly hit, she decided. The burn seemed to be a glancing surface sear with no depth. A few inches lower, and she would have nothing much worth mentioning left of her leg or of her innards. Heavy or light, the damn thing hurt like all the hells, and she was glad just to lie here and get her breath back without having to fight again.

She sighed. She could not sit here pampering herself for the remainder of the night. A little white cat needed her, and she had promised Lem Tubbit that she would return to him as quickly as possible. There would be an interstellar transceiver aboard the pirates' starship. She could make her report from there and then head back after augmenting her food and medical supplies from the fighter's stores.

The sergeant braced herself and scrambled to her feet. She winced at the effort and stumbled when she did come erect, but she soon steadied. After a couple of minutes of testing herself, she nodded in satisfaction. She could function well enough for the little that remained to be done here.

She turned back for one last look at the chaos she had wrought, and her eyes widened in pure horror.

Two figures were standing on the roof of the blazing warehouse, one of them supporting the other. The scene around them was something out of nightmare or a madman's vision. The materials comprising the shell of the building were flameproof—they had to be to withstand the effects of potential planeting accidents—but the violent explosions rending the interior had holed the walls and roof in several places, and the three skylights giving both light and emergency access to the place had been blown out. Flame was venting high and fierce through every opening like geysers from a savage hell. There was little safety anywhere on that roof, and soon there would be less or none whatsoever. It could not be all that much longer now before the whole or most of the expanse collapsed into the inferno beneath.

Even as the seed of a plan formed in her mind, the shock of a massive explosion flung her to the ground. A wave of heat and open flame shot over her. It was far above, but she buried her face in her arms in instinctive terror.

When Morrigan looked up again, nearly the whole of the warehouse was cloaked in heavy fire. A great part of the left wall had been blown away, and it seemed that most of the roof—all the center—was gone. The roar of the flames as they responded to the sudden surge of fresh oxygen was so monstrous, so utterly overpowering, that she had heard nothing of the great mass's fall.

At first glance, she thought that the raiders were gone, but then she saw them, huddled at the very edge of the roof, trying to keep as far as their precarious perch would permit from the great tongues lashing the heavens so horribly near.

The Ranger's black eyes were cold and hard as titanone. Those two had the answers to a lot of questions that were not likely to be resolved if they died, and they were not far from that now. Even if the place where they were standing did not collapse under them, either the ever-expanding flames would get to them or the heat itself would sear the life out of them. The temperature up there would soon match that of a starship's drive tubes.

She clambered to her feet, cursing the pain the effort wrung from her hip, but she started running for the sound warehouse as soon as she was standing. She was going to have to ignore more than this if she was to get that pair down.

Morrigan drew her weapon as she neared the door in case she should have to blast her way in but holstered it again when she found the entrance unlocked. She hurried inside, sliding the door closed behind her to stop sparks or flame from gaining access to this building as well.

She paused, studying the interior, then nodded in satisfaction as she spotted the long ladder depended from the first of the warehouse's skylights. She went to it. It was movable to permit its use for other purposes, but whether it was light enough to be maneuvered as she must do was another question.

Morrigan did not take long to reach the top even with the pain the movement cost her. The catch holding the skylight closed was stiff, but after a couple of minutes, she freed it. After that, the whole piece swung up, allowing her body easy passage.

Hauling the long ladder up and drawing it out onto the roof through the narrow opening proved difficult. It was tense work as well. If she dropped the ladder back into the warehouse, her hope of effecting the rescue was gone.

Lizard raised it some five feet without mishap, but then she twisted too violently in her struggle to continue lifting it and to keep it angled correctly at the same time. The sudden surge of pain rippling through her injured hip equaled that of the initial laser strike, and she stumbled under the shock of it. Her hands released their hold as they instinctively shot out to break her fall.

The ladder slithered back over hard-won feet. Morrigan leaped for it, almost throwing herself down the skylight as she saw the topmost rung drop beneath its rim.

Her right hand closed over it, stopping its fall with a shoulder-jarring wrench. She fought it back into place with the one hand until she was able to get the second on it as well.

She worked with greater care after that, and in the end, she had the ladder lying beside her on the roof.

Was she in time?

Aye, the pair were still there. They were very close to the edge now and were obviously contemplating jumping. The certain death they would meet on the pavement below was preferable to that closing in behind them. She shouted a warning to stay where they were and when she had their attention told them to move as near as they could to the corner, the point where the blazing warehouse most closely approached the uninvolved building.

She was near enough to see the pair now. The sound one was a woman. The other, whom his companion appeared to be more than half carrying, was male.

To her credit, the former did not abandon her comrade although the fire was pressing them hard. Her lover perhaps. These vermin had certainly shown no soft feeling for the men, women, and children they had slaughtered here.

The Ranger shuddered when she got a full look at the injured pirate. Anyone burned that badly should be dead. He probably was as good as dead, but the poor devil was somehow still conscious and still fighting to avert the remainder of his fate. Space scum these raiders might be, but no one dealing with or against them could term them cowards.

Courage or no, would he be able to make the crossing? His whole left side was charred, blackened almost beyond anything recognizably human. The clothes were gone, and Morrigan could see carbonized flesh curling, flaking away from seared bone. Both the arm and leg, what remained of them, were useless or nearly useless.

The Ranger-sergeant hoisted the ladder up. Silently praising Tybault's gods that the two roofs were even with each other, she shoved it toward the imperiled couple. Miraculously, its end fell at their feet on the first attempt, and the pirate woman drew it farther in to better secure it.

"Send him over first," Lizard shouted when the raider straightened again. She did not relish the idea of having the sound renegade behind her here on this roof while she tried to help her probably dying companion. The pirate might well decide to sacrifice him to get at the one who was still her foe despite her present role. She would not be so inclined to make any such move against the Ranger—and chance throwing down her only avenue of escape—while the fire was still licking at her own heels.

The raider nodded. This was precisely the way she would have handled the rescue, and she wasted no time protesting.

"Lie on your right side," Morrigan directed the man. "Crawl. I'm coming over for you, but you'll have to help. Just try to hang on until I get to you. You, help him. It'll be safer if you wait until we're completely across, but if you're too hard pressed, come on. Just do it gently."

The renegade signaled her agreement and maneuvered her companion into position.

Lizard groaned to see how small the ladder appeared beneath him. He would have to be a large man, she thought grimly. That just about trebled their danger. They had no margin whatsoever for mishap or error.

The pirate struggled to move as instructed. His ruined body responded sluggishly, but he got himself into position and steeled himself for the effort he would have to make when the Ranger reached him.

Morrigan started to creep toward him. Her stomach lurched in pure terror as the ladder wobbled beneath her, but she kept her eyes open and kept on moving forward.

Every inch gained required a battle against herself. Height itself was no problem to her, but she preferred a more stable route, and something very basic inside her rose up violently against going any closer to the conflagration she had inadvertently begun. Her injured hip was not functioning as well as it should, either, and she feared that too much greater stress would cause it to give or to lock, that or jolt her into overbalancing herself. It was more than painful enough to do that if she made too sudden a movement. The sergeant reined that line of thought, ashamed that she was so considering her mere discomfort in the face of that man's awesome suffering.

She reached the pirate at last and, instinctively cringing, caught hold of his blackened left arm. She began to draw him back along the ladder to the safety of the untouched roof, moving slowly and as smoothly as possible so that he could keep pace with her. Her mouth was dry with fear, and her heart slammed against her ribs with every lurch of their support. If her charge fell now, she was almost certain to go down with him.

She trembled in her heart to think of what this crawl could be costing the other and hoped that he was feeling relatively little of it. There should be few nerves left alive to transmit pain in flesh so charred . . .

So great was her concentration on what she was doing that she started almost disastrously when her boots struck a hard surface under the rungs in stead of the familiar emptiness. She steadied herself, compelled herself to continue moving at the same careful, even pace until she was secure once more on the firm roof.

She did not pause even then but continued to draw the man along until he, too, rested on the hard, broad surface.

That done, she motioned to the second pirate to begin. She obeyed, seemingly with scarcely a moment to spare. A wall of flame was advancing on her so closely that the heat of it must have been singeing her flesh, yet she had held to her place. The woman must have solar steel for a spine, Lizard thought numbly. There was no way that she could imagine herself holding out that long had their positions been reversed.

She dragged the man farther back so that one of those gigantic tongues would not reach him should any of them chance to sweep out in this direction. When she again looked back, she saw that the pirate woman was definitely having trouble. The Ranger-sergeant realized that both her hands and knees were burned and perhaps a good part of her legs. She would have to help her, or she might go down.

Before she started for the ladder, Morrigan removed the male raider's blaster and cast it over when she reached the edge of the roof. She wanted no chance of treachery while she was helplessly suspended above that drop.

Lizard once more mounted the makeshift bridge. Her passage across it was less nerve-wracking this time. She was not heavy, and the other woman weighed only slightly more and was in greater control of her movements than her comrade had been. The ladder seemed wider by comparison, and it trembled less violently beneath them. The pirate made no mistake. She advanced carefully, keeping her movements smooth and even despite the agony of her burns.

The Ranger caught her wrist. Raw hatred blazed in her eyes, but she accepted the aid and support Lizard offered. She knew she was unlikely to complete this crawl without that help, whatever the strength of her will. The body could be forced only so far, and she was close to the limit of her endurance. Morrigan felt no anger, although she read what was in the other easily enough. She would sooner face the pirate's hate and what might logically spring from it than try to outguess an unnatural lack, or seeming lack, of response against her.

Slowly, they worked their way back to their refuge. At last, Liza once again felt the welcome resistance of a solid surface beneath her boots. Seconds later, she had gained her feet, and minutes after that, she was steadying the pirate, that and deftly slipping the blaster from her holster before the woman could move to stop her or draw it herself.

The raider nodded, as much acknowledging defeat to herself as to the Ranger. For now, at least, she was beaten. "Why?" she asked dully, looking from the blazing warehouse to the ladder. "Why the save?"

Liza Morrigan shrugged. "I'm Stellar Patrol. It was my job."

Lizard studied the man who had just entered her cabin on the *Altair Rose*. Tubbit, cleaned up and dressed in the clothes the spacers had given him, seemed older than she had first imagined, nearer to elderly than middle-aged, but that might be the effect of what he had just gone through. He must be feeling the full impact of the disaster by now. His physical injuries, of course, had been erased after a few minutes under the starship's renewer, even as her own had been.

She sighed in her heart. In a sense, the settler was fortunate. He had merely worked for Ken Eddy. There was no wife or child or grandchild of his numbered among the slaughtered.

She smiled. "It's good to see you, Mr. Tubbit. How are you?"

"Healed up. Yourself?"

"I'm fine." She tapped her hip. "There's not even a scar."

"What about the two you pulled off that roof?"

"They're well enough, better than might have been expected. We got the man under regrowth treatment fast enough that he'll live to stand trial. The renewer was sufficient to take care of the other one."

"It doesn't matter much, does it, apart from easing their suffering? They'll both be executed."

"Within the next couple of months."

"So soon?" Tubbit asked in surprise. "Aren't they facing a civilian court?"

"Oh, aye. Tatarina did that much good. Even the weeping hearts in the inner systems have no use for space pirates. They'll get a just hearing, but no one will have any patience with patent delaying tactics and even less with attempted circumvention on the part of their lawyers."

"Is there hard evidence enough to convict them?" he asked bluntly.

"Plenty. Their own log speaks loud and clear on that point. Besides, we've already begun to run a check on them. Rest assured they're wanted in more than one place throughout the ultrasystem, either by us or by surplanetary authorities. There'll be meat in plenty for multiple convictions in the unlikely event that we fail to secure this one."

"You're in contact with your headquarters. Have your people learned anything? About the other pirates, I mean?"

Morrigan shook her head. "Not yet as far as I know."

"So we execute two raiders, and all the others go free as space so they can murder still more helpless people," he said bitterly.

"Give us time, Mr. Tubbit. Our prisoners haven't even reached Deneva for interrogation. All Intelligence has at the moment is that copy of their log that I fasmitted, and even at that, we can make some pretty good guesses."

The sharpness in the Tybaultan's tone had caused the gleaming cat stretched out on the bunk to raise her head and meow inquisitively. In the cramped cabin, it was easy for Liza to swivel her chair and reach over to run a reassuring finger between Survivor's ears.

Tubbit frowned. "Your cat?"

"Aye. Our medics advocate keeping a pet." Lizard fought to block the defensive note in her mind from reaching her voice. She and Survivor were bonded, damn it, and the poor little animal already suffered the loss of everyone on whom she had depended. She was settled in well with her, and it would be savage to wrench her away again, even if she was also a survivor of the Tybault colony.

She saw in the next moment that her worry was needless. Tybaultans as a rule had placed little value in companion animals. Survivor's caregivers had been very much an exception in that respect. The old man simply shrugged and dismissed the feline from his attention once more. "You mention some guesses?"

She nodded. "Aye. Think about it. How does inheritance work on Tybault? What if a whole family dies, as can happen on a first-ship colony?"

"The next closest person on-world gets everything. No so-called kin who wouldn't come with us are going to get any benefit out of us whether we win or lose . . . I'll be a son of a Scythian ape!" he gasped as the import of what he had just said struck him. "The whole planet?"

"Hopefully not. The search teams should turn up some others, especially in areas distant from the capital. However, aye, a large portion of Tybault of Alor is yours."

"What use is it?" he asked dully as the excitement in him faded. "I'm not a young man. I have no kin even in the stars, and the neighbors, the friends, I would have liked to help are all dead."

"That's for you to decide, Mr. Tubbit. There are a great many worthy causes and worthy groups." She paused. "Having rights is one thing. Claiming and exercising them may be another."

He frowned. "What do you mean?"

Liza hesitated, then went on. "What would have happened if the whole colony, every single person, perished?"

"Tybault would revert to her original owners." His eyes widened. "Sergeant! That's a huge interstellar corporation!"

"Obviously, we believe that only a very few people are involved, probably no more than a single individual."

Tubbit was silent a while. "But why?" he asked at last. "Tybault of Alor is no prize, not to the usual brand of settlers who want to carve a comfortable niche for themselves in the Federation trade economy. Her developers were lucky to find us, and they may have to wait a long, long time before they can unload her again."

"That may not be the plan. Exploration continued after the initial sale as part of their contract with you. Tybault's former owners might have turned up something that they would prefer to exploit themselves. A gem or mineral deposit comes to mind, but it could be any number of things. The point is, they, or someone there, wanted the planet back real bad, bad enough to hire that wolf pack to clear her off for them."

"You sound like it's proven fact, not just a guess," the settler accused.

"Proven, no, but it fits. Tybault was no target to attract raiders on her own. They had to be acting on commission, and a fleet like that would not have come cheap. Only greed or hate would fire that kind of an outlay, and the last isn't likely. Your people, from what we've been able to dig up thus far, are neither malignant nor controversial, and you certainly weren't wealthy, not after having shelled out to buy a planet and establish yourselves there. That leaves Tybault herself."

"It's a hell of a long shot," he said after another long silence. "If it were me and my butchers had been caught, I'd swallow my losses and stay low."

"Forget a desire so compelling that it drove him to annihilate an entire colony?" The Ranger-sergeant shook her head. "We're putting credits down that he'll make a move as soon as the excitement appears to have died down. Our people intend to let him feel nice and safe, give him lots of line, and haul him in as soon as he has properly strangled himself with it."

Lem's eyes narrowed. "And you bastards are planning to set me up as bait?"

"If you consent," Lizard responded evenly. "We'll do everything in our power to protect you, but we can't be absolutely certain of being able to do it, not when we don't even know at this point whether we're dealing with a sane opponent or a madman."

"Suppose I don't cooperate?"

"You'll still be in danger, and we'll still try to protect you. We'll just probably be a lot less effective. We could also keep you in hiding and try to set up a trap with a fake survivor. That would probably be your safest course."

"You'd go to some other Tybaultan first, assuming there are any more of us left."

"Probably," she agreed. "We want the one who did this."

He stared at her coldly but then shrugged. "No. I'm old, and no one's heart is going to break if I die. A lot of good folks, nice, fine folks, were butchered.

You can use me to avenge them. I've got nothing better to do with myself now."

"Thank you, Mr. Tubbit," she said quietly.

He studied her. "What about you, Sergeant? Are you still in?"

Morrigan's face hardened, and she nodded. A colony had been slaughtered, people, innocent human beings, savagely cut away from life and hope. She had seen babies dead in their cribs, and not all of them had perished in the aerial attack. She had seen Survivor's original caregiver's pathetic little body. There was a hatred in her that would be extinguished only when the one who had conceived and commanded those deaths walked or was dragged into an execution chamber and was carried lifeless out of it, and it was a satisfaction to know that her efforts would be instrumental in bringing him—or her—to that end. "Aye, I'm in. As a Ranger, my part would normally be over, but I requested and received reassignment to the investigation team for the duration. I'll see this through."

A flicker of movement caused her eyes to turn to the sleeping cat. Survivor was at peace, contented and safe, and a sudden warmth filled Lizard. She would help bring this ghastly business to a close, aye, and to such a close that other potential villains would think again about perpetrating a similar atrocity, but then she would put hate behind her and return to her own job, to her true mission of giving fledgling Rangers the skills they would need to meet and surmount challenges such as she had faced on Tybault of Alot. Her head raised in pride. It was important work, essential to the Rangers and to the ultrasystem itself, and it was infinitely important to her. She would be glad to shoulder it once more.

Elizabeth Moon's mother was an engineer and a single parent back when both were made even more difficult for a woman than they are today. Elizabeth grew up to join the U.S. Marine Corps, where she reached the rank of lieutenant. Later, she served for six years as an emergency medical technician on a rural Texas ambulance crew. Elizabeth and her physician husband have adopted a learning-disabled son, whom Elizabeth home-tutors. Her views on women in the military and women in combat show up in a number of books, including the fantasy trilogy *The Deed of Paksenarrion* and the space adventure series that began with *Hunting Party.*

About "Hand to Hand" Elizabeth writes: "For a change of pace, this story looks at one of the traditional assumptions of military power: the people a soldier protects (at the cost of blood) should be grateful for such protection, that the culture that is saved should serve its saviors. It is not a pacifist or a militarist story; it is a tale of the tangles humans get into when they don't examine their assumptions, emotional as well as political."

—LMB

Hand to Hand

Elizabeth Moon

Ereza stood in the shadows at the back of the concert hall. She had promised to be silent, to be motionless; interrupting the final rehearsal would, she had been told, cause untold damage. Damage. She had survived the bombing of her barracks; she had survived being buried in the rubble for two days, the amputation of an arm, the loss of friends and all her gear, and they thought interrupting a rehearsal caused *damage?* Had it not been her twin onstage, she might have said something. But for Arlashi's, sake she would ignore such narrow-minded silliness and do as she was told.

She had seen concerts, of course; she had even attended the first one in which Arlashi soloed. This was somewhat different. From the clear central dome the muted light of a rainy day lay over the rows of seats, dulling the rich colors of the upholstery. The stage, by contrast, looked almost garish under its warm-toned lights. Musicians out of uniform wore all sorts of odd clothes; it looked as if someone had collected rabble from a street fair and handed them instruments. Ereza had expected them to wear the kinds of things Arlashi wore, casual but elegant; here, Arlashi looked almost too formal in purple jersey and gray slacks. Instead of attentive silence before the music, she could hear scuffing feet, coughs and cleared throats, vague mutters. The conductor leaned down, pointing out something to Arlashi in the score; she pointed back; their heads finally moved in unison.

The conductor moved back to his podium and tapped it with his baton. "From measure sixty," he said. Pages rustled, though most of the musicians seemed to be on the right one. Silence, then a last throat clearing, then silence again. Ereza shifted her weight to the other leg. Her stump ached savagely for a moment, then eased. Arla, she could see, was poised, her eyes on the conductor.

His hand moved; music began. Ereza listened for the bits she knew, from having heard Arla practice them at home. Arla had tried to explain, but it made no sense, not like real things. Music was either pretty or not; it either made her feel like laughing, or crying, or jumping around. You couldn't say, as with artillery, what would work and what wouldn't. This wasn't one she knew without a program. It sounded pretty enough, serene as a spring evening in the garden. Arla's right arm moved back and forth, the fingers of her left hand shifting up and down. Ereza watched her, relaxing into the sweetness of the music. This was the new cello, one of only four wooden cellos on the planet, made of wood from Scavel, part of the reparations payment imposed after the Third Insurrection. Cravor's World, rich in military capacity, had far too few trees to waste one on a musical instrument. Ereza couldn't hear the difference between it and the others Arla had played, but she knew Arla thought it important.

Her reverie shattered as something went drastically wrong with the music. She couldn't tell what, but Arla's red face and the conductor's posture suggested who had caused the problem. Other instruments had straggled to a halt gracelessly, leaving silence for the conductor's comment.

"Miss Fennaris!" Ereza was glad he wasn't her commanding officer; she'd heard that tone, and felt a pang of sympathy for Arla. Somehow she'd thought musicians were more lenient than soldiers.

"So sorry," Arla said. Her voice wavered; Ereza could tell she was fighting back tears. Poor dear; she hadn't ever learned toughness. Behind her twin, two other musicians leaned together, murmuring. Across the stage, someone standing behind a group of drums leaned forward and fiddled with something on the side of one of them.

"From measure eighty-two," said the conductor, this time not looking at Arla. Arla had the stubborn, withdrawn expression that Ereza knew well; she wasn't going to admit anything was wrong, or share what was bothering her. Well, musicians were different, like all artists. It would go into her art, that's what everyone said.

Ereza had no idea what measure eighty-two was, but she did recognize the honeyed sweetness of the opening phrase. Quickly, it became less sweet, brooding, as summer afternoons could thicken into menacing storms. She felt breathless, and did not know why. Arla's face gave no clue, her expression almost sullen. Her fingers flickered up and down the neck of the cello and reminded Ereza of the last time she'd played the game Flight-test with her twin, last leave. Before the reopening of hostilities, before some long-buried agent put a bomb in the barracks and cost her her arm. Arla had won, she remembered, those quick fingers as nimble on the controls as on her instrument.

Suddenly the impending storm broke; the orchestra was off at full speed and volume, Arla's cello nearly drowned in a tumult of sound. Ereza watched, wondering why it didn't sound pretty anymore. Surely you could make something stormy that was also good to listen to. Besides, she wanted to hear Arla, not all these other people. Arla was leaning into her bowing; Ereza knew what that would mean at home. But the cello couldn't dominate this group, not by sheer volume. The chaos grew and grew, very much like a summer storm, and exploded in a series of crashes; the man with the drums was banging away on them.

The music changed again, leaving chaos behind. Arla, she noted, had a moment to rest, and wiped her sweaty face. She had a softer expression now and gazed at the other string players, across from her. Ereza wondered what she thought at times like this. Was she thinking ahead to her own next move? Listening to the music itself? What?

Brasses blared, a wall of sound that seemed to sweep the lighter strings off the stage. Ereza liked horns as a rule, but these seemed pushy and arrogant, not merely jubilant. She saw Arla's arm move, and the cello answered the horns like a reproving voice. The brasses stuttered and fell silent while the cello sang on. Now Arla's face matched the music, serenity and grace. Other sections returned, but the cello this time rose over them, collecting them into a seamless web of harmony.

When the conductor cut off the final chord, Ereza realized she'd been holding her breath and let it out with a whoof. She would be able to tell Arla how much it meant to listen to her and mean it. She was no musical expert, and knew it, but she could see why her sister was considered an important cultural resource. Not for the first time, she breathed a silent prayer of thanks that it had been her own less-talented right arm she'd lost to trauma. When her new prosthesis came in, she'd be able to retrain for combat; even without it, there were many things she could do in the military. But the thought of Arla without an arm was obscene.

The rehearsal continued to a length that bored Ereza and numbed her ears. She could hear no difference between the first and fifth repetition of something, even though the conductor, furious with first the woodwinds and then the violas, threw a tantrum about it and explained in detail what he wanted. Arla caused no more trouble—in fact, the conductor threw her a joke once, at which half the cello section burst out laughing. Ereza didn't catch it. At the end, he dismissed the orchestra and told Arla to stay. She nodded, and carried her cello over to its case; the conductor made notes on his papers and shuffled through them. While the others straggled offstage, she wiped the cello with a cloth and put the bow neatly into its slot, then closed the case and latched it.

Ereza wondered if she should leave now, but she had no idea where Arla would go next, and she wanted to talk to her. She waited, watching the conductor's back, the other musicians, Arla's care with her instrument. Finally all the others had gone, and the conductor turned to Arla.

"Miss Fennaris, I know this is a difficult time for you—" In just such a tone had Ereza's first flight officer reamed her out for failing to check one of the electronic subsystems in her ship. Her own difficult time had been a messy love affair; she wondered why Arla wasn't past that. Arla wisely said nothing. "You are the soloist, and that's quite a responsibility under the circumstances—" Arla nodded while Ereza wondered again *what* circumstances. "We have to know you will be able to perform; this is not a trivial performance."

"I will," Arla said. She had been looking at the floor, but now she raised her eyes to the conductor's face—and past them, to Ereza, standing in the shadows. She turned white, as if she'd lost all her blood, and staggered.

"What—?" The conductor swung around then and saw that single figure in the gloom at the back of the hall. "Who's there? Come down here, damn you!"

Ereza shrugged to herself as she came toward the lighted stage. She did not quite limp, though the knee still argued about downward slopes. She watched her footing, with glances to Arla who now stood panting like someone who had run a race. What ailed the child—did she think her sister was a ghost? Surely they'd told her things were coming along. The conductor, glaring and huffing, she ignored. She'd had permission, from the mousy little person at the front door, and she had not made one sound during rehearsal.

"*Who* told you you could barge in here—!" the conductor began. Ereza gave him her best smile, as she saw recognition hit. She and Arla weren't identical, but the family resemblance was strong enough.

"I'm Ereza Fennaris, Arla's sister. I asked out front, and they said she was in rehearsal, but if I didn't interrupt—"

"You just did." He was still angry but adjusting to what he already knew. Wounded veteran, another daughter of a powerful family, his soloist's twin sister . . . there were limits to what he could do. To her, at least; she hoped he wouldn't use this as an excuse to bully Arla.

She smiled up at her sister. "Hello again, Arlashi! You didn't come to see me, so I came to see you."

"Is *she* why—did you see her back there when you—?" The conductor had turned away from Ereza to her sister.

"No." Arla drew a long breath. "I did not see her until she came nearer. I haven't seen her since—"

"Sacred Name of God! Artists!" The conductor threw his baton to the floor and glared from one to the other. "A concert tomorrow night, and you had to come now!" That for Ereza. "Your own sister wounded, and you haven't seen her?" That for Arla. He picked up his baton and pointed it at her. "You thought it would go away, maybe? You thought you could put it directly into the music, poof, without seeing her?"

"I thought—if I could get through the concert—"

"Well, you can't. You showed us that, by God." He whirled and pointed his finger at Ereza. "You—get up here! I can't be talking in two directions."

Ereza stifled an impulse to giggle. He acted as if he had real authority; she could just see him trying that tone on a platoon commander and finding out that he didn't. She picked her way to a set of small steps up from the floor of the hall and made her way across the stage, past the empty chairs. Arla stared at her, still breathing too fast. She would faint if she kept that up, silly twit.

"What a mess!" the conductor was saying. "And what an ugly thing *that* is—is that the best our technology can do for you?" He was staring at her temporary prosthesis, with its metal rods and clips.

"Tactful, aren't you?" She wasn't exactly angry, not yet, but she was moving into a mood where anger would be easy. He would have to realize that while he could bully Arlashi, he couldn't bully her. If being blown apart, buried for days, and reassembled with bits missing hadn't crushed her, no mere musician could.

"This is not about tact," the conductor said. "Not that I'd expect you to be aware of that. . . . Arriving on the eve of this concert to upset my soloist, for instance, is hardly an expression of great tact."

Ereza resisted an urge to argue. "This is a temporary prosthesis," she said, holding it up. "Right now, as you can imagine, they're short-staffed; it's going to take longer than it would have once to get the permanent one. However, it gives me some practice in using one."

"I should imagine." He glared at her. "Now sit down and be quiet. I have something to say to your sister."

"If you're planning to scold her, don't bother. She's about to faint—"

"I am *not,"* Arla said. She had gone from pale to a dull red that clashed with her purple tunic.

"You have no rights here," said the conductor to Ereza. "You're just upsetting her—and I'll have to see her later. But for now—" He made a movement with his hands, tossing her the problem, and walked offstage. From that distance, he got the last word in. "Miss Fennaris—the *cellist* Miss Fennaris—see me in my office this afternoon at fourteen-twenty."

"You want lights?" asked a distant voice from somewhere overhead.

"No," said Arla, still not looking at Ereza. "Cut 'em." The brilliant stage lighting disappeared; Arla's dark clothes melted into the gloom onstage, leaving her face—older, sadder—to float above it. "Damn you, Ereza—why did you have to come now?"

Ereza couldn't think of anything to say. That was not what she'd imagined Arla saying. Anger and disappointment struggled; what finally came out was, "Why didn't you come to see me? I kept expecting you. . . . Was it just this concert?" She could—almost—understand that preparing for a major appearance might keep her too busy to visit the hospital.

"No. Not . . . exactly." Arla looked past her. "It was—I couldn't practice without thinking about it. Your hand. My hand. If I'd seen you, I couldn't have gone on making music. I should have—after I beat you at Flight-test I should have enlisted. If I'd been there—"

"You'd have been asleep, like the rest of us. It wasn't slow reflexes that did it, Arlashi, it was a bomb. While we slept. Surely they told you that." But Arla's face had that stubborn expression again. Ereza tried again. "Look—what you're feeling—I do understand that. When I woke up and found Reia'd been killed, and Aristide, I hated myself for living. You wish I hadn't been hurt, and because you're not a soldier—"

"Don't start that!" Arla shifted, and a music stand went over with a clatter. "Dammit!" She crouched and gathered the music in shaking hands, then stabbed the stand upright. "If I get this out of order, Kiel will—"

Ereza felt a trickle of anger. "It's only sheets of paper—surely this Kiel can put it back in order. It's not like . . . what do you mean 'Don't start that'?"

"That *you're not a soldier* rigmarole. I know perfectly well I'm not, and you are. Everyone in the family is, except me, and I know how you all feel about it."

"Nonsense." They had had this out before; Ereza thought she'd finally got through, but apparently Arla still worried. Typical of the civilian mind, she thought, to fret about what couldn't be helped. "No one blames you; we're *proud* of you. Do you think we need another soldier? We've told you—"

"Yes. You've told me." Ereza waited, but Arla said nothing more, just stood there, staring at the lighter gloom over the midhall, where the skylight was.

"Well, then. You don't want to be a soldier; you never did. And no need, with a talent like yours. It's what we fight for, anyway—"

"Don't say that!"

"Why not? It's true. Gods be praised, Arlashi, we're not like the Metiz, quarrelling for the pure fun of it, happy to dwell in a wasteland if only it's a battlefield. Or the Gennar Republic, which cares only for profit. Our people have always valued culture: music, art, literature. It's to make a society in which culture can flourish—where people like you can flourish—that we go to war at all."

"So it's my fault." That in a quiet voice. "You would lay the blame for this war—for that bomb—on me?"

"Of course not, ninny! How could it be your fault, when a Gavalan terrorist planted that bomb?" Musicians, Ereza thought, were incapable of understanding issues. If poor Arla had thought the bombing was her fault, no wonder she came apart—and how useless someone so fragile would be in combat, for all her hand-eye coordination and dexterity. "You aren't to blame for the misbegotten fool who did it, or the pigheaded political leadership that sent him."

"But you said—"

"Arlashi, listen. Your new cello—you know where the wood came from?"

"Yes." That sounded sullen, even angry. "Reparations from Scavel; the Military Court granted the Music Council first choice for instruments."

"That's what I mean. We go to war to protect our people—physical and economic protection. Do you think a poor, helpless society could afford wood for instruments? A concert hall to play in? The stability in which the arts flourish?" Arla stirred, but Ereza went on quickly before she could interrupt. "I didn't intend to lose a hand—no one does—but I would have done it gladly to give you your music—"

"I didn't ask you for that! You didn't have to lose anything to give me music. I could give *myself* music!"

"Not that cello," Ereza said, fighting to keep a reasonable tone. She could just imagine Arla out in the stony waste, trying to string dry grass across twigs and make music. Surely even musicians realized how much they needed the whole social structure, which depended on the military's capacity to protect both the physical planet and its trade networks. "Besides—war has to be something more than killing, more than death against death. We aren't barbarians. It has to be *for* something."

"It doesn't have to be for me."

"Yes, you. I can't do it. You could fight—" She didn't believe that, but saying it might get Arla's full attention. "Anyone can fight, who has courage, and you have that. But I can't make music. If I had spent the hours at practice you have, I still couldn't make your music. If I die, there are others as skilled as I am who could fight our wars. But if you die, there will be no music. In all the generations since Landing, our family has given one soldier after another. You—you're something different—"

"But I didn't ask for it."

Ereza shrugged, annoyed. "No one asks for their talent, or lack of it."

"That's not what I mean." Arla struggled visibly, then shrugged. "Look—we can't talk here; it's like acting, being on this stage. Come to my rehearsal room."

"Now? But I thought we'd go somewhere for lunch. I have to leave soon."

"Now. I have to put my precious war-won wood cello away." Arla led the way to her instrument, then offstage and down a white-painted corridor. Ereza ignored the sarcastic tone of that remark and followed her. Doors opened on either side; from behind some of them music leaked out, frail ghosts of melody.

Arla's room had two chairs, a desk-mounted computer, and a digital music stand. Arla waved her to one of the chairs; Ereza sat down and looked over at the music stand's display.

"Why don't you have this kind onstage? Why that paper you spilled?"

Her attempt to divert Arla's attention won a wry grin. "Maestro Bogdan won't allow it. Because the tempo control's usually operated by foot, he's convinced the whole orchestra would be tapping its toes. Even if we were, it'd be less intrusive than reaching out and turning pages, but he doesn't see it that way. Traditionally, even good musicians turn pages, but only bad musicians tap their feet. And we live for tradition—like my cello." Arla had opened the case again, and then she tapped her cello with one finger. It made a soft *tock* that sounded almost alive. With a faint sigh she turned away and touched her computer. The music stand display came up, with a line of music and the measure numbers above it. She turned it to give Ereza a better view.

"Do you know what that is?"

Ereza squinted and read aloud. "Artruud's Opus 27, measure seventy-nine?"

"Do you know what *that* is?"

Ereza shook her head. "No—should I? I might if you hummed it."

Arla gave a short, ugly laugh. "I doubt that. We just played it, the whole thing. This—" She pointed at the display, which showed ten measures at a time. "This is where I blew up. Eighty-two to eighty-six."

"Yes, but I don't read music."

"I know." Arla turned and looked directly at her. "Did you ever think about that? The fact that I can play Flight-test as well as you, that my scores in Tac-Sim—the tests you had me take as a joke—were enough to qualify me for officers' training if I'd wanted it . . . but not one of you in the family can read music well enough to pick out a tune on the piano?"

"It's not our talent. And you, surrounded by a military family—of course you'd pick up something—"

"Is war so easy?" That in a quiet voice, washed clean of emotion. Ereza stared at her, shocked.

"Easy! Of course it's not easy." She still did not want to think about her first tour, the near disaster of that patrol on Sardon, when a training mission had gone sour. It was nothing she could discuss with Arla. Her stump throbbed, reminding her of more recent pain. How could Arla ask that question? She started to ask that, but Arla had already spoken.

"But you think I picked it up, casually, with no training?"

"Well . . . our family . . . and besides, what you did was only tests, not real combat."

"Yes. And do you think that if you'd been born into a musical family, you'd have picked up music so casually? Would you be able to play the musical equivalent of Flight-test?"

"I'd have to know more, wouldn't I?" Ereza wondered where this conversation was going. Clearly Arla was upset about something, something to do with her own wound. *It's my arm that's missing,* she thought. *I'm the one who has a right to be upset or not upset.* "I'd still have no talent for it, but I would probably know more music when I heard it."

"Yet I played music in the same house, Eri, four to six hours a day when we were children. You had ears; you could have heard. We slept in the same room; you could have asked questions. You told me if you liked something, or if you were tired of hearing it; you never once asked me a *musical* question. You heard as much music as many musicians' children. The truth is that you didn't care. None of our family cared."

Ereza knew the shock she felt showed on her face; Arla nodded at her and went on talking. "Dari can tell you how his preschool training team pretended to assault the block fortress, and you listen to him. You listen carefully, you admire his cleverness or point out where he's left himself open for a counterattack. But me—I could play Hohlander's first cello concerto backward, and you'd never notice. It's not important to you—it's beneath your notice."

"That's not true." Ereza clenched the fingers of her left hand on the arm of the chair. "Of course we care; of course we notice. We know you're good; that's why you had the best teachers. It's just that it's not our field—we're not *supposed* to be experts."

"But you are about everything else." Arla, bracing herself on the desk, looked almost exultant. Ereza could hardly believe what she was hearing. The girl must have had this festering inside for years, to bring it out now, to someone wounded in her defense. "You talk politics as if it were your field—why this war is necessary, why that legislation is stupid. You talk about manufacturing, weapons design, the civilian economy—all *that* seems to be your area of expertise. If music and art and poetry are so important—if they're the reason you fight—then why don't you know anything about them? Why don't you bother to learn even the basics, the sort of stuff you expect Dari to pick up by the time he's five or six?"

"But—we can't do it all," Ereza said, appalled at the thought of all the children, talented or untalented, forced to sit through lessons in music. Every child had to know something about drill and survival techniques; Cravor's World, even in peacetime, could be dangerous. But music? You couldn't save yourself in a sandstorm or grass fire by knowing who wrote which pretty tune, or how to read musical notation. "We found you teachers who did—"

"Whom you treated like idiots," Arla said. "Remember the time Professor Rizvi came over, and talked to Grandmother after my lesson? No—of course you wouldn't; you were in survival training right then, climbing up cliffs or something like that. But it was just about the time the second Gavalan rebellion was heating up, and he told Grandmother the sanctions against the colonists just made things worse. She got that tone in her voice—you know what I mean—and silenced him. After that he wouldn't come to the house; I went into the city for my lessons. She told the story to Father, and they laughed together about the silly, ineffectual musician who wouldn't stand a chance against real power—with me standing there—and then they said, 'But you're a gifted child, Arlashi, and we love it.' "

"They're right." Ereza leaned forward. "What would a composer and musician know about war? And it doesn't take much of a weapon to smash that cello you're so fond of." She knew that much, whatever she didn't know about music. To her surprise, Arla gave a harsh laugh.

"Of *course* it doesn't take much weaponry to smash a cello. It doesn't take a weapon at all. I could trip going down the stairs and fall on it; I could leave it flat on the floor and step on it. You don't need to be a skilled soldier to destroy beauty: any clumsy fool can manage that."

"But—"

Arla interrupted her. "That's my point. You take pride in your skill, in your special, wonderful knowledge. And all you can accomplish with it is what carelessness or stupidity or even the normal path of entropy will do by itself. If you want a cello smashed, you don't need an army: just turn it over to a preschool class without a teacher present. If you want to ruin a fine garden, you don't have to march an expensive army through it—just let it alone. If you want someone to die, you don't have to kill them: just *wait!* We'll all die, Ereza. We don't need your help."

"It's not about that!" But Ereza felt a cold chill. If Arla could think that . . . "It's not about killing. It's protecting—"

"You keep saying that, but—did you ever consider asking me? Asking any artist, any writer, any musician? Did you ever consider learning enough of our arts to guess how we might feel?"

Ereza stared at her, puzzled. "But we did protect you. We let you study music from the beginning; we've never pushed you into the military. What more do you want, Arlashi?"

"To be myself, to be a musician just because I *am,* not because you needed someone to prove that you weren't all killers."

That was ridiculous. Ereza stared at her twin, wondering if someone had mindwiped her. Would one of the political fringe groups have thought to embarrass the Fennaris family, with its rich military history, by recruiting its one musician? "I don't understand," she said, aware of the stiffness in her voice. She would have to tell Grandmother as soon as she got out of here, and find out if anyone else had noticed how strange Arla had become.

Arla leaned forward. "Ereza, you cannot have me as a tame conscience . . . someone to feel noble about. I am not a simple musician, all full of sweet melody, to soothe your melancholy hours after battle." She plucked a sequence of notes, pleasant to the ear.

"Not that I mind your being soldiers," Arla went on, now looking past Ereza's head into some distance that didn't belong in that small room. Ereza had seen that look on soldiers; it shocked her on Arla's face. "It's not that I'm a pacifist, you see. It's more complicated than that. I want you to be honest soldiers. If you like war, admit it. If you like killing, admit that. Don't make me the bearer of your nobility, and steal my own dark initiative. I am a person—a whole person—with my own kind of violence."

"Of course you're a whole person—everyone is—"

"No. You aren't. You aren't because you know nothing about something you claim is important to you."

"What do you want me to do?" Ereza asked. She felt grumpy. Her stump hurt now, and she wanted to be back with people who didn't make ridiculous emotional arguments or confuse her.

"Quit thinking of me as sweet little Arlashi, your pet twin, harmless and fragile and impractical. Learn a little music, so you'll know what discipline really is. Or admit you don't really care, and quit condescending to me."

"Of course I care." She cared that her sister had gone crazy, at least. Then a thought occurred to her. "Tell me—do the other musicians feel as you do?"

Arla cocked her head and gave her an unreadable look. "Come to the concert tomorrow, Eri."

"I don't know if I can—" She didn't know if she wanted to. A long journey into the city, hours crammed into a seat with others, listening to music that didn't (if she was honest) interest her that much. She'd already heard it, parts of it over and over. "How about tomorrow's rehearsal?"

"No. The concert. I can get you in. If you want to know how musicians think, and why . . . then come."

"Are the others—?"

"I don't know. Grandmother usually comes to my performances, but the others less often. I wish you would, Eri."

Ereza sat in the back row of the concert hall, surrounded by people in formal clothes and dress uniforms. Onstage the orchestra waited, in formal black and white, for the soloist and conductor. She saw a stir at the edge of the stage. Arla, in her long swirling dress, with the cello. The conductor—she looked quickly at her program for his name. Mikailos Bogdan.

Applause, which settled quickly as the house lights went down. Now the clear dome showed a dark night sky with a thick wedge of stars, the edge of the Cursai Cluster. The conductor lifted his arms. Ereza watched; the musicians did not stir. His arms came down.

Noise burst from speakers around the hall. As if conducting music, Bogdan's arms moved, but the noise had nothing to do with his direction. Grinding, squealing, exploding—all the noises that Ereza finally recognized as belonging to an armored ground unit in battle. Rattle and clank of treads, grinding roar of engines, tiny voices yelling, screaming, the heavy thump of artillery and lighter crackling of small arms. Around her the others stirred, looked at one another in amazement, then horror.

Onstage, no one moved. The musicians stared ahead, oblivious to the noise; Ereza, having heard the rehearsal, wondered how they could stand it. And *why?* Why work so for perfection in rehearsal if they never meant to play? Toward the front, someone stood—someone in uniform—and yelled. Ereza could not hear it over the shattering roar that came from the speakers, then—low-level aircraft strafing, she thought. She remembered that sound. Another two or three people stood up; the first to stand began to push his way out of his row. One of the others was hauled back down by those sitting near him.

The sound changed, this time to the repetitive *crump-crump-crump-crump* of bombardment. Vague, near-human sounds, too . . . Ereza shivered, knowing before it came clear what that would be. Screams, moans, sobs . . . it went on far too long. She wanted to get up and leave, but she had no strength.

Silence, when it finally came, was welcome. Ereza could hear, as her ears regained their balance, the ragged breathing of the audience. Silence continued, the conductor still moving his arms as if the orchestra were responding. Finally, he brought the unnerving performance to a close, turned and bowed to them. A few people clapped, uncertainly; no one else joined them and the sound died away.

"Disgracefully bad taste," said someone to Ereza's right. "I don't know what they think they're doing."

"Getting us ready to be ravished by Fennaris, no doubt. Have you heard her before?"

"Only on recordings. I've been looking forward to this for decads."

"She's worth it. I heard her first in a chamber group two years ago, and—"

The conductor beckoned, and Arla stood; the gossipers quieted. Intent curiosity crackled around the hall, silent but alive.

"Ladies and gentlemen," Arla said. She had an untrained voice, but even so it carried to the back of the hall. "You may be wondering what happened to the Goldieri Concerto. We chose to make another statement about music."

The conductor bowed to her, and signaled the orchestra. Each musician held an instrument at arm's length; at the flick of his baton they all dropped to the floor, the light rattling cases of violins, the softer boom of violas, the clatter and thud and tinkle of woodwinds, brasses, percussion. A tiny round drum rolled along the floor until it ran into someone's leg and fell over with a final loud tap. Louder than that was the indrawn breath of the audience.

"I'm Arla," she said, standing alone, facing a crowd whose confusion was slowly turning to hostility. Ereza felt her skin tingling. "Most of you know me as Arla Fennaris, but tonight I'm changing my name. I want you to know why."

She turned and picked up her cello, which she had left leaning against her chair. *No,* Ereza thought, *don't do it. Not that one. Please.*

"You think of me as a cellist," Arla said, and plucked three notes with one hand. "A cellist is a musician, and a musician—I have this from my own sister, a wounded veteran, as many of you know—a musician is to most of you an impractical child. A fool." She ran her hand down the strings, and the sound echoed in Ereza's bones. She shivered, and so did the people sitting next to her. "She tells me, my sister, that the reason we're at war right now—the reason she lost her arm—is that I am a mere musician, and need protection. I can't protect myself; I send others out to die, to keep me and my music alive." Another sweeping move across the strings, and a sound that went through Ereza like a jagged blade. All she could think was *No, no, don't . . . no . . .* but she recognized the look on Arla's face, the tone of her voice. Here was someone committed beyond reason to whatever she was doing.

But Arla had turned, and found her chair again. She was sitting as she would for any performance, the cello nestled in the hollow of her skirt, the bow in her right hand. "It is easy to make noise," Arla said. With a move Ereza did not understand, she made an ugly noise explode from the cello. "It takes skill to make music." She played a short phrase as sweet as spring sunshine. "It is easy to destroy—" She held the cello up, as if to throw it, and again Ereza heard the indrawn breath as the audience waited. Then she put it down. "It takes skill to make—in this case, millennia of instrument designers, and

Barrahesh, here on Cravor's World, with a passion for the re-creation of classic instruments. I have no right to destroy his work—but it would be easy." She tapped the cello's side, and the resonant sound expressed fragility. "As with my cello, with everything. It is easy to kill; it takes skill to nurture life." Again she played a short phrase, this one a familiar child's song about planting flower seeds in the desert.

"My sister," Arla said, and her eyes found Ereza's, and locked onto them. "My sister is a soldier, a brave soldier, who was wounded . . . she would say protecting me. Protection I never asked for, and did not need. Her arm the price of this one—" She held up her right arm. "It is difficult to make music when you are using your sister's arm. An arm taught to make war, not music. An arm that does not respect music."

She lowered her arm. "I can make music only with my own arm, because it's my arm that learned it. And to play with my arm means throwing away my sister's sacrifice. Denying it. Repudiating it." *No,* Ereza thought at her again. *Don't do this. I will understand; I will change. Please.* But she knew it was too late, as it had been too late to change things when she woke after surgery and found her own arm gone. "If my sister wants music, she must learn to make it. If you want music, you must learn to make it. We will teach you; we will play with you—but we will not play *for* you. Good evening."

Again the conductor signaled; the musicians picked up their instruments from the floor, stood, and walked out. For a moment, the shuffling of their feet onstage was the only sound as shock held the audience motionless. Ereza felt the same confusion, the same hurt, the same realization that they would get no music. Then the catcalls began, the hissing, the programs balled up angrily and thrown; some hit the stage and a few hit the musicians. But none of them hurried, none of them looked back. Arla and the conductor waited, side by side, as the orchestra cleared the stage. Ereza sat frozen, unable to move even as people pushed past her, clambered over her legs. She wanted to go and talk to Arla; she knew it would do no good. She did not speak Arla's language. She never had. Now she knew what Arla meant: she had never respected her sister before. Now she did. *Too late, too late* cried her mind, struggling to remember something, anything, of the music.